THE
MEASURE
OF
SILENCE

THE
MEASURE
OF
SILENCE

A NOVEL

ELIZABETH LANGSTON

LAKE UNION
PUBLISHING

Published by Lake Union Publishing, Seattle

www.apub.com

Amazon, the Amazon logo, and Lake Union Publishing are trademarks of Amazon.com, Inc., or its affiliates.

ISBN-13: 9781662510632 (paperback)
ISBN-13: 9781662512094 (digital)

Cover design by Kathleen Lynch/Black Kat Design
Cover image: © Nicole Matthews / ArcAngel; © Jena Ardell / Getty

Printed in the United States of America

To Angela—storyteller, seeker of justice, friend.
You are missed.

CHAPTER 1

November 22, 1963

It would be hard to say whether Mariah was more excited about seeing the Kennedys or getting married. But if she were forced to choose? Honestly, the Kennedys would win. Not that she would ever tell Hal.

It was his fault. She hadn't known the president would be in Dallas until Hal surprised her with breakfast in bed and the morning paper. Her attention had locked on a photograph of the first lady, radiant in a chic white dress, beside a headline that read, Thousands Expected to Greet JFK.

Hardly daring to breathe, Mariah had asked, "What's this?"

Hal scooted onto the bed beside her, bare chested, fresh from the shower. "The Kennedys will be riding through Dallas around lunchtime, close to the courthouse. I thought we could leave early and see them. Maybe grab a bite after." He kissed her shoulder. "Then say *I do*."

She'd given him an enthusiastic yes without saying a single word.

The drive downtown had been an adventure, but they'd found a not-so-legal parking space near the end of the motorcade route and walked as fast as possible to Dealey Plaza. And so here they were, standing behind the swarm of people at Elm and Houston, waiting for a glimpse of the Kennedys.

She so admired Mrs. Kennedy and aspired to be like her. A wife adored by her man. A loving mother to beautiful children. And—as Mariah had happily pointed out once to her unyielding father—a successful *career* girl, who'd made her mark with a camera!

But there was more to her fascination with the Kennedys than the wonderful model of womanhood from the first lady. It was the way the president looked at her. Whenever Mariah opened a magazine with the Kennedys on its cover, there would be a shot of the president smiling in delight at his wife, his expression showing his pleasure in having her at his side. That she made a difference in his life. Mariah hoped Hal would want that kind of marriage with her.

A bystander pushed past her, fighting for a better spot at the curb, knocking her into Hal.

"Whoa, darlin'," he said. "Careful."

She didn't want to be careful, nor did she want to be crowded. They would have to find another spot where there were no bodies, no talking, and no straining to see. "We have to move."

"Huh?"

She nudged him with her elbow. "Go."

"Whatever you say." He took her hand and led her up the incline to a stretch of open lawn. With no one else around, she wouldn't worry about being jostled or blocked. But were they in the best spot? This close to the street, it would be over too quickly. If they were too far away, the first lady might not notice her.

"Let's back up, Hal. Just a little."

She paused three steps later, her view clear from the intersection to the bridge. "This is it."

"Happy now?" There was laughter in his voice.

"Yes." *Please hush!* What were the chances that she'd ever see Mrs. Kennedy or the president again? She had to remain focused with all her senses. Savor the moment and remember it forever.

A match rasped. Cigarette smoke curled around her. She shifted from the smell as she took in the details of the scene, determined to remember every second of the most thrilling experience of her life. Even though it had rained earlier, the weather had turned lovely. The air buzzed with conversation. The mood was festive. Their president had come to Dallas, and he'd brought the most elegant woman on earth with him.

Mariah couldn't imagine a more perfect day for her wedding.

After months of resisting Hal's proposals, she'd finally agreed. He'd chosen his very next day off—the Friday before Thanksgiving—to schedule the ceremony downtown, not taking a chance on her changing her mind.

"Hey, Mrs. Highcamp."

Tossing her head, she said pertly, "I'm Miss Byrne for two more hours."

"Countin' down." He nuzzled her neck. "You are beautiful."

She felt beautiful, and that was because of her dress. She'd found it at the Goodwill store, hanging on the bargain rack, similar to something Mrs. Kennedy had worn on the cover of *Life*.

This wouldn't be the wedding of Mariah's childhood dreams. As a little girl, she'd pictured the ceremony in a cathedral, with her in a gown of satin and lace, the groom in a tux, and Father Tim performing the sacrament. But when she'd escaped North Carolina last spring, when she'd disappeared before dawn to flee with her man, she'd made new dreams.

Even though she'd only said yes a week ago, she'd managed to put together the right pieces.

Something old: white boots, a bit scuffed.

Something new—at least, new to her: an off-white wool crepe dress, tailored to fit her shape, its neckline grazing her collarbone with a cute fringed tie.

Something borrowed. Well, *borrowed* wasn't exactly true. More like taken from her mother's jewelry box years ago and never returned. A starburst brooch, sparkling with crystals, pinned to the bodice of the white wool dress to cover the reason it had been a bargain. A red wine stain.

Something blue: a beaded headband holding back her short flip of black hair.

Pa would be appalled if he could see her. A bride with an uncovered head. A courthouse instead of a church. A Baptist groom. *Good Catholic girls don't . . .*

There were so many things good Catholic girls didn't do. Mariah had done them all.

She peeked over her shoulder at the boy she'd followed to Texas. Her groom in his best pants and sweater. "You're lookin' pretty handsome yourself."

The roar of the crowd refocused her attention. On the opposite side of the street, people stood in clusters. A family with two little boys. Three women chatting, their knees bouncing with anticipation. A man holding an umbrella, even though the rain had stopped hours ago.

"I have to get ready." She withdrew the heavy movie camera from her purse. Something else borrowed, this time with permission. Squinting through the viewfinder, she panned the street, establishing the scene as she'd been taught. A few seconds of footage would be enough. The crowd was so heavy on Houston, she couldn't see the road. Along Elm, it was sparser. She swept past Umbrella Man to another photographer standing on a wall, his own camera raised. She ended with a final shot of the intersection.

"Your arms are gonna get tired." Hal's strong body steadied hers. "I got you."

She shivered. Wished for time to slow down. The air was fresh, the sky was blue, and the day held such promise.

"Darlin', you won't be able to see much with that thing in front of your face."

Darn it all, but he was right. Mariah bit her lip and lowered the camera. She'd come to make eye contact with the first lady, if only for a moment. But if she held the camera too low, would the framing be off?

Screams and cheers erupted from Main Street, rolling over them in a wave of noise. There was no time left. She nestled the camera against her chest.

A white Ford drove past, but she hardly noticed. The nose of a dark limo, its top down, flanked by motorcycle cops, was surging around the corner like an awkward ship.

Pink! Mrs. Kennedy was wearing her pink Chanel suit! The one with the navy-blue collar and the cutest pillbox hat. Mariah *loved* that outfit.

The limo was nearly even with them. Was Mrs. Kennedy looking at her?

Yes! Yes, she was. The first lady waved. Mariah waved back.

Pop.

She stilled in confusion. Mariah had grown up in rural North Carolina. She recognized the crack of a rifle.

Hal's arms tightened around her. "What the . . . ?"

Pop.

The president clutched his throat. The first lady whipped around to face her husband.

Pop.

Mariah's brain recorded what happened next like a series of snapshots, all in crystal-clear focus. The red mist. The president slumping sideways. Mrs. Kennedy crawling on all fours onto the limo's trunk. A man leaping on as the limo sped away.

"Down, Mariah, down!" Hal yelled, slamming her to the ground, knocking the breath from her, tilting her view.

While the world exploded into chaos around them, she lay motionless, eyes dry and wide, her fingers tangled in grass greener and silkier than she would've expected.

"Darlin', what did we just see?"

It was a stupid question. Because they knew. They'd witnessed the murder of the president.

Pain radiated up her spine as if someone hammered at its base. She welcomed the pain. It reminded her that she could feel. That what she'd seen hadn't dulled her senses. Muffled sounds pressed against her ears. The sobs of the hordes. The shrieks of police cars. The whistle of a breeze. Her body ached fiercely, surrounded by the scent of moist dirt, Hal's sweat, and the noxious fumes of motorcycles and fear.

She closed her eyes but couldn't hide from the scene seared into her brain. Gaping mouths rounded by screams. Mrs. Kennedy's horrified stare. The aftermath of three gunshots.

Why had this happened? One moment there had been joy, excitement, innocence. And hope. The next, all was lost, leaving sorrow, terror, and despair. It had taken only seconds for the world to split into *before* and *after*.

CHAPTER 2

Sixty years later

Jessica Elliott arrived at the door of her sister's condo carrying a black dress encased in a dry-cleaning bag. She rapped once and entered, her gaze sweeping the living area. She'd only been here a handful of times in the year her sister had owned the place. It hadn't changed much. The furnishings were good quality but minimal. No artwork adorned the walls. But there were curtains, presently drawn. The great room was cool, dim, and low-key.

Raine stood at the kitchen island, dropping her phone into a purse.

"From Mom," Jessica said, holding up the coat hanger. "She didn't think you had a black dress."

"She's right, but I'm ready."

When her sister turned, Jessica got the full effect. Brown eyes solemn and shadowed. Lips pale and thin. No makeup, but her brown hair had been brushed smoothly along her jaw. Her sister wore a Windsor blue silk sheath with cap sleeves. It was pretty and festive. Better suited to a cocktail party than a funeral. Did she realize that? "Uh, Raine?"

"Papa liked me in this dress," she said, her tone resolute. She strode past Jessica and out the door.

Jessica folded the unneeded dress over her arm and followed. They waited silently, side by side, at the elevator.

As the door pinged open, Raine asked, "Are we picking up Mom and Mariah?"

"No, they're already at the chapel." *And we're behind schedule.* "Luke will drive us there, then to the cemetery."

Raine stepped all the way to the back of the elevator and tucked her chin. Avoiding eye contact. Avoiding conversation.

Jessica pressed the lobby button and faced forward, preparing, like her sister, for the ordeal ahead.

◆　◆　◆

As the priest's resonant voice flowed over her, Jessica fixed her gaze on the spray of stargazer lilies covering Papa's casket. It was a lovely day for the graveside service, mild for a May afternoon, not the heavy heat they'd had the week before. The national cemetery was serene, its trees tall and green against a Carolina-blue sky.

It had been exhausting to squeeze the funeral details into three days. Her grandfather had outlined exactly what he'd wanted, and she'd made it all happen. Arranged transportation for the Armenian Apostolic priest to travel to Raleigh from Richmond. Contacted the military for an honor guard. Coordinated with the funeral directors about a visitation (yes) and a postservice reception (no).

Her mother had been too distraught to help. Raine had completely withdrawn from the world. And nobody could tell if their grandmother remembered that her husband had died. So Jessica had ended up running the show. After a decade in TV news production, she'd become skilled at objectivity, at taking herself out of the story. But she would go home soon, and, without the goal that had consumed her since Tuesday, she would be *in* the story again.

"Would anyone like to say a few words?" the priest asked.

She glanced over her shoulder and nodded at Phil Jones—the former supervisor of Papa's construction company and one of his best friends.

Phil sent her a reassuring smile and stood. "Well, now," he said, "Gregor didn't much like mistakes, 'specially in himself."

Everyone laughed at the understatement.

"I won't quote him directly, 'cause Gregor could get a bit salty when he was mad, and with Mariah listening . . ."

Her grandmother chuckled, still hunched over, still clutching the folded American flag like a lifeline. Jessica exhaled slowly. Phil's anecdote was perfect. She'd known she could count on him.

One by one, people took turns sharing a memory.

Someone from his bowling league. *Gregor played to win.*

A neighbor. *Gregor sure loved driving that old Impala.*

She'd never appreciated how important this part of a service was. Her news-producer brain kicked in, as if each tale were a scene she could storyboard into a documentary of Papa's life. Her eyes welled. *Not now.* It would be over soon.

The "spontaneous" storytelling drew to a close. Prayers were spoken. And Papa's graveside service was done.

Jessica was done too. Once her husband had helped her up, she leaned into him and stifled a groan. Her body ached. She hadn't expected the physical toll grief took.

"Do you know where Raine is?" Her sister had never made it to the front row.

"Under the magnolia tree behind us."

Jessica felt the bite of impatience, then shook it off and scanned the trees until she spotted her sister. She'd had it drilled into her from an early age to look after Raine. To smooth her path. *Your sister thinks uniquely,* their mother would say. *You have to be a good big sister for her.* A hard habit to break now that Raine was an adult.

Jessica looked away. What else needed handling? Not her mother, who had already crossed to the priest, both hands outstretched. Her grandmother remained seated as she gazed across the lawn, brow creasing, as if bewildered by where she was or why she was here. It was good that no one approached her. Fortunately, only family and close friends had come to the cemetery. The few who lingered were fidgeting, waiting to be greeted. Jessica released Luke's hand and maneuvered to a spot between the grave site and the lane lined with cars. One by one people came by, patting her hand, murmuring words of sympathy. She smiled through the condolences, masking her fatigue.

When the last mourner had moved on, Luke drew her to his side. "What can I do for you?"

"Exactly what you're doing." Resting her head against his shoulder, she closed her eyes and enjoyed the touch of his hand at her waist. The fresh scent of his body wash. The silky feel of his jacket beneath her cheek. He looked so good in his dark suit. Well, actually, he looked good in anything. Or nothing.

Jessica opened her eyes reluctantly, ready to leave. Her father and sister had emerged from the shade of the magnolia and were heading toward them. Jessica had called him yesterday and encouraged him to come, not simply out of respect for his former father-in-law but also because she'd wanted him here for his daughters. Raine especially. Both sisters had been doted on by their parents and grandparents. But Jessica had been closer to her mother and grandmother. And her sister to Dad and Papa. With Papa gone, Raine needed Dad.

As glad as Jessica was that he'd come, she'd overlooked a major detail: warning Mom, who was still bitter fifteen years after the divorce. Any joy at seeing Dad was fractured by the dread of Mom's reaction.

Jessica wasn't done after all. She had an explosion to defuse.

Her father removed his sunglasses as he arrived. "Jessie," he said, the hint of a smile on his lips.

Before she could respond, Mom stalked over. "You weren't invited, Donovan."

Jessica stifled a sigh. They'd been so close to making it through the funeral without a scene. "Mom, please. He doesn't need an invitation. He's part of the family."

"No, he is *not*." She glared at him. "Why are you here?"

His blue eyes narrowed on her. "Nice to see you too, Stephanie."

"Cut the crap. Why did you come?"

"Gregor was my father-in-law."

"*Ex*-father-in-law."

"And the grandfather of my daughters."

"He had no relationship with you."

"That's where you're wrong—"

"Stop!" her grandmother hissed.

The single word had an electric effect. It was the first time Mariah had spoken since the memorial service. They all turned to her, holding their collective breath to see what she'd do next.

She offered her cheek to her former son-in-law. "Dear one," she said, the endearment she used for someone she recognized but whose name she could no longer recall.

"Mariah, I'm so sorry." Dad kissed her cheek.

"Hmm." She tolerated the contact, her eyes wide and dry and restless.

Into the strained silence, Raine asked, "Can I see the flag?"

Their grandmother clutched it tighter. "No."

They laughed, which didn't break the tension but cracked it somewhat. Dad whispered briefly into Raine's ear and then turned to Jessica and opened his arms. She walked eagerly into their comfort.

"How are you holding up?" he murmured.

"Okay. Thank you for coming." Jessica stepped back while her husband and father shook hands.

With the greetings behind them, they stood awkwardly, unsure what to do.

"Are you ready to go home, Mariah?" Raine asked.

Jessica flinched inwardly whenever her sister used her grandmother's name. It felt, somehow, disrespectful. But that wasn't fair to Raine. She was just being pragmatic. Their grandmother often forgot she had grandchildren, but she always responded to *Mariah*. Yet Jessica clung stubbornly to *Mima* and *Papa*. *Papa* and *Mima*. She should let it go.

Mima shook her head. "I have to say goodbye." She wrapped a hand around Luke's arm and, with a regal tilt of her head, allowed him to escort her to her husband's casket.

The rest trailed after her, all but Raine. The funeral home staff moved a considerate distance away as the family gathered round. No one spoke, wondering what Mima would do.

Stifling a yawn, Jessica focused on the cemetery spreading about her. It was only seven acres, with six thousand white markers and a red-brick wall separating it from the noise of the city. When she'd arranged the burial, she learned the cemetery was near capacity. Her grandfather would be one of the last veterans laid to rest here.

"He was a good man." Mima spoke into the silence, shuffling closer to the casket.

Jessica hoped her grandmother would keep talking. She'd been so quiet since they'd broken the news to her, as if it hadn't sunk in. They'd worried she didn't really understand that Papa had died. But it would seem she did, and she was handling the loss in her own way.

Jessica dabbed fresh tears from her cheeks. "Was it love at first sight?"

"No, not at first. It was more like lust."

There was a stunned pause, then everyone laughed.

Mima's lips curved into an impish smile. "There was this one time that he—"

"You can stop anytime," Jessica said. "Please."

Her grandmother chuckled. "TMI?"

"Exactly."

Mima's smile slipped. "He commanded my attention from the moment we met." She brushed her fingertips over the dark wood and pressed them to her lips. "Goodbye, Gregor. I will miss you," she said softly. "My best love."

Jessica heard a strangled sob behind her. Raine stood a few feet away, arms rigidly straight, hands clenched, head bowed, her grief so thick and fierce that Jessica's breath caught. She grabbed her father's arm. "Dad," she whispered urgently.

He looked down at her, then over her shoulder, and stiffened. "Got it."

CHAPTER 3

Raine had been fine until her grandmother spoke, and now she could barely hold it together.

Goodbye, Gregor. I will miss you.

Footsteps shushed through the grass, approaching her. The breeze brought a whiff of her father's aftershave. Just knowing he was there restored part of her control.

"Hey," he said. "Do you need a ride home?"

She nodded, grateful for the offer.

He dropped a firm hand on her shoulder and guided her to his car. Dazed, she climbed in and, after buckling up, closed her eyes, unwilling to take in another image of the gravesite or the mourners or the quiet beauty of this place.

Dad pressed a tissue into her hand before driving noiselessly down the lane. She mentally traced the route he was taking toward downtown and her condo.

"When was the last time you ate?" he asked.

"Breakfast."

"We'll stop."

When she opened her eyes again, they were parked in front of her favorite Greek restaurant. She exchanged a faint smile with him. He'd chosen the only place where she would actually order something. Soon, she was eating soup and nodding at his feeble dad jokes.

"The funeral went smoothly," her father said.

"Agreed." She wouldn't have expected anything less. Jessica had choreographed it, and she didn't make mistakes. Raine felt a twinge of guilt over disappearing in the days following Papa's death, but it had been for the best. Jessica liked everything done a certain way, and Raine would've been too frozen from grief to do her assignments right.

Dad drove her home but didn't simply drop her off. He followed her up, talking nonstop to fill the silence. When they entered her condo, he took a few steps in and looked around. It had been new and empty the last time he'd been here. The look had been upgraded from *nothing* to *spartan*. A petite couch, a recliner, two tables, a lamp, a wall TV. All in soothing shades of blue, gray, and green. She was committed to the concept of *less furniture equals less to clean*.

"Are you all right?" he asked.

"Not yet." If a person could be a refuge, Papa had been hers. She didn't know who to turn to now.

"Let me know how I can help." Dad gave her a hug. "Before I go, I have a legal thing to mention."

Her attorney father was about to give her something to do. That she applauded. "About Papa's will?"

"Yes. How soon could we get started?"

"Give me a few days to catch up with work."

"Tuesday?"

"Sure."

"I'll text the details."

Once he left, she changed into shorts and a T-shirt, then returned to the great room. Craving a distraction, she paced while listening to her Broadway Favorites playlist on Spotify, letting the music fill her and the lyrics claim her thoughts.

Mom's ringtone sounded. Raine considered ignoring the call, but her mother would keep at it until she answered. She paused the music and put the phone on speaker. "Yes?"

"Do you want to come over? The neighbors brought a lot of food, and I've set out a buffet. Jessica and Luke are here. And Phil."

"No thanks. I've eaten."

"Oh. Good." Mom hesitated. "Alone?" she added too casually.

Raine closed her eyes briefly. Her mother had to suspect whom she'd eaten with, and she wasn't in the mood to manage divorced-parent rancor. "With Dad."

"He left you by yourself? Really, Raine, you shouldn't be there—"

"Mom. I'm fine, and I *need* to be by myself. Thanks for calling."

Raine flopped onto the couch, head lolling against the cushions. Her parents had separated sixteen years ago, divorced a year later. After Dad moved out of the family home, Mom had holed up in the den, weeping into her wine. Jessica stayed at school, the cheeriest cheerleader ever. And Raine retreated into silence. Nobody would tell her why Dad had left, so she made up the reasons. They all involved her, and they all hurt.

Then one gloomy day, she heard a car honk as she walked out to the school bus lane. Papa waved from his pickup truck, shouting, "Hop in." Suddenly the world felt less gloomy. He'd taken her to his house, nodded at Mima as they passed her parlor, and headed for his study. While he sat at his desk, tapping at his computer, she'd collapsed into a wing chair, hidden from his view, and started her homework.

After an hour of silence, she knelt in the chair and peered over its back. He hadn't asked her how she felt, so she told him. "I miss my dad."

Papa looked up. "He misses you too." He sounded convincing, and she wanted to believe.

Each school day for a month, her grandfather showed up. Then Dad began to visit regularly. Mom found an interior design job. Raine joined the backstage crew for the fall musical. And slowly her afternoons in Papa's study had trickled to an end.

The pattern repeated five years ago when she'd dumped her college boyfriend. She'd received a text from Papa the next day.

My house is a no question zone

Exactly what she needed. She'd driven over, and they'd sat quietly in his study. No pressure. No expectations. Only this time, he'd just moved his wife into a memory-care unit. The healing went both ways.

Now *he* was gone. She'd have to get through this on her own.

Raine spent the weekend recovering the best way she knew how—with action. Saturday was devoted to spring-cleaning her condo. Anything that didn't move was eligible. Crown moldings. Trash cans. Ceiling fans. TV remotes. She might not have much furniture, but what she did have was vacuumed or scrubbed. She fell into bed at nine, exhausted. Sore in a good way.

Sunday was all about baking. Cookies. Muffins. Pie. She even experimented with bread, which was a bust, but at least she knew with absolute certainty never to try it again.

Raine resumed work on Monday. As a freelance forensic accountant, she had flexibility with her schedule. It was one of the things she liked best about freelancing. She also liked the commute, twenty steps from her bedroom to her home office. Today, the commute included a detour to the condo's balcony, where she nursed a cup of coffee and waited for dawn. She loved watching sunrises and sunsets. She'd always been intrigued by transitions . . . until she found herself in one.

Since Papa died in his sleep last week, she'd been stuck in transition. She'd read up on the stages of grief and thought she'd passed through denial, but she seemed to be in a loop.

Unfolding her legs from the wicker love seat, she continued to her home office, opened her laptop, and brought up her to-do list, the items sorted by urgency. She had two projects due by the end of the month. For the insurance fraud claim, she sent a status update letting them know the analysis would be available next week. The divorce attorney had emailed to learn whether she'd found a cheating husband's hidden assets yet. She had and was sure there were more. She scheduled the requested Zoom meeting.

If Raine had been asked in college what she planned for her accounting career, she would've predicted a more conventional path than freelancing. Then Coulter happened. He'd been another teaching assistant in graduate school who'd barged his way into her life. For someone who'd never really been on a date, she'd been flattered by his persistence. Before Coulter, she'd only been kissed once, and that had been, frankly, disgusting.

She must've been an easy target for him. Innocent, curious, and needy. An enticing combination for a controlling guy on the hunt. She'd stayed in the relationship for nearly a year, against the advice of family and grad school friends and her own good judgment.

Fresh with her master's, she'd received multiple job offers, including one at a big firm where she'd interned. But when her ex got a job offer there too, she'd gone with a smaller firm. It was there that she'd discovered forensic accounting. After the firm folded during the pandemic, she'd accepted a freelance contract to stay afloat, only to find that she loved the clearly defined expectations, the challenge, and the pay. One contract had led to another, and she was hooked. Freelancing became a choice.

Papa had been the biggest advocate of what Mom called "the itinerant stage." So when he'd invited Raine to dinner two nights before he died, she'd been taken aback by the topic.

"I know you like freelancing, but perhaps it's time to pursue something more permanent. Have you considered a job with any accounting or law firms?"

Why was he asking? Didn't he support her anymore? She'd broken eye contact. "They would prefer that I'm certified."

"How close are you to certification?"

She wouldn't lie. She had the business experience, the education, and her CPA. Only one requirement stood between her and applying to be certified in financial forensics. "I haven't taken the CFF exam."

"What's holding you back?"

She was. "I haven't signed up."

He'd shaken his head. Deception by omission. "Why, Raine?"

The short answer was fear. Once she was certified, she would have the credentials to serve as an expert witness. When her cases went to trial, she might have to testify, and the idea unsettled her. She had daymares about falling apart as she was grilled on the witness stand or being confronted by people whose lives had changed for the worse based on her analysis. Until she could manage her fears, she wasn't willing to take the exam. "I'm not ready."

"You should just get it done. If you like, I'll help you open your own business," he'd said proudly. "You could be in charge."

Loners should never be in charge. One of Coulter's unwelcome criticisms that popped up sporadically in her thoughts. He'd sometimes substituted *losers* for *loners*.

"No, Papa. Not yet."

When they'd parted that night, both had been disappointed. She, because Papa had misread her so badly. She would be terrible at running a business, not because she was a loner but because she would hate the administrative noise.

He'd left disheartened that his granddaughter allowed fear to block her from fully embracing a career she loved.

It was the last time she'd seen him.

Her laptop dinged, a reminder for the Zoom meeting. She pushed away the memories and got back to work.

When Raine entered her father's law office on Tuesday, a chime sounded in the back. While she waited, she looked around the lobby. It sent the right kind of message for a family-law practice—welcoming all who came with sturdy furniture, popular magazines on a table, a corner devoted to building blocks and board books, and live plants in ceramic pots.

On the wall opposite the door was a piece of artwork she loved. Photography on canvas, the image taken at sunset with the sky a fiery mix of red and orange and, in stark silhouette, a family of four strolling on the beach.

"Mariah took that," her father said from the hallway behind her.

Something clicked. "They're us?"

"Yes."

She studied the image in awe, seeing it with fresh eyes. Jessica ran boldly at the water's edge, followed by their parents holding hands. Toddler Raine rode high on her father's hip, enjoying a different perspective.

So beautiful. So bittersweet.

She'd been in this lobby a hundred times and never made the connection of that photo to her family. To her, it had been a dramatic sunset. The stick figures in the corner were noted but not really considered. Why did Dad keep a record of when his family had been whole? How did it not hurt to see it each day?

She crossed to him. He was dressed in suit pants, a long-sleeved shirt rolled up his forearms, and no tie. Casual enough for nervous clients. Easily transformable for those who would expect more. "Hi, Dad."

He hugged her. "Ready for this?"

"No." She'd agreed without hesitation when Papa asked her to be his executor. She hadn't anticipated how hard it would be to do the work while mourning him.

"Understood." Dad dropped his arms. "We'll meet in the conference room."

The office manager had everything prepared when they walked in. Coffee and pens at her designated seat. A stack of papers at her father's. A box of pastries between them.

"Thanks, Marco," Dad said, his attention already on the paperwork and his daughter. "As executor of Gregor's estate . . ."

The process was simple. He described a document, she signed it, and the next document was produced. When they were done, she checked the wall clock. It had only taken half an hour. She liked efficiency.

He squared the corners of the stack. "There won't be much passing through the will."

"What about the contents of the house?"

"Whatever remains belongs to you and Jessica. It's why Gregor added you both to the title. To make the transfer easy." He looked up. "Any questions?"

Plenty. "Papa set up a trust for Mariah?"

"He did. Your grandparents had a complex estate, but Gregor planned carefully. The people he loved most will be fine."

"Is Mom the trustee?"

"And me." His tone was neutral, but sharing the responsibility with his ex-wife had to hurt. Fireworks erupted whenever her parents were near each other, with Mom lighting the fuse and Dad taking the hits stoically. Yet he hadn't refused Papa.

She'd wanted to ask, *Why, Dad?* so many times. Why had he pushed for the divorce when Mom was so opposed? Why had Raine never seen him date? Why had he opened a law practice in Chapel Hill—a city thirty minutes from his daughters?

And why did he have a photo with his ex-wife, taken by his ex-mother-in-law, hanging prominently on the lobby wall?

But Raine would never ask those questions, worried she wouldn't like the answers. Something awful had happened between her parents, and she didn't trust her reaction if she ever learned who did what to whom. Ignorance was safer. "Are we done?"

"There's one more thing. Your grandfather left a final wish for you and Jessica." He slid over a yellow envelope with *For my grand girls* written in Papa's beautiful handwriting.

A final wish? She opened the clasp, and a vintage skeleton key fell onto the tabletop. "Do you know what it's about?"

"He didn't say, exactly."

She met her father's gaze. "Can you guess?"

"I have suspicions."

She fought a scowl. His reticence was annoying, but she wouldn't push yet. "Do you know what the key goes to?"

"Gregor said everything you need is in his study."

"When did he give the key to you?"

"A couple of months ago. Not long before he moved into the senior community."

Papa had cleaned out his house, except the study, and left the key behind. The final wish was strange and, she had to admit, strangely exciting. "What does Mom think?"

"She doesn't know." Dad jammed his fists into his pockets. "I recommend not saying anything to her until you understand what Gregor wanted."

Even more curious. A wish for his granddaughters that Dad knew about and Mom did not. Raine really ought to go home, but she couldn't resist heading straight to Papa's house. "Okay. Guess I'll find out."

Dad walked her to his office door. As she started down the stairs to go outside, he said, "Call me when you need me."

When. Not *if.*

When she arrived at Papa's house, there was a contractor's truck in the driveway. She parked behind it but didn't get out immediately. She hadn't been here since he died. She would allow herself a moment to prepare for how she'd feel.

Papa had built this house in the sixties. From the street, it appeared to be a one-story ranch, modest for the now-exclusive neighborhood, but there were actually two stories. The upper floor held the living spaces. The bedrooms were downstairs in the walk-out basement.

Her grandfather had moved to an apartment in the Larkmoor Senior Living Community in April, wanting to be nearer to Mariah. Once the house was empty, he'd decided to renovate it into sellable condition and asked Raine to manage the project. They'd all been surprised. Her mother was an interior designer. Jessica had serious project-management skills. But he'd explained his decision by saying, "Raine is the one who loves the house."

Totally true. Neither Mom nor Jessica liked midcentury modern architecture. Raine didn't care what style it was. She found everything about the house Papa built to be awesome.

Papa had hired a former construction employee to complete the renovations. Once Damian was done, they would be putting the house on the market. Raine had told Damian to take his time and fit it in around his other contracts. She hoped it took him forever.

Hauling her backpack onto a shoulder, she slid from her SUV and walked along the sidewalk. But as she fumbled with the house key, she wondered how she'd react to seeing the changes. Knowing the ultimate goal was to sell. This house had been a refuge throughout her life. Letting go of it would be hard.

Coulter had often needled her about being emotionally stunted.

Does anything matter enough for you to cry?

Oh yes. Many things mattered to her. Her family. Her career and seeking justice. And, apparently, this house.

If her ex could see her now, he'd learn how wrong he'd been. Her problem wasn't about *feeling* emotions. It was about having so many at once she didn't know what to do with them.

Inside, she paused in the foyer, assessing what she could see of the top floor. To her left was her grandmother's parlor, a room so like Mariah: elegant, understated, lovely. The rest of the house might look lived in, a consequence of two adored granddaughters with few constraints, but a higher standard existed for the parlor. If Mariah was there, rocking quietly, staring out the window with that faraway look on her face, Jessica and Raine had known not to enter.

Now it looked forlorn. Shelves without books. A mantel without pictures. Raine hoped a fresh coat of paint and refinished hardwoods would be enough to restore its charm.

Across the foyer, the dining room was unrecognizable. Bare wires had replaced the brass-and-Murano-glass chandelier. The molding had been peeled from ceilings and floors. The formerly red walls had been primed, awaiting their new life in light gray.

A loud banging came from the lower level. Damian was prepping the downstairs bathroom. She wouldn't bother him today. She trusted his work. Besides, she didn't want to be distracted from her purpose.

Straight back were the kitchen and sunroom, but her destination was midway down the hall. Papa's study. She hesitated outside its closed door, resting her hand on the knob, drumming up the courage.

A twist of her wrist, a slight push, and she was inside.

It was hushed in this private place where no one had dared enter without invitation. She squirmed under the weight of memories. It might be a room, but it had been his, and his personality—his *presence*—occupied it still.

She continued in until her shoes brushed the faded woolen carpet. Little had changed. There was mahogany furniture covered in worn burgundy leather. Objects crowded low tables that small hands and curious hearts could not destroy. High on the outside wall, a long rectangular window clung to the eaves, filling the room with soft light. A wall of shelves was crammed with well-loved books.

She crossed to the desk and perched on its edge, seeing the room from Papa's viewpoint. When she'd been little, he would pull her onto his lap, and they'd sit there together while both did their "work." He'd be looking at documents, his pen scratching at intervals. She'd added columns of numbers, happy when he'd glance over and grunt in approval at correct answers.

As she straightened, something caught her eye on the desktop. At one corner was their last family portrait, taken at her sister's wedding in January. Dad and Luke had worn dark suits and matching ties. Jessica looked gorgeous in Mariah's lace wedding gown. Mom and maid of honor Raine were both in blue cocktail dresses, thankfully not matching. Papa and Mariah had sat in front, holding hands.

Beside the picture frame lay an envelope, addressed by Papa to his grand girls. She ripped it open and drew out a single sheet of paper.

> My dearest Raine and Jessica,
> Our family has a story that the two of you don't know. Your Mima and I wish for you to work together to seek the truth.
> Everything you need to start lies within Mima's hope chest. Explore the contents and follow where they lead. Be patient and thorough. Reserve judgment until you've finished.
> Parts of the story will be hard to accept. You may be disappointed in us, and for that I'm sorry.
> Once you know all, claim it as your story and do the right thing.
> With love,
> Papa

A story she and her sister didn't know? A truth that would disappoint them?

Papa wasn't one to exaggerate, but a hunt for secrets seemed a bit . . . extreme. She refolded the letter, returned it to the envelope, and slipped it into her backpack. Then she crossed to the hope chest and inserted the vintage key. When the lock clicked, Raine raised the lid until the hinges popped and held. Inside were three cardboard cartons, each labeled *For Raine and Jessica*. Papa had numbered them one, two, and three.

The first carton held four photo albums: *Gregor*, *Mariah*, *Courtship*, and *Our Family*. Raine parked her butt on the carpet and pulled out each album, lining them up in a row. As she flipped through a few pages of *Gregor*, she smiled. She couldn't remember seeing any of these photos or albums. It would take a while to go through them, and it would be a pleasure.

Carton two contained dozens of reels of eight-millimeter film and a home-movie projector in pristine condition. She replaced the lid and opened the third carton. It held an accordion file with documents and letters in archival sheeting, organized by years, 1963–1986. Beneath the file was a stack of magazines and newspapers.

She felt a tickle of interest. Why had he begun in 1963? Papa and Mima met in 1964. And why end in 1986? She was tempted to look further, but . . . No. If she'd received these materials in a forensics case, she would've resisted the obvious attempt at providing a process. But from her grandfather, she considered the order instructive. There was a reason behind the numbers. She should honor it. His wish, his way.

Correction, *they* should honor it. Because, yes, this project was designed for two. She didn't get why Papa had included Jessica. Raine preferred to work alone, and Jessica barely had enough time for the people in her top tier of importance. There wouldn't be any to spare for Raine. But Papa had decreed it, so Raine would clue her sister in. She pulled out her phone.

Are you busy?

Yes

Well, cool. No guilty conscience about getting started. Raine wasn't waiting until her sister was free. Which never happened. Jessica managed to fill all her time.

A banging started directly beneath her. Damian must be destroying something in the guest bathroom, and Raine couldn't think through the racket. The cartons were going home with her. She had old photos to review and a family story to expose.

CHAPTER 4

Jessica had to hurry or she'd be late for the afternoon meeting. But as she wove her way through the newsroom, the assistant news director came out of his office, his gaze laser-focused on her. He sent her one of his rare smiles, his energy high and positive.

"Walk with me."

"Sure." She matched her stride to his. "What is it?"

"I have some personal news." Swiping on his phone, he held it up for her. A blurry gray-and-white sonogram. The outline of a tiny head. An elbow. A leg. "My daughter's pregnant. She's due in October."

Jessica had often wondered why people showed off sonograms. Fuzzy gray-and-white blobs that no one could interpret except medical staff. But she'd always dutifully oohed and aahed whenever friends had proudly displayed them. She'd do the same for Charlie. "That's great. You'll make a wonderful grandfather."

"Thanks." He continued toward the conference room, chatting on about his daughter's search for a bigger home in Santa Fe. His son-in-law's family living nearby. Their jobs and childcare and—

Wait. Back up. "You're moving to New Mexico?"

His smile vanished. "Yeah. My wife can't stand the idea that the other grandparents get more access to the baby than we do."

"When?"

"I haven't announced it yet, but I'll retire in August."

"Congratulations." She was happy for him. She was also aware his departure would lead to a reshuffle with cascading promotions.

He gestured her into the conference room and muttered as she walked past, "You have a strong chance at a promotion to senior producer."

She swallowed a gasp, hurried to the nearest empty chair, and wished he hadn't said anything right before the meeting. How did he expect her to concentrate?

The meeting flowed around her, but she didn't hear a thing, too busy thinking about this news. After taking a lateral move to the Raleigh station, she'd had to adjust her career plan. Optimistically, she hadn't expected a promotion for another two years, but Charlie said she had a strong chance. Senior producer was in sight!

Mima had once served as a senator in the state government. Teen Jessica had watched news coverage of her grandmother with frustration. She'd known how hard her grandmother worked to get things right. To improve special education for the children of North Carolina. Jessica would get angry at how twisted and wrong the TV coverage would come across. She'd known then that if she ever landed her dream job leading a news team, she'd want to be known for beautifully written stories told with compassion and humanity.

She'd never actually told anyone that. It would sound hopelessly idealistic. And now, she might be one rung closer up the career ladder. She couldn't help a smile.

"Jessica?" her executive producer asked. "Do you have anything to add?"

She looked up from the doodle on her notepad. All eyes were on her and her huge smile. She had no idea what they'd been discussing. "No. Nothing to add."

When Charlie winked at her, she tried not to laugh, but she did tune back in.

As soon as the meeting ended, she made her way to the break room but found too many people crowded around the coffeepot. So she headed outside to the blissfully empty patio and a quiet chance to think without an audience.

A promotion would be recognition for her hard work and commitment to quality, but it would also bring higher expectations, more responsibility, and more *hours*. Since she'd joined the six o'clock team, she'd made it a habit to observe her senior producer. RJ was always available for advice. Never hesitated to step into a gap. Breaking news didn't fluster him. And his ability to run interference between the team and their overanxious executive producer was a marvel.

On the downside, RJ was at the station before she got in and after she left. He was divorced with no kids, the type of private life common up the management chain. Only a few had partners or children.

In an ideal world, she could manage the increased responsibility of a promotion and a family—Luke and, someday, kids. But in reality, she hadn't quite figured out the right balance with him yet. They barely saw each other on weeknights.

She reentered the building, deep in thought. Luke knew she was ambitious, but she hadn't told him much about her specific career goals. They'd only been a couple for nine months, not enough time to share a possibility that had been—she assumed—years away. They'd have to talk about it now. Once Charlie's retirement was announced, change would come fast.

Jessica left the booth after the six o'clock news ended and returned to her desk long enough to get her purse. She hadn't seen Mima since the funeral and wanted to squeeze in a brief visit on the way home.

As she navigated through evening traffic, her mind was drawn back to the possibility of a promotion and when to tell Luke. It had to be an honest conversation, complete with the pros and the cons, but those depended on which part of the day had positions available. More hours were a certainty, but stress levels would be different in the morning versus the evening. Should she wait to introduce the contentious parts until she had details?

A simple heads-up would let him prepare for when she knew more. She would share only the announcement tonight and the heavier stuff this weekend.

When they'd first started dating last summer, it hadn't been so hard to schedule time together. With public schools on break, he hadn't been teaching. Even the fall hadn't been too bad because Luke had accommodated her.

Then the spring semester brought small, incremental changes. Luke had chaperoned the Spanish club to Puerto Rico over spring break. When he'd returned, the high school baseball season was ramping up, and he attended as many of those games as he could.

She'd planned to go to the team's evening games, but that hadn't worked out. April brought bad storms, a deadly tornado, and a trip from the president. Her free time had been claimed.

Not that she minded. She *loved* her job.

From the first moment she'd watched a TV reporter interview her grandmother, Jessica had known she'd found her calling. Once, as she and Mima were walking out of the North Carolina state legislative building, a news team ran up to her. The reporter stuck a microphone in her face and asked about her vote on a recent bill.

"Senator Azarian, you've been accused of flip-flopping."

She'd given him a withering look that would've had Jessica shaking in her sandals.

"Senator?"

"I'm waiting for the question."

"Did you flip-flop on the bill?"

She sighed. "Compromise is key to good governance. It strives to ensure the most good for the most people. Did I compromise for the most good? Yes, I did."

The reporter waited.

"You have your sound bite. Move along." Then she'd nodded at Jessica and continued down the steps, swinging hands.

Ten-year-old Jessie had loved the interview while it happened, but when it aired, she'd been amazed by the difference in what she'd witnessed live and what was portrayed on TV. In Jessica's opinion, Mima had been witty, but the edited clip made her seem arrogant. Jessica had grown intrigued by the production process, from shooting the interview to editing it into a few informative seconds for the newscast. She'd wanted to be *behind* the scenes. Producing the show. Writing the stories. Making sure video, graphics, and words came together into a fair and cohesive whole.

By high school, she'd mapped out a career plan. Journalism degrees. The right internships. Jobs in small markets to build skills and connections.

She'd been in Virginia for four years when a news producer job opened up at a station in Raleigh. She accepted the position to be closer to her aging grandparents and, of course, for the potential for advancement.

But the family plan had fewer specifics. Marriage by thirty and, after a brief period of adjustment, the first of their charming children.

Then she met Luke, and he'd shown her that love didn't follow a plan.

It was actually her sister who brought them together. Raine and Luke had hung out in the same circle in high school. Geeks on the track team. They'd both gone to colleges nearby and stayed in touch after Raine entered graduate school and Luke joined the National Guard.

The Luke that Raine introduced to Jessica fifteen years ago had been a shy, skinny freshman beginning his growth spurt, with a bad haircut, acne, and soulful brown eyes. That same image of him had lingered in her mind throughout his teen years, college, and military deployment. She'd been in Virginia Beach at her first full-time news producer position when he'd been sent to Afghanistan. Other than an occasional photo or a greeting in passing, she hadn't seen him again until nine months ago.

He'd cold-called her last August at the station. "Jessica, this is Luke Rivera."

She'd frowned, almost asking *Who?*, when the name clicked. *Raine's Luke.* "Oh. Hi?"

"I was talking with Raine last weekend, and she thought you might help me with a project I'm working on."

What was he doing now? Teaching high school English, if she remembered correctly. "Sure."

"I'm in public affairs for the National Guard. A unit's just back from Africa, and I'm editing a video clip . . ."

Her initial reaction had been that there might be a story there, so she'd agreed to meet. The reality of Luke in uniform, strong and ripped and confident, was breathtaking. How had she never noticed . . . *that*?

It only got better as they sat side by side while she coached him through the video-editing software on his personal computer. He was ridiculously good, given the resources available to him. She'd enjoyed the project—and him. Here was a guy who understood her profession and had zero interest in competing with her.

She'd pitched the story without success, but her interest in Luke stuck. When he'd asked her out for coffee, she'd agreed. He'd arrived at the shop ahead of her, held her chair, and paid obvious attention to what she'd said. She'd been hooked.

On her way home that night, she'd debated whether to call her sister. Since Raine didn't like talking on the phone, Jessica hadn't spoken with her sister in a couple of weeks. But curiosity overcame reluctance. She placed the call.

Raine answered immediately. "Yes?"

Might as well jump right in. "I went on a date with Luke."

"He told me."

That was all. No emotional shading to her voice. No reflection of her opinion. Jessica pressed. "What do you think?"

"It's cool." A pause. "He's a great guy, Jessica. Be good to him."

That last statement sounded ominous. "Why wouldn't I be?"

"Your job is your one true love. If you can't prioritize him . . . Just be careful."

Jessica couldn't argue with her sister's assessment, but it had made her acknowledge how much she wanted Luke in her life. She was a woman who created plans for everything, but no plan could've accounted for how hard and fast she fell for him. By the weekend, they'd met for a late dinner, left separately, then FaceTimed until 2:00 a.m. They were engaged after a month and married on New Year's Day.

In retrospect, it was amazing they'd found the time to fall in love. Their schedules hadn't aligned well. He was up at dawn and teaching teens before she awakened. If she got home at a reasonable hour, he was likely grading papers, only taking a break while they ate.

Jessica learned a lot about Raine's past from Luke, often hiding her surprise when he commented on things he'd assumed a sister would know. Like when he'd fallen at a track meet and wanted to give up, Raine had jogged beside him until he crossed the finish line. Or how their circle of friends had gone to prom together as one big group date. Or about a night in college where he'd been the getaway driver for Raine as she broke up with her emotionally abusive boyfriend.

Raine hadn't shared those stories, maybe because Jessica had been too engrossed in her own goals to draw out a sister who was notoriously cryptic about her life.

They were complete opposites in personality. Jessica loved being around people. Raine liked solitude. Jessica wanted to climb the ladder. Raine preferred where she was. Jessica's job was all about the power of words. Her sister, the power of numbers.

Their greatest commonality was Luke.

After parking in Larkmoor's visitor lot, Jessica walked briskly along a slate pathway to the three-story stone-and-cedar main building. The front doors swooshed open, and she stepped into the deserted lobby, with its chic charcoal-and-lemon furnishings. Laughter burst from her right, from the independent-living wing. Where Papa had moved just before his death.

As she passed through the windowed corridor to the memory-care unit, she spotted her grandmother plodding along a paved path in the enclosed courtyard, pushing her walker. Okay, a deep breath that her grandmother was in a good mental place today. Jessica exited through the automatic doors. "Mima?"

She paused, her frown wary. "Are you talking to me?"

"Yes, ma'am." Jessica had to start using her given name. "Mariah."

With an approving nod, she resumed her measured progress along the path, looking primly stylish in a red silk blouse, black linen pants, pearls, and leopard-print flats. She'd always been perfectly put together except for one thing that didn't quite fit, one thing she slipped in to give harmonious dissonance. When Jessica had been a child, it had been one of her favorite things about Mariah. Like *Goodnight Moon*'s mouse appearing on each page in a different place, there was always something to look for with her grandmother. Serpent hair clips. Skull buckles on her shoes. Thumbnails painted with whichever constellation was Raine's favorite that week.

Mariah hadn't cooked much, although she was good at it. She hadn't shown up at recitals or sporting events, usually because she was giving a speech to the NC General Assembly or meeting with constituents. But Jessica hadn't minded. She'd never felt unimportant. Her grandmother hadn't forgotten, no matter how long it took. "Excellent, Jessie. Let's do something special afterward" was all she'd needed.

Now that her grandmother's mind was faltering, now that she was no longer Mariah Azarian—that mighty force who kicked ass in a man's world and giggled over brownie sundaes in theirs—it had become their job to keep her special.

When Mariah reached the fountain at the courtyard's center, she scooted backward until her legs touched a wrought-iron bench. She inched down and shoved the walker to the side. "You may sit."

"Thank you." Jessica sat, close but not touching, and waited for signs her grandmother would welcome affection. There were none. Jessica looked at the garden instead, seeing why Mariah loved to sit here. It was peaceful in this place with the soothing symmetry to its beds, the fragrance of flowering herbs, the whispering waterfall and pond with lazy koi.

Her grandmother hummed "Soak Up the Sun." When she reached the refrain, she sang the lyrics, each word clear and correct. She ended abruptly midstanza and folded her hands in her lap. She had short, thin fingers, the veins like twisty blue twine. The skin would be velvet soft if anyone dared to touch.

"Why are you here, dear one?"

Dear one. Some days, Jessica wished she could do or say something to rewind Mariah's fading memories. What about the museums they'd gone to, hand in hand? The ballets and concerts? All her political campaigns, where Jessica had first become fascinated with television news? "I wanted something to do."

"You need more imagination."

Jessica laughed as she relaxed against the bench, for the first time in days able to enjoy the evening's warmth, the sounds of twilight.

"Speak up, dear one. I'm all ears."

Should she share her worries? Her grandmother wouldn't tell anyone else, even if she remembered. She'd always been good at keeping secrets.

"I have a career that I really love, and it requires a lot of hours."

"Is that a problem for you?"

"Not for me. But I've recently married, and I have to consider my husband. I feel like I'm neglecting him, and it worries me." She'd never spoken that thought aloud. It was achingly true.

"Hmm. Are you ambitious?"

"Sure."

"Be ambitious for both."

She straightened at the revelation. Was she ambitious for her job? Absolutely. She was making steady progress along her career plan. But ambitious for her marriage to Luke? She'd never thought about that, and she should have.

Mima clicked her fingernails impatiently on the bench. "Is there more?"

"My schedule isn't all that flexible," Jessica said, thinking out loud, "and neither is his. We're both so busy. I don't know how to spend more time with him and be good at my job."

"Tricky. What do you do?"

"I'm a journalist. In TV news."

"A journalist?" Mariah's voice was soft. "I wanted to be a photojournalist."

Jessica's visceral reaction was to deny the statement as another misfiring of her grandmother's broken mind. But maybe it wasn't so far from the truth. Mariah had been good for an amateur photographer. Jessica would play along. "What stopped you?"

"My father."

Her grandmother had been a steely-eyed force in the mostly male world of politics, supported by an indulgent and equally steely husband. But attitudes toward women had been far different in the fifties and sixties, especially when a father was the obstacle. "I don't think I've ever heard you mention him."

"No, I don't suppose you have. I try not to speak of him." With a sigh, she fumbled slowly to her feet. "It is late. I wish to go in now."

With Mima safely in her suite, Jessica returned to the visitor lot. As she was getting into her car, her phone pinged. A text from her husband.

We won

She stared at the two words in disbelief. She'd missed another baseball game?

How could she have forgotten? If she'd gone straight to the field after the newscast, she could've been with Luke for the final few innings.

She was eating a slice of cold pizza when the garage door whined up. A minute later, he came through the mudroom and crossed to the refrigerator.

"I'm sorry about the game, Luke."

He grabbed a bottle of water. "What happened?"

She winced at the quiet resignation in his tone. "I was with Mima."

He nodded soberly. "How is she?"

"Good."

"Okay. Maybe next time." As he walked past her, he said, "I have lesson plans to review." His footsteps thudded up the stairs.

She watched him go uneasily. He was disappointed she hadn't come to the game. Although she'd like to tell him her good news, now wasn't the right moment to broach the topic of a promotion guaranteed to consume more of her hours. Instead, she ought to be thinking about how to rebalance their lives. Their marriage was too new to be this starved for time.

CHAPTER 5

September 1960

Mariah's brother Stephen introduced her to the magic of a camera before she was old enough to go to school. Before her fingers were strong enough to click the shutter. She would trail after him, running to catch up with his long strides as they tramped through the woods or climbed in the barn, using the viewfinder to see the world differently. It was only practice, though. Film was too expensive to actually load in the camera.

In the beginning, Pa was indulgent. Her "hobby" didn't cost him anything, and it made her happy. Each Sunday before Mass, as he brushed her glossy ringlets, she would tell him adventures of frog parties in the creek or mushroom kingdoms on a log. He'd listen and chuckle, later telling Ma, "That girl has imagination."

But his indulgence ended when the twins were born. Ma was sick in bed for *so long*. Granny came to stay awhile, but after she left, Mariah had lots more chores. A first grader was plenty old enough to shoulder more of the women's work. Playtime was over.

The first time she'd finished her chores extra fast, she'd pleaded with Pa to let her practice with Stephen's camera. But all that earned her was a smacked mouth and bed without supper. She'd been shocked, 'cause she didn't think little girls got hit for punishment. But she knew better now.

Then one day, an empty Kleenex box appeared beneath her pillow. A hole had been cut in the bottom, the size of a viewfinder, to make a cardboard "camera." Joy—sweet and thick like warm syrup—flowed through her veins. She skipped to the kitchen. "Thanks, Ma."

Ma's free hand stroked the top of her head. Pulled her closer. "Okay, now. Go finish your chores."

"Yes, ma'am." Each day, after her homework and chores were done, Mariah would take her cardboard camera outside to practice and imagine.

◆ ◆ ◆

Mariah was twelve when Stephen graduated from high school. The ceremony had hardly ended before Pa kicked him out of the house.

"Make your own way, boy."

She would miss her brother *so much*, but she wouldn't miss the shouting and shoving and naughty words that made her hide in her room whenever Pa got mad at Stephen.

After her brother had packed his bags and tossed them onto the back seat of his Ford, he'd sent one last glance back at Ma and Mariah, his wink seeming to say, *I won't go far.*

That fall, she'd walked out of Mass one Sunday morning to find him waiting. After greeting Father Tim, he'd turned to his parents. "I can bring Mariah home. We'll take a ride through the country first."

Before Pa could bark out a refusal, Father Tim clapped Stephen on the shoulder. "What a good brother you are."

Pa closed his mouth, glared at his son, and stalked away. Ma and the twins followed like ducklings.

Stephen had driven her to the ocean. She loved it there. Fresh air with a briny scent. Sand, sea grass, and shells. People strolling and laughing, carefree. There wasn't much carefree in her life.

From the back of his Fairlane, he pulled out a fancy new camera. When she begged to hold it, he handed her his old Brownie instead. "It's yours now," he said, blue eyes sparkling.

She was *almost* speechless.

They'd wandered the beach. He snapped photo after photo of shells at the water's edge or dolphins playing in the waves. But she was stingier. Her babysitting money wouldn't stretch to developing many rolls of film. She agonized over what to take and limited herself to two shots.

After an hour, they sat side by side on the sand, staring out to sea.

"What did you shoot today, Rye?"

"The pier and the man helping his son build a sandcastle."

"Take whatever you like. You don't have to be so careful." He sucked deeply on his cigarette and blew out a stream of smoke the wind snatched away. "I've bartered with a photography studio. I help them out, and they let me use their darkroom. Whatever you shoot, I'll be able to develop."

After that, Stephen would pick her up after Mass on the last Sunday of the month, spend an afternoon hunting for interesting places to capture, and return her again before supper. Her father didn't like it but didn't interfere either. Stephen was bigger and stronger than Pa.

One summer morning, while Pa was taking the twins to a baseball game, Ma knocked on her bedroom door. "Can I see some of your pictures?"

Mariah gaped, shocked her mother even knew. "What . . . ?"

"Stephen told me. He says you're really good."

So she reached under the mattress and pulled out her *Very Best* folder. While Ma sat beside her on the bed, Mariah explained each photograph. They all had stories behind them, and Ma wanted to hear.

It was one of the happiest hours of Mariah's life, but it ended when gravel started popping in the driveway. Pa and the boys were home. She and her mother jumped off the bed, hurrying to hide the photos. As Ma left the room, they exchanged conspiratorial smiles. Their little secret.

◆ ◆ ◆

Saint Adalbert's Catholic School stopped at eighth grade, so her freshman year Mariah had to transfer. She would leave behind so much that was familiar. Seeing Father Tim and the three sisters each day. Wearing school uniforms. Starting each morning in worship. But she was excited too. The public high school would be an adventure.

Pa was uneasy about sending his daughter there. "A girl as pretty as you will attract attention. You have to be careful, or boys will find a way to sully your good name." Pa knew this because her brother Mitchell's sole claim to high school fame had been sullying. "Don't give them the chance."

He didn't have to worry. She'd never felt so free. She wasn't giving that up for a boy.

She made a beeline for the clubs bulletin board on her first day and hungrily looked for an outlet to use her camera. And there it was: the yearbook staff. She flipped through the past two yearbooks and discovered, to her chagrin, that her *Very Best* weren't the kind of shots a high school yearbook needed. And the staff had no girls.

Mariah made a plan, giving herself two years to practice. She patiently took her camera to school most days, buried deep in her bag, and focused on portraits. A weary librarian reshelving books. The janitor sneaking a smoke behind the gym. Students flirting on the patio outside the cafeteria. In a stroke of luck, there had been a rare snowstorm in the winter, and she'd captured a wonderful shot of the high school towering above the lawn like an icy castle surrounded by a skirt of pristine snow.

On the first day of her junior year, Mariah was ready. She shoved her portfolio into a three-ring binder and carried it around all day. When the final bell rang, she made her way to the yearbook advisor's classroom and waited until he was alone. He'd never had a girl photographer. She wanted to break the record.

Mr. Dolan welcomed her warmly, then flipped quickly through her photos. When he was done with one complete pass, he pursed his lips, looked through them again, pausing to study the photos that were her personal favorites. Hope tingled.

He spread the best of her *Very Best* on his desk. Shuffled them around. "Where did you learn to do this?"

"Stephen taught me," she said with pride. Her oldest brother claimed that he and Mr. Dolan had a mutual admiration society.

"Your work is . . . quite good." He looked up. "Tell me why you're here."

Mr. Dolan was being kind. She soaked it up like she was parched. Kindness was a rare treat in her life. "To be a yearbook photographer."

He closed his eyes briefly. "Mariah, yearbook photographers must be willing to accept any assignment. That includes after school and at night. No exceptions."

Her smile faded. Pa didn't allow her to go to football games or clubs or anything, really, outside school hours. "Good Catholic girls" didn't need temptation. "I don't think I can."

"You have more talent than I've seen in a month of Sundays, but my hands are tied. The principal won't let me bend the rules. Especially not . . ." He shook his head.

Especially not for a girl?

Or especially not for *her*—a *Byrne*?

It had to be the latter. Mitchell had been in constant trouble at school, and her father had stormed up there often to "straighten out those people." Now that the school was finally rid of Mitchell, no one wanted to tangle with Pa again. But Mariah wasn't prepared to give up easily. "Please, Mr. Dolan. I'll do whatever you need during the day."

"Mariah." He sighed. "I'd love to have you, but . . ."

"Please."

"Okay, let me think." He stacked the photos into a neat pile, then handed them back to her. His eyes held regret. "See if you can get your father to agree to home games."

In other words, no.

She spoke in a voice thick with disappointment. "Thank you."

For the rest of the afternoon, she trembled with nerves. Such a conversation with Pa would be foolish. He was bound to refuse, and he would learn he'd been deceived.

Should she ask?

No, she shouldn't. Too much risk.

But if she didn't, she'd be giving up. A quitter. Stephen wanted to be a photojournalist, and she thought she might like it too. To make her mark by telling stories with pictures. But journalism was a hard career. Journalists had to fight to get noticed. It'd be even harder for a woman. If she couldn't stand up to her own father, how could she hope to stand up to people in the business?

Throughout dinner, she listened to the scrape of forks as her brothers and father shoveled in their meal. She toyed with her food and pep-talked her way into courage. She could do this. Doubt meant certain failure.

When at last her father finished, she pounced. "Pa, can I join the yearbook club?"

He folded his napkin into a precise square and dabbed at his mouth. "Why?"

"To be one of the photographers."

"No use wasting your time with a hobby."

"It's not a hobby, Pa. People make good money with photography. Senator Kennedy's wife was a camera girl."

"Not anymore. She's a wife and a mother. And I expect she'll be the first lady too." He reached for his water glass. "What would you be taking pictures of?"

She was afraid to hope. "Candid shots around school. At plays and concerts."

He grunted and sipped.

"The games."

He frowned. "Football? At night?"

41

She nodded, fingers twisting together under the table.

"No."

"But, Pa—"

"End of discussion."

Her plans, her future, her *freedom* were all at stake. Ignoring her mother's warning pats on the knee, she pushed harder. "I'm good. Mr. Dolan says so."

Pa's pupils looked huge behind his glasses. "How did you get good?"

Too late she realized her error, and she was about to make it worse. The only person who tried her father's patience more than his daughter was his oldest. "Stephen's given me lessons."

At her brother's name, Pa set down his glass with a menacing click. "Has he, now?" He turned to his wife. "Did you know?"

Ma's face flushed guilt red. The look Pa shot her promised bruises tomorrow.

He stood, the chair shrieking against the linoleum, and limped down the hall, the special shoe replacing his missing foot clomping loudly on the floorboards. The door to her room creaked. A drawer in her dresser screeched open. Slammed shut.

Oh please. No.

Open. Shut.

The bottom drawer squawked. It didn't shut.

Had he found it? Her Brownie? When she got home this afternoon, she'd put it in her underwear drawer instead of the good hiding place. Surely he wouldn't touch her private things—

A foot stomped. Then . . . crunch. Crackle. The sound of a dream breaking.

She leaped from the table, too horrified to stay until dismissed. Racing to her bedroom, she halted in the doorway. The shattered remains of her Brownie lay on the floor. A spool of exposed film curled around her father's foot as he ground it into the floorboards.

"Like I said, girl. End of discussion."

She looked from the Brownie's destruction to his face. He watched her reaction, smirking.

He wouldn't see her cry. She blanked her face, her thoughts spinning. The camera's loss was a huge setback. A cruel act to thwart her. But her father was a fool to think he had. She was determined and patient. If something was worth having, she could wait.

There would be other cameras. Other opportunities to hone her skill. She would become so good that photography would make her money—and let *her* make a difference.

For Pa, this might be the end of the discussion. But for Mariah, it was the beginning of a better dream.

CHAPTER 6

Raine hauled Papa's cartons onto the bed in her home office, then paused to study them, itching to get started. But discipline won out. She had contracts to complete.

She brought up the to-do list on her laptop and hesitated. Should she add items about the certification exam?

Her shoulders slumped. Why did the thought of completing her certification twist her into knots? All she needed was the exam. She didn't like taking them, but it wasn't that big of a deal. Certainly not an even trade for letting down Papa or herself.

Okay, enough. She typed in three items: *access materials*, *study*, *take exam*. Then she went back to making progress on her freelance projects.

After dinner, she indulged her need to work on Papa's wish. After crawling onto the guest bed, she plumped the pillows behind her back, opened carton one, and lifted out the *Courtship* album. She riffled through its paper pages, getting an initial impression. Scallop-edged snapshots attached with yellowing Scotch tape. There were numerous candids of her grandparents partying. Papa with a drink and a cigarette. An astonishingly beautiful Mariah standing beside him with flawless skin, pouty red lips, poufy dark hair flipped up at the ends, and cautious brown eyes heavily highlighted with mascara and eyeliner.

Big, impersonal parties yielded to more intimate events. Two pages had been devoted to a backyard barbecue. A door lay across a pair of sawhorses, piled with burgers, chips, and sodas. The decorations and Papa's captions proclaimed it a Fourth of July party for his construction crew and their families. Mariah wore a hard hat painted with **BOSS OF ALL**.

Near the album's end was an eight-by-ten of Papa in a suit, standing in front of a house under construction, smiling as if he was struggling to control laughter. On the opposite page, the same photo appeared on the cover of a local magazine, dated May 1965.

The final pages focused on their engagement. There were snapshots of her grandparents outside the Armenian Apostolic church in Richmond. A professional portrait claimed its own page. Papa's smile was huge and proud. Mariah's was more typically muted, yet sweet. Tucked in the back pocket were a newspaper clipping of their engagement announcement, a pressed rosebud, and, inexplicably, a black-and-white shot of Dorton Arena. Why had Papa kept *that*?

In a forensic accounting investigation, Raine flagged anything that stuck out as curious, memorable, or out of place. She would use that same technique with Papa's wish, and she was curious enough about the Dorton Arena photo to set it aside.

She yawned, stretched, and checked the time. It was after eight. She'd been immersed in her grandparents' courtship for more than an hour. If the date stamps on some of the photos could be believed, they'd married within four or five months of when they first started dating. Jessica had inherited the fast-romance gene.

Logic said that the *Gregor* album would hurt most, which was why she would review it next. She plopped it on her lap. It was slimmer than *Courtship*. Its opening page held two black-and-white prints. A baby dressed in tiny shorts and suspenders, with slicked-down hair and a wide-eyed look of wonder. Next, a grumpy toddler, hands reaching for something unseen. Both images were unmistakably Papa.

There were photographs with clusters of solemn people, all taken outside, always with a couple and a small child in the middle. Papa and his parents? Abruptly, the album skipped forward to the 1940s. Since his father had been killed in World War II, the remaining family portraits showed Papa with his mother and younger brother, the boys in starched shirts with dark ties and pants hemmed not quite long enough for their legs. The final page had Papa in an army uniform, head nearly bald, fear embedding wrinkles in his brow.

She closed the album. It had been a pleasure to see those photos, but poignant too. She wished she could've gone through them with Papa. However, nothing had stuck out, which was curious in itself. This album would get a second review.

She yawned again, weariness washing over her. She'd been plagued by insomnia lately, her brain too busy with whirling thoughts to let go. If she didn't sleep soon, she'd be worthless tomorrow.

Well, maybe she could squeeze in one more. She reached for *Mariah* next. What would this album reveal about her grandmother?

Raine had been so comfortable in Papa's presence. He'd gotten that her love of solitude didn't mean she was lonely. She simply liked being alone. He'd accommodated her preference for serenity and order, but they'd had laughter too.

Her relationship with her grandmother had been more . . . formal. It was Jessica who shared a stronger bond with Mariah. Whenever the two of them had been together, they'd get all giggly and girly and spontaneous. Raine had approached Mariah with awe—this heavenly creature so perfect that Raine had feared touching her, worried she might mess something up. Raine adored Mariah, but it had been overwhelming to be her granddaughter.

Wedged into the album's front pocket was a loose eight-by-ten of a model-beautiful woman with a 1940s-era hairstyle—a fat roll of hair framing her face. She wore a white jacket, a black skirt, and gloves. In her arms was an equally beautiful little girl in a frothy dress, shiny black shoes, and lace-trimmed socks. Although the photo was in sepia tones, someone had added touches of . . . watercolor? Blue eyes, blonde hair, and red lips for the woman. Dark-brown eyes and hair with a pink polka-dotted dress for the toddler.

On the portrait's back was stamped a Wilmington address and *1946*. It had to be her grandmother and great-grandmother. Raine knew little about the Byrnes other than Mariah's oldest brother. Uncle Stephen had died during the Vietnam War. Mariah's parents were also deceased, but she had been estranged from them since her teens. The only other family name she'd ever mentioned was "Uncle-Duane-we're-not-close."

Was Raine about to learn more about the Byrnes?

Another loose photo slipped out onto the bedspread. A black-and-white candid showed seven people. Five males of various sizes, each in buzz cuts and suits. Two females in formfitting dresses with short sleeves. Mariah was in the middle. Raine would recognize that look of aloof defiance anywhere. A young man towered behind her, definitely older, probably Uncle Stephen. Another lounged against a brick wall, smirking. Short, identical twin boys stood in front of her. On one side of the children was a frowning man, his face partially shadowed by his hat. On the other, her namesake, Great-Grandma Lorraine, her face in profile as she smiled at the twins.

One of the unidentified boys was likely the phantom Uncle Duane. And the other two? Were they friends? Or did Mariah have two never-before-mentioned brothers?

If this was the family secret, it was more sad than shocking.

Raine had her first real lead to follow. She could take the loose photos on tomorrow morning's visit to her grandmother and hope that Mariah would remember.

Raine was enjoying a rosy dawn on her balcony when her phone buzzed. A text from Luke.

I'm at Uncommon Grounds. Want coffee?

A rhetorical question. She tapped a reply as she walked into her living room, scanning for her flip-flops.

Sure. Be there in 5

Before leaving, she filled a paper bag with an assortment of muffins and grabbed her purse. Three minutes later, she was entering the coffee shop. Her brother-in-law had claimed a table by the window.

She slid onto the opposite chair and returned his smile. It was past time to emerge from her haven. "Morning." She handed him the muffin bag.

"Hey." He pushed over a to-go cup. "Have you been in contact with your family?"

"I'm talking to you right now. That counts." She sipped her coffee. *Mmm, perfect.* "Yesterday, I saw Dad and texted your wife."

He made a show of checking his watch. "So that makes three days completely alone?"

It was her most successful coping strategy, as Luke well knew. Nice of him to worry, though. "I required silence to process Papa's death."

Luke checked the contents of the paper bag. "And baking therapy."

Okay, he wasn't letting this go. She would add another reason. "Papa and I had a conversation we didn't finish. Now we never will."

Luke's face softened. "You baked muffins instead."

"And cookies and pie and bread." Her smile widened. "I won't repeat the bread mistake."

"You should've called me."

"I wasn't ready to interact with my family."

"We've been *friends* for fifteen years."

"You've been promoted." She and Luke had met at a high school known for its overachievers. Both had been misfits. Luke because he'd been a wary transfer student. Raine because she'd been a geek in recovery from her parents' divorce. But despite their differences, they'd become friends. He'd tutored her in English and Spanish. She'd tutored him in math. When they'd joined the track team together, they found themselves absorbed into a diverse athlete clique.

Through college and career and the churn of becoming adults, their friendship had held. Until his "promotion" to brother-in-law. Raine had known that marriage for either of them would create change. But with Luke married to Jessica, their relationship had to shift even more. Sharing private details might be okay with a friend, but it was just awkward with your wife's sister.

He poured cream into his travel mug. "So you've communicated with Donovan and Jessica."

"Yeah." Raine leaned forward, resting her arms on the table. "Dad told me that Papa left his grand girls a last wish."

Luke's eyebrows rose. "What is it?"

"To learn the truth about a family secret. But instead of simply telling us, he wants us to figure it out."

"Jessica hasn't mentioned that."

"She doesn't know."

"Why not?"

This would sound like a criticism of his wife. Which it was, actually. But it was a commentary on Raine too. She could've tried harder to get her sister's attention. "When I texted her, she said she was busy."

He sipped his coffee. Frowned. "That's the default for her."

"Too busy for you too, huh?"

"Yeah." He opened his mouth. Closed it.

She understood his hesitance. The Luke who'd been her friend since high school would've said more, but her brother-in-law could not. A transition in progress.

He gave a slight shake of his head. "What am I saying? We're both too busy. It'll get better this summer. So really, how are you doing?"

"Bruised but not broken." Next he might try to bring up feelings or something. *Nope.* "Don't you have a bunch of teenagers somewhere to teach?"

"Yeah, I ought to go." He stood and picked up the travel mug and the bag of muffins. As he opened the coffee shop door for her, he asked, "Can I tell Jessica about the wish?"

"There's nothing I say to you that you have to keep a secret from your wife."

He shot her a smile as he turned toward his car.

Raine worked until midmorning before leaving for Larkmoor. When she arrived at the memory-care unit, an aide directed her to the recreation room. She walked into subdued lighting and the scent of lavender, vinegar, and stale sweat. A few people gathered around a large TV, watching an Alfred Hitchcock movie. Mariah sat alone at a table, pulling cards from a deck, slapping them down, moving things around, following a set of rules known only to herself.

Raine pulled out a chair beside her. "Hello, Mariah."

Her grandmother side-eyed her, then frowned at the card game. "Why are you here, dear one?"

"Visiting my grandmother."

Mariah stole a surreptitious glance around the room at the other grandmother-aged women in view. "Have a lovely time."

Raine sucked up the pang of sadness. By the time she'd been old enough to feel completely comfortable around her grandmother, Mariah's mind had begun to slip. Now it was too late. "What are you doing?"

"Playing cards."

"Who's winning?"

"The cards."

Raine laughed. It was one of her grandmother's good days.

Mariah threw the deck on the table and sighed loudly. "Why are you here, dear one?"

Had she repeated the question for emphasis? Or had she forgotten she'd already asked? Raine had her attention, either way. While her grandmother was unlikely to remember this morning or last week, she might remember sixty years ago. Pulling the photos from her backpack, she spread them on the table.

Mariah inhaled deeply and leaned forward on her arms. "Hmm."

"I'm curious about these photos. Do you recognize them?"

"Yes."

Excitement prickled. "Why would your husband keep a photo of Dorton Arena?"

"It's where he asked me to marry him."

"Really?" Raine tried to visualize Papa popping the question in the stands among a cheering crowd. "Like during the circus?"

"No, he had connections." Her grandmother smiled dreamily. "We were there alone with a picnic basket and champagne and a rose."

Aww, that was a romantic and believable explanation. Papa did have connections. Raine would like to hear that story, but it would have to wait until she asked about the other two images. She pushed over the shot of Great-Grandma Lorraine with toddler Mariah. Raine had put it in a frame to be a keepsake if her grandmother wanted. "How about them?"

"My mother and I. She was stunning, wasn't she? Too bad."

"Why is that too bad?"

Mariah traced a fingertip across her mother's red lips in the photo. "It's a terrible thing to be a beautiful woman with a jealous husband."

Raine frowned. Her grandmother didn't speak often of her father. Were the Byrnes part of the puzzle? "Would you like me to leave this photo?"

"Please."

She pushed over the picture of the group of seven. "Is this your family?"

"Yes. My parents and brothers." Her grandmother's nose wrinkled like she'd sniffed something foul. "You can keep that one."

Mystery solved. Mariah had four brothers, and her granddaughters had only known of two. Why?

Okay, slow down. Papa had expected them to reserve judgment, and she would, but great-uncles she'd never heard of was certainly a surprise. "Do you know their names?"

"Of course I do. Mitchell, Douglas, and Duane." Her expression softened as she touched the guy standing behind her. "Stephen."

"Stephen is the only one you ever discuss."

"He is the only one I care about."

He is. Present tense. "What happened to the others?"

"Casualties of war."

Wow. All of them? That was awful. Was that why they hadn't heard of them? Did she find it too upsetting to speak of? "Which war?"

Her lips twisted bitterly. "The war with my father."

A "war" with her father and two brothers Raine had never heard of? She'd definitely found her first clue to track down.

CHAPTER 7

Jessica had been busy this morning putting the evening newscast together, looking for ways to better present the stories, arranging them in the rundown. And the piece on baby goats? She might have reviewed its video more than once, just to be sure they were still adorable.

Pushing from her desk, she went to the break room in search of caffeine. As she was walking back out again, her phone rang.

"Hi, Jessica," her mother said. "Can you talk?"

"Briefly."

"Have you heard from Raine?"

"Yeah." The call was about her sister. No surprise. Mom tended to flutter when her youngest showed signs of distress. "We texted yesterday." Jessica had to get back to Raine when she wasn't busy.

"Okay, I thought I'd check."

Jessica halted at the entrance to the newsroom and looked around. The energy had intensified. The executive producer was gesturing for her. Something was up. "Sorry, Mom. I have to run."

A sigh. "Bye."

In an instant, everything changed. An armed man had robbed a bank, then fled on foot, triggering a lockdown of all schools within a ten-mile radius. One of the station's teams had been coincidentally at the closest elementary school on a feature story and got caught up in the breaking news. They'd shot some excellent footage. Racing police cars. Shouted commands to hide. Small, frightened faces pressed to windows before their teachers pushed them to safety. Although the robber had been apprehended, he'd come too close for comfort. A sobering reminder of the dangers that lurked.

Jessica didn't catch her breath again until midafternoon. She slumped wearily in her desk chair, ignored her growling stomach, and skimmed her messages. Another text from her sister.

Are you still busy? I actually have something important to tell you

I'm due a break. Why?

Papa left us a final wish

Succinct without being clear. That was just like her sister. Jessica's plate was full. She didn't have time for dragging out the information.

What kind of wish?

I'll show you when we talk. Can I come there?

Raine wanted to *talk*? Like, in person? Her sister tended to avoid face-to-face conversations. Jessica glanced at her watch. She had a meeting in an hour.

I'm free until 4

Hungry?

Yes

I can be there in 10 minutes. I'll bring lunch

Raine never dropped by the station because she hated the chaos. They should meet outside.

Ok. Meet me in the rear garden

When Jessica entered the garden a few minutes later, she found Raine standing by a shaded picnic table, dressed casually in black calf-length yoga pants and an oversize tee. She didn't look sloppy. She was too careful for that. It was just that, as short as she was and with her hair in a bob, she looked about half her age.

As Jessica drew near, Raine pointed at two to-go cups and a giant cupcake on a paper plate. "Lunch."

"The best kind." Jessica slid onto the bench and watched as her sister divided the cupcake. Red velvet with cream cheese frosting. Her favorite. She broke off a piece, then checked the time. "What's up?"

Raine licked frosting from her fingers, wiped them on a moist towelette, and pulled a white envelope from her backpack. "It's in here."

"The final wish?"

"Yes."

Jessica held the envelope as if it was a fragile thing, feeling weepy to see Papa's nickname for them in his gorgeous, calligraphy-like handwriting. He'd used his fountain pen, the nib pressed so firmly that she could trace *grand girls* with her finger. She drew out a sheet of heavy white vellum and read.

My dearest Raine and Jessica . . .

Grief quivered deep inside her. He'd written those words knowing they wouldn't read them until after his death. She pushed on until the end, then read the letter again. The wish was uncomfortably vague.

Jessica folded the letter and slid it back into the envelope. They'd been given a joint project to discover a story they didn't know that would disappoint them? The whole thing unsettled her. "When did you find this?"

"Yesterday morning."

"Why did you wait to tell me?"

"I didn't. You said you were busy."

"But—" She stopped. Her sister had texted, and Jessica had brushed her off. Because she *had* been busy. Too busy. Between catching up after her bereavement leave, Charlie's announcement, visits to Mima, breaking news, and Luke, it would've been hard to schedule anything else. Raine had done her a favor by not adding to the load. "Is this all we have to go on?"

"The letter's more of a kickoff. The contents of the hope chest are clearer. Three distinct steps."

"You've opened the hope chest?" *Without me?*

"Well, yeah."

"What did you find?"

"Three cartons filled with artifacts. Photos. Eight-millimeter films. Documents."

"Where are the cartons?"

"They were in Papa's study. They're in my condo now."

Jessica stifled a flash of irritation as she took in the shadows under her sister's eyes. The determination in the set of her jaw. For the past nine days, Jessica had leaned on her husband. And her sister had leaned on . . . whom? Jessica sagged at the thought of one more thing to do, but there was no choice. She couldn't let her sister grieve alone anymore. "Okay. When do we start?"

"I already have. Carton one has the photo albums." Out from the backpack came two albums, one thick, one thin. "I saved these for you to go through."

"Wait." Jessica frowned at the albums, then at her sister. "Are you in charge?"

"In charge?" Her sister's lips pinched. "Yeah, I guess I am."

"Why?"

"Someone has to be." Raine tilted her head back and looked up at the sky. "Papa left the key for me, so he wanted me to be the leader. I'm not sure why. Maybe because you're busy, and I'm not . . . quite as busy."

Jessica couldn't argue the point. May was ratings month, which put more stress on her job than normal. Now, she would have to add Papa's final wish. It would take time, a commodity she had precious little of. "Can the albums wait until June?"

"If that's your preference, I'll keep these." Her sister stuffed them back into her backpack. "It's my preference to make progress. Let me know when you're available."

Jessica dropped her head forward, weighed down by all she had to do. This was the first time she'd seen her sister since the funeral. She hadn't seen her mother at all. And she never saw enough of Luke. She had to rethink her priorities. "Is there something simple I can do?"

"Sure." Raine tapped on her phone. "I've sent you a link to a share-able folder. I've been putting notes and images there. Check out the photo of Mariah and her four brothers."

"Four?" Jessica clicked on the image. A teenage Mariah stood in the midst of six other people. Parents and four brothers? Odd that she'd never seen a picture of Mariah's family of origin. Nor had she ever really wondered why she hadn't. "I only knew about two of them."

"Me too, but Mariah identified them. Stephen, Mitchell, Duane, and his twin Douglas. It'd be great if you could uncover more about them."

"Wait." This was too much, too fast. "You haven't searched for them yet?"

"Actually, I have. Uncle Stephen's at Arlington Cemetery. There's a Duane Byrne in a small town outside Wilmington who's a possibility. For Mitchell and Douglas, the number of links was unmanageable. I thought I'd leave them for you."

Not much of a task, but she could handle it at home. "Text me what you have, and I'll see what I can find." She held out her hand impatiently. "What about the albums? What can I do with them?"

Raine gave an exaggerated sigh. "Review. See what sticks out or anything else TV news types do when they smell a story."

"Hand them over. I'll find the time." Jessica kept her expression neutral, but the dismissive attitude toward her career field stung. Once she had the albums in her arms, she stood. "I should get back. Thanks for lunch."

Her sister joined her on the path back to the building. "When will you get to the photos?"

"By Saturday."

Raine started to respond, then shrugged. "Okay." She tossed trash into a receptacle and stopped beside her car. "Is something going on? You're acting different. More preoccupied than normal."

Jessica halted. Really? Her sister had picked up on that? "The assistant news director is retiring soon."

"Wow, that's big. People will shift around. There will be promotions."

Sometimes Raine seemed to not get it, and other times, scarily tuned in. "Yeah, there will be."

"Is this sooner than you expected?"

Jessica nodded, already regretting that she'd shared anything. Her husband should've been the next to know.

"This changes your career plan and family plan."

She'd never mentioned the plans out loud. Not even to Luke. "How do you know about them?"

"You spill your guts when you're drunk."

"When have I ever been drunk around you?"

"Six years ago, when Curtis broke your engagement. You drove all the way home from Virginia Beach to tell Mom, then came to my apartment, drank hard cider like it was water, and talked nonstop. Curtis screwed with your heart, and you were going to *Show. Him.* Then you told me every stop along your career ladder, with flexibility for where 'Mommy' fit between the various levels of news producer. I was glad when you passed out."

Jessica suppressed a groan. She didn't remember much about that night, including the reason she couldn't remember. Why had she spilled so much about something so private?

Curtis had been a big mistake, Jessica's uncharacteristic foray into dating someone she worked with. He'd been another news producer, whose career was two years ahead of hers—and therefore, in his mind, "more important." He'd accepted a promotion at a TV station on the West Coast before discussing it with her—mainly because he didn't want her to go. Her pride had been more wounded than her heart, but it had still hurt.

She glanced at her watch. Ten minutes until the afternoon meeting. She had to shut down this conversation until she shared the plans with Luke. "I was twenty-six. Things change."

"Not *your* plans. You've clung to them like they're imprinted on your soul. Have you told Luke about the promotion?"

"I will." She would have already if life hadn't gotten in the way.

Her sister rolled her eyes.

"What?"

"He has a career plan too. Grad school."

"I know. My getting promoted won't change that."

"Maybe." Raine opened her car door. "Be careful. Tell him soon."

"I am. Tonight." Jessica hurried into the building, irritated with herself when she saw the conference room was already full. She hated to be late, but she couldn't let go of what Raine had said. *Careful.* She used that word often when talking about Luke. Jessica had always thought *careful* was a warning for his sake. But maybe it was a warning for *hers*. Her husband was a man of infinite patience. Was her sister suggesting that might not always be the case?

She made it home for dinner at a decent hour and was greeted with delicious smells. "What's this?" she asked, stopping beside Luke to peer in the skillet.

"Chicken tikka masala. It'll be ready in about ten." He pressed his lips to hers.

She leaned into the kiss, then broke away reluctantly. "I'll change and be right down."

When she returned, he had two places on the bar with a platter of rice and chicken and a bowl of salad.

"Mmm. This is nice." She slid onto a stool, looking forward to an evening meal with her husband. "Why don't you tell me about your day?"

His smile was wide. "It's possible the baseball team will make it to the playoffs."

"That's great news." She had to attend one of his games. "When will you know?"

"Next Wednesday." He launched into other school news, ending with the senior projects. He was the senior advisor this year, and he'd been delighted with the quality of their work. "Oh. Um, I want to show you something." He bent over his messenger bag, and out came a folded slip of paper, ripped from a spiral notebook, addressed in cramped writing to Mr. Rivera.

She smoothed it open.

Thank you for being the hardest teacher I've ever had . . .

The letter continued in the same vein. Luke had encouraged the student in his creative writing ability, cheering the kid past his insecurities and disinterest from home. Something Luke said must have really connected, because the young writer's emotions leaped off the page.

"Wow, Luke. This is amazing."

He blushed with pride.

Her husband had been a finalist for Wake County Teacher of the Year before, so she'd known his peers regarded him highly. But to be so good a student felt compelled to commit their feelings to paper? Teaching was more than something Luke did. It was who he was. Her attitude toward his job shifted, like tiny pieces in a kaleidoscope clicking into place. The image was still beautiful, but there was a new pattern to take in.

She collected their dishes and dropped them in the sink, her thoughts tumbling. What mattered to him had to matter to her too. She had to do better. To be *careful*.

As she added water, he slid an arm around her waist. "Let them soak. I haven't picked up the mail today. We could walk up to the mailbox kiosk together."

How out of control had their lives become when a trip to get the mail felt like a date? "Sure."

As they strolled toward the neighborhood clubhouse, holding hands, he said, "Tell me your news."

"Okay." A beautiful night and a relaxed hour together made for the perfect opportunity to talk. "Charlie's planning to retire."

"Wow." Luke glanced down at her. "What will that mean for you?"

She smiled. It pleased her that he got it. "A promotion is possible."

"That's great. When will you know?"

"Nothing's official, so no details yet. Could be soon." Moving on to the next big item. "Raine came to the station today. We shared a cupcake."

"So she told you about the family secret."

Her sister had told her husband first? "You knew?"

He nodded. "I met Raine for coffee on the way to the high school this morning. She said she contacted you."

"Her first text didn't mention it was important."

"When does Raine ever text about unimportant things?"

Jessica's irritation deflated. He was right. Her sister was too frugal with communication to squander it on trivial things. "She showed me a letter Papa left us. I saw his handwriting and . . ." She swallowed over the lump in her throat. Such a simple thing to stir up her grief. "Anyway, we're to uncover the whole truth behind family secrets before passing judgment."

"Together."

She looked up at him. "Yes."

"That'll be good for both of you."

"It'll be frustrating for me."

"Why?" His inflection was odd.

"She has her preferences for how to do things."

He grinned. "That may run in the family."

"True." She didn't bother to roll her eyes. He wouldn't be able to see them in the dark.

"Jess." He pulled her to a stop under a streetlamp. "Teachers are taught in neurodiversity training to accept people where they are. There are many ways to think and act and be." He smiled. "You and Raine can have different approaches to your grandfather's wish. View your differences as strengths."

After they'd collected their mail and were turning toward home, Luke said, "Your grandfather worried about how distant you and Raine are." At her look of astonishment, he added, "I'm worried too, Jess. Sometimes it feels like I'm a go-between for the two of you, and it doesn't have to be that way. This is your chance to be friends."

Friends with Raine? Jessica got along with her sister just fine. They shared a bond of history. But friendship? She'd have to give that some thought.

CHAPTER 8

Raine checked her business messages Thursday morning and found a text from one of her favorite clients. Patrick owned a forensic accounting firm in Durham, and he sent a lot of great projects her way.

Have time to handle a second opinion?

She liked writing second opinions on another forensic accountant's report. Besides offering her insights into how others attacked problems, she wouldn't have to testify. She would work this in.

Patrick often followed a freelance request with a question about when she would be certified. It had been two weeks since her final visit with Papa, and she hadn't acted yet. Why not just do it? She brought up the certification website, downloaded the exam outline, and paid for the review course.

She would start studying . . . soon.

Time to reply to Patrick's message.

How fast would you need it back?

He answered within a couple of minutes.

End of June

Yes, I can do that

He was texting again. It took a while, but the question was predictable.

Do you have your CFF yet?

She was glad she had a better answer than *no*.

Starting the exam process

When you have it completed, let me know

Why? Would he send her different types of projects afterward? Maybe offer her a job? She mulled over the latter possibility. She liked working with him, but *for* him?

Okay, no use wasting time on hypotheticals. Back to work. She had a due date looming on the insurance fraud report.

The pinging of her phone startled her, dragging her from deep concentration. It was her mother.

Want to join me for lunch?

They hadn't seen each other since the funeral, and Mom must be worried. It was unlike her to hold off this long from checking on her younger daughter. Lunch would be nice. Although Raine had her afternoon obligated, she could fit in an hour break.

Sure. When?

As soon as you can get here

On my way

As she drove to her mother's town-house community, she pondered what to do about Patrick. She was pretty sure she'd like working for him. He was relaxed and reasonable. She wouldn't have to seek projects anymore because he would find them. His firm would provide a benefits package and handle the noise of managing taxes and such, all desirable aspects of being employed. However, since the certification part was so important to him, he'd expect her to be willing to testify. Was that something they could negotiate?

No, probably not, but it couldn't hurt to ask.

Raine banished the Patrick dilemma to a corner of her mind as she tapped in the security code of her mother's ranch townhome. The deadbolt snicked back, and she went inside. Mom's home was in its typical company-ready condition. The great room looked designer perfect with its love seat and chairs in pink, coordinating prints topped with an abundance of lace-trimmed pillows. Scented candles lined the mantel. Walls teemed with photographs in matching frames. A restful place to be. "Mom?"

Her mother rushed from her bedroom to give her daughter a perfumed hug. Raine held her breath.

"Thanks for coming over, sweetie. Tuna salad sandwiches okay?"

Better than okay. "Sure."

Mom went into the kitchen and assembled the ingredients. Homemade bread. Tuna salad. Mayo. Tomato. "How are you feeling?"

"Moving in the right direction." Raine dropped her purse on the couch and joined her mother at the kitchen island. Better distract her mother before she pursued feelings any deeper. "How's the house-staging job?"

"Going well." Mom's smile was smugly satisfied. "I'm known as the budget stager. I have a talent for making great finds at flea markets and overstock stores." She gestured toward the refrigerator. "Fix the tea, please. And chips are in the pantry."

Raine finished her part of the lunch setup, then sat on a barstool.

"Here you go." Mom set a plate before her daughter, the sandwich cut into four triangles.

No crusts. Serious concession to how Raine preferred sandwiches. Habit or bribe? "Did you invite me over for a reason?"

Mom sat on the other barstool and stared with an exaggerated tilt of her head. "Did you give Mama the photo of Great-Grandma Lorraine?"

"Mm-hmm," Raine mumbled, savoring her first bite, then washing it down with tea. "I found it in Papa's study."

"His study?" Her mother stiffened. "I thought the house was empty."

"It is, everywhere but the study."

"What else did you find?" she asked, her eyes narrowing.

The edge to Mom's attitude seemed out of proportion. Interesting. "Four photo albums. *Gregor*, *Mariah*, *Courtship*, *Our Family*."

"They should be mine. When can I get them?"

Raine ate another bite, buying herself time to process the change in Mom. She was more bothered than the information deserved. Raine would have to proceed cautiously until she knew why. "As soon as I've finished scanning the photos in."

"You don't have to do that."

"But I will."

"It's not necessary."

"Jessica and I would like copies." In a forensic investigation, Raine had learned the value of choosing the right time to share information. This felt like one of those times. She pulled out her phone, hunted for the Byrne family image, and held it up. "Here's a photo I found."

Mom glanced at it. Sniffed. Looked away.

"Did you know Mariah had four brothers?"

"Of course I did." She crunched a chip primly.

"Why have you never told us?"

Mom finished chewing the chip. Wiped her fingers on the cloth napkin. Picked up her sandwich. "It wasn't pertinent."

"How can it not be pertinent that we have extended family?"

"Mama's estranged from them. I've honored her wishes."

Our family has a story . . .

What else did Mom know? "Any ideas where the brothers are?"

Her mother shrugged, then made a show of enjoying her sandwich.

Raine waited. Silence was an effective tool with her mother.

"Okay," Mom said in a huff. "Two are dead. I think the other two are still alive, but I don't know anything about them." Sliding off her stool, she took her plate around the island and dumped the remnants into the trash.

"We'll find them."

"We?"

"Me and Jessica."

Mom crossed her arms. "I don't see the point of dragging this up."

"But we will."

"Listen, sweetheart," she said, voice softening. A change in tactics. "It's just family history, and it's distressing for Mama. Why bother?"

"It's my history too. I have the right to know." She might not like what she uncovered, but she was determined to try. Dad had been right to warn her about being careful with Mom. Raine would leave out the part about the wish. "Will you at least confirm what I learn?"

"I won't help you at all." Mom scrubbed at a spot on the counter, her tone carefully mild. "There's nothing to be gained from pursuing this. You have to stop."

Raine slipped from the stool, puzzled by her mother's reaction. But also intrigued. Why was she so insistent? "Thanks for lunch." After grabbing her purse, Raine let herself out of the townhome.

But as she drove home, she reviewed the conversation. Stephanie Elliott had been the fun, upbeat mom. Willing to help anyone, anytime. It was why her parents' divorce had been such a shock. Sure, there had been tensions. Arguments that stopped abruptly the instant her parents realized they had an audience. Then cheerful Mom had returned and smoothed everything over.

Until Dad moved out.

Raine hadn't tried to understand. It had been easier to hide the pain and confusion behind classes and friends and track meets—anything to be away from home while her mother fought the divorce.

Raine had been relieved when her mother finally gave in. She'd come home from a track team practice one Saturday, and Mom had just been . . . not normal, exactly. More like making an effort. She'd dressed up, served a homemade lunch, asked questions, and showed real interest in Raine's responses. Mom's mood had turned a corner. Not perfect, but on the way to a pleasant stasis.

She'd followed a similar strategy today. Lunch, low-key curiosity, then pointed interest in the most pleasant of terms. The ploy wouldn't work. Mariah had been estranged from her extended family, and Raine was determined to uncover why.

CHAPTER 9

May 1962

Mariah would graduate tonight, and oh, was she ready. She wouldn't miss anything about high school, not the teachers or the classes or the students. But what she looked forward to most was what the ceremony meant. After today, she would be free. She could go anywhere she wanted. Be whatever she wanted to be.

Well, that wasn't entirely true. Pa thought college was a waste for a woman, and she couldn't afford to attend without his help. She'd applied to the teachers' college in Greenville in secret, hoping that if she got in, he'd relent. She didn't really want to be a teacher, but he might change his mind for a ladies' job.

Since she couldn't count on college, there would have to be a new plan. She couldn't bear to live in this house any longer. No privacy. No freedom. A pretty creature locked in a redbrick cage. But where could she go?

Stephen had experience with the world outside their little town. He would be coming over for dinner. He would advise her.

For tonight's ceremony, Mariah had sewn a new dress of navy cotton. The dress fit her figure nicely and had a rounded neckline that hinted at her bosom and cap sleeves that left her arms bare. With Pa being so particular about how his women dressed, he was only letting her wear it since she'd patterned it after something the first lady had modeled in a magazine. For him, Mrs. Kennedy set the standard for style.

Mariah went into the kitchen to help her mother with dinner. The pan of meatloaf steamed a delicious aroma into the air. She tiptoed closer to the stove and peered into the pots. Creamed potatoes. Green beans cooked to mush. Her mother had made her favorite meal. "Thank you, Ma."

"You're welcome." Ma kissed her brow and whispered, "I'm so proud of you." Ma rarely gave praise, as if reluctant to express an opinion lest it be ridiculed. But its rarity made her praise all the sweeter.

Mariah dropped a large dollop of margarine on the potatoes and carried the bowl to the table, smiling with anticipation for the food and the evening that followed. Her brothers clattered in and watched with hungry eyes as she returned with the platter of meatloaf and the bowl of green beans. Pa limped to his chair and sat, rubbing his damaged leg, groaning from the lingering ache of his old war injury.

Once Ma had set a basket of hot rolls on the table and taken her seat, Pa intoned, "Bow your heads."

Mariah gritted her teeth, then looked from him to the door. He knew Stephen was coming, and Pa wasn't waiting.

She fisted her hands against her belly while Pa prayed. Beside her, Doug squirmed, impatient to eat. Mitchell caught her gaze and sneered. Ma kept her hands out of sight under the table, picking at her cuticles.

"Amen."

When Mariah raised her head, Pa was staring at her. With a flick of his wrist, an envelope flew at her and landed on her plate. "Do you know what that is?"

She read the return address. A letter from the college? She tamped down her excitement, afraid for Pa to see how much this could mean to her. But this letter was what she'd been waiting, hoping, praying for! *Please, please, be good news.* She lifted it reverently, memorizing every detail. It had a typed address. *Miss Mariah Helen Byrne.* Postmarked on . . .

She swallowed a groan. April! It had arrived weeks ago. She shot an accusatory glare at her mother, who looked down guiltily. Ma had handed it over to Pa, and he'd withheld it. Until now.

"Go ahead," he commanded.

Mariah's heart fluttered with worry. She'd applied behind his back after he'd specifically told her not to. Why was he being so matter-of-fact? Why hadn't he punished her as soon as it arrived?

The envelope was slit open. Her parents already knew the results. The college must not have admitted her. Punishment enough. She drew a single page from the envelope, smoothed it, and read.

> Dear Miss Byrne,
> Congratulations . . .

Gasping, she read that wonderful word again. They *did* want her. She looked up in feverish joy. A nasty smile curled Pa's lips. Ma was picking her cuticles bloody. What was wrong with them? Would neither cheer her terrific news? Their reactions were stealing her pleasure.

Hands shaking, she continued to read.

> Please inform us of your decision no later than . . .

The deadline had passed. Yesterday.

Her chest heaved with the effort to breathe. That . . . bastard. She would rather have been rejected. Or never to have known. Pa had smashed her future and waited until mere moments before graduation to hand over the shards.

"Thought you were being smart."

Cold fury drenched her body. Pa had ruined what should've been the best night of her life. "I *am* smart, Pa." It was a wonder her snide tone didn't get her mouth smacked. "I don't have to think it."

The twins and her mother froze. Mitchell mouthed, *Someone's gonna get it.*

"Watch it, girl. I won this one." Pa reached for the potatoes and slapped a heaping spoonful onto his plate. "I'll win them all."

No, he would *not*. In a few hours, she would be a high school graduate. He couldn't control her anymore.

While she waited for the men to fill their plates, she lowered her gaze, stared defiantly at the tablecloth, and pondered escape.

She'd barely had time to choke down two bites of meatloaf before Pa was pushing his plate away. "Delicious, Ma. Thank you." He patted his wife's hand, then turned to his daughter. "Did you ask Mr. Franklin about that job?"

Mariah didn't have a plan yet, but once she did, it wouldn't include a job at Mr. Franklin's drugstore. She'd had all of Scottsburg she could stand. "I won't be in town this summer."

The silence greeting her words pulsed with shock.

"Where do you expect to be?" Pa asked.

"Anywhere else."

"You're not leaving. Your ma needs help with the twins."

Did he really believe she would simply stick around to be an unpaid servant? She glanced at the others for help or sympathy or encouragement, but there was none to be found. No one met her gaze except Mitchell, and he watched with glee, enjoying her misery. The bastard-in-training.

She was on her own. She faced her father and lifted her chin, her silent rebellion clear.

"Fortunately for you, I did the asking. Mr. Franklin is expecting you tomorrow at three. You'll work the soda fountain."

"Pa, you better not let her walk home down Main Street," Mitchell said.

Her father's gaze lingered on her. "Why?"

"That Highcamp boy works at the gas station."

Color flushed hot in her cheeks. She willed it away, but too late. Pa's expression hardened.

"Why does that matter?" Pa's voice was soft and scary.

"Because he pants after her."

She glared at Mitchell. With only twenty seniors at the high school, of course she and Hal knew each other. Had taken classes together. And yes, she liked to watch Hal, and she was pretty sure he liked to watch her back. But they'd done nothing more than look. How could Mitchell know? He'd graduated four years ago. Did he have spies?

"Is that true, Mariah?" Pa asked.

"I barely know him." This topic had nowhere good to go. She stood and stacked the dirty dishes. Putting distance between her and Pa might lessen the chance of a bad result.

Mitchell smirked. "He sure knows you."

Shut up. But she suppressed the words, not wanting her mouth washed out with soap. Why had Mitchell even come over tonight? She didn't want him around. Maybe tormenting her had been the reason. *Jackass.* She stalked to the sink, set the dishes in, and turned on the water.

"Are you calling your brother a liar?" Pa spoke from behind her, his spittle peppering her neck.

She felt her first fissure of fear. Pa was getting wound up. She'd have to tread carefully through the booby traps of his mood. "No, sir."

"Do you deny enticing the boy?"

"I do deny it." Pa's opinion of Hal was undeserved. Just because he drove around in a snazzy Impala, a cig in one hand and a Pabst in the other, Pa called him the high school bad boy. But she knew differently. Hal was the kindest guy in her senior class, and she was a sucker for kindness. He didn't seem to care much about school, though, barely making the grades to graduate. They'd never spoken to each other outside of a classroom, but his sweet smile and those sexy eyes had managed to burrow under her skin anyway. "I think he's handsome—"

"Stop right there."

"I think Elvis is handsome too. That doesn't mean I stand a chance with him."

"Stay away from the Highcamp boy."

If she wanted her father to leave her alone, the wise response was to say nothing. She wasn't feeling particularly wise. She spun around. "Why?"

"He's not a nice boy."

"He's the nicest boy I know."

"He's not Catholic." The ultimate sin, in her father's estimation.

"Neither was Jesus."

Horror whistled through the kitchen like a gale. The twins flushed and bowed their heads. Her mother clapped a hand over her mouth, her face whitening. Even Mitchell gaped.

What have I done?

Pa grabbed her ponytail. "You're showing your butt to me, girl."

"I'm not, Pa. Please—"

He yanked hard. Agony snapped down her neck.

"You know what comes next."

Yes, everyone knew *what comes next*. She hadn't had a whupping since . . . She couldn't remember when, but she could remember how it felt. Painful. Humiliating.

"What's going on in here?" Stephen asked, his voice lethally soft.

They all looked toward the doorway.

His gaze surveyed the room, taking in the dirty dishes, the stark fear on Ma's face, and the shock from the boys, finally landing on Pa's grip on Mariah's ponytail.

If she didn't do something quickly, there would be bloodshed.

"Oh look. My ride's here," she said with false brightness. "Stephen's driving me to the high school."

Her brother stared their father down, eyes narrowed to slits, daring him to continue. Pa released her hair and stepped back.

"Okay, everyone," she said, her voice shaking, "we'll see you there." She sidled around Pa on rubbery legs, squeezed past her brother, and hurried to the door.

A moment later, Stephen came charging after her. They got into his Fairlane and stayed silent as he reversed onto the lane and gunned it for the highway.

She shifted on the seat, breathing hard, grateful for the reprieve, terrified a worse punishment awaited her return, mortified her brother had witnessed that.

"If he touches you again, let me know."

No, not gonna happen. If she did, they'd fight over her, and everyone would lose. She'd have to keep her mouth shut or do a better job of tiptoeing around Pa's moods. "Don't provoke him, Stephen."

"Why not? His opinion means nothing to me." He snorted in derision. "I take that back. His opinion does matter. If he hates something, I know I'll love it."

"We're supposed to honor our father and mother," she said halfheartedly.

"I do honor Ma. But not him." He glanced at Mariah, his lips twisting into something deeply sad. "He's not my father."

She stared at him, aghast. "What did you say?" Stephen was Ma's son, but not Pa's?

He faced forward, gaze glued to the road, a tic in his jaw. "She had to marry someone. Pops picked your father."

Not even for a moment did she doubt her brother. She looked out the side window at the tobacco fields they rushed past. Details clicked into place like pieces in a puzzle. Stephen was, by far, the tallest Byrne. His hair was light brown, and his eyes were blue—lighter and brighter than Ma's. The rest of them had eyes and hair that were nearly black.

This explained her mother's doting looks. Stephen was her clear favorite. Whenever she looked at her oldest, she glowed with pride and wonder.

It was incredible news. Ma had been an unwed mother.

Had the man loved Ma, or had he tricked her into sinning? Because Mariah was sure Ma would never have *done that* unless she loved him.

Why hadn't she married the baby's father? Had he refused?

Or had *she*?

That had to be it. Ma had refused. "Your father isn't Catholic," Mariah stated with absolute certainty.

"No, he isn't."

What a heartbreaking decision for Ma. No matter how much she'd loved the man, she was a devout Catholic. If Stephen's father wouldn't convert, Ma would've seen her options as limited. Either she had to find a willing husband in the church or end up in a home for unwed mothers. And if she'd done the latter, she would've feared they would take her baby.

"Do you know who?"

"Her high school sweetheart." A sigh. "I shouldn't have told you, Rye."

"I'm glad you did." He trusted her with the knowledge, which made her feel more grown-up than knowing she was about to graduate. Oh, how she craved a reminder there was a bigger world awaiting her than the tiny, petty place where she lived. "Stephen? I need the ocean."

"You might be late for the ceremony." There was a smile in his voice.

"What a shame."

With an exultant whoop, he slammed on the brakes and fishtailed into an expert U-turn in the middle of the highway. "Sure thing."

They stayed on the beach as long as possible, staring at the horizon as endless waves foamed and nipped at their feet. But at last they left, forced to race along back roads to reach the high school on time. The lot was already packed, so they parked at the far end and ran. When they drew even with the crowd streaming into the gym, she spotted her parents near the door. Pa stomped at the crumbling edge of the asphalt, his limp exaggerated as he puffed a cigarette down to the filter. Mitchell snickered with friends and eyed the girls whose fathers couldn't control them. Ma was cajoling the twins to behave while she watched the two stragglers approach.

"I want you out of that house," Stephen said, his pace slowing.

"I'll leave." As soon as she came up with a plan.

"Did you get into college?"

She toyed with lying, but it was better for *her* to tell him than Mitchell. "I did, but I won't be going."

"Why not?"

She would give an answer that was completely true but leave out the part that would get Stephen and Pa into a public brawl. "Can't afford it."

"I'll help you." Stephen ignored their parents and strode with her toward her classmates lining up at the entrance to the gym.

"How can you? You work at a restaurant. You barely make enough for you."

"I have an idea. If it works out, I'll earn good money, with some to spare."

She pulled him to a stop, suspicious. "How?"

"I plan to enlist in the army." He jutted out his chin.

"Stephen, no. *Don't.*"

The glint in his eye was resolute. "I'll be fine, and this way, I'll get to choose what I want to do. Now, come here, graduate." He pulled her into a hug.

"We're not done with this conversation," she whispered.

"I think we are." He kissed her forehead. "Get out of here."

Inside the gym, it was moist, hot, and noisy. She exchanged smiles with Hal Highcamp as she found her spot in line, three graduates ahead of him. She located her parents and the twins up high on the bleachers. Pa was talking with the family next to them. Big smiles, big gestures. Ma was focused on the twins, her smile adoring.

Did Ma have regrets? She'd fallen for someone who didn't share her faith, made the best choice she'd thought she had, and was still paying for the decision twenty-five years later. Were her children compensation enough?

Ma watched *The Donna Reed Show* faithfully. Tried to mimic the television model of what the perfect housewife should be. Just as Donna's home was spotlessly clean, so was the Byrnes'. Everything matched. Kitchen counters were gleaming and empty. Tablecloths and napkins were laundered and pressed. The table waited in a perpetual state of readiness for the finest in home-cooked meals.

Yet in Ma's kitchen, the forest-green curtains made the room somber and hushed. Was that what she liked, or did she need *somber and hushed* to survive a meal? Because that's all their family did in there. Pray. Eat. Survive.

Maybe Ma dreamed of a life like Donna Reed, where problems solved themselves, people apologized, and life returned to serenity in thirty minutes.

But Donna Reed didn't have ragged cuticles, and Ma would never have serenity.

Neither would Mariah if she stayed.

She would bide her time and do as Pa demanded. Work hard. Avoid Hal. Hide as much of her paycheck from her father as she could. And when she'd saved enough money not to starve, she would leave this town. Forever.

CHAPTER 10

When the email announcing Charlie's retirement came out Friday afternoon, Jessica heard a buzz spread across the newsroom. Speculative glances followed cries of surprise. It was distracting. Unfortunately for Jessica, too much so.

The six o'clock newscast went smoothly until the final piece. The caption for a politician's interview read "Lie Goals" instead of "Life Goals." Jessica and two others had proofread the graphics. All three had missed the error, but she was the news producer. A mistake had been made, and she would offer no excuses. Her responsibility. Her fault.

The calls poured in. Comments flooded the message board. It was excruciating. She never made mistakes like that. When it was time to make decisions about promotions, this incident would be fresh in everyone's minds. A senior producer who couldn't proofread?

Not unexpectedly, the executive producer called an emergency meeting to dissect the error, and Jessica had to be there. Luke had National Guard duty this weekend, and she hated to miss the night before, but she couldn't help it.

The meeting ran long. So, so long.

When Jessica made it home after eight, she could hear the shower running. In the oven, homemade shepherd's pie stayed warm. She was setting the table when he came down and grabbed a pair of pot holders.

"So, *lie goals?*" Luke chuckled.

She sighed. "After the meeting I just went through, not funny."

"Sorry, Jess, but it really is funny."

Maybe one day she'd see it that way, but not now. "Will your drill weekend be busy?"

"Yes." He didn't elaborate, and she knew not to ask. He had to be careful about what he shared.

"What about dinner tomorrow night?"

"I expect to be home at a decent hour."

"Okay." Good. She would cook dinner, something that could be easily reheated if necessary.

"Have you heard anything else about promotions?"

"No, although they announced Charlie's retirement today."

"Right before your show?"

"Something like that." She tried to shrug it off and almost succeeded. "There will definitely be a senior producer position available."

A proud smile lit his face. "And you're eligible."

"Yeah." She smiled back. Just the reaction she'd hoped for. It would pave the way for the bad part. "I have a good chance too." If today's error didn't ruin it.

"That's amazing, Jess." His gaze dropped to her fingers, which were pleating her napkin. "Is there a 'but'?"

Nodding, she pushed the napkin aside. Why did this topic make her so nervous? He had to know promotions came with changes that might impact their lives. "A promotion brings more responsibility and money. But also more hours."

He homed in on the big con. "*More* hours?"

"Yeah."

His smile dimmed. "We hardly see each other during the week already."

"Which is why we have to talk about it." She pressed her hands to her waist against the clenching in her stomach.

He pushed back his chair, gathered their dishes, then proceeded to scrape, rinse, and load them in the dishwasher.

She followed him into the kitchen, stifling her frustration that he'd walked away at the first sign of trouble. "Luke?"

He went to the refrigerator and got a beer. After walking over to the bay window, he stared out into the night and drank deeply.

She crossed to his side. "Can we talk now?"

"No, Jess. I have prep work for the Guard and a kit to pack."

"Then when?"

He heaved a sigh. "I don't know. You just sprang this on me." When his phone buzzed, he drew it out and frowned at the screen. "It's my boss at the Guard. I have to answer it." He headed to the stairs.

She didn't want him disappearing until he'd committed to a time. "Sunday night?"

He paused. "Okay." Clamping the phone to his ear, he took the stairs two at a time.

She wandered out to their screened porch and over to the glider she'd "inherited" from her grandparents. Before Papa moved to Larkmoor in April, he'd let his girls choose any furniture left in the house. The glider had been one of the few she'd requested. She swayed in it now, the movement recalling long-ago sleepovers and Popsicles and laughter, all memories that filled her with peace and joy and a sense of rightness in the world.

Thinking back to the conversation she'd just finished with her husband drained her sense of rightness. It hadn't ended well. She would be stewing all weekend. Not the best environment for a crucial conversation.

When they'd become engaged in November, they'd originally planned the wedding for this summer. But she'd moved it up when she'd remembered how her grandparents had married after a four-month courtship. They'd had the perfect marriage for almost sixty years. Why wouldn't it work for Luke and Jess?

She'd rescheduled the wedding for January, which hadn't left much time to learn the little details of combining two lives. Had that been a mistake? Should they have given themselves longer to understand what they were taking on?

Closing her eyes, she blocked out the beautiful starry night. She loved her husband, family plan or quick wedding or not. They needed to put their marriage back on solid ground. Something felt cracked, and they had to repair it. Fast.

◆　◆　◆

Her eyes popped open at five thirty. She was alone in the bed, although there were muffled sounds down the hall. To avoid disturbing her, Luke left his Guard uniforms and kit in the guest bedroom. He was preparing to leave.

Unease lingered from the night before. Could she make it better before he left?

She could try. Yanking on a robe, she headed downstairs to the kitchen. An inventory of available ingredients gave her options for breakfast. Scones were one of the few things she made well from scratch. She whipped up a batch, slid them into the oven, then brewed a pot of coffee. She was scrambling eggs when she heard the door to the guest bedroom close. He was on his way down.

"Hey," Luke said. He looked amazing in his military uniform.

"I made breakfast." She pulled the tray from the oven. The scones were a perfect golden brown.

As he perched on a stool, she handed him a plate and a travel mug of coffee.

"Thanks." He picked up his fork and attacked the eggs.

She plated a scone for herself and sat beside him, needing a final moment of connection before they were apart for the day.

"You've never done this before." He said it like a statement, but it felt like a question.

Her job was all about words. Why was it so hard to find the right ones this morning with her husband? "Things didn't end as I'd hoped last night."

He nodded. Swallowed. "We'll work it out, Jess. Don't push."

She flinched. Was that how it was coming across? Not her intention. "I'm not pushing."

He put his fork down and shifted toward her. "Okay, look. You've earned whatever promotion they offer you, but the 'more hours' part bothers me. I know you want to talk about the promotion, and we will. But we should also discuss how we are now. You and me. What we expect from our marriage. How we can act more like a couple."

She agreed. That was the point of tomorrow night's conversation. Not just *How do we react to a promotion?* but *What kind of family do we want to be, and will a promotion fit into that?* If he didn't like the way things were now, he had to *tell* her. Not make her drag it out of him. "We can make adjustments."

"Adjustments? I was thinking an overhaul."

She choked on a gasp. An overhaul? Really? An overhaul meant major cracks. Was he that worried about their marriage? As she searched his face, his gaze held hers steadily. He was serious. "If you felt that way, why haven't you said anything?"

"When? We're both so busy. We slot an hour or two into each other's schedules when we're not doing something else."

"We have the weekends." When he wasn't gone. Or if she wasn't on call.

"Some, yeah, and that's the best part of our marriage. I don't want to spoil it by complaining." He stood and reached for his kit.

"Luke, please. I don't want you to walk out of here today without knowing . . ." She stopped, not sure what to say. She was committed to him and their marriage, but an overhaul required time—the one thing she had the least of. There would be even less while she worked on the family secret. He'd encouraged her to work with Raine, but had he considered its effect on *them*?

"I love you, Jess." He cupped the back of her head and kissed her. "We have to fix this." He grabbed his travel mug and was gone.

She stayed where she was long after the garage door whined down, sipping cold coffee, crumbling the scone, reliving their brief dialogue. She'd known things weren't perfect, but she'd thought he was happy.

Did all new couples go through these kinds of growing pains? Or was this specific to them?

CHAPTER 11

When the sun rose Saturday, Raine had been on her balcony for an hour, coffee at her side, computer on her lap, immersed in her exam studies. The ding of her email app announced the arrival of a new message. She welcomed the distraction.

Jessica had sent the kind of no-nonsense email Raine liked best. It had a concise subject line: **Byrnes**. And a message body full of embedded links and no unnecessary commentary.

> Stephen and Douglas died in Vietnam. You can find them on the Arlington National Cemetery site.
>
> Stephen Thomas, 1938–1966.
>
> Douglas Arthur, 1951–1971.
>
> There are too many Mitchell Byrnes in the US to narrow down. None in North Carolina are the right age.
>
> Duane Allen Byrne, born 1951. Voted as recently as November 2022. His last known address is in Scottsburg, near Wilmington. He is a retired

pharmacist, owns a drugstore, has 3 children and
at least 5 grandchildren.

Terrence Byrne, 1914–1978

Lorraine Byrne, 1920–1996

Raine had been a toddler when her great-grandmother died.
Her sister would've been four. Had they ever met? She fired off a text
message.

Do you remember meeting Great-Grandma Lorraine?

Her sister was already typing a response.

Wow. It was six thirty on a Saturday. Jessica must've gotten up with
Luke before he left for the Guard. Good. Luke would've loved that kind
of send-off for his weekend.

No, but I've seen a 4-generation picture with both of us

Lorraine was rarely mentioned. Duane and his family lived barely
two hours away and had been ignored. Now that Raine knew of his
existence, she had questions. Why were they estranged? What happened
with Lorraine? What in Mariah's life had caused her to distance herself
from her family of origin?

Since Mom refused to help, the answers would have to come from
someone who'd been there. Raine clicked on the link her sister had supplied and landed on the website for Byrne's Pharmacy, opening in three
hours. She set a timer for nine thirty. While she waited, she resumed
her studies.

When the alarm sounded, she picked up her phone but didn't call.
She didn't like talking on the phone, and this had the potential to be

uncomfortable. What reception would she get? Did they resent the lack of contact? Did they know about her?

All right, she should just call and satisfy her curiosity.

"Hello, Byrne's."

A young female voice. Obviously not her great-uncle. "Is Duane Byrne there?"

"No, he's retired. May I help you?"

She hoped she wasn't making a mistake. "I'm Raine Elliott—"

"Aunt Mariah's Raine?"

Wow. She sucked in a breath. Had the estrangement been one sided? "Yes."

"I'm Cheslyn Byrne. Your second cousin."

A second cousin? Raine and Jessica—the daughters of two only children—had cousins. That was cool, but frustrating too. Why had they been kept in the dark? "I was wondering if I could speak with Uncle Duane."

"By phone or in person?"

She hadn't expected in person, but she could make that work if he was comfortable with it. "Either way."

"I'll ask him and call you back."

She saved the number in her contacts, then walked out to the balcony. Apparently, Papa had intended for them to discover unknown uncles and cousins. Had he expected them to connect with their extended family? Were people typically close to second cousins? She kind of doubted it.

What had Papa's goal been? And why now?

Her phone rang. "Yes, Cheslyn."

"He'd like to meet you. Are you free today?"

Today? That was fast. Was he curious to meet her? Or did he have things to say that might contribute to the family story? She should jump at the chance. "Yes. I could be there a little after noon."

"I'll text directions."

"Thanks."

After hanging up, she went inside to gather her things, then frowned guiltily at her phone. Should she include her sister? Jessica would want to talk in the car, which wouldn't be fun. But she might manage the interview with Uncle Duane, which would be great. And teamwork *was* part of the wish.

Raine would ask.

Are you there?

Yes

I'm going to meet Uncle Duane. Want to come?

You're meeting Uncle Duane today?

Hoping to leave in a few minutes

The phone rang. "Yes?"

"Why?"

"Papa asked us to follow through on what we found in the cartons. Missing uncles stick out to me. I'd like to meet Mariah's brother and learn the reason for their estrangement. Maybe he'll tell us something that helps us understand better what Papa wanted us to discover."

There was a pause. The clink of a mug hitting a glass tabletop. "Yes. I'll go. Can you pick me up?"

"See you in fifteen minutes." Raine smiled, glad she'd invited Jessica and glad she'd agreed.

Half an hour later, they were on I-40 East, windows up, air conditioner on, no other sound.

"So how did you work out today's visit?" Jessica asked.

Raine's hands gripped the steering wheel. She preferred silence while she was driving. Paying attention to traffic was all-consuming. At least her sister had waited until they were past the construction zone.

"I called the pharmacy. His granddaughter offered to ask Uncle Duane when I could come, then called back and said today would be good."

"Do they know I'm coming?"

"No."

"How did the granddaughter sound?"

"Her name is Cheslyn. She seemed nice. I didn't notice anything negative."

There was a pause. "Do you plan to record the interview?"

"No."

"Why not?"

Should they? Raine considered the idea, then decided that, no, it felt like too much. "We're not interrogating him. We're talking."

"Good point. Would you rather be quiet now?"

"Of course."

Failing to conceal a smile, Jessica slipped on headphones and looked out the side window.

Once the traffic thinned out, Raine let her thoughts drift to Uncle Duane. She was curious about him but also wary. Her grandmother was a nice woman. Accepting of everyone. It hadn't mattered to her whether a person was homeless or the governor. Mariah Azarian would smile kindly, listen, and promise to see what she could do.

When Raine had been five or six, she'd witnessed how kind her grandmother could be. That day, Mom and Dad had been busy. Jessica had been at some type of practice. Soccer or piano or dance. So Mariah volunteered to babysit. Raine had been sprawled on the floor of her grandmother's legislative office, browsing a book, when there was shouting in the hall. The commotion grew louder until it stopped outside their door.

"Raine," her grandmother said, rolling back her chair. "Under the desk."

She'd crawled underneath and waited in the dim cave. It had been kind of cool, actually. Even when Mariah rolled her chair back in, there had been enough light. "Is this a game, Mima?"

"No, I have a visitor. A constituent. This will only take a moment. I need you to be quiet."

The door banged open. She hadn't liked that, but her grandmother had slipped off her shoe and firmly pressed their feet together. It felt good.

The man shouted. Mariah responded, her voice low and calm. Raine could hear their words but didn't understand, so she went back to her book. The shouting faded. More voices joined the conversation. Then the door closed, it grew quiet again, and the chair rolled back.

"Are you okay down there?"

"Yes, Mima. Can I stay here?"

"Be my guest."

Mom had been furious about the "danger." She'd never allowed Mariah to babysit in her office again. Raine learned later that the man had been angry about a stance Mariah had taken on a new law. She'd faced him down, explained her viewpoint, and listened to his. While he left not quite voluntarily, they'd parted on polite terms.

But Raine's lasting impression was that Mariah got along with everybody, even political foes. Yet she hadn't gotten along with her family of origin. If she'd been estranged from her brother, Raine was inclined to believe the fault was his. Maybe they'd find out today.

An hour after they left Raleigh, Jessica removed her headphones and shifted sideways in her seat. "Can we discuss how to handle the interview?"

Raine had a tentative plan, but it made sense to pass it by Jessica. "You should be the one to start."

"Sure. But why?"

"You'll do a better job."

"Huh." Jessica toyed with her headphones. "I will do a good job, but you have experience with interviewing too."

"I'm in forensics. My experience is with potential criminals, which Uncle Duane is not."

"Valid point. So what do we want to know?"

"About his brothers. Mariah's childhood. Why she left. Why she stayed away."

"Well, that about covers it. I'll refine the way I pose those questions."

It wasn't long before they pulled into an old neighborhood off a deserted two-lane highway, then up the gravel driveway of a compact ranch. A porch stretched the length of the house, dotted with rocking chairs and small metal tables painted the same bright blue as the front door and shutters.

The lawn was freshly mowed. The flower beds and bushes were mulched and clipped. The yard appeared to be several acres, fenced, with trees. A barn sat off to one side, dark red, with a glimpse of a green tractor in one of its stalls. A vegetable garden lazed in the sunshine near the barn, the smudges of red, green, and yellow suggesting it was busy being productive. If the yard reflected their great-uncle's personality, he would be neat, precise, and colorful.

They both got out. Over the top of the car, Jessica said, a quaver in her voice, "Here's my suggestion. I'll start with easy questions while we're all in the getting-to-know-you stage."

"A conversation with family."

"Yes. Then we'll move into the uncomfortable territory. You should jump in whenever it feels right. We'll both follow where he leads."

Raine nodded in relief. A simple, respectful plan. "Sounds good."

A screen door thwacked, and an older gentleman stepped onto the porch. He would've been tall in his youth, but he was stoop-shouldered now, with a thick mane of white hair, bushy eyebrows, and brown eyes the same color and shape as Mariah's. He wore a smile that seemed to restrain ready laughter. Beside her, Jessica had caught her breath. Yeah, Raine felt it too. It was a small moment that felt pretty huge. They were about to meet their grandmother's brother, a man who looked like a nice guy eager to welcome them.

The first sentence out of his mouth was, "You came for answers."

"Yes, sir," Raine said, stepping forward.

He swung his hand in an arc and clasped hers firmly. "Duane Byrne."

"Raine Elliott." She inclined her head toward her sister. "Jessica Elliott."

"Come in, ladies."

The interior belied the view from the road. The living area was wide open, with comfortable chairs and a couch facing a large TV over a brick fireplace. The kitchen had granite countertops, stainless-steel appliances, and slate floors. In the dining room stood an older woman with skillfully dyed brown hair.

"This is my wife, Susan." He gestured with his head. "My great-nieces, Raine and Jessica. Mariah's granddaughters."

"Hello." Susan's expression showed neither surprise nor welcome.

"Can you bring us some tea, Sue?"

Raine was taken aback at his gruff, demanding tone, but his wife seemed relieved at having something to do.

He waited until the sisters were seated on the couch to back into a recliner. "My sympathies for your grandfather. Greg was a good man."

"You knew him?" Raine blurted, surprised. Had everybody known everybody else—except the sisters?

"Yes, but not well." Their great-uncle frowned. "How's Mariah?"

She glanced at her sister, who was leaning forward, looking purposeful. Raine would shut up now.

"She's in a slow decline," Jessica said.

"I'm sorry." He tipped back slightly in the recliner and stared at the cracks in the ceiling. "I've lived in this house most of my life, but Mariah couldn't wait to escape."

Raine looked around, the past weighing heavily. They were in the house where her grandmother had been raised. The renovations had included modern updates without sacrificing charm. Nice for an older couple. But it would've been cramped for seven. Whatever had gone on all those years ago had been so oppressive her grandmother left forever. The thought gave Raine goose bumps.

Jessica continued. "Did you inherit it from your parents?"

"I bought it from my mother after Pa died. I was already a pharmacist in town and wanted a house for my family. Ma moved to Wilmington. Got a nice place with a view of the Cape Fear River." He smiled. "It was a good life for her, and she deserved it. She made friends. Had a beau. Her high school sweetheart."

Mariah had hard words for her father but hadn't said much about her mother. Lorraine Byrne was a mystery. Yet Raine carried her name. With hardly a two-hour drive separating them, there hadn't been much contact. Complicated dynamics there. Raine couldn't imagine excluding her parents and grandparents from her life.

"Well now, ladies." His grin encompassed them both. "What else would you like to know?"

"When did you last see your sister?" Jessica asked.

"It was just before she moved into the place she is now." Duane's grin grew strained. "Did she ever say anything about me?"

Raine felt sorry for him. He was eager to hear something positive. Hopeful. But they wouldn't be able to deliver that.

"She's mentioned you and Stephen," Jessica said, "although we knew you weren't close."

"One of my biggest regrets." The color rose in his face, but he didn't volunteer a reason.

Duane's wife entered the living room, her face tightening at her husband's words. She handed out three glasses of tea and left again.

Jessica shifted on the couch, crossed her legs, and looked at Raine. Well, that was clear. Her turn. "Tell us about your brothers."

A shadow crossed his face. He gulped his tea and set the glass down again on a coaster. "Stephen was the oldest. He was good to Mariah. She worshiped him.

"Mitchell was second. He left in his twenties, and we haven't seen much of him since. Ended up in Florida, as far as I know. He has two step-kids but never any of his own. Or none that he claims. Drove an eighteen-wheeler all over America. Married at least three times, although I don't understand how he fooled that many women. He was always mean as a snake.

"The youngest was Douglas. My twin." Her great-uncle clamped his lips, damming a rush of emotion. "Our draft number came up. We went to 'Nam in '71. Douglas was killed in action a few months later." He stopped again. Breathed open-mouthed. "He was a good man. A good brother."

More than fifty years had passed, and he still grieved. When Jessica murmured, "I'm so sorry," Raine nodded her agreement.

"Mariah came to his funeral. I hafta say that for her. She do come to funerals. 'Cepting Pa's." Duane's hand shook, the ice cubes in his glass clicking.

Raine shivered. Felt it in Jessica too. Her grandmother hadn't completely ignored her family of origin. She'd just never included her granddaughters.

Jessica widened her eyes in an *I got this* look, then asked, "Can you tell us more about Uncle Stephen?"

They'd rarely spoken of Stephen with Mariah. His flag might hold a place of honor in her home, but conversations about him had been too painful for her.

"He died in 'Nam, same as Douglas. Stephen volunteered for the army, so he got to stick around in the States for a couple of years. Didn't go over to 'Nam until '65. And he was killed in the spring of '66. We all went to Arlington for the funeral. Mariah too. First time I'd seen or heard anything about her in three years. Ma knew she was living in Raleigh, but the rest of us didn't. Mariah was expecting. Little thing like her looked all belly." He released a mournful sigh. "I'd never seen her so shaken. It was bad enough for us. It must've been horrible for her." He lapsed into silence, lost in the past.

How devastating for Mariah, traveling all that distance to say good-bye to her brother, then having to share the ordeal with a family who'd been so awful she'd had to escape them.

"Uncle Duane?" Jessica prompted gently.

"What?" He looked up, his gaze out of focus, wisps of memories fading away. "Oh yes, sorry. Where was I?" He cleared his throat. "So . . . Stephen and Mariah were always close. He was six when she was born. Ma had a hard time getting back on her feet, so he did what he could. He used to say Mariah was *his*. Called her Rye. When she was a baby, he changed her diapers, fed her, rocked her to sleep. Each morning before school, he made sure her uniform was pressed and her hair braided. He took better care of her than, well, our parents."

"Did she come to his funeral alone?"

"No, Greg was with her. We hadn't known she was married. Stephen did, of course. She woulda made sure he knew wherever she was. He left everything to her. She even got the flag. Pa was furious. Said it was disrespectful to Ma. When Mariah showed up, he shouted that she didn't belong there, which was backward. She deserved to be there more than him." Duane looked out the window, as if something in the distance had caught his attention. "When Pa started to get ugly with her, Greg looked about ready to punch something, but she just squeezed his arm, then snubbed Pa like he wasn't even there. Perfect thing to do. Made him furious. I was proud of her."

Raine met her sister's gaze and gave a nod, accepting the handoff. "How often have you seen Mariah since then?"

Her great-uncle turned to her. "At Douglas's funeral and Ma's. Mariah came to my first wedding. Sometimes, she and Greg would stop by on the way to Emerald Isle. Or I'd go by if I was up in Raleigh for the state fair. But not much." He sighed. "Not much."

So their grandmother hadn't completely cut off her brother. Estranged but not quite. Forgiven but not really. Raine wondered how much of a role their vile great-grandfather might have played. "Your father died in 1978."

"Yeah. From lung cancer. He served in World War II. Six months after he got to Africa, his foot got shot off. Never really recovered from that. Ma used to say he was different before the war. That when he lost his foot, he lost his peace of mind."

Raine felt a twitch of sympathy for the man. The war had left him disabled and probably struggling with PTSD. But only a faint twitch. What he'd been through wasn't an excuse for treating others badly. "Do you resent that Mariah left?"

"No, never have. I don't blame her. Our father bullied her."

"Physically?" Raine shuddered.

"Sometimes. Not hard. Didn't draw blood often . . ."

Mariah had been abused? Raine gaped at her uncle, at the bland way he'd relayed something so awful. Did he actually believe her abuse had been no big deal? Did he realize that the effects of abuse didn't go away after the fists stopped—or the *words* stopped? Raine's breathing sped up. Bracing her arms on her knees, she hunched over, bathed in chills as she fought mental images of Mariah being punished to the point of drawing blood.

Jessica laid a hand on her shoulder. Solidarity.

"But Mariah definitely had it tough here. The only one who had it tougher was Stephen. She was so pretty and sweet. Pa thought all the boys wanted her, and it was his job to protect her from ruination. But he was the one who pushed her away. I'm sure that's how Hal happened."

Who? Raine straightened, met her sister's gaze, recognizing the surprise. What were they about to learn?

"Tell us about Hal," Jessica said, her voice remarkably calm.

"Hal Highcamp. Mariah's first boyfriend. He was a nice guy, but Pa hated him. When he tried to keep them apart, she and Hal ran off to Texas."

CHAPTER 12

March 1963

Mariah had long planned to leave her hometown, to flee to somewhere she could be safe and happy and free. What she hadn't expected was that she would leave North Carolina too.

It had taken ten months to reach the breaking point. Throughout the summer of '62, Mariah had honored two of her goals. Work hard. Hide her tip money. But the third goal had changed. Instead of avoiding Hal, she had to avoid Pa finding out about her and Hal.

As her father had decreed, she worked at the drugstore, serving milkshakes, hot dogs, and pimento cheese sandwiches. When fall rolled around, business thinned. Convenient, since she only cared about one customer.

Hal had a smile so sweet that every time he sent one her way, her heart flipped. He came in Friday nights at closing and ordered a chocolate malt, then stuck around while she cleaned up. The first time he'd asked her on a date, her smile nearly split her face in two. But she'd refused, of course. Pa would never allow her to date *that Highcamp boy*.

Hal didn't give up easily. By October, they'd created their own way to be together. He'd wait for her in the alley behind the drugstore at ten past nine. After she locked up, he escorted her home, watching from a street corner as she finished the final quarter mile alone.

Their relationship consisted of twenty-minute "dates," six nights per week, strolling in the dark while they talked about everything. Their conversations always ended with plans for escaping Scottsburg. She hoped to use photography to tell stories. He longed to own a shop to restore old cars to their former glory.

It wasn't much, but it was all they had. Talk, walk, hold hands.

Until Stephen intervened.

One cold November Sunday, her brother announced after Mass that he and Mariah were going on a photo shoot at the beach. Father Tim was listening. Pa didn't argue.

As she slid into Stephen's Ford, she asked, "Which beach today?" It had been months since they'd done this.

"Your favorite." He revved the engine. "And there's a surprise."

They parked on the shoulder at North Topsail and climbed over a dune. As the slope gentled, they stopped. The beach was empty except for one lone man, his back to them.

Her heart was beating so hard it nearly flew from her chest. Mariah turned to her brother. "Hal?"

Stephen smiled. "Meet me back here in an hour."

Would she really have an hour alone with Hal? Had she ever been so happy? She ran toward the water, calling out. He whipped around, caught her in his arms, and swung her in a circle while they laughed themselves breathless. Hands firmly clasped, they ran along the waterline until they could no longer see Stephen, then ducked behind a clump of seagrass. They kissed among the dunes, the vast ocean spread before them, the sky blue and clear.

But meeting at the beach only happened once. Stephen left two weeks later for army boot camp.

Soon after the beach date, Pa started picking her up after work. "Too cold for you to be walking home," he'd said the first time.

Did Pa know?

He must, but he hadn't punished her. That bothered her more than a whupping would have.

Her dates with Hal went from twenty-minute walks to stolen moments between customers.

When the drugstore reopened after Christmas, Hal entered an hour before closing. After it was empty, he gestured for her to join him at the back and gave her an utterly delicious kiss, then begged her, "Meet me on New Year's Eve."

"What?" That would be reckless. "I can't."

"Please. You can slip out at midnight."

She wanted to. So much. But if she were caught? It would be so, so bad.

Oh, stuff it. Why was she letting fear dictate her actions? "Okay. The woods behind my house."

A bell tinkled as another customer came in. Giddy at the thought of a forbidden date, she headed back reluctantly to make more hot chocolates.

Time passed in an agony of anticipation. By New Year's Eve, her excitement was at a fever pitch. Pa's suspicious scowl sobered her. She reined in her emotions by remembering the terrifying possibilities, like getting caught.

That evening, she went to bed early and sat in the dark, waiting for her parents to trudge past. The twins giggled in their room until Pa rapped on their door. After that, the house went silent in minutes.

Just before midnight, Mariah crawled through her bedroom window and dropped to the ground, glad she'd made sure earlier to brush aside crunchy leaves. She darted into the line of trees along the fence line and continued through the shadows to the rear of their property. She knew where Hal was from the glowing orange tip of his cigarette.

He cupped her head between his hands and kissed her. She was on fire for more and pressed against him, the air cold and his body warm. She closed her eyes, dizzy from his kisses and the scent of smoke, English Leather, and safety. She was so tired of watching what she said, what she did. Even what she thought, lest it show on her face. With Hal, she was free.

"It's 1963, darlin'."

This would be the year she asserted herself. It wasn't her destiny to live in Scottsburg, barely earning a dollar an hour behind a soda counter. In 1963, she would defy her father.

"I was fired."

She jerked back. "That's terrible. Why?"

Bitterness pinched his lips. "A customer accused me of cheating him when I made change."

"Do you know who?"

"Your father."

Fury blazed in her belly. Her father had found out about them and punished Hal instead of her. Did Pa think this was a game? That if he raised the stakes, she'd fold? Well, the joke was on him, because his actions would have the opposite effect. She'd never been more determined to be with Hal. "What will you do?"

"Look for a job, anything I can get."

"Maybe it would be better if you stayed away from me."

"Better for who? Not for me. I'll find a job, but I can't lose you."

She melted against him, shivered in his strong embrace. New Year's Eve was about making resolutions. And she was *resolved*. Her father had declared war. He'd attacked an innocent person to get at her. It was her move, and when the time was right, she would make it.

Now she just had to figure out what she'd be willing to do.

She figured it out a couple of months later.

Hal's optimism faded with each week that passed. He couldn't get a job at another service station, so he was bagging groceries at a store in Wilmington. She hated to see how sad and bewildered he was.

Then, one night early in March, he strolled into the drugstore near closing time and headed to the farthest corner. After her customer left, she rushed over to Hal, straight into his arms.

His kiss held desperation. "Aunt Rosalie is selling her house and moving to Virginia." He'd been living with his mother's sister for the past ten years, since a tornado had killed his parents in Texas.

"Where will you go?"

"Dallas. My uncle Fred has a Sinclair station, and he knows I'm a good mechanic. He's giving me a job and a place to stay."

She hadn't seen Hal this excited in months. She should be happy for him, right? But she couldn't be. Her heart was breaking. "When do you leave?"

"This weekend." He buried his face in her neck.

He was moving to somewhere big and bold. A beautiful new life without her. How could she bear it? She'd thought they would be together forever. *Unless . . .*

They could be, if she went too. "Hal. Take me with you."

"What?" He leaned back. Checked to see if she was teasing. "Really?"

"Yes. *Please.*"

He laughed. "Are you sure? Just like that?"

Her mouth went dry. Had she meant it? Could she really go . . . just like that?

There was nothing keeping her here. She longed to flee this town, and now she had the chance. To escape to Texas with the man she loved. And it wasn't as if they'd be alone. His uncle and aunt and cousin lived there. A built-in family.

"What will your uncle Fred think?"

Hal's face fell instantly. He ran a thumb over his lower lip. "Well, now," he said. "It'll be a shock, that's for sure. He's not much for surprises."

Hal's reaction dented her enthusiasm. She wouldn't be welcome? That could be bad—

"Nah, darlin'. It'll be fine." His smile reappeared.

That happy smile dissolved her doubts. "Then I'll come."

He whooped and kissed her breathless until the bell chimed, announcing customers.

They sprang apart. "I'll get rid of them," she whispered.

At the counter, she struggled to mask her impatience when the young couple took too long to make a choice. Once they'd been served, she urged them out the door and flipped the sign to **CLOSED**. As she returned to Hal, thoughts tumbled through her head, already making plans. Already wondering how hard it would be to walk away from her family.

She wouldn't miss her father. Leaving him would feel like being reborn.

Not Mitchell either. She didn't care to ever see him again.

She'd make sure Stephen knew where she was. Always. He'd escaped himself in December and joined the army. He was loving California, and Texas was a whole lot closer to him than North Carolina.

But her mom and the twins? She loved them so much. How could she say goodbye? Without her sinful nature diverting Pa, Ma's life would get harder. The twins would be okay. They had each other and would forget her. They would have to, because if she left, it would be forever. Her father would forbid her return.

Hal smiled as she approached, eyes full of love, the kind of wild abandon that sappy books hawked and romantic movies promised. She was making the right decision. "When do we leave?"

"Really?" He cupped her face in his hands and stared deeply into her eyes. "You'll come?"

"I will."

He kissed her with such exquisite tenderness that she almost wept.

"Okay, darlin'. Here're the plans. We leave Saturday morning, long before sunrise. How 'bout I pick you up at four, where your lane meets the highway?"

She laughed, feeling reckless and bold and alive. "Get out of here, then. I'll see you Saturday."

The next twenty-four hours raced by in a flurry of details and secrets. Outwardly, she acted the same. She did her chores, ate quietly. But behind her closed bedroom door, she packed jewelry, makeup, and her favorite clothes inside a denim duffel bag.

Just before three on Friday afternoon, she left the house as usual to walk to the drugstore, stopping at the post office to mail Stephen a letter with her plans.

She worked her best that night, making the yummiest hot chocolate ever, flirting with the old guys, adding extra whipped cream for the kids, cleaning everything when no one was about.

Her only regret was quitting without notice. Mr. Franklin had been nice to her. He didn't deserve this. But if she told him her decision, he might tell Pa. She couldn't allow that.

Her shift ended at nine, and for the last time, she locked up, emptied the cash register, and took the funds to the office. Mr. Franklin owed her fifty dollars in wages. She'd take twenty-five of it from the cash bag, and he could keep the other half. The thought soothed her conscience. After putting the rest of the money in the safe, she wrote a note to apologize for leaving without warning and left it on the desk.

Pa picked her up, raking her with a hard stare as she got in. Did he suspect anything? She hid her shaking hands in the pockets of her sweater, relieved when they spent the whole ride home in brooding silence.

Inside the house, light spilled from the kitchen. When she hesitated in its entrance, Pa pushed past her and went to his chair. Ma handed him a piece of apple pie.

"'Night, Ma," Mariah said, her voice cracking.

Her mother spun to face her. "Honey, is something wrong?"

Mariah cleared her throat. *Don't mess up now.* "Nothing's wrong."

"You look sad."

Sad wasn't the right word. More like melancholy mixed with elation. An odd combination, but true for her. She pasted on a fake smile. "No, ma'am. Just tired."

Ma nodded, then scrubbed a spot on the counter with bleach.

Will I ever see her again?

Mariah heard the clink of a fork. She glanced over her shoulder. Pa ate a bite of pie, chewed, and stared at her, like a predator eying his prey.

She turned away. Outside the twins' room, she paused. They were seated on the floor, re-creating a World War II battle with toy soldiers. She longed to hug them, but it would be unlike her to love on them at night.

Doug looked up suddenly and smiled. She smiled back and then stumbled into the shadows of the hall, choking on a sob. Twisting the crystal knob on her bedroom door, she entered, shut the door behind her quickly, then halted in horror.

The scent of Ivory soap lingered in the room. Her father had been in here.

Heart racing, she tore into her closet and looked around. Her shoes were askew. The books stacked on the floor had been shifted. He'd been in her closet and touched her things.

Had he found the packed bag?

She ripped the lid off the dirty clothes hamper. It looked undisturbed. *Please, please.* She removed the small pile of "dirty" clothes, hauled out the duffel bag, and unzipped it.

The insides looked intact. Her legs gave out, and she sagged to the floor. Slowed her breathing. Willed the shudders to cease. She had much to do. She needed her head clear.

Everything looked fine. Did he know?

No, not likely, but he might suspect something was up. She'd have to take precautions. After donning her street clothes, she pulled a flannel pajama top over them, slid into bed, and pulled the covers to her chest.

The light went out in the hallway. Ma tiptoed past. Then Pa's heavier, uneven tread. Their door shut.

Minutes passed. Fifteen. Twenty. Quietly, she slipped from the bed, crossed to the door, and pressed her ear to the crack. Pa was snoring to wake the dead. She let another twenty minutes pass before setting the duffel bag on her bed. She added the camera Stephen had given her for Christmas, her two favorite books, her rosary, cash, and her *Very Best* folder of photographs.

Should she write a note?

Yes, but that would be best done right before she crawled through the window. Back in bed, she turned her body toward the window to track the nearly full moon across the sky.

At three thirty, she rolled from bed, traded the flannel top for a heavy sweater, and crossed to the window. Ever so slowly, she eased the window up, praying it wouldn't squeak. Rain-fresh air wafted in. Grimacing, she pushed her duffel bag out, listening as it fell with a faint plop and a wet rustle of leaves. She froze, straining to hear any sounds.

The house was silent, save for the hum of the boiler coming on.

She released a shuddery breath. All that remained was the note— and to go.

Writing the note was more difficult than she'd anticipated. There was much in her heart to say. She composed phrases in her mind, then discarded them. Why was she trying so hard? Pa would destroy the note after he'd read it. Best to keep it simple and brief.

I've moved to Texas with Hal. I'm fine and will write when I can.

Mariah

She'd just propped the note on her dresser when her parents' bedroom door slowly squeaked open. She snapped off the flashlight, shaking with fear.

Pa's limping gait passed by and continued to the bathroom. There was a tinkling sound in the toilet. It flushed. He returned to his bedroom.

She was running out of time, but she had to give her father a few minutes to fall asleep again. She watched the clock, mouth dry, wondering when to leave. Too soon and Pa might awaken. Too late and Hal might think she'd changed her mind.

At five minutes till four, Mariah couldn't wait any longer. She crawled through the window and picked up her bag. The damp cold wrapped around her, seeping through her sweater. She crept along the shadows, looking over her shoulder, but the house remained dark. She hurried down the lane and stopped at the edge of the highway, staring down the rain-slick asphalt. Twice, she looked back at her home, torn by her decision, the knowledge she could never return, the worry that she was making a rash and foolish choice.

Then headlights pierced the gloom. The rumble of an Impala drew closer. She squared her shoulders against the doubts. That was only fear talking. Staying meant more misery. Leaving gave her the hope of freedom.

When Hal pulled up, she tossed her bag in the back and hopped in. "Hey, darlin'." He grabbed her chin and kissed her hard. "Ready?"

"Uh-huh." Her response sounded breathless. Scared. Triumphant.

They roared off into the dark, heading west to their destination. Dallas.

Mariah and Hal cheered as they crossed into South Carolina. Once their laughter died away, though, she glanced at her watch. Her parents would be awake now. If they hadn't already seen the note, they would soon.

The euphoria of escape had dimmed by Georgia, as the magnitude of her decision intruded. Would she ever see her mother or the twins again? She brooded over that question as the boring miles passed, taking her closer to Texas and what awaited her there.

The novelty of seeing new places had utterly dissipated by Mississippi. She'd traveled through more states that day than she'd been to in her entire life. With Louisiana and Texas left to go.

Would Hal's family like her? He'd assured her that they would welcome her. But his gut reaction when she'd asked two days ago had been worried. What lay ahead?

She and Hal hadn't made plans, other than to leave North Carolina. She'd thought no further than making the rendezvous on time without getting caught. How incredibly impulsive she'd been. They weren't making a drop-by visit or attending a slumber party. This was *life*.

Hal had a job ready. She'd need one too, but what could she do? Babysit? Serve chocolate malts?

Where would they live? He'd planned to stay with his uncle, but that wouldn't happen now. No way would his uncle and aunt allow an unwed couple to live in their home. She and Hal would have to rent. What could they afford on a mechanic's wages?

She put it from her mind. She would find out soon enough.

They stopped for the night in Shreveport, pulling into a cheap-but-clean motel overlooking the Red River. She entered their room first, holding her purse protectively over her chest, her attention nervously fixed on the double bed. They hadn't discussed sex, but it was a certainty. She had mixed feelings. Excitement to finally know what the fuss was about. Fear that she wouldn't like it. Apprehension about going to confession and telling a priest.

"Nice room." Hal slid his arms around her waist and kissed a shivery spot beneath her ear.

She lost her virginity ten minutes later. The first time was painful and overwhelming. She'd heard so much about the act. It was supposed to be holy. Something so special that it should be reserved for marriage. What they'd done had been neither holy nor special. It just hurt. Afterward, she rolled to her side, facing away from Hal, hiding her tears.

He spooned her with gentle arms. "It'll get better, darlin'. I promise."

Turned out he was right. She was ready to try again in the morning, and it was *more* than better. It left her drunk with pleasure. She finally got why people hungered for sex.

CHAPTER 13

May 1963

Mariah's first two months in Dallas had been islands of happiness in a sea of misery.

News from North Carolina had been upsetting because there had been no news. She'd sent a letter to Ma every week, and days later, the envelope would reappear, unopened, marked *Return to Sender*. Mariah hadn't relinquished hope, but it was waning.

She'd also hoped that Hal's family would become hers, but she'd learned quickly enough it would never happen. On the day they'd arrived in Dallas, as she'd walked up the Highcamps' driveway for the first time, Uncle Fred had come out, taken one look at Hal's hand holding hers, and sent her a glare so vicious she'd stumbled. Mariah had never before been loathed on sight.

Uncle Fred's hostility hadn't abated. He'd made big plans for Hal, which a girl somehow thwarted. So she tried extra hard to be the perfect girlfriend. She was polite to Uncle Fred and helpful to Aunt Vera. After she and Hal rented a tiny duplex not far from the service station, Mariah had done her best to keep it clean and feed him well. She was already bringing in pocket change through steady babysitting jobs in their neighborhood.

It wouldn't be long before Uncle Fred had even more reason to hate her.

The Highcamps were celebrating Mother's Day with a barbecue at Fred and Vera's house. Mariah and Hal had been assigned potato chips and deviled eggs. She'd come home from church to the smell of boiled eggs. It made her nauseous.

Many things made her nauseous now. Her boobs hurt. She tired easily. Most telling, she'd missed two periods. Next Mother's Day, she would be a mother.

She smiled to herself. Her pregnancy might be a surprise, but it was a scary, exciting, wonderful surprise. For both of them. They hadn't told anyone, although Hal really wanted to. But she'd convinced him to give it some time. She wasn't ready to answer questions, especially, *When are you getting married?* A sore point between her and Hal. When he'd proposed, she'd said no. She wanted their kids to grow up Catholic, but he refused. They'd had a huge disagreement over it, and neither would compromise. Until he saw things her way, she wasn't getting married.

They listened to the radio on the drive to the Highcamps' house. Hal chain-smoked. She hung her head out the open window. When they pulled up, his cousin's car was parked at the curb.

"Reggie invited his new girlfriend," Hal said.

"Cool." She jumped out of the Impala as quickly as possible. Eggs and smoke. Gag. "I'll take the chips in."

It was a hot, humid day, and inside the house, it wasn't any better. In the foyer, she wavered on her feet rather than go into the living room and sit on the heavy mustard-yellow couch or the brick-hard chairs. All were as stodgy and oppressive as the people who lived there.

Voices rose and fell in the kitchen. She preferred not to be around Uncle Fred without her guy, but okay, she could do this. Gritting her teeth, she marched through the living room and into the dining room. She'd almost reached the kitchen doorway when Fred's muttering halted her.

"Why does Hal have to bring that useless Catholic slut with him?"

"Fred, really."

"She does nothing but sit on her fanny and spend his money."

Her cheeks burned with humiliation.

A floorboard squeaked in the mudroom, and a Marilyn Monroe look-alike sauntered into the kitchen. "Anything I can do to help?"

"No, doll," Fred said, oozing appreciation. "We're fine. Can I get you anything?"

"Tea would be nice," the woman drawled. She glanced over his shoulder into the dining room, her gaze connecting with Mariah's. She'd overheard his *slut* remark too.

Mariah backed up slowly and was standing by the front door when Hal came in.

"Hey, darlin', why didn't you—?"

Before he could say more, she kissed him quiet. "Just waiting on you," she said softly.

"Well, then." He looped an arm over her shoulders. "Let's have some fun."

Mariah smiled throughout the afternoon, despite her discomfort. The heat made her sticky with sweat. She kept having to pee. And the tea was too sweet. She sat in a lawn chair in the shade, alone, energy flagging, watching the others have fun.

Reggie's bombshell beauty of a guest was named Ida Mae Collins, a pediatric nurse, born and raised in Dallas. Tall and slim with enormous boobs, she was wearing a cute dress made of white cotton printed with cherries, full-skirted with off-the-shoulder sleeves. The kind of thing Mariah couldn't afford even if it showed up on the bargain rack at the Goodwill. Ida Mae claimed to be two years older than Reggie's twenty-three, although Mariah would estimate their age difference at closer to five times two.

While the men were gathered around the grill, spatulas in hand, Ida Mae crossed the grass, pulling a lawn chair with her. "You okay, hon?"

"Yeah." Mariah averted her face from the cigarette poised daintily between Ida's lacquered nails.

"I wouldn't take what Fred said personally." The woman gestured toward the older Highcamps, flicking ash. "They're old fashioned. They don't get the idea of living in sin."

Mariah didn't respond. Their opinion didn't matter much, and she wouldn't discuss something so personal with someone she barely knew anyway.

"So Hal won't pop the question?"

Her hackles rose, but she made an effort to smooth them down again. Mariah didn't want to air their religion argument, but it wouldn't hurt for the others to know they'd talked about marriage. She was confident the other woman would pass along whatever she said. "He's already proposed."

"You're engaged, then?"

"No."

"You turned him down? Well, hon, you got more backbone than I woulda thought." Ida's thinly plucked eyebrows peaked. "If you don't want him, can I have him?"

Mariah gaped at the woman, too astonished to mask her reaction. "What did you say?"

"Just teasin'," the woman said with a laugh. "Reggie's enough for me. The Highcamps make fine-looking men, though, don't they?"

Mariah stared a moment longer. Teasing? But the woman smiled so blandly that she wondered if she'd overreacted. It had to have been a joke, 'cause no one would be so bold.

"Mariah?" Aunt Vera called. "Would you take a picture of the family?"

Groaning, she pushed out of the chair. "Sure."

As the rest of the family lined up, Reggie handed her a camera. "Dad gave Mom a new Polaroid that makes color pictures. Let me show you."

Mariah had never seen anything like it. The photo came out and developed itself right then. It was a fab idea.

"Okay, let me get you posed." She grouped Fred, Reggie, and Hal around a beaming Vera.

"You come too," Fred said to Ida Mae.

Mariah pasted a smile on her face and stared through the viewfinder, waiting as Reggie yanked his date into his arms and pulled her tight. She snapped the shot.

She lowered the camera, hoping for an invitation to join them, expecting Hal to notice and remind them. But it was too late. Fred stalked off immediately, lighting up another Camel. Vera made a fuss about getting the food put away.

Reggie's new girl had been allowed in, but not Mariah. The Highcamps didn't want to include *her*. At least she understood why now. She wouldn't have if she hadn't eavesdropped earlier. Her nausea swelled, this time from dejection.

Ida sauntered over, picked up the photo, and peeled off the paper. The picture looked as good as it could for the kind of film it was. Mariah had caught them all at the perfect moment. Ida laughing as Reggie rested his chin on her shoulder. Uncle Fred trying not to scowl. Vera exuding maternal joy. And Hal, beaming at the camera with lover-like pride.

Ida held the photo between two cherry-red nails. "Reggie says you like to take pictures?"

"Yeah, I do." Mariah felt her first spurt of enthusiasm since she'd arrived. "It's a hobby of mine."

"I have a friend who owns a photography studio downtown. Mowry's. They mostly do portraits and weddings. They're looking for help."

A job with a photographer? That was almost too good to be true. Since she wasn't showing yet, they couldn't hold her pregnancy against her. "Really? Would they consider someone like me?"

"Sure thing, hon. It's office work to start, but it might grow into more. You can find them in the yellow pages. Ask for Lance. Tell him I sent you."

"Thank you." On impulse, she gave Ida Mae a hug. "This will be great."

◆ ◆ ◆

Mariah had an interview the next day. She ironed her one nice outfit, the navy dress she'd made for graduation, and slipped her feet into sky-blue flats, her cutest and most comfortable dressy shoes. It was a three-block walk to the bus stop and a thirty-minute ride to downtown, but she showed up well before her scheduled appointment and hovered outside on the sidewalk.

"Miss Byrne?"

She turned. The man in the studio doorway was at least twice her age. He was dressed sloppily in a rumpled brown suit with an orange shirt and no tie. She wasn't sure what she'd expected, but he wasn't it. "Mr. Mowry?"

"Come on in. You're punctual."

She smiled, unsure if that was good or bad.

"I like punctuality. *Brides* like punctuality."

She followed him in, masking her wince. The floor desperately needed a mop. Papers teetered in piles on the desk. Cigarette ashes spilled from overflowing ashtrays. A bookshelf was covered in dust.

Her gaze landed on a wall calendar that had appointments in most squares. The man had lots of business. He must be so good his customers didn't care about how awful the place looked.

He gave her a tour of his studio. Rooms had been set up to take portraits of families, children, and brides. There was a storage room with cameras and equipment. They had their own darkroom.

Excitement tingled. "What would I be doing?"

"Answering phones. Scheduling appointments. Making sure we never run out of film." He waved his hand at the lobby. "Fixing up the place."

She could do all those things. Reaching into her purse, she pulled out her *Very Best* folder. "Can I ever help with taking photographs? I brought some examples of my work."

"Baby doll, I don't need another photographer." He chuckled. "My brother handles what I can't get to. You'll just be a receptionist. We pay a dollar an hour. Come in Mondays and Wednesdays. Saturdays, too, when there are weddings."

Only a dollar an hour? She'd been hoping for at least minimum wage. But if she had to be disappointed about the money, at least she'd be working in a photography studio. And the Lord knew, she and Hal could use whatever she brought home. "Okay, I'll take it."

"Good, and call me Lance. Can you start now?"

"Yes."

"Good. Put your things in there." He pointed at a filing cabinet. "And, um . . . get at it." Lance scurried down the hall to the back.

She put her purse in a drawer and looked around. He hadn't said what to do first, but the lobby was a mess. That's where she'd start.

The door chimed as she was sweeping.

"Well, hello," a man said, taking off his sunglasses.

She smiled, gripping the broom. "Hello. May I help you?"

"Maybe. I'm Paul Mowry." The man resembled his brother superficially. Everything about Paul was more refined. He was younger, shorter, more slender, and handsome in a magazine-model way. He wore narrow, neatly pressed pants in pale yellow with a snug black polo shirt and loafers. Simple and fab. His smile was friendly. Nothing more.

"Oh, hi. I'm Mariah, your new receptionist."

"Ah." He flicked a glance at her bare ring finger. "We haven't advertised the opening yet. How did you find out about it?"

"Through Ida Mae Collins."

"Unexpected." He cocked his head. "You don't look like a typical friend of hers."

"We aren't friends," she blurted. At his laugh, she relaxed. "She's dating my boyfriend's cousin, for now."

"For now," he echoed, then grinned. "How much guidance did Lance give you?"

"Not much."

"Okay. Stick with me." When the phone rang, he held up a finger, then reached for the receiver. "Mowry's Studio. Hmm?" He glanced at the calendar. "Sure, how about . . . ?"

She listened to him handle the call. Politely businesslike. She could do that.

After he hung up, Paul hesitated, his attention caught by her *Very Best* folder. He looked through the photos. "Did you take these?"

"Yes."

"Did my brother look at them?"

"No." She held her breath.

Paul spread them out. Tilted his head. Separated out two and studied them. "You have talent. Tell me about your training."

After she explained about her lessons from Stephen, Paul probed with more questions. "Ever assisted in a darkroom while someone developed photographs?"

"No."

"Filmed anything with a movie camera?"

"No, but they're both things I'd like to try."

"Hmm. How old are you?"

There was so much to learn here. She couldn't wait. "Eighteen."

He let out a low whistle. "Okay, Mariah. Here's our deal. Around Lance, you're the receptionist. For me, you're my assistant. As long as you keep the office work caught up, you can tag along to weddings." He held out his hand. "Welcome aboard."

She gripped his hand and returned his smile, happier than she'd been since moving to Dallas. She'd have a job with someone who seemed kind, thought she was talented, and planned to teach her more. Even better, this place would be somewhere she could escape the dreary duplex and Hal's dreary family. Until the baby came, the studio would be her haven.

CHAPTER 14

Raine glanced at her sister and saw the same shock. Mariah had fled abuse as a teen and moved to another state with her boyfriend? Here was a major clue in the hunt for secrets. "When did she run away, Uncle Duane?"

"Winter of '63. She was eighteen."

"What happened to her in Texas?"

"'Fraid I don't know anything about her life out there."

Jessica set her empty glass on a coaster and reached for her purse, actions that indicated the interview might be coming to a close. *No.* Raine had another question to ask. "What caused Mariah to stay away?"

He exhaled noisily. "I don't know the reason for Ma. She never said, but it weighed on her. It must've been bad." His face flushed with shame. "For me and Doug? That was our fault. After Mariah ran off to Texas, she wrote letters to Ma for months. Sent packages too. Pa . . . rewarded us for intercepting them from the mail. When Mariah found out what we'd done, she told us she understood 'cause we were young. She knew how hard it was to be on Pa's bad side. But . . . she never got over it." He lapsed into silence, wilting.

Raine softened toward her great-uncle, another victim of abuse. As a tween, he'd been coerced into betraying his sister, which he'd done as a matter of survival. Mariah had tried to forgive but had been unable to forget. Terrence Byrne had orchestrated an estrangement that lasted a lifetime.

Jessica shifted forward, taking over. "Before we go, we'd like to hear about your family. Can you tell us about them?"

"What would you like to know?" Duane's energy revived.

When she gestured at a wall of photographs, he sprang from his chair and led the way over. "Now this here is my grandson Troy . . ."

Both sisters were silent for the first half hour of the trip home to Raleigh, lost in their own thoughts. But at a grumble from her stomach, Raine pulled off the interstate and stopped for a late lunch at a seafood restaurant overlooking a river.

After they'd placed their orders, she waited for the inevitable recap of their interview with Uncle Duane. Her sister, however, was absorbed in her phone. Jessica tapped, smiled, read, and tapped some more.

"Are you texting with Luke?"

Jessica dragged her gaze up. "What?"

Raine pointed at the phone. "Luke?"

"Yeah." Her sister flipped the phone over on the table. "He's checking in."

"It was a good idea to get up with him this morning."

Jessica cocked her head. "How did you know . . . ?" She stopped. Answered her own question. "I responded to your text."

"At six thirty on a Saturday."

"I made him breakfast. It was nice." She frowned at her glass of tea. Drew a circle in the condensation. "I'm worried about Luke."

Raine clamped her lips. She did *not* want to get into a personal discussion about Luke with her sister, even though she was right to be worried.

Jessica continued, as if she hadn't noticed the reluctant silence. "I think he's unhappy."

"To put it mildly." Raine swallowed a groan. Why had she let that slip out?

Her sister's head jerked up, cheeks flushing. "What do you know? Has he said something?"

It had been a mistake to respond, but now that she had, she might as well finish. "He doesn't have to say anything. I can see that he's not happy."

"You didn't answer the question."

Raine rolled her eyes. "We don't discuss your relationship."

"Then how do you know?"

Okay, she should just put it out there. "It's more about the lack of what he says. He's a naturally happy guy. He's not smiling as much lately. He doesn't say much about you. Which implies there aren't many happy things to say."

Jessica gasped. "Any advice, oh wise one?"

"Damn, Jessica, even I know this one. Treat him like he's a priority. Show up at things that are important to him because you want to be there, not because you're ticking an item off a checklist."

"Wow, Raine. Don't hold back."

"I am, actually." She paused, surprised at how much she was saying, but if she could help Luke, she should, and her sister had asked. "You've hurt him. He rates better, and you know it. But you'll have to figure this out on your own because I'm the last person anyone should come to for relationship advice."

Jessica's eyebrows peaked, her attention diverted. "Why shouldn't you give relationship advice?"

"Please."

"No, really, I want to know." She leaned back as their food was served. When they were alone again, she asked, "Is this about Coulter?"

Raine controlled a flinch. "It would have to be. He's the only guy I've ever dated."

Her sister's eyes widened. "The only?"

"Yeah." And that was enough about her ex. "Now, I'd like to finish eating."

Thankfully, they didn't speak again until they were back on the interstate. Midafternoon on a Saturday, traffic was flowing toward the beach, not away from it like they were. It made concentrating on her driving easier.

Jessica waited until a relatively empty stretch of road before asking, "Is it okay to talk?"

Better now than in the never-ending construction zone around Raleigh. "Yes."

"Do you think Papa intended for us to meet Uncle Duane?"

"If Papa left us a loose photo of Mariah's family, it wasn't random. Talking with Uncle Duane was part of the process."

"Okay, I'll buy that, but we could've asked Mom."

"I did, and she refused. She asked me to honor Mariah's wishes and stay away from the Byrnes."

"But we *are* honoring Mima's and Papa's wishes."

"Exactly, except I didn't tell Mom that part."

Jessica pursed her lips. "Maybe she was afraid of what he might tell us."

"The boyfriend," they said in unison.

"Something big happened in Texas." Jessica tapped text into the notes app on her phone. "Do you think she married Hal?"

That would be hard to stomach, but Raine doubted it. "It would've been hard to fit a marriage and a divorce into the time between Hal and Papa, but it's worth researching."

"She was more religious back then. She probably would've viewed cohabiting as less problematic than divorce." Jessica sighed. "What's in the other two boxes again?"

"Films and documents."

"Raine, let's jump straight to the documents."

She shook her head firmly. "No. Papa wanted us to be patient and follow where the contents lead. We have to trust his process. Remember what he used to say about truth?"

"Facts and truth aren't the same thing."

"So, yeah, I agree that the final facts are likely in carton three, but if we don't get there the way he set it up, we might gloss over the truth."

Jessica sighed. Squirmed in her seat. "Fine. I have a couple of other things I'd like to mention."

Raine didn't like the sound of that, but okay. "What?"

"If we interview together again, we ought to coordinate our styles."

"Would you rather I stay silent?"

"No, you drew out some good information. It's just . . ."

"You're more diplomatic than I am." Just as her sister was being now.

"Yes, and you ignored my handoff signals."

"No, I didn't *ignore* them. I didn't *see* them." They'd lived together for sixteen years. How had she not noticed? "Communication can be exhausting for me. If I'm concentrating on a person's words, I don't have any energy to spare for their body language."

"Then how—?" Jessica stopped, her hands steepled as if deep in thought. "How can we be clear when to hand off?"

"Don't be subtle. Shift toward me. Cross your legs. Touch my arm firmly." Traffic was thickening as they neared downtown Raleigh. Raine had to steer the conversation to something less intense. Something requiring less focus. "Want to tell me how things are going at the station?"

"I'd rather circle back to Coulter."

Her sister's persistence implied lack of knowledge. Had Luke not filled in the details? That was loyal. While Coulter was hardly her favorite topic, Jessica ought to know. "Okay."

"What happened with him?"

"He was emotionally abusive, and I dumped him." Eventually.

"He's really the only person you've ever dated?"

"Yes. I wasn't interested during high school. There was so much going on, it took all I had to get through the day." High school would've been a living nightmare without her sister or Luke. "People thought I was weird, and some bullied me." At her sister's gasp, she added, "Or they tried, until you or your friends stepped in and kicked ass." Raine slowed onto the off-ramp leading to Jessica's town house. "After you graduated, Luke and our friends on the track team took over."

"So Coulter showed up while I was in Virginia and Luke was deployed?"

Multiple factors played into letting Coulter past her defenses. She hadn't been in grad school long enough to have developed friends she trusted. Luke's deployment to Afghanistan had brought constant concern over the dangers he faced. Mariah's dementia had been worsening. Raine had needed someone to lean on, and Coulter had stepped into the gap. It had taken a while to appreciate that she was better off alone. By the time Luke returned, she'd been extricating herself. "Yeah."

"That was a long time ago."

The five-year break wasn't only about Coulter. It was about her. There had been a couple of guys she almost went out with but decided against. Saying yes would've been about worries she *ought* to be dating, not because she actually wanted to. If she ever felt a genuine desire to accept a date again, she would. Until then, she liked being single. "Sometimes I'll get curious about a guy, but never more than that."

"What's more than curious?"

"Interested." They were pulling into the driveway of Jessica's town house. Conversation over, which was a relief. Raine had reached her limit on talking about relationships.

Her sister unbuckled and opened the door. "Thanks for driving."

"Want to get into carton two tomorrow? We can have a movie marathon at my place."

"That works. When?"

"If you get up again with Luke," Raine said with a smile, "come over early."

CHAPTER 15

Jessica had dinner in the oven and beers chilling. The only thing missing was Luke.

He should be getting home soon from the Guard. While she waited, she would add her impressions from today's interview to the notes the sisters were collecting. Picking up her iPad, she opened her sister's shareable drive and clicked on the *Duane Interview* file. But a quick browse showed there were no gaps to fill. Raine's notes were remarkably detailed. A near-perfect transcript of the conversation with their great-uncle.

Mariah's time in Texas had been a black hole to Duane. Had Papa left the Texas puzzle pieces in cartons two and three? He'd planned the hunt with care. The movie marathon would likely reveal more.

Jessica next selected the *Timeline* file, a spreadsheet of the people and places they'd discovered, sorted by date, with insightful comments sprinkled throughout.

It was a marvel how well Raine had the data organized already. Had Papa counted on her love of order?

Yes, of course he had. Putting Raine in charge had been a careful choice, one that Jessica would honor.

She reopened the *Duane* file. They'd uncovered a lot of new information. The physical abuse by Mariah's father. Running away with the boyfriend. The lack of protection from her mother. Learning her brothers had played a key role in separating her from their mother. Mariah must have felt so alone and betrayed to have remained distant throughout her life.

They had extended family on Papa's side, had visited his mother and brother in Richmond often. Great-Gran Azarian had lived in a musty old house, where the cloying scent of lilies hung in the air. She would sit enthroned on an overstuffed armchair, a crochet hook flying, wearing flowy dresses with knee-highs peeking out from the hem and a plate of delicious treats on the table. But after she passed away, they hadn't returned to Richmond much.

In Raleigh, they'd been their own little family unit of six. Parents, kids, grandparents. That had been enough for Jessica. She'd never wondered about the Byrnes, and the oversight bothered her.

She glanced at the clock. Where was Luke? A peek in the oven showed a beautifully roasting chicken. She turned on the burner under the pot of peeled potatoes.

Did she have time to squeeze in some research? She signed in to Ancestry.com. A quick query found a Harold "Hal" Highcamp from Dallas. There wasn't much information on him, none confirmed with documentation. He was listed as being born in 1944. Married to Ida Mae Collins in October 1964. His wife died in 1972, and he died in 1986.

Raine was right. It seemed unlikely Hal and Mariah had enough time to marry and divorce.

Armed with Mitchell Byrne's age and last known location, she located him in Daytona Beach. Alive and living with a woman named Daisy Byrne, twenty years his junior. Presumably his wife, since Uncle Duane didn't think he had kids.

Jessica picked up the *Our Family* album and skimmed through it. The pages were filled with lovely, sentimental photos of a family enjoying a quiet life in the last few decades of the twentieth century. There were several photos of family trips to the zoo, memorable because her mom had never particularly liked going to zoos. Jessica would add them to the image gallery on the shareable link.

Her phone beeped. A text from Luke.

I'll be another hour or two. Paperwork to complete

It was their fourth drill weekend since the wedding and the third time he'd done this. She hadn't adjusted to the role of military spouse. Smothering her disappointment, she went into the kitchen, turned off the boiling potatoes, and lowered the oven temperature. The meal would have to wait.

Luke made it home later than he'd thought, worn out and quiet. After they'd finished eating, they'd ended up on the porch, side by side on the glider, swaying in the moonlight until his head dropped against her shoulder. She continued to rock, listening to his even breathing. Glad to be the person he came to for rest. Empathizing with the frustration he must feel on the weeknights she came home late, then afterward wasn't fully present.

Jessica got up early Sunday and made breakfast again for Luke. A lot of effort for fifteen minutes with him, but worth it. Maybe this was good practice for her possible future with a morning show.

When she entered her sister's condo later that morning, she breathed in the scent of warm apples and cinnamon. Her sister's amazing coffee cake was one of Jessica's favorites. A small but touching gesture. Raine showed emotion through action, and Jessica had really needed that message of inclusion today.

"I have a snack ready." Raine pointed at the island. "How was your evening?"

Small talk too? Controlling her surprise, Jessica poured cream in her coffee and said evenly, "It was quiet."

"Guard kept Luke late?" At her nod, Raine said, "You gotta get used to that."

"I know." Jessica's smile was pained. Would she ever?

"He's doing a good thing."

"I know." She'd known it would be lonely on his drill weekends, but the reality was harder than she'd expected.

Raine scrunched her brow. "Okay, I have something to say about him."

"Luke?" Jessica froze. What was she about to hear?

"He and I have been friends a long time, but . . ." Her sister stopped and stared up at the ceiling. "It's been different since you married. I get that. I'm not sure he does yet."

"What do you mean?"

"We can't be the same. Brother-in-law is more . . . formal than friend." She met Jessica's gaze. "You asked yesterday about whether he's told me he's unhappy, and he hasn't. He might've in the past with other relationships, but not with you. And that's the way it should be for his wife." Her voice echoed with melancholy. "Especially when she's my sister."

Jessica hadn't thought of it from her sister's perspective. Luke was one of the few old friends Raine kept up with. Of course their relationship had to change. "Thank you for telling me. Are you okay with it?"

Raine shrugged tightly. "I will be eventually. Sister-in-law isn't so bad. Now, bring your snack." She carried her plate and mug to her office. "We'll watch the movies in here. I have room-darkening shades."

Jessica followed her sister. The film projector sat on a low table, facing a blank wall. Well, really, all four walls were blank. Raine had no artwork or decorations in here. It had only four pieces of furniture: a nightstand, a double-size bed (currently covered with albums, home movie canisters, and a carton), an ergonomic chair, and a sleek desk holding top-quality computer hardware and a framed eight-by-ten of the family portrait from Jessica's wedding.

She sat on the bed and placed her plate on the nightstand. "While I'm not as committed to Papa's process as you are, I do think there's a purpose to the photos. They're setting the stage. Giving us a sense of nice people living ordinary lives. Have you watched any of the films?"

"More than half. I've looked at all the *Stephanie Firsts*. Bath, birthday, ballet. Mostly, they're bloopers. All adorable. All well done. I'm pretty sure Mariah took all the footage."

"Makes sense," Jessica said. "Papa stayed out of the film business until camcorders appeared."

They laughed at the memory. Papa had chased them around when they were little, overcapturing their childhoods. Technology had delighted him.

Jessica took a bite of the apple-cinnamon coffee cake. *Mmm, delicious.* "I wonder where all those tapes are."

"Mom's getting them converted to DVD." Raine dropped onto the carpet beside the projector. "We should look at the 1963 reels first. There are six of them. All from Dallas. All on holidays. I've queued up Memorial Day."

Mariah's favorite subject in the film was a handsome man with a deep tan and bright-blue eyes. Always smoking. Always smiling at the camera with a sheepish kind of tenderness. It had to be Hal Highcamp. Interesting that Papa would've willingly kept films that featured another man.

Mariah had also focused on another couple. The second man appeared to be a slightly older version of Hal. Similar builds, smiles, and distinctive blue eyes. Attractive in a laconic way. The woman looked like a 1950s pinup girl. Tall. Hourglass curves. Bleached-blonde hair in bouncy curls. Trying hard to be pretty and mostly succeeding.

When the film ended, Raine handed the reel to Jessica, who popped it into its canister.

"What next?"

Raine handed over a clipboard. "We could go in chronological order, or you could pick whatever you want. Here's a list of the reels."

Jessica read through the list of 1963 films. Memorial Day, Fourth of July, Labor Day, Halloween, Nov 22, Christmas.

Wait, what? Gasping, she reached for the second-to-last canister. On it, Papa had written:

Nov 22, 1963

Dallas, TX

Her pulse raced. A strange coincidence, surely. She handed over the reel. "This one, Raine. Now."

"What's wrong?" Her sister narrowed her eyes in concern. "The Thanksgiving one?"

"That's not Thanksgiving. It's the day John F. Kennedy was assassinated."

Raine's movements became brisk. She threaded the *Nov 22* film into the projector and looked over her shoulder. "Ready?"

Jessica nodded, her whole focus on a square of white light on a blank wall.

The projector stuttered. Images rolled of people lining both sides of a city street. The crowd had been sparse near the photographer—their grandmother—and heavier up the block.

The location was familiar. Chills swept her body. Mariah had been a *witness*! Jessica braced. "Raine, if you've never seen the raw footage before, it's graphic."

A white four-door car drove past slowly, then out of the frame. The camera shifted toward a dark convertible flanked by motorcycle cops. As the limo cruised by, the first lady, in her vivid pink suit, turned to face Mima and waved. At her side, the president jerked. The camera bobbled slightly while staying on Jackie Kennedy's bright smile. JFK jerked again and . . .

The scene transformed into a chaotic mess of racing cars and motorcycles. Blurry humans running. The camera tilted sideways and dropped toward the ground. A few seconds of grass. Then black.

Jessica could hardly breathe.

"Mariah was there." Raine's tone was hollow.

"Yeah." *Okay.* What they'd just seen was either real or one of the best fakes Jessica had ever seen. Her mind flicked through the implications. Mima had witnessed—and filmed—one of the most devastating moments in US history. She'd been a teen, possibly with her boyfriend, watching what should've been a joyful occasion, given her extreme admiration for Jacqueline Kennedy, until the moment turned catastrophic before her eyes.

Mima had never spoken of it. How could she have remained silent about something so . . . huge?

Did Mom know? It seemed unlikely she'd keep a secret this big, but this quest for the family's story was leading them into unbelievable territory.

Papa had known and left this shocking footage for them to find amid mundane glimpses of an ordinary life. Had that been the goal? To shock his granddaughters like Mima had been shocked?

Sliding from the bed, Jessica paced around the room, her thoughts racing. Her grandparents had made an unfathomable choice to hide this footage. What if it contained information that could've changed what the world believed about the assassination? What if it could've put an end to conspiracy theories? Or showed evidence of a second gunman? Yet they'd withheld it from history. They hadn't even told their journalist granddaughter, who would've grasped its significance and had ideas for what to do.

The film's existence didn't bother her as much as her grandparents' silence. Mima made sure, as far back as 1963, no one got their hands on this.

In college, Jessica had been fascinated with JFK's assassination—which both her grandparents knew. She'd taken a class on how the story had been covered. Lapped up every documentary and movie about conspiracy theories. Pored over the Warren Commission report. Read the FBI interviews from every witness they could find. If Mima's name had been listed anywhere, Jessica would've noticed. She went back to the bed. "Let's watch again."

Raine rewound the reel and replayed it. It was similar to the famous Zapruder film, except Mima was positioned on the opposite side of the street with an unobstructed view. Filmed on a better-quality camera.

"Again," Jessica said quietly, forcing herself to observe it in news-producer mode.

There was an establishing shot.

The lead car passed.

Next came the president's limo, smoothly in frame, trailed by motorcycle cops.

Even without audio, the excitement of the cheering crowd was palpable.

The film captured the first lady's charming smile, as if Jackie had been looking directly at the photographer. The camera jerked. The smile faded from Mrs. Kennedy's face. Her head whipped around as the film recorded, in gory detail, what happened over the next several seconds. A Secret Service agent charged the limo as Jackie climbed onto the hood. Even as the agent was launching himself onto the vehicle, it accelerated.

"Mima witnessed JFK's assassination *and* took footage no one knows about."

"We do," Raine said, her voice cracking. She dropped her head against the bed and closed her eyes, clearly shaken. "I'd never seen . . . all that before."

Jessica wanted to comfort her sister but wasn't sure how. She lowered herself to the carpet, close to her sister but not touching, supporting Raine by just being there.

As the silence lengthened, Jessica grappled with her thoughts. Mima had been at Dealey Plaza, watching as the gruesome scene played out. The fear. The manhunt and confusion. Seeing the assassin murdered on national TV in real time. The loss of innocence. Only 9/11 could come close to being comparable to how the world had ground to a halt.

As the journalist in her kicked in, her first reaction was to send this to an institution that could prove its authenticity. The JFK Library or the Smithsonian? The FBI?

But she trusted her gut, and it was telling her to wait until they knew more. "I don't understand why they never spoke about it."

"I do. She was traumatized," Raine said dully. "*I* don't want to speak about it, and I wasn't even there."

Valid point. "What should we do about the reel?"

"They've had this for decades. They knew its significance. There must be a compelling reason to hide it."

"I agree. They could've destroyed it, but Papa wanted us to know."

"Do you think she remembers?" Raine lifted her head. Winced. "What am I saying? I don't see how anyone could forget."

"We have to ask her." They had to seek confirmation from their grandmother, and it ought to be done together.

Raine met her gaze. Nodded her understanding. Looked away. "When?"

"I can't today." She had the promotion discussion pending with her husband tonight. "I want to be home when Luke arrives. Tomorrow?"

A long, impatient sigh. "Sure."

"After I get off work. That'll be past seven."

"Okay." Raine stood abruptly. "We're done here. I need a break."

Jessica had dinner warming and the porch table set when Luke walked in after seven. Fatigue shadowed his eyes.

"Hi," he said quietly. "Give me a few minutes to shower."

"Okay." She was serving the chicken when he jogged down the stairs, dragging a T-shirt over his head.

He carried their plates out to the screened porch. She followed with two bottles of beer, sat, took a couple of bites, then folded her hands in her lap. The events of the day had stolen her appetite.

"Has something happened?"

She looked up, still in a daze. "We did more work on the wish today. A box of old home movies. One was hard to watch. I'll tell you more after confirming a detail with my grandmother." She reached for her bottle and rolled it between her palms, her mouth curving up in a half smile. "There was one nice thing, though. We met in Raine's condo. I know how much she likes her solitude."

"That she does." He picked up his fork.

She pretended to eat another bite, then gave up, reclined into her seat, and sought the pleasure of hearing her husband talk. "Tell me about your weekend."

"It was good," he said eagerly. "Took some great video. Made plans for the summer."

"You have units going to Botswana in July?"

He nodded. "A civil engineering team needs to practice repairing roads. Might as well practice somewhere it builds goodwill with a partner country."

"And Public Affairs will be there to cover them." Her interest stirred. If she pitched the story at the station, would they air it?

"We'll send units to Moldova too." He ate a bite of chicken. "Mmm."

"Moldova?" That was news to her.

"Yeah. It was FOUO until this weekend."

"FOUO?"

He grinned. "For official use only. But we can talk about it now." He ate a forkful of mashed potatoes and groaned with appreciation. "We made plans for the hurricane season. It could be a busy one."

Hurricanes had the station's attention too. She could be camped out at the station while Luke was away helping with weather events. Something they'd have to deal with for years. He wouldn't be eligible to retire until he was thirty-eight. It would be an issue they'd have to resolve before having children. "What does that mean for you?"

"If the Guard gets called up, I go. Mostly to counties on the coast. But it could be to other states or the Caribbean. Depends on where we're sent and how many PA teams they need."

When they finished, they cleaned up like a well-oiled machine. She packed up the leftovers while he cleared the dishes. But once he hit the start button on the dishwasher, he remained where he was, his back to her, staring out the kitchen window.

She studied him. His stillness. The tension in his shoulders. Was he, like her, in the grip of what had happened to him over the weekend? "Luke, are you ready to talk about how a promotion might affect us?"

"Sure."

She crossed to the couch, still agitated over Mima's traumatic experience. Luke seemed distracted too. Not the best of circumstances to make decisions. She should limit the scope. "Why don't we educate each other on the issues tonight? Then we can take a few days to mull things over."

Nodding, he sank onto the opposite end of the couch. "You first."

"I've already mentioned the big pros and cons. What I didn't say was how much I would enjoy being a senior news producer. I'd be working similar tasks to what I do now, only focusing on the parts I like best. Like breaking news and helping other staff."

"Sounds great. Why wouldn't you want it?"

It was a good question. She sorted through her concerns. "More responsibility means more stress. There are no details yet, but I suspect I'd move to a different part of the day. Probably the morning." She was hardly a morning person, but she would like having afternoons free. And the morning team was staffed by fun, talented people. "I might like it, though, once I got used to getting up early."

He picked at the label on his beer. "What are the hours?"

"I'd probably leave by three a.m. and return around lunchtime."

"With the rest of the day free."

"Yes, but I'd have to go to bed earlier on weeknights." That might not be so bad. They often ended apart late at night. While she did her news catch-up downstairs, he handled schoolwork upstairs. With the morning show, she would do their apart time asleep.

He frowned at his hands. Breathing steadily. Brow creased in concentration.

"Luke? Any questions?"

He looked up. "Would morning shows be less stressful?"

"Probably, but that's relative." She paused, giving him time to ask something else, but he just shook his head. "Okay," she said, "it's your turn. Tell me about grad school."

He faced her. "The application's ready, but I haven't submitted it yet. There's another month until the deadline. I've narrowed the choice to Global Literacies or Curriculum and Instructional Leadership."

"Which way are you leaning?"

"The global program is really new. It sounds exciting, but the C&I program would open more career opportunities in the future. I'm weighing them both." He rubbed the back of his nearly bald head.

Her husband was wearing down, and so was she. This was a good place to stop. "What do we do next?"

"Talk through it. Make a plan." He rose, then leaned over to kiss her. "But not this week. I have a National Guard brigade to post online about, fifty high school seniors relying on me to grade their projects, and a baseball team to coach to the playoffs. Let me get past that."

"Okay." She had to work on Papa's wish too, and the intensity was increasing. Given what they'd seen today, she worried about what might be inside carton three.

"Jess," Luke said hesitantly. "I have a meet and greet at the high school Tuesday night. We've invited the incoming freshmen and their families. Can you make it?"

"What time?"

"Six to eight." He tensed, as if expecting disappointment.

"Yes. I'll get there as soon as I can." And she would keep her promise.

CHAPTER 16

Raine had a restless night, her dreams filled with dark convertibles and ladies in pink suits.

After awakening with the need to outrun the gruesome images in her head, she went to the fitness center and worked off her agitation on a treadmill until her body protested at the punishment.

Back in the condo, she opened her exam-review course, then immediately set it aside. Any attempt to concentrate would be futile.

Mariah had witnessed something horrific. At nineteen. She'd been distant from her family. Uncle Stephen was in the army. Hal had been a teen too. Who had she turned to? Who helped her to heal? There would've been no therapists or mother or brother.

How did a person ever get over something that traumatic?

But hiding the reel, not turning it over to the government, still didn't make sense. Once it was out of her possession, she wouldn't have to think of it again. Keeping it seemed counterintuitive.

Raine got why people committed financial crimes. Greed. Revenge. Desperation. But the behavior always trailed the money. She didn't get this behavior. Why had Papa and Mariah withheld that film from a world that might profit from the knowledge?

They were missing something big. Would Mariah be able to tell them? Or would they find it in the remaining reels and a carton?

She wrenched her thoughts away to refocus on work, not stopping until after dinner to check in with her sister.

Are we still on to visit Mariah?

I can't go today. I have to stay late at the station

I'll go without you

The phone rang. Jessica was calling to argue.

"Don't, Raine. I don't have time for this, okay? There's too much going on." Her sister's voice was strained. "Maybe Mariah will remember something useful, but it'll be more efficient to open carton three."

Normally, pulling the efficiency card carried a lot of weight with Raine. But not today. "Papa and Mariah wanted us to know the truth. He gave us the clues in this order for a reason."

"The real mystery will be in those documents."

"You're probably right, but maybe there's something we need to know first. I trust Papa's process."

"Wait," Jessica said, lowering her voice. "My executive producer is headed this way." She muted her end. Seconds later, she came back on. "I've been called to the EP's office. I'll leave as soon as I can afterward. Don't go in without me."

Raine was sitting in her car in the visitor lot when her sister parked beside her. They got out in unison and hurried along the path to the main building.

"What did your boss want?" Raine asked.

"I can apply for the promotion soon. She wanted to counsel me."

"About the *lie goals* thing last Friday?"

Jessica stopped on the veranda and gaped. "Do you watch the six o'clock news? I thought you hated the news."

"I do." Raine went through the door. "Yours is palatable."

"Is that your version of a compliment?" Jessica asked as they walked into the memory-care unit.

"Sure." And Raine meant it. She could always tell when someone read her sister's words because they were more . . . lyrical. Compelling. "The anchors sound better on your show, and I like the little things at the end."

"Like the goats?"

"And the puppies."

"Thanks." Jessica gave her a bright smile outside their grandmother's door. "Okay, what's the plan?"

Her sister had never asked her that question before. She'd never really minded in the past. Jessica's plans were always good, and Raine rarely balked at using them. It wasn't efficient to argue over who had come up with an idea if it worked. But the glow of pride at being asked was unexpected and . . . nice. "I took a few images from the home movie. The quality isn't great, but it's discernible. I also found a few more online that we could show her. You should take the lead on the interview until we can tell how receptive she is to returning to those memories. I'll jump in if I need to."

When they entered their grandmother's suite, Mariah was standing by the bookcase with her walker. She frowned at them over her shoulder. "Who brought me to a hotel? Take me home."

Jessica murmured, "I've got this." Then stepped closer. "You are at home, Mariah. You're not in a hotel."

"This doesn't look like my house."

"It is, I promise. The bookcase has your pictures and Papa's flag and Uncle Stephen's. A hotel wouldn't have them. You *are* at home."

Mima studied the flags for a long moment. "Okaaay," she said skeptically.

Raine had a sinking feeling about this. "Hotel" was a new complaint. Mariah had never liked living here, but the house had become a dangerous place for her. She'd burned pots on the stove. Fallen on the stairs. Strolled into the neighborhood and forgotten where she was. Papa had had no choice but to move her somewhere safe.

"Mariah," Jessica said gently, "why don't you sit?"

Her grandmother backed up to a chair and eased down, then looked from one sister to the other. "What is it, young ladies?" Her grandmother's tone was clipped. Impatient. *Young ladies*—a term she reserved for strangers.

They both sagged onto the love seat. They'd known this day would come, but who could be prepared for how much it stung?

"We thought we might talk about when you lived in Dallas."

Mariah made a rude sound with her lips and picked at her cuticles. "Why would I want to talk about that?"

"You don't have to. Your choice."

Mariah made a dismissive sound.

"We could go outside for a walk," Jessica said.

"No."

"Do you want us to leave?"

A long sigh. But that wasn't a yes. The sisters exchanged a glance and waited. They would let their grandmother make the next move.

Mariah held up her hands and studied them. Folded them in her lap. Rolled her head away from them and looked out the window. "What do you want to know?"

Jessica touched Raine's arm, passing the baton. "You lived in Dallas in 1963."

Her grandmother inhaled an audible breath. "I did."

"Did you have a movie camera?"

"I did, yes. Well, I worked at a photography studio, and they had several." Mariah smiled smugly. "I was hired as a receptionist, but I made myself more."

Raine nodded at her sister. Suspicion confirmed. "What exactly did you do at the studio, Mariah?"

The cuticle picking resumed. "I helped one of the photographers—the good one—with weddings and babies."

It was the opening they needed. "Can I show you some photos?"

"*May* I?"

"May I show you some photographs?"

Mariah gave a curt nod.

Raine got out her tablet and brought up an image of the man they presumed to be Hal, his arm slung around his look-alike companion. "Do you know these people?"

Her grandmother pointed at the companion. "Reggie Highcamp. Such a joy." She touched the boyfriend's face. "Hal. He's a good man. One of the finest I've ever known."

Uncle Duane had called him a good guy too. Mariah might have been raised by a jerk, but it hadn't harmed her ability to judge fine men. Raine swiped to a second image. "Here's Reggie with a woman."

Mariah's face hardened. "Ida Mae. Bitch."

Her sister stiffened beside her. Their grandmother never swore. Mariah's life in Texas was proving to be a minefield. Raine would proceed cautiously.

She hesitated to show the last image, the one from the JFK footage where the limo had just straightened on Elm. The final seconds of Camelot. "While you were in Dallas, you went to Dealey Plaza with your camera."

"I wanted to see the first lady." Mariah's eyes welled with tears. A few escaped. Dripped onto her blue silk shirt.

Raine pulled the cover over her tablet. Enough images. She turned to her sister.

Jessica said, "You filmed the motorcade."

A barely perceptible nod.

"Then what?"

A deep breath. "Jacqueline Kennedy is such a beautiful lady. So elegant. So . . . radiant. She smiled at me and waved. Then . . ." Mariah's face crumpled. "It all started there." A sob burst from her lips. "It all started there."

CHAPTER 17

November 22, 1963

It was a nightmare getting out of the center of Dallas. Terror stripped away civility.

Mariah's back ached fiercely. She squirmed, unable to get comfortable, but it was a godsend too, because it kept her mind off what they'd witnessed.

Hal had a white-knuckled grip on the steering wheel as he listened to the radio and the wild theories being bandied about. Fear had carved deep creases into his face, erasing the laugh lines. It had taken just minutes to age a decade.

"President Kennedy has been taken to Parkland Hospital," a tinny voice intoned, "where the doctors are doing their best . . ."

What idiots the reporters were. Everyone at Dealey Plaza had seen the man die. "There's nothing the doctors can do for him."

"I know, Mariah. I was there too." Glaring at the gridlocked intersection, he picked up his pack of Marlboros, shook one out, and clenched it between his lips. He didn't reach for the cigarette lighter.

"You never liked him anyway."

"I wouldn't say that." Hal spat out the words. "I wouldn't have voted for him, but I wouldn't have wished . . . *that* on him."

She closed her eyes against the images seared into her brain, but they didn't stop tormenting her. Mrs. Kennedy's horror. Screams and fumes and abject terror. Three pops. The president . . .

Mariah pressed both hands to her mouth, holding in sobs.

He parked before their duplex and came around to her side to get the door. Gripping his hand tightly, she tried to pull herself from the car. Her legs wouldn't cooperate.

"You okay, darlin'?"

She was too tired, too wobbly to even nod. "A little shaken."

He cradled her against him, a firm arm around her waist. "Did I hurt you back there? When I pushed you down?" Guilt roughened his voice.

"No, you protected me, and I love you for it." She leaned against him as she walked up the sidewalk, her legs quivering like Jell-O.

After he helped her onto the couch, she lay on her side, her breaths shallow. The pain from her back radiated around her sides, then tightened across her belly. Something wasn't right, and it scared her to think what it might be. She didn't say anything to Hal. Not yet. Maybe it would go away and she wouldn't have to tell him.

He had the radio going in the kitchen, frightened voices filling the air with strident words to stave off the truth. She was glad she couldn't hear them clearly.

The other half of the duplex had a TV set on loud, a cycle of droning announcements, gasps, and wails. Hal came into the living room and loomed over her, hands shaking. His agitation was making hers worse. She closed her eyes against the sight.

"I wanna know what's happenin', and the neighbors have a color TV. I'm going next door." The screen door thwacked after him.

She didn't want to know. Didn't want to remember. The ache in her back was worsening. At least pain gave her something to focus on besides what they'd witnessed.

Was she having contractions?

No, that couldn't be right. The baby wasn't due for another month.

She wished she could ask her mother, but that option was blocked forever. Every letter she'd sent had been returned unopened. She'd even sent a package from a fabric store. A beautiful length of rayon in black with an iridescent blue sheen. More expensive than Mariah could afford. The shopgirl had wrapped it in an official-looking box and mailed it for her. Mariah had slipped a note in before they taped it shut. It hadn't been returned, but still no response.

She would have to go through this alone. As she waited out the next contraction, she let her mind shift to the baby. After months of arguing over raising their children in her faith, Hal had finally given in. They should be married now. They'd planned the ceremony for two o'clock . . .

◆　◆　◆

"Mariah?"

Her eyes slitted halfway open. Hal was kneeling beside her.

"What?" she asked, her throat raw.

"Walter Cronkite says LBJ is the president." Hal laid his head on her breast, his cheeks shiny and wet.

She lifted a hand—a heavy, trembling hand—and smoothed his hair. Nobody cared about political or religious disagreements today. Whoever had done this had done it to America.

"Have they found . . . ?"

"The killer? Yeah. Some weaselly little creep." Hal pushed up and walked out of her view. The shower started. He needed to wash off the events of the day.

That would've sounded good to her too, if she could've moved.

She'd been pretending to herself that her backache came from being knocked to the ground and pinned under Hal, but she couldn't pretend any longer. She was in labor, and it was too soon. The baby was supposed to be their Christmas miracle.

Water seeped between her legs, saturating her underwear, soaking into her beautiful wedding dress. The prettiest thing Mariah had ever owned, and now it was covered in grass stains, dirt, and . . . something else. Still she lay, staring hot-eyed at the dingy carpet.

Hal reappeared in fresh jeans, a long-sleeved shirt, and bare feet. "I'm making macaroni and cheese." He went into the tiny kitchen.

"Hal," she called.

"Gimme a second." Water gurgled from the faucet, making a hollow metallic ping as it hit the pan.

"Hal."

A cabinet door opened. Closed.

"*Hal.*"

"Darlin'." He stood in the entrance to the kitchen and frowned at her. "Don't look like that. Get it out of your mind."

"He's coming."

"Who?"

"The baby."

"I know. In a month."

She raised her frightened gaze to his. "No, Hal. Now."

He charged over to the couch. "Are you sure?"

"Yes," she panted.

He hustled her into the car, backed out without even looking, and raced through the empty streets. She lay on her side in the front seat, her cheek on Hal's thigh, and drew up her knees. It relieved the ache for a minute, but the pain returned with the next contraction. She was exhausted, scared, confused. This couldn't be happening. It was too soon.

He screeched to a halt outside the emergency room. "Come on, darlin'. Sit up."

She wobbled upright, eyes closed, gasping.

They stumbled in together, Hal practically carrying her. The lobby was empty. The desk, deserted. He helped her into a chair, then raced away. "Hello?" he shouted. A door banged open and a radio blared. He shouted again.

She wasn't sure how much time had passed in the eerie silence of the place, but suddenly she was surrounded by noise and hospital staff. They were lifting her onto a gurney as Hal hovered nearby.

"Ma'am, when did your water break?"

Her eyelids fluttered as she tried to think. A sea of people crowded above her, bright lights behind them, their faces in shadow. "I don't know. An hour?"

A hand slid under her dress. She winced at the discomfort.

"She's close," someone shouted.

Hal gripped her hand. "What's happening?"

"Sir," a firm female voice said, "you have to move your car."

"What?" Hal was smoothing the hair from her face. "No, I don't want to leave her."

"Move your car, sir. Now."

"Okay." He leaned over her and kissed her temple. "I love you, Mariah. I'll be right back."

She grabbed for him, terrified to be left alone with these strangers with their ravaged expressions and tear-streaked cheeks. "Please don't go."

He kissed her knuckles and smiled reassuringly. "I'll be right back. Wait for me."

She tried to chuckle at the little joke, but couldn't. The gurney was whisked away, through quiet hallways, the lights hurting her eyes. She shut them tightly.

Someone shook her shoulder hard. She opened her eyes to a room with even brighter lights. People were tugging at her clothes, cutting them off.

"Stop." Tears spilled from her eyes. Not her beautiful wedding dress.

A man leaned over her. His face was covered by a mask, except his eyes, which were brown and red-rimmed. "It's time, Mrs. Highcamp."

No, she thought, *I'm still Miss Byrne.* "Time for what?"

"Your baby is ready now," he said sharply. "We have to take it."

"Where's Hal?"

"He's nearby. In the waiting room."

When the man straightened, the overhead lights blazed in her eyes. She closed them again. Her head ached, and she wanted Hal.

A rubbery mask was placed over her nose and mouth.

Were they trying to gas her? "No," she said, but the word went nowhere. She batted at the mask. "Stop." She shook her head violently. "Get that off me."

"You need this, Mrs. Highcamp."

"No, I don't want gas . . ." She fought the hands and the mask and the pain. A contraction hit, rolling over her, leaving her gasping.

They took advantage of her distraction, clamping the mask on again. "Breathe, Mrs. Highcamp."

Mariah shook her head again, feebly now. Belly tightening. Legs trembling. Hands throbbing . . .

◆　◆　◆

A ticking clock awakened her to a large dim room. She should probably sit up, but she preferred to lie there, arms folded over her belly, praying for the worst headache of her life to go away.

Her hand itched fiercely. When she reached to scratch it, her fingers brushed a needle taped down. Her belly wasn't as big anymore either, and it felt puffy, like a deflated ball.

What happened?

It all flooded back. The assassination. The hospital. The baby.

A chair squeaked. She rolled her head toward the sound.

"Hey, darlin'." Hal stood, smiling faintly. "We have a boy."

A son. Their Christmas miracle. Or more like a Thanksgiving surprise. She breathed in the knowledge and smiled. That was good. So very good. She would've been glad with whatever they had, but a boy was better for Hal. It was what he wanted, and she understood boys. With four brothers, how could she not?

Their son was the only light in a day of devastating darkness. "Where is he?"

"In the nursery. He's small, bald, and he can let out a loud shriek."

"Is he handsome?"

"Oh yeah. Takes after his dad."

She sighed in relief. "Baby boy Highcamp."

Hal chuckled. "He needs a better name than that."

"Harold," she said.

He kissed her forehead, then her lips. He tasted of tobacco and coffee and pride. "How about Kenneth, after my dad?"

"Harold Kenneth Highcamp. It's a fine name." She struggled to sit, wincing at the pain. Hal helped her, plumping pillows behind her, smoothing the sheet. "When can I see him?"

"How about now?" a nurse called, walking in the door, a bundle in her arms. She crossed to the bed and handed over the newest Highcamp.

Mariah smiled into her son's face, love coursing through her body, pure, sweet, all-consuming. Was this how her mother had felt when she first saw her daughter? Mariah kissed her son's brow and thought him the most beautiful baby she'd ever seen.

Grief had hung over the maternity ward all weekend like a thick fog. From the nurses to the janitors to the visitors, everyone had stumbled about. Sobbing. Dabbing at their eyes. Speaking in tragic whispers.

Mariah and the baby were going home today, and she was ready to get out of this place. But she had to change clothes first, and there was no one to help her. The president's funeral was being broadcast, and the hospital staff were glued to the black-and-white television in the waiting room.

After slipping out of her hospital gown, she gingerly put on the fresh clothes Hal had brought her. Without guidance, he'd picked the wrong things. Maternity pants—too loose. A shirt from before her pregnancy—too tight across her boobs. But the bedroom slippers were just right. When she was done, she stared at her reflection in the mirror. No makeup. No accessories. Her hair, dull and flat. Her eyes, bloodshot. She didn't look her best.

She had one last thing to do before they left. Ask someone in charge about Kenny. He had jaundice. She'd been complaining about it to anyone who would listen, but they weren't taking her seriously. They were more interested in the television than her son.

"Mrs. Highcamp," a candy striper said in a singsong voice, pushing a wheelchair into the room. "Are you ready?"

"Mr. Highcamp isn't here yet."

"Would you like to wait in your room?"

Absolutely not. "In the hall, please."

The girl pushed her to the nursery and stopped before the windows. A nurse came out, the baby bundled in a blanket. "Here you go," she said. "Such a pretty boy."

In a world drenched in sorrow, her son brought so much joy. Mariah hugged Kenny to her chest and kissed his sweet brow. But after peeking into his face, she looked up in alarm. "He's still too yellow."

"Don't worry. He'll get better. They always do."

The staff thought she was overreacting. As if being nineteen meant she was stupid about babies. With all the babysitting she'd done, she'd been around newborns before, and they did *not* look like Kenny. "You said he'd be okay by Sunday, and he wasn't. Then you said he'd be okay by today."

"Give it time—"

"*No*. Stop treating me like a dunce." Tears trembled on her lashes. She wasn't used to being pushy, rude, *strident*. But this was her son. "He's worse."

"Jaundice is common—"

"I *know*. What did the doctor say?"

Rather than answer, the nurse flushed.

"Has Kenny even seen a doctor?"

"Well—"

"Hello," a commanding voice interrupted. "Is there something I can help with?"

A nurse Mariah didn't recognize appeared beside the wheelchair. Her starched cap nestled atop curly gray hair barely restrained by bobby pins. The woman wasn't smiling, but her eyes were kind.

"I'm sorry, Mrs. Adams," the other nurse started. "Everything is fine."

"No, it is *not*." Mariah would pin her hopes on the new nurse. Maybe she would listen. "I've been telling them all weekend that my baby is too yellow, but no one will pay attention to me. Please look at him."

"Certainly. Let me see." Mrs. Adams leaned over, studying Kenny's face. She opened the flaps of the blanket. Ran gentle hands down his body. Frowned at his squeaky cry. "May I?" she asked, lifting him into her arms. "Gladys," she said, shooting the younger nurse a steely-eyed glare. "Is Dr. Cooper on the floor?"

"I think so," the girl said in a chastened voice.

"Tell him to join me. *Now*." To Mariah, she said, "Your son won't be going home today."

"He shouldn't be that yellow."

"No, I'm sorry. He shouldn't."

A tall, white-haired man in a white coat came out of the nursery, his long strides bringing him swiftly to them. Nurse Adams joined him. As she spoke urgently in a low tone, he examined the baby, his face tightening.

He nodded grimly at Mrs. Adams. "Back to the nursery. I'll be right there." He closed the distance to Mariah. "Ma'am, I'm Dr. Cooper. I'm not your son's pediatrician, but I'll be taking over his care."

"Thank you." She licked her lips, frightened by what was happening. "It's serious?"

"Yes."

"Will he be okay?"

He looked down. Blew out a puff of air. Met her gaze again. "We'll do our best. I'll let you know something when I can." He hurried back through the nursery door.

The elevator pinged, and off stepped Hal and Reggie.

"Here, darlin'." Hal handed her a bouquet of mums. "Where's my boy?"

Mariah cradled the bouquet to her chest and cried.

CHAPTER 18

Jessica watched uneasily from the door to her grandmother's suite. Mariah had wailed so loudly that a nurse's aide had come in to soothe her. After several agonizing minutes, she was finally calming down. The woman gestured that all was well as she pushed Mariah's wheelchair into the bedroom.

"I hate that this happened," Jessica said to her sister. "It was a mistake to come and hurt her like that. We need to move on to carton three."

"We will. Tomorrow. You can come to the condo after work."

"I can't. I'm going to a meet and greet at Luke's school."

Before her sister could respond, high heels snapped down the corridor, drawing rapidly closer. They turned to look. Mom was hurrying toward them in a sparkly blue top over a swishy black skirt, as if she'd come straight from a party.

"Who called her?" Raine muttered.

"She probably left instructions to be contacted if Mima gets upset."

Raine sighed. "I'll fall on the sword."

"Why?"

"It's easier for her to believe I'm the screwup."

Jessica stared at her sister in astonishment. Did she really believe that? Because Jessica didn't think it was true. Mom had always worried more about her younger daughter.

Raine had already taken a half step forward. "Everything's okay, Mom. Mariah got upset when we were talking with her."

Mom's eyes narrowed warily. "About what?"

"Texas," Jessica said.

Their mother blanched. "How did you find out about Texas?"

So Mom did know. How many other secrets was she party to?

"Uncle Duane told us," Raine said flatly. "We met him this weekend."

Their mother looked ready to ignite. "What exactly did he tell you?"

"Everything he knew," Raine answered truthfully.

Emotions flitted rapidly across Mom's face. Annoyance, fear, ending with resolve. She glared at her younger daughter. "I asked you to drop that."

"I told you I wouldn't."

Mom snorted. "Okay, then. Care to share details?"

Jessica would toss out a bit of information and see where it led. "He said Mariah ran off with a boyfriend as a teen. We asked her to confirm, which she did, and the memories upset her."

Some of the tension drained from Mom's face. She pushed past them, then halted in the doorway to the suite. In a low, tense voice, she said, "Girls, stop asking questions. Leave this alone." The door closed behind her.

Jessica's mind raced as she and her sister walked through the parking lot. When they reached their cars, they stopped and turned to each other.

"That was odd." An understatement. Jessica had rarely seen their mother so perturbed. "She knew Mima lived in Texas, and she was relieved we don't know specifics. What is she worried about?"

"She's told us twice to stop. I'm not asking her anything else until we know more."

"Okay." Jessica was confident she could wring information out of their mother, but that conversation would have to wait. For now, if Mom chose to be an obstacle, they'd go around her. "*It all started there.*"

Jessica repeated the last words Mariah had spoken before melting down. "It's more than a confirmation."

"It's a direction." Raine stared at the night sky. "So what's the plan?"

Jessica was eager to push forward. She could feel them closing in on something bigger than an unknown recording of JFK's assassination. But not tomorrow. "Open the rest of the films and carton three. But you'll have to do them without me."

Raine sighed with relief. "Good. I get why Papa asked us to do the teamwork thing, but you slow me down."

"Aww, thanks," Jessica said with a laugh. "Glad to help." Then she sobered. "I can't let Luke down. I've already missed every one of his baseball games."

"Wow, Jessica, major error. He's really proud of those kids. They had talent last year but no discipline. No . . . spirit. He's worked hard with them. You need to get to a game."

"I know. I want to do better. I just . . ."

"Have too much going on, and sometimes you prioritize wrong."

That surprised another laugh out of her. "Thank you for that succinct yet highly accurate summarization of my life."

Raine's lips twitched as she got into her car. "I'll start on the other stuff and let you know what I find."

"Sounds good," Jessica said with a goodbye wave. But as she drove home, her sister's statement lingered on her mind. For the first time, instead of viewing Raine's friendship with her husband as irritating or (Jessica was embarrassed to admit) threatening, she saw it as a gift, and that brought relief. Someone else understood—without questions or explanations—what she was navigating in her marriage.

CHAPTER 19

After returning from Larkmoor, Raine viewed the final four 1963 reels.

Three were mundane. What Jessica called "setting the stage."

The Fourth of July footage showed a basic cookout with cake and candles, probably a birthday celebration for both Mariah and America.

Labor Day had a bunch of stylish, laughing people at a wedding reception.

Halloween presented a predictable party with people wearing costumes and drinking beer.

Only the Christmas movie grabbed her interest. Before a decorated tree, Hal and Reggie flanked Ida Mae, who cradled a baby in her arms. There had been no reference to a baby before. Was this reel mundane? Or something more? Raine placed it on the *maybe* pile for her sister.

Carton one had revealed an important discovery: Uncle Duane. Carton two: the JFK film. If Papa's pattern held, they had one more major discovery to go.

Her sister was right. It was time to take the next step.

They were a team now. Raine would ask.

Nothing on the other 4 films. Are you sure that I should keep going?

Yes. I don't think we should wait

Ok. I'll let you know what I find

She'd get to it in the morning. But as she prepared for bed, she thought about all the time she'd spent with Jessica in the past few days. When she'd first read Papa's expectation for the sisters to work together, she'd been seriously worried it would be hard to break the habits of a lifetime. For so long, she'd looked up to her older sister—literally and figuratively. But in less than a week, their sisterhood felt more equal. Raine only took the lead when a fast decision was necessary. If this was a taste of what it was like to be in charge, she didn't mind it so much. And Papa had given this to her.

As eager as Raine was to open carton three in the morning, self-discipline won. There were assets to be found in the divorce case. She made it until ten thirty before curiosity won out. She would call it an early lunch break.

She lifted the accordion file out of the carton. It wasn't particularly heavy, merely awkward to maneuver. Propping herself against the head-board of the guest bed, she set the file between her legs.

The 1963 pocket was a bit boring. Three newspaper clippings about the assassination. A ticket stub from a football game. A cigar wrapper.

The 1964 pocket wasn't any better. It held a library card, a one-dollar bill, a Greyhound bus ticket, and an index card written by Papa announcing the job of secretary at his construction company. She smiled at that. Mariah had saved the want ad she'd answered that had led her to the man she would marry.

More pockets continued in that vein. Memorabilia that was sometimes cute, sometimes weird.

She drew out the contents from the 1972 section. It was thicker than the others had been. There were newspaper clippings about desegregation in North Carolina after a 1971 Supreme Court case involving the Charlotte-Mecklenburg Board of Education. Even more articles describing local efforts to merge the Wake County and Raleigh city school systems. A folded receipt. And two envelopes, both postmarked in Dallas and addressed to Papa.

Why were envelopes from Texas addressed to Papa? Not Mariah?

Okay, that stuck out. Heart pounding, she pulled a letter from the first envelope and smoothed the yellowed piece of lined paper. The handwriting was squashed and painstaking.

September 14, 1972

Dear Mr. Azarian,
My husband's name is Hal Highcamp. He's the father of Mariah's son. I'm sure you don't know about Kenny.

Wait. What had she just read? Her grandmother had a son? Her mother had a brother?

What?

Raine's hands shook so badly she dropped the sheet of paper. In the space of one sentence on a faded letter, her grandmother had become a person she no longer recognized.

She slid off the bed and stumbled to the guest bath. The face looking back at her from the mirror was pale, wild-eyed, despairing. *How could you, Mariah?*

Raine's beautiful, wonderful, amazing, truly perfect grandmother had had a baby before Mom. Before Papa. With a boy named Hal she'd run off with as a teen. And nobody had ever told them.

Papa had nailed it when he'd said they'd be disappointed. Actually, maybe not. This was more than disappointing. It was horrible.

Mariah had been unlike other grandmothers, the kind who baked cookies and took their grandchildren to the park and gave birthday presents kids actually liked. No, Mariah had done none of those things. She was too busy downtown, meeting with the governor, pushing bills through the general assembly, modernizing how children of all abilities were educated in North Carolina. Her efforts had made a difference.

And she'd had a son Raine had never heard of.

She splashed cold water on her face, dried with a hand towel, returned to the bed, and picked up the letter. There was more.

> Mariah made us promise to never tell you, but I'm too sick to take care of him anymore, and we can't afford for Hal to quit his job.
> Please help us.
> Sincerely,
> Ida Mae Highcamp

It was hard to breathe through the knowledge. When Papa received the letter, he and Mariah would've been married for seven years. Had it been a surprise? Because that would've destroyed him. Had he opened a letter one autumn day more than fifty years ago and discovered his wife was a liar?

With clammy hands, Raine reached for the second letter. This one had a document attached.

October 1, 1972

Dear Gregor,
It was nice of you to come and meet Kenny. He liked you. That don't happen much with strangers.

Thanks for the check. Aunt Vera and Reggie's wife, Karen, are willing to help Ida Mae with Kenny if I'm at work. It'll be good to pay them.

Here is a copy of his birth certificate, like you asked.

I'm sorry my wife contacted you. She should never have said anything. We would have made do. Mariah and I had things worked out between us. That's always been fine. I don't want nobody to pity my boy.

Sincerely,

Hal Highcamp

Raine unfolded the birth certificate, looking for any detail that might absolve her grandmother, but her hope went unrealized. Harold Kenneth Highcamp had been born on November 22, 1963, in Dallas, Texas, to Mariah Helen Byrne and Harold Alvin Highcamp.

Mariah had a baby son on the day JFK died. Three years before Mom.

Disbelief ached in her head, invaded her limbs. She sucked in a slow breath to steady herself and smoothed open the folded receipt. It was a lease for an apartment on Glenwood Avenue. Papa had moved out ten days after the first letter was sent.

Her grandparents had separated over the revelation. For how long? What had brought him back?

Her mother had been six, old enough to notice him gone. Had Mom known *why* Papa left?

This was . . . awful. No, worse than that. Despicable.

How dare they drop this bomb on their granddaughters with no warning?

How dare they hide Kenny from his nieces?

How. Dare. They?

CHAPTER 20

February 1964

Stephen picked the worst possible day to meet his nephew.

Hal left after breakfast, his lips flattening at the kitchen mess and her stained robe. But he said nothing, just gave her that hard, critical stare. He lit another Marlboro as he plodded down the driveway and into Reggie's truck, idling at the curb.

The snug fit of his uniform pants suggested that Hal had been putting on a few pounds. Mariah, however, had lost weight. Too much. Since Kenny's birth, she'd had no appetite. She was having to use Hal's belts to keep her pants on now.

Hal's cigarette habit had worsened since . . . Dealey Plaza. And the beer. So much beer. It was ruining their food budget. No eggs or produce for them until Hal was paid on Friday.

They hardly spoke now, and when they did, the conversation descended quickly into arguments about money, Kenny, meals, or housework. They avoided topics like the news or his family, too sensitive when minds were fogged over and bodies were barely holding on.

She filled a jelly-jar glass with water, took an aspirin, and sat on the linoleum floor, leaning her head against the cabinet. She'd been awakened at three by a nightmare and had decided not to go back to sleep. But a catnap might help. She shut her eyes and waited for the most reliable alarm clock around. Kenny.

A shriek roused her. She rolled to her knees, grabbed the edge of the counter, and dragged herself to her feet. She'd slept ten minutes. Better than nothing.

In the bedroom, she could see his little fists wobbling wildly, but he calmed when she said softly, "Kenny, Mommy's here." As she bent over him, tears plopped onto his tiny nightshirt. Would he grow up believing mommies always cried in the morning?

"Hi, sweetie," she said as she lifted him, hugged him close, and sniffed his body. A bath was necessary.

Kenny loved splashing in the tub but afterward grew crabby from his cold. He didn't want to be left alone, and chores were piling up. There were dishes stacked in the sink, clean clothes lying unfolded on a chair, and a bed still unmade. But the dirty diapers stinking up the bathroom were the absolute worst. Everything else could wait.

After a morning at the laundromat, Mariah paced side to side in front of the couch, with her miserable son in her aching arms. He'd just relaxed when someone knocked on the door.

Who could it be? Nobody ever came here during the day. Hal's family shunned her, and their neighborhood was too poor to be worth a door-to-door salesman's effort.

Maybe it was Ida Mae. Anger flared. Mariah was sick of her coming by. Even though Reggie had broken up with her more than a month ago, she kept coming 'round. Mariah shifted her son onto one shoulder, pasted on her fiercest frown, and cracked the door. "What do you—?"

A tall man in an army uniform grinned down at her. "Mornin', Rye."

She hadn't seen her brother in fifteen months, not since he'd left for boot camp, and here he was, without warning or fanfare. She burst into tears.

Stephen nudged the door wider, tossed in his duffel bag, and wrapped his arms around her, baby and all.

"Hey, hey, hey. Not the greeting I was expecting," he said, kissing her forehead. "What's going on?"

She cried harder, pressing her cheek against the wool of his jacket. For three months, she'd been alone each day with the baby. She rarely ate, rarely slept, rarely thought. Hal's obvious disappointment hung around like a dark cloud, but she was often too numb to care. Kenny came first and took all her focus. Nothing else mattered.

She would never complain about her life out loud. Not even to Stephen. But having her brother here made her feel less alone.

"All right, hand him over, Rye. I want to inspect my nephew." Stephen cradled the baby high on his chest and made tick-tock sounds with his tongue. Kenny stared, mouth open, then his lips relaxed into the sweetest baby smile. "Handsome kid. You did well."

She swiped at her cheeks. "You're a natural at that."

"Lots of practice. I was thirteen when Duane and Doug were born." He looked around. "Is there somewhere I can change?"

Anxiety made her want to puke. Not the bathroom. She'd have to scour it first. That left the bedroom, but it was a disaster. The sheets hadn't been washed in . . . She couldn't remember. Everything smelled. The carpet was grimy. Oh God, Stephen would see what a failure she was.

"Rye, relax and look at me."

She met his gaze.

"Pick a room. Any room. But not this one. Too many windows."

Her lips curved into a half smile. "The bedroom. Straight back."

He handed over the baby, grabbed his bag, and took off down the hall. She surveyed the living room in shame. There was so much she'd let go. Laying Kenny on the floor, she made a circuit of the room, shoving clothes and papers behind chairs and under the couch.

"Rye, stop."

She jerked at the sound of his voice. Her brother appeared beside her in jeans and a long-sleeved shirt. He held Kenny against his shoulder.

"Don't clean up."

Ignoring him, she headed for the bathroom and hastily wiped the counters and toilet down before tossing used towels and rags into the tub. Then she pulled the shower curtain closed and returned.

Stephen was holding the baby at arm's length. "Love ya, kiddo, but not enough to change his diaper."

She smiled, glad he'd come. Glad to be around someone who sought her out, who enjoyed her company. Glad to feel a spark of happiness.

While she sat on the carpet, cleaning up the baby, Stephen lounged on the couch, long legs stretched before him. "Tell me, Rye. What's going on here?" His voice was soft, firm, demanding honesty.

Where to start? *We're hungry and tired and broke. We don't have time for fun or, well, anything other than survival.* But she'd say none of that. "It's hard."

"Yeah, I can see that. Where's your help?"

The question startled her. "What help?"

He sucked in a deep breath. Released it in a hiss. "There should be family and friends who come over to clean for you, cook for you, hold the baby so you can rest."

She shook her head.

"Doesn't Hal have family here?"

"Yes."

"Then where are they?"

She shook her head again. They didn't come over, which was good. The idea made her ill. She didn't need any more frowns of disapproval.

Stephen shot to his feet. Stalked over to the sliding glass door. Stood there, hands on hips. "How long have you been doing this alone?"

"Since around Thanksgiving."

"When your son was a few days old. That's unforgivable," Stephen growled low in his throat. Faced her. "Do you remember how sick Ma was after the twins were born?"

"Yes."

"I heard Granny call it 'baby blues.' Maybe you have that. You should ask a doctor."

Mariah nodded, as if she'd take his advice, but she wouldn't. Their money wouldn't stretch to another bill.

"Ever hear from Ma?"

"No."

"Does she know she's a grandmother?"

"No."

Snorting in disgust, he came over and squatted before her. "How are you really doing?"

"Okay." Her face burned at the lie.

"I don't believe you. Rye, you haven't written about the assassination since December. I'm here now, and I'm listening."

He'd used *the word*. That bald, terrible word. "I can't. Not yet." Not *ever*.

"Why not?"

"It . . . I . . ." Three pops of a rifle. And screaming. So much screaming. The fumes. Motorcycles racing. Mariah lying in the grass, Hal pressing her down, reeking of sweat and aftershave. She couldn't stand the smell of English Leather anymore. "Please don't make me."

"Do you still have nightmares?"

Every night. "Sometimes."

"Uh-huh. So you're not sleeping either." He leaned forward and kissed the top of her head. "Okay, I'll leave the topic for now, but we're not done with this conversation. Got any beer?"

His request was a relief, because it meant he would stop prying, but it was also bad since there was only one Pabst left. They'd had to ration the supply after the medicine for Kenny's ear infection wiped them out. "I'll get you a beer."

"No, I can."

He stepped into the kitchen and opened the fridge. Whistled. Frowned at her over his shoulder. Yeah, she knew it was sparse. Milk, margarine, eggs, and bologna. So much bologna. It'd been on sale, and she'd stocked up.

He peeked in a few cabinets. Said a filthy word she'd never heard from him before. "Where's the closest grocery store?"

She should refuse his generosity, but she wouldn't. It was hard to feel shame on an empty stomach. "Go back to the main drag. Turn left. Three blocks."

He returned to the living room and lifted the baby. "So here's what's happening next, and no arguments."

Her lips edged into a tentative smile.

"Ken and I will have some uncle-nephew time together. You'll just get in the way, so I'd suggest a nap."

Sleep in the middle of the day without a snuffling baby on her chest? Turn everything over to her brother so she could relax? Too good to believe. "Okay."

"Up on the couch."

She crawled onto it and curled on her side. With one hand, he expertly snapped open a blanket and draped it over her. Her last thought as she drifted off was that she would give herself over to her brother's care for now and scold herself later for her weakness.

The creak of the front door awakened her. She peered through half-closed eyes as Stephen backed into the room, pulling the buggy piled high with groceries and Kenny cuddled against his shoulder. She shut her eyes again and listened. Her brother talked softly, his deep voice rising and falling in a one-sided conversation. Paper bags rustled. Cabinet doors squeaked open and shut. The fog in her brain took over again, and she fell back asleep.

"Mariah, what happened in here? Where's the baby?"

Hal's angry voice yanked her from a pleasant dream. She sat up yawning, pushing hair from her face, and looked around. The living room and kitchen had been transformed. Laundry put away. Furniture dusted. Floors swept. Dishes washed. The duplex hadn't looked this clean since Thanksgiving. "I, uh . . ."

Hal was kneeling by the couch. "I know *you* didn't do this," he bit out. "Where is the baby?"

"I'm not sure—"

"God. What the hell is wrong with you?"

"I, uh . . ." She shook her head, hardly able to concentrate. "My brother—"

"Hal, it's been a while," Stephen said as he emerged from the bedroom. He carried a freshly changed Kenny over his shoulder.

"What are you doing here?" Hal rose, his smile genuine. "When did you get in?"

"This morning."

"I didn't know you were coming." Hal's glare was heavy with accusation.

"I didn't either until yesterday, and I didn't let Rye know 'cause I didn't want to disappoint her if my plans fell apart." He walked into the kitchen and returned with a platter of steaks, enough for several meals. "Hey, I hope you have a grill."

"Sure. Yeah. There's one out back."

"Great." Stephen went outside, talking to the baby. The door banged shut.

"Mariah? You couldn't have called me? Let me know he was here?"

"No." Her jaw flexed at his tone. "Uncle Fred won't let you take my calls."

"What?"

"You haven't noticed you never get calls from me? It's a rule. No talking unless it's an emergency. I don't bother anymore."

"I didn't know that." He rubbed his face. "I'm sorry. I'll talk to him." He walked into the kitchen. "I need a beer."

"Wait, Hal—"

The fridge door opened. He groaned. Cursed. A cap popped. He came out again, a bottle in hand. "Did Stephen go shopping?"

She nodded.

"Did you ask him to?"

"*No.*"

"Why didn't you get groceries?"

"With what, Hal? We don't have any money."

He drank half his beer in a single gulp as he perched on the arm of the couch. "Where's it all going?"

Before the baby, they'd had two people living on two paychecks. Now they had three people living on one. What did he expect? "Kenny costs a lot. We run out of money between paydays."

Hal's shoulders rounded in defeat. "This was nice of your brother." The harshness in his voice had mellowed. The beer and the promise of a good meal must be working its magic.

It had been months since she'd heard echoes of the old Hal, the relaxed Hal from before. "Why don't you go outside? Keep him company?"

"Sure, but I don't know how to thank him."

"You don't have to."

"Okay." He leaned over and kissed her softly on the lips. "I love you."

She shivered. It had been so long since he'd kissed her or said those words. Not since the day their son was born. The day they should've married. "I love you too."

The evening had been nice. Kenny usually shrank from strangers, but not Stephen. Her son had been content to be held by his uncle, and Mariah had been content to sit on the carpet and lean against the wall, a spectator detached from the action.

Unlimited beer and beef had loosened Hal's tongue. His laugh. He told her brother funny anecdotes of customers at the service station. Then the two of them got into a war of words over their cars. Stephen boasted about his Fairlane. Hal was certain his Impala could "take you on any time."

She closed her eyes, listening to her three best guys.

"Mariah," Hal called gently. "Let's get you to bed. Stephen's bunking out on the couch."

She blinked in the lamplight and clasped Hal's hand. "Where's Kenny?" she asked, wobbling to her feet, her gaze seeking her brother's.

"Fed, changed, and sleeping in his bassinet." Stephen winked at that last word. Their bassinet was an empty dresser drawer.

"Okay." She hugged him tightly. "Thank you. For everything."

"Yep. Good night."

She headed to the bedroom. Hal was already undressing. She put on a nightgown, checked on her son, then slid in beside her fiancé.

He flung an arm around her waist and pulled her closer. "I talked with Stephen tonight," Hal said quietly.

She nodded, afraid of what she might hear next.

"He wanted to know about . . . Dealey Plaza. I told him no."

"Yeah, me too." To talk was to remember, and that would be . . . destructive.

"Then he jumped on me about how little help you get. I didn't know, darlin'. I thought Aunt Vera was helping out."

Mariah shook her head. Not since December.

"I'll talk to them."

"Don't. They don't like me. It's why I let you and Kenny go to Sunday dinner without me. I'd rather be alone than get the *slut* stares."

"What?" Hal rose up on his elbow and frowned down at her, his eyes gleaming in the light filtering in through the blinds. "Has anyone called you that?"

"Hal, don't say anything. Please." If he did, he would be told lies, and she'd be the one punished. Not him.

"We'll see." He made a noncommittal grunt. "Stephen says you hate bologna."

Her brother had a big mouth. "So?"

"It's the only meat we have. What are you eating?"

She loved her brother, but she wished he'd mind his own business. Well, no, she didn't. "Steak for the next few days."

Sighing, Hal wiggled closer and cuddled her. She never slept much, but she surely wouldn't now, not while Hal was holding her. He gave all his tenderness to their son. Being held like this was too novel to miss a single second.

◆ ◆ ◆

Three days went by too fast. Mariah struggled not to blubber the entire drive to Love Field. As Stephen drove the Impala into the airport drive, he touched her arm.

"Don't come in, okay?"

He was right. She'd make a scene at the gate, otherwise.

After parking at the terminal, he got out. She waited for him at the curb.

He held his duffel bag in one hand and reached for Mariah with the other. "Love ya, kiddo."

She nodded against his chest. The impossible felt possible when her brother was around. And when he walked away from her, she'd go back to being an exhausted mother who never did anything right, with a baby who never stopped crying and a daily existence that would never match her dreams.

"I got something for you."

She stepped back, dabbing at her eyes. "What?"

He handed her an envelope. It was full of ten-dollar bills.

"Stephen?" Really, she should refuse, but they needed it too much.

"If it helps with groceries, fine. But use some of it for you."

"Like what?"

"College."

She shook her head. When she'd hopped into Hal's car on a dark highway a year ago, she'd said goodbye to college.

"You'll get there one day. Save some for that." He kissed her forehead. "See you later." Then he spun on his heel and strode away.

She stood by the fence along the runway, waiting until his flight took off. Long after the tiny speck of an airplane disappeared into the wide blue sky, she gripped the fence, yearning for her brother, clinging to the sliver of hope he'd brought with him.

CHAPTER 21

March 1964

If Stephen hadn't come, if Mariah hadn't caught the baby's cold, if Jack Ruby hadn't been found guilty of murdering JFK's assassin, her Saint Patrick's Day would've gone very differently.

The problems started when she woke up with a pounding headache and a throat on fire.

Hal came out of the bathroom, rubbing his clean-shaven jaw, smelling of Aqua Velva. He kissed her forehead. "You're warm. You feeling okay?"

She wouldn't admit to being sick. They couldn't afford for him to stay home from work. "Yeah, I'm fine."

"Okay, darlin'. See you tonight."

As if the baby realized what a bad day it was, Kenny was being sweet. The TV was off because there was nothing on but Ruby's verdict and more footage from the president's assassination. She could not bear to watch another second. But the woman next door had her TV blaring, the words clear as a bell through the thin walls. Mariah had to get away from it before she screamed.

She wiped Kenny's snotty nose, wrapped him in a blanket, put him into the baby buggy, and went out. She couldn't go shopping, but walking past the shops was free.

The peace that Stephen's visit brought had vanished with him. If anything, everything was worse. While Stephen was there, she'd been reminded how good it felt to not be hungry. To feel rested. To joke and laugh. That was all gone now. Those three lovely days had shown her how bleak her life was.

She pushed the buggy to the main drag, then past a children's clothing store, a bicycle shop, and a travel agency with shamrocks taped to the windows. She stopped. Backed up. She'd forgotten what day it was. On impulse, she went inside and picked up a brochure for Hawaii. The beaches were unlike anything she'd ever seen. Sand and shells and waves and beautiful blue water. She missed the beach.

She missed her mother. She was homesick.

Mariah was in-every-way sick.

The travel agent eyed her skeptically, and Mariah understood. She didn't look like someone who would ever visit Hawaii, but the man dutifully handed over a stack of brochures and said, "We hope to see you back."

A bad round of coughing scraped her throat and sent her home. She fixed herself a hot honey-lemon-whiskey toddy, laid Kenny on the carpet with a pacifier, and thumbed through the brochures showing tropical scenery and happy people in tiny swimsuits lazing on white sand.

Another brochure slipped out. Galveston. Mariah's interest stirred. The closer, more affordable beach for those Texans who would never reach Hawaii. And it wasn't so far, was it? Hal could drive them there someday. It would be good for them. A reminder of what it had been like before.

Her daydreaming interlude ended when Kenny spat out his pacifier like a rocket and let out a shriek. Setting down the brochures, she lifted him and paced in front of the couch, until his snuffling at her neck let her know he'd drowsed to sleep.

She laid him on a blanket on the floor, stretched out beside him, and tried to nap.

When the front door creaked open, Mariah jerked upright and slid the brochures into a thumbed-over copy of *Good Housekeeping*. No sense in upsetting Hal.

"Happy Saint Patrick's Day," Ida Mae sang out as she sailed into the duplex without knocking. "I hope you don't mind that I let myself in."

Mariah did mind. She didn't want that woman in her home. As long as Ida showed up, Reggie wouldn't, and he was the only friend Mariah had here. Why did Ida come anyway? Hal was taken, and Ida and Mariah would *never* be friends.

The woman walked over and perched on the couch, smoothing her pink plaid miniskirt over a pair of pale-green stockings. She looked dressed for a party. "Hon, you look close to breaking. Do you want me to take him?"

Mariah had been close to breaking for months, like she was holding herself together with baling twine and Scotch tape. "No, I'm okay."

Ida sniffed. "When's the last time you did anything just for you?"

"Christmas." Mariah closed her eyes. A tear squeezed past her defenses.

"Hey, hon. How 'bout I babysit tonight? I can stay for a couple of hours."

Longing swamped her. A free babysitter? Oh, what she wouldn't do to accept! "Don't you have somewhere to go?"

Ida flicked her wrist dismissively. "I can be late. Why don't you go take a bath? Get all dolled up. When Hal gets home, the two of you go on a date, to a bar for a beer or something."

Mariah was almost afraid to breathe. To believe. An actual date, for the two of them? "Hal won't go for that."

"I bet he would. He'd love for you to try again. Look, hon, I know you must feel like a failure, but don't give in. You'll get better at all this. Nobody'll ever call you a bad mother to your face, 'cause we can tell you're trying the best you can. Now go out. Have fun. Show everybody they're wrong."

Other people talked about her? They thought she was a bad mother? How did they even know? No one ever came over but Ida, and Mariah didn't go out much.

Was it Hal? No, she couldn't believe that. He wouldn't.

She did try to be a good mother. Really she did. She loved her son so much. But how could she be good when she could never put him down? When there was no money after groceries and formula and medicine? When, between nightmares about gunshots and his little wails, she never got enough sleep?

"Here, let me take him." Ida Mae reached for Kenny. "Now go have a soak."

A long bath sounded wonderful. Mariah shuffled down the hall, stopped, and peeked back. Kenny was staring up at Ida Mae's face, eyes wide, lower lip trembling. But no screams yet. Mariah waited another anxious minute. But as the silence lengthened, she continued down the hall. Ida Mae was a nurse for kids. She knew how to handle them.

Mariah fetched a robe from the bedroom closet, then went to the bathroom and locked the door. As the tub filled with hot water, she added some Ivory dish soap and sank beneath the bubbles. For the first five minutes, she soaked and cried. As the heat of the water soothed her, she closed her eyes and imagined her little family in one of those pictures of Galveston. The three of them laughing into the wind, the huge expanse of the Gulf of Mexico spreading before them.

She and Hal would go out tonight. Drink beer. Talk. Maybe even plan a trip to a park. Or the lake. Palm Sunday was this weekend. She could pack a lunch. It would only cost a tank of gas for a few hours of fun.

When she heard voices in the living room, she sat up. The water had cooled, sloshing as she rose. Drying quickly, she hurried to the bedroom. No need to wonder about what to wear. She only had one decent dress. So she put it on over hose. After applying makeup and tying on the scarf Hal gave her for Christmas, she was ready.

She was so excited. She needed this night off *desperately*.

In the drawer with her period underwear, she'd hidden Stephen's envelope of cash. She looked at it now with a pang of guilt. That money could make life so much easier for them, but she hadn't told Hal, afraid if he found out, some would end up paying for cigarettes and beer. She was holding on to it for emergencies, taking a little whenever the grocery money ran out too soon.

Tonight was an emergency. She couldn't bear it if she didn't have something nice to look forward to.

How much for a few drinks? Five dollars? She took a ten, then recklessly added a second. After stuffing them into her purse, she threw in some toilet tissue for her drippy nose and walked out to the living room, quivering with anticipation. A date with her man. An escape to a bar instead of a beach, but at least it was happening.

Hal sat on the couch with Kenny in his lap, making faces at him. She loved the sight of them together, envious the baby was so good for his father.

Or maybe the father was good for the baby. Her smile trembled at the thought.

Hal looked up and whistled. "Darlin', you are beautiful."

"Thanks." She bobbed a curtsy.

"What's the occasion?"

"We're going out."

"We?"

"Ida Mae is babysitting so we can have a date." Mariah looked around. The other woman was missing. "Did she go outside for a smoke?"

"She had to leave. As soon as I walked in, she handed me the baby. Kenny spit up all over her clothes. She went home to change for a party. I don't think she's coming back."

His words were like a punch to the gut. Mariah couldn't breathe. Turning away, she choked back sobs. No more night out for a drink with her fiancé, like they were a couple again.

"Darlin', it's okay. Why are you so upset?"

"I was looking forward to it," she said, gasping out the words. "Ida said she'd watch the baby so we could go on a date. She took him so I could bathe and change and . . ." Mariah's legs gave out, and she crumpled to the floor.

"Go, darlin'. Okay?" He came to sit on the carpet beside her.

She shook her head, hands clapped to her mouth, trying not to heave. This was so, so bad. She wanted a little fun. Just a little. That wasn't too much to ask, was it? One night to leave these four walls, to stop the constant TV coverage of her nightmares, to feel pretty, to laugh.

To not be a failure.

"Mariah. Darlin'. If it means so much to you, go out. Have some fun. Kenny and me, we'll play some poker and have a few drinks. We'll be fine."

Mariah smiled through her tears. He'd never offered before. Was this real?

It took a few minutes more of pleading from Hal and resisting from her before she agreed. For an hour. Maybe half an hour.

She walked down to the corner bar. It was noisy and full of life. She stepped inside and hovered by the door. Couples crowded the tables, laughing, talking, drinking. There was one lone seat at the bar. And four men, puffing cigarettes, playing pool, eyeing her.

Hesitating, she stayed by the door, somehow feeling sadder in this crowded bar than she had at home. She was nineteen and a mom—a *bad* mom—and she didn't want to be here without Hal. Running back outside, she shivered in the brisk March wind. Should she go back to the duplex?

No.

Hal had the baby, she looked nice, and she hadn't had time to herself since . . . before. She was so damn tired of everything going wrong.

Behind her came the hiss of a bus slowing to a stop. She climbed into its warmth and leaned her head against the window. The lights of

Dallas slid past, although she didn't really see. Just sat there, warm and alone and free.

"End of the line," the driver called. They were at the bus terminal.

She followed the stragglers off and huddled in the corner of the waiting room. This late, it would take forever to get home. Should she splurge on a taxi?

No, she shouldn't waste money that way. But what other option did she have? Call Hal and have him drag out the baby to pick her up?

No good choices. What should she do?

"Ma'am, can I help you?"

She looked up, confused. "What?"

A stoop-shouldered man in a bus company uniform was giving her a friendly smile. "Do you have somewhere you want to go?"

She wanted to scream *yes*. If only for one day, she wished she could be somewhere with good food and clean clothes and nice furniture and plush carpet and a baby who didn't wail because he had a *bad* mother.

She looked at the money clutched in her hand. "I don't have enough to go very far."

"That'll get you to Houston and back. Or Galveston."

Galveston!

She was on the beach by sunrise.

CHAPTER 22

Raine fled to the living room, unable to share the same space with two letters, a birth certificate, and a lease.

It had been years since she'd felt such intense anger. She had to calm down. After drawing the shades and dimming the lights, she burrowed in her recliner, tuned in to Spotify, and closed her eyes.

But she couldn't evade her thoughts.

She had an uncle. If he was still alive, where did he live? Texas? North Carolina? Somewhere else?

Did her parents know about Kenny?

Mom had been horrified her daughters knew about Texas. Dad had said, *Call me when you need me.* When, not if.

They knew. A conspiracy of silence.

This was bigger than she could handle by herself. She had to tell her sister. But when? Once Jessica found out about their uncle Kenny, the news would consume everything. Her mood. Her thoughts. Her emotions. Raine couldn't tell her now. Her sister was at work, with a mistake behind her and a promotion decision looming. Not tonight either. It might ruin the meet and greet, and Raine wasn't doing that to Luke.

But she couldn't sit here in a dim room, brooding. She had to uncover more facts before she shared this news. Jessica idolized Mariah.

Raine could use help, though. She fired off a text to her sister.

What's your best trick for discovering if someone is alive?

Check voter records

A few seconds later, a second text arrived.

Dare I ask why you want to know?

I'll let you know soon

First, she tried Texas, whose voter lookup was impossible. But North Carolina's was scarily easy, and she found him. Harold Kenneth Highcamp voted regularly in Lee County, no more than an hour away. How dare they?

She controlled the urge to jump in her car and drive somewhere, anywhere to outrun her distress. But she wouldn't. It would be dangerous. A classic case of driving while distracted. Instead, she texted her father.

Call me

She was out on the balcony, hoping the view would ease her mind, when her phone rang.

"Hey," Dad said. "I have ten minutes until my next appointment. What's up?"

"I know about Kenny."

Her father sighed heavily. "I'm sure you have questions."

"I do indeed." There was a sick feeling in the pit of her stomach. She hated the idea of questioning her father like this, but she had no choice. "Will you answer them?"

"I'll try."

"Tell me about where he lives."

"It's a residential facility for adults with disabilities about an hour southwest of Raleigh—called Alder Creek."

She took a slow breath. Steadied herself. "What's your role in this?"

"I drew up his trust."

"You knew. You let them lie to us all these years." She clapped a hand over her mouth to hold in a sob.

"Raine. I'm sorry. I . . ." There was a pause. His voice was husky when he spoke again. "It wasn't my choice."

"Then why not tell us?"

"Let's call it a form of attorney–client privilege."

"Which is superior to daddy–daughter privilege?"

There was silence from his end.

"I'm sorry, Dad. I shouldn't have said that."

"Understood. Trust me."

This phone call was exhausting her. "How much more is there to this story?"

"I'm not sure. I've only been told a small part."

"Mom knows."

"Yes . . ."

Raine sat on the wicker love seat, overcome by the emotions warring inside her. Mom knew. They *all* knew. They'd all hidden Kenny from his nieces.

"Although the only person who knows everything is your grandmother."

Which meant the rest of the story was in danger of being lost forever. Were there any more revelations out there lurking? "We should speak in person."

A pause. "I can be free for a late lunch."

Her sister wouldn't be free until later tonight, and the search had just grown more urgent. Raine would have to collect this data on her own. "When?"

"One fifteen to two thirty."

"I'll bring food."

She ordered online from a sandwich shop near her father's office. Then got in her car for the half-hour drive to Chapel Hill.

When Raine walked into the hushed recesses of the law office, Marco gestured toward the conference room. Dad was setting bottled water and napkins on the table. She added the paper bag from his favorite sandwich shop. "Turkey or roast beef?"

He reached into the bag without looking.

Folding her hands in her lap, she focused on her breathing. The drive over hadn't done much to calm her down, but Dad didn't deserve to bear the brunt of her anger. She didn't agree with his decision to remain in the conspiracy, but he should have a chance to explain.

She handed him a bag of chips and a cookie before unwrapping her sandwich. "What can you tell me?"

Dad finished arranging his meal. "I know about Kenny, but only the minimum necessary to complete the trust and wills. Have you found anything else?"

"Yes." But she didn't elaborate. Nothing could top the big lie.

"Then you already know more than me."

She nodded, tore her sandwich into pieces, composed her thoughts. "You said Kenny is disabled. What does that mean?"

"He has intellectual and developmental disabilities. He completed high school, worked most of his adulthood detailing cars, and retired a couple of years ago."

She bit into her sandwich. She'd checked out Alder Creek's website. The photos looked amazing, but that could be hype. She'd be paying them—*him*—a visit soon.

Dad glanced at his watch. Yeah, the clock was ticking. She sorted through her other questions, ordering them by priority. "Are there any living relatives?"

"Kenny has a cousin in Texas. They keep in touch. Other than that, we're his family."

And he hasn't really had us, but that's about to change. "What role does Mom have?"

"She's Kenny's legal guardian now, and one of the trustees of his trust fund."

Mom was in this all the way. Their mother had deceived them their entire lives. When Raine felt anger threatening her control, she shoved it to the side. To be processed later. "How long has she known?"

Dad's jaw tightened. "You'd have to ask her."

Maybe there was worse. "Who are Kenny's other trustees?"

"Just me." He opened his mouth. Closed it. Shook his head. Done.

Raine swallowed a final bite of the sandwich, rewrapped it, and pushed it to the side. She'd lost her appetite. "When did Uncle Kenny move to North Carolina?"

"After Hal Highcamp died in 1986. It was Kenny's choice to move here."

So he'd lived nearby for thirty-seven years. Papa had accepted the disabled stepson he hadn't known existed until Kenny was eight years old. "Has our family been involved with him?"

"Gregor visited regularly. I think Mariah did too."

Something else to pin down. "And you?"

A hesitation. "Our relationship is mostly professional."

"You don't visit?"

"Not often. I'm Stephanie's ex-husband, and she—"

"Doesn't?"

"You'd have to ask her."

The list of questions the sisters would have for their mother was multiplying. "How long have you known he existed?"

Her father cleaned up the trash around him with methodical attention. Reclined in his chair. Frowned. The longer he took to respond, the more her agitation grew. She wouldn't like the answer.

"Sixteen years."

Sixteen? Raine knew the significance of *sixteen*. Too well. "When you separated." At his nod, she asked, "Is that why you divorced?"

"The timing is no coincidence." Dad looked steadily at his hands. "It wasn't the sole reason. Just the last straw."

She heard the pain in his voice. He'd gone through what she was going through right now, only his must've been an order of magnitude worse because he'd been betrayed by his *wife*, the person he should've trusted most. Just like Papa had been betrayed.

The most nightmarish change in her life had stemmed from this secret. She'd been so upset with Dad sixteen years ago and had never quite forgiven him for leaving them. She'd blamed her father for something that hadn't been his fault.

"I'm sorry, Dad." For what he'd gone through. For taking her teenage despair out on him. "You know how I'm feeling."

He nodded, his expression hinting at sad memories. She'd seen that look all those years ago and hadn't understood it. She'd desperately needed therapy and had trouble finding the right therapist. But Dad had patiently taken her from office to office until she found a good match. Whenever she would walk out to the lobby after a session, he'd be waiting, a tight set to his face, his gaze bleak. "Why didn't you tell us?"

"It was their lie. Their story to tell. You deserved to hear it from them." His lips thinned into a grim line. "It crushed me, Raine. It altered my life and the lives of my children. I couldn't be the person who crushed my girls."

His explanation resonated. She would hate being the person to tell Jessica. She looked into her father's face and saw his suffering. "I get it, Dad. And I'm sorry I didn't understand back then."

"Thank you." He cleared his throat. "I'm so sorry you're having to go through this now."

She was too. "They were *wrong* to do this to us."

"They were," he said quietly. "I caution you to slow down, though, and learn more. Good people do bad things, but their reasons matter."

Be patient and thorough, Papa had warned them. She let that settle in. He'd known what he was revealing. That his granddaughters would be hurt by the knowledge.

She couldn't see what other conclusions there were to draw, but Dad was right. She hadn't found the reasons.

Facts and truth aren't the same thing.

She folded her arms on the table, laid her aching head on them, and considered the timeline. Kenny had lived with his father until he was twenty-three, then near her grandparents for almost forty years. They had married in 1965, which meant Mariah moved from Texas when Kenny was a baby. That made no sense. Raine shook her head, saturated with bad news. "What do I need to do for Kenny?"

"Be his niece." Dad smiled lightly—no strain or hesitance.

His statement made her want to weep. Kenny had nieces he hadn't known. Did he think they'd stayed away deliberately?

Why had anyone thought this was okay?

Well, this was about to end. Kenny would have Raine and Jessica in his life now.

CHAPTER 23

Luke didn't remind Jessica about the meet and greet. Was he afraid that if he did, she would tell him she couldn't make it? Not an unreasonable assumption. Her heart ached for what that meant.

If she was promoted to senior producer, would she have to let him down more?

After the evening show ended, Jessica left the booth and returned to her desk, anxious to leave. She sent Luke an "On the way" message, gathered her purse, and was locking her computer when Charlie strode up to her desk.

"You leaving?"

"Yes."

His eyebrow rose. "I'd like to chat about what happened Friday night."

Her face flushed. The "lie goals" would haunt her forever. "I made a mistake."

"Yes, you did. How?"

"I don't know. No excuses." She took a quick look at a wall clock.

Charlie noticed, his lips tightening. "Got plans?"

"Yes."

He lowered his voice. "The application period begins tomorrow. It's not the best time to be ducking out early."

Maybe so, but tonight, she was keeping her promise to Luke. "Thanks for letting me know."

She drove across downtown, plunging through one-way streets as she navigated around congested areas. The Raleigh downtown had gone through a slow but effective transformation. South of the State Capitol, there were great restaurants on highly walkable streets, a performing arts center, convention center, and an outdoor amphitheater.

The high school where her husband taught was a few blocks north of the government complex. The streets were jammed with cars, not all legally parked. Raleigh PD must be looking the other way.

She found a spot easily, since people were already beginning to trickle out. After locking the car, she hurried to the athletic field, toward a tent that had been set up in its center. Would any of the people streaming past her have Luke next fall? They'd be lucky if they did.

She smiled as people passed, knowing she looked out of place at this casual event in her lemon linen dress. Like her grandmother, she had a collection of brooches. For Jessica, it was always something from the sea. Today she wore a coral-pink starfish. A gift from Luke.

He stood near the edge of a tent, surrounded by an audience, mostly kids, but a few parents hovered. Had his fan club for next year already started?

She approached slowly, studying his profile. He answered questions, hands gesturing as he spoke. While the people around him laughed, he turned slightly, scanning for something. Her? She shifted her path to come into his line of vision, wanting to see his face when he realized she'd come.

His smile broadened, his posture broadcasting the news that his attention had been caught. The group turned to see what had caused the change.

He drew her to his side, grinning down at her. The only thing standing between them and a hot, hot kiss was the audience.

"Everyone, this is my wife." His voice held pride and maybe a hint of relief.

She was so sorry about that. He couldn't count on her. Of all the times he'd asked her to come to the school, this was the first one she'd made. If she'd known the warmth shining from his face and the possessiveness in his touch were the reward, she would've tried harder.

"Hi, everyone." She smiled at the crowd.

There was a chorus of "Hi, Ms. Rivera." She felt Luke's glance when she didn't correct them.

"It was great to meet you," he said to the people clustered around him. "I look forward to seeing you this fall." With that, they turned away. "Want something to eat?"

"Yeah, I could eat." She was starving.

Linking their hands, he led her to a table that held remnants of a catered meal. The table had multiple sections. Vegan, vegetarian, allergen-free, and eat at your own risk.

He watched as she added a few things to her plate and then sat with her, hip to hip, at an empty picnic table.

"Thank you for coming, Jessica."

She nodded, so glad she'd made it.

It didn't take long for two other teachers and their partners to join them. Luke made the introductions. Maybe it was her imagination, but they all seemed to be staring. Why? Because they'd never seen her here? Had he told them she worked in TV news?

No, that was an excuse. They were all busy. It didn't matter who her employer was. It only mattered that her husband had wanted her here and she had finally come.

She ate as the teachers teased each other about their summer plans, then grew more serious about active-shooter training they would have at the end of the month. She was startled to learn that Luke would be one of the instructors.

She bowed her head to hide the strain she was sure was reflected on her face. Why had missing out on this part of his life been okay with her?

After the crowd was nearly gone, Luke walked her to the car, their arms around each other. She was feeling disoriented. She understood the roles of daughter, sister, grandchild, and news producer, but she'd been slow at growing accustomed to the role of wife. Tonight she'd only been Mr. Rivera's other half. Something she wasn't used to. Something she was proud to be.

He stood in the open driver's-side door. "It'll be another hour before I get home."

"I'll be waiting."

He leaned forward, surrounding her with his body and scent. His lips brushed hers. A kiss chaste enough in public. Hot enough to suggest more later in private.

She drove away. Glanced in her rearview mirror. He was bathed in the light of a streetlamp, watching her leave. This was what she wanted to get back to in her marriage. The good part, where she didn't feel anxious or separate or afraid.

◆ ◆ ◆

Jessica was walking into the town house when a message came in from her sister.

Are you home from the high school?

She replied with a yes and continued upstairs to change. Her phone rang as she entered the bedroom.

"Is Luke there?" Raine asked without preamble.

"No, he's still at the school."

"Good. We need to talk. In person."

"You opened carton three." Jessica had a bad feeling about this. Her sister didn't sound right.

"Yes." A car door clicked open. Outside noises buzzed in the background.

Whatever her sister had found, it couldn't be good if she was coming over here this late to share in person. "When will you be here?"

"Ten minutes."

She fidgeted while she waited. Poured two glasses of tea. The doorbell rang, and Raine strode in, a manila folder in one hand, her tablet in the other. She made a beeline for the couch.

Jessica joined her, placed the glasses on coasters, then sat, hands clenched nervously in her lap. Her sister was acting stiff and detached. Kind of scary. "Luke's on his way home. We have less than an hour."

"Fine." Her sister set up her tablet between them. "I have a video clip to show you. It's not good quality, but you'll get the gist."

Raine played a short clip of two men and a woman in front of a Christmas tree, passing around a baby.

"From Texas?"

"Yep."

Poor quality was right. "Did you turn on the projector and record with your phone?"

"Yes. Now pay attention. These people are important. You may recognize the guy on the right as Mariah's boyfriend, Hal Highcamp, and the other guy as his cousin, Reggie." Raine pointed at the woman holding the baby. "That's Ida Mae."

"The woman who married Hal."

"Yeah, but I'm pretty sure she dated Reggie first." Her sister's voice was flat. Relentless.

"What about the baby?"

"Hal was his father."

"Mima's boyfriend had a baby?" Jessica hadn't seen a child referenced on Ancestry.com.

"Yes. Harold Kenneth Highcamp. Called Kenny. Ida Mae was his stepmother." Raine released a shuddery breath. Closed her eyes. When she opened them again, they looked wet.

Jessica felt a buzzing in her ears. "Who's his mother?"

Her sister flipped open the folder. It held three documents in archival sheeting. Raine tapped the top one. "That's the baby's birth certificate."

Jessica picked it up with shaking hands. Father's name was Harold Alvin Highcamp. Mother's name . . .

She gasped, dropping the document as if it had burned her. Surely she'd read that wrong. "Our grandmother had a son?" she asked hoarsely.

"*Has* a son."

She'd never felt so stupid in her life, because her brain wasn't processing this properly. "Our grandmother had a child while she lived in Texas?"

"She did. Born on November twenty-second, 1963."

The day JFK died. A week ago, she would've laughed off this news as a bad joke. But no longer. "What happened to him?"

"Kenny lived with Hal and Ida Mae in Dallas until they both passed away. He moved to North Carolina in 1986 and now lives in a residential facility. Alder Creek is in Lee County."

A memory snapped into place. A white building, rose arbor, water fountain, sticky heat, chocolate cupcakes, and yellowjackets. A man had been there too. She'd noticed his grease-stained fingernails and not much else.

Raine folded the cover over her tablet. "He's a fifty-nine-year-old man with intellectual and developmental disabilities."

"No, that can't be right." This was horrible. They had an uncle. How was it even possible to hide something like that? Jessica didn't want it to be true. She didn't doubt it either.

Mariah, no.

Her grandmother had been the model of everything Jessica wanted to be. A strong career woman. Adored by her husband and family. Kind. Fair. Gracious.

Unable to sit still, she launched off the couch and stalked to the opposite corner of the room. A wave of nausea rolled over her, and she leaned against the wall for support.

How did this happen? She couldn't reconcile their amazing grand-mother with someone who would walk away . . .

No, she couldn't let her mind think the words. "Does Mom know?"

"I met with Dad today. He and Mom are the trustees of Kenny's trust fund."

Jessica buried her head in her hands. Her parents and her grandpar-ents had hidden this from them. No, wait. Not *this*. A man. Their uncle.

The memory returned. Sharpened.

Papa, can we stay at our house for America's birthday next time?

Okay, Jessie. That's fine.

"We were there once," she said.

Raine stiffened. "We were?"

"I think so, and I didn't like it." She flushed. It had been an odd day. Burning hot. Aggressive insects. And an unidentified man she hadn't been curious enough about to remember his name. "I complained so much that Mima scolded me." The man had been her uncle, and she'd sensed nothing special. "Who else have you told what you've found?"

"Besides Dad, only you."

"I don't know what to say." Jessica shook her head against the knowledge. Mariah had spent her professional life championing mar-ginalized children, yet she'd hidden her own son. "Who made the deci-sion to keep him away from us?"

"Not Dad. He learned about Kenny right before he separated from Mom. There's a causal relationship there . . ."

The divorce had happened because of the secret? Another blow. She could hardly bear it.

"And Papa was in on it for most of their marriage."

Please stop. "I don't want to believe this." Jessica returned to the couch and reached for the other two documents. Read them silently. Letters addressed to Papa. Mariah and Mom had both concealed the truth from their husbands. Mariah for seven years. Mom for seventeen. And they'd all hidden it from Raine and Jessica their entire lives. Until now. "This is the family story we didn't know."

"Papa's final wish." Raine's voice was flat.

Jessica took a deep breath. She needed to think clearly. They had facts without motivations. Who could they trust now? How could they untangle the story? Because Jessica didn't want to believe what the raw facts whispered. "What do we do next?"

"'Claim' the story as our own and 'do the right thing.'"

Jessica shook her head. "It's too soon to claim this story. It's incomplete."

Raine's face creased with a new kind of grief. "We have to meet Uncle Kenny."

"Agreed."

"Saturday?"

Jessica hesitated. If Luke's team won tomorrow, they'd go to the playoffs this weekend, and she had to go to a game. She was swamped with priorities, and her marriage deserved a place at the top. "Let me check with Luke."

"I don't know if I can wait." Her sister bent at the waist and hunched forward. "Why did Mariah abandon her son?"

Abandon scraped against Jessica's heart. She wasn't ready to accept that word. Not yet. "Until we know why this happened, let's use a different term."

"Okay. Yeah." Raine nodded, then tried again. "Are there any good reasons for leaving her son behind?"

"I can't think of any, but there are different degrees of bad." Jessica leaned closer to her sister and gave her a hug. Her sister didn't resist.

"Papa asked us to do this," Raine said. "He and Mima must've planned it, knowing we'd be horrified. What was going on in their heads? Why not tell us instead of leaving a bombshell to find after they're out of reach?"

The door to the garage creaked, and Luke walked in. After tossing the keys onto the counter, he came into the living room, his smile fading when he took in their expressions. "What's wrong?"

Jessica shot him a pleading glance. "I'll tell you later."

He gave a curt nod. "Back soon," he said and charged up the stairs.

"Time for me to leave." Her sister picked up her tablet.

Jessica followed her sister to the door. "I'm sorry you had to deal with this alone today."

Raine shrugged, her lips pressed together.

Jessica wished there was something she could do to make it easier on her sister, on both of them. "We won't give up. We'll look for people with information they're willing to share."

Her sister nodded, walked slowly to her car, and got in. Jessica stayed by the front window until the taillights disappeared.

Luke joined her, sliding an arm around her waist. "Can you tell me anything?"

She melted into him, so grateful for having him here to hold her. "My mother has an older half brother. Mariah has a son."

The news rippled through him. "The family secret."

She nodded against his chest. "Raine confirmed it with Dad. We don't know much more than that." Her eyes welled with tears.

"Have you talked with Stephanie?"

"Not yet. Raine wants to meet our uncle Kenny first." She looked up at Luke. "What do you think?"

He kissed her forehead. "I think you've received a terrible blow that shakes up everything you believe about your family. You need to process it your way, and let Raine process it hers." He stepped back and captured her hand. "Want to sit on the porch? You can talk and I'll listen. Or we can be silent. Whatever you need."

They went out and snuggled on the glider. She found herself musing out loud. She and Raine would have to view what they knew as objectively as possible and choose carefully where to head next. Papa had warned them they'd be disappointed and to reserve judgment until they had all the pieces. So many questions needed answers. And the first question on Jessica's list would be: Why had Mariah left Texas without her son?

CHAPTER 24

March 1964

A squawking seagull and the squeal of brakes yanked Mariah from sleep. Her eyes were crusted shut. As she pried them open, she straightened on the bench. Had she slept? Her first thoughts were . . . how lovely the beach was in the daylight. And the Gulf of Mexico wasn't as ferocious as the Atlantic Ocean, but it was mighty in its own way.

Next came disgust at her clothes. Her one good dress, and it was grubby and speckled with bird doo.

She bent double as a cough racked her body. After wiping her mouth on her sleeve, she looked out at the water again.

The water?

No, no, no. What had she done?

Guilt slammed into her. What craziness had grabbed ahold of her last night? Ending up on the beach wasn't merely a nightmare, but a disaster she'd created herself. She'd caught a bus to Galveston. Left her fiancé and baby alone.

They didn't know where she was. Hal must be frantic. She had to get back. Thank God she'd bought a return ticket. She'd call him from the bus station. Say she was on the way home. Apologize. Beg his forgiveness.

She reached for her purse, but it wasn't there. She looked around. Her purse?

Oh, dear Lord. Where was it? She jumped up. Looked under the bench. Around. Up and down the sand. It was nowhere. Had someone stolen it? From her arm while she slept?

An even worse disaster had begun.

She spent hours at the police station, reporting the theft, trying to figure out what to do. They were sympathetic until they realized she was a "runaway" mother. Then the sympathy dried up. They wouldn't help her, although they did allow her to place one collect call.

When the phone rang in the duplex, Ida Mae picked up.

"Where are you?" she demanded.

What was Ida Mae doing in her home? "In Galveston. My purse was stolen, and I can't get back."

"What do you want us to do about it?"

Us? "Tell Hal I'm here. Tell him I need him to come and get me. Or wire me the money for a bus ticket."

"Where is *here?*"

"I don't know where. I'm at a police station now."

"You won't be much longer," the desk sergeant said. "You can go to the Baptist Mission." He quoted an address.

"Baptist Mission," Ida Mae said. "Right."

"How is Kenny?"

But Ida Mae had already hung up.

Mariah trudged for what seemed like hours to a dreary building on a dirty street. Inside, she signed her name in the book, barely able to hold up her aching head. Dropping the pen, she looked up, shivering violently. She had to get back to her son. He needed her. "When my fiancé calls, will you fetch me?"

"Sure, dear." The woman cocked her head. "Are you okay? You look flushed."

"Just a cold."

The woman picked up a key and said, "Follow me."

She was taken to a small, neat room with four twin beds. Cots, really. "Does it matter which one I use?"

"Whichever you like. Look, dear, you're sick."

In so many ways. "I'm fine." She punctuated her statement with a cough.

The lady laid a hand to her forehead. "You're burning up with fever. Lie down. I'll bring an aspirin."

Mariah curled up on a cot. Had a fit of coughing. She felt awful. Kenny hadn't been this sick. She was glad about that. Now, if she could only sleep . . .

When she awakened, it was morning. Without moving, she looked around, huddling under a warm but scratchy blanket, still in her nasty clothes. Her fever and headache were gone. But not the sore throat or the coughing.

A different volunteer appeared in the door. "How are you?"

"Better." The words came out in a croak, scraping her throat. It hurt to talk. "Did my fiancé call?"

"No." The lady came over and laid a skirt and a long-sleeved shirt on a chair by the cot. "Why don't you take a shower and put on fresh clothes? I'll bring you some aspirin and soup in half an hour. Okay?"

Once she was clean and had slurped down some soup, she laid her head on the pillow. The next time Mariah woke up, it was turning dark out. She went down to the front desk. "Has my fiancé—?"

"No. Would you like to try again?"

This time, she tried the service station. Maybe Reggie would answer. But Fred picked up, worse luck, although he did surprise her by accepting the charges.

"Uncle Fred, please put Hal on the phone. It's an emergency."

"I ain't letting him talk to you."

"I can't get home without bus fare."

"You made your bed. You can lie on it."

She panted with desperation, ready to beg. "Please tell him I'm at the Baptist Mission in Galveston. It's not far from the water. Maybe he can drive down here to get me. Please."

The handset banged.

She called the duplex again, waiting until Hal would be home. Reggie picked up instead, accepted the charges, then hissed, "Where the hell are you?"

"In Galveston." She didn't want to waste time on a collect call with explanations. They could come later. "How's Kenny?"

"He's fine. Do you care?"

"Yes." It choked her up to hear the question. How could anyone think otherwise? A foolish decision didn't change her love for her son. "Where is he?"

"My mom took him out for a walk."

Good. Aunt Vera was good. "Can I talk to Hal?"

"I don't think that's such a good idea. Just come home."

"I can't. I'm stuck. I need bus fare. Or someone to get me. I'm at the Baptist Mission."

"The Baptist Mission? Why didn't you let us know? No, don't answer that." Reggie muttered a curse word. "Tell me how much and where to wire it. You'll get it tonight."

The return bus trip Friday morning took hours, long enough for Mariah to sit in her seat, shredding a tissue, trying to hold her emotions together, working herself up into a frenzy. It had been a stupid, stupid mistake. A simple longing to feel normal again. To evade the nightmares. To remember peace. But it was like her mind wasn't in control any longer, and she didn't know who or what was.

She was scared. Hal would be furious, and nothing she could say would make this better.

When she got to Dallas, she transferred to a city bus and stepped off at the corner nearest the Highcamps' service station. Smoothing the ill-fitting blue tweed skirt over her thighs, she blinked in the bright afternoon sunshine. Now that she was here, her courage faltered. She had to explain. Her world wouldn't be right until apologies were offered and accepted.

She walked to the station and paused on the sidewalk. The bays were full—cars floating high in the air while mechanics in greasy coveralls worked underneath.

Hal was outside, pumping gas for a lady in a red convertible, his envious gaze drinking in its sleek lines. When he was done, he took her cash, smiled, and stepped back. As it pulled away, his gaze swept over the street, snagging on Mariah. His eyes flashed with joy, but the light quickly died. He swallowed hard, glanced over his shoulder at the station, then back at her. He plodded over on leaden feet.

"Where is Kenny? Is he all right?"

"He's safe. He's with Aunt Vera." His stare was unyielding. "Been having fun in Galveston?"

"No. It wasn't fun at all." How could he think that? She hadn't stayed away by choice. His attitude was feeding her desperation. "You didn't return my calls."

He shrugged, like it was okay she'd been stranded there. She would've been home the next morning if he'd helped.

Okay, she should calm down. She'd made the decision to go. It was her fault. A longing to erase the past few days rushed over her. "Hal, we need to—"

"No. Whatever you're gonna say, I don't wanna hear."

Behind him, his uncle stepped out of a bay, fists clenched. She dragged her gaze back to the man she loved. "Please, Hal. Can we talk? Just the two of us."

He pulled a pack of Marlboros from his shirt pocket, shook out a cigarette, rolled it between finger and thumb. "Why are you here?"

"I know what I did—"

"Stop." Hal shook his head, slowly at first, then rapidly, as if he was denying the past. Denying *her*. "You left me and Kenny to go on a vacation. Ida Mae found a brochure. You been planning that long?"

"The brochure? I got that on Tuesday. For *us*. I wanted our family to go on a trip."

"Then why did you go alone?"

"It was an impulse. As soon as I got there, I wanted to come home."

"Three days don't sound 'soon' to me."

Anger flared. Why was he being like this? "My purse was stolen. They got my return ticket and all my cash. There was no way to get home. I called three times, and you never called back."

"Three times? Why didn't you leave a message?" He closed his eyes briefly and groaned. "You called here, and Fred wouldn't let you talk with me."

"And home. I left a message with Ida."

"She never said." Hal ran shaking hands through his hair, paced out to the street, then back again. When he spoke, his voice was soft and sad. "Okay, so you tried, but you wouldn't have had to if you hadn't gone."

"I'm sorry. It was stupid. I don't know what got into me, but I'm back."

"Sure. You are now. But how long before you get another impulse?" He shuddered. "I don't think I can ever trust you again."

Not trust her? He could. She'd made a mistake. People made mistakes. "What are you saying?" She reached a hand to him.

He flinched. "Don't touch me."

"Hal. Please." Dread clamped around her chest like a vise. He'd never acted this way with her before. "I love you. I love our son."

"You shoulda remembered that before you abandoned us."

"I didn't *abandon* you." That word horrified her. No, she had *not*. Abandonment wasn't just about physical distance. Abandonment started in the heart, and her guys were always there.

But putting all those miles between them? She had no idea how that had happened. It was like she'd become a puppet with someone else pulling the strings. Deep in her soul, she understood Hal's worries. She wasn't sure she could trust herself anymore, that she might make even more decisions that made no sense. "Something crazy came over me. It was only supposed to be overnight."

"You left us, Mariah." He tapped the cigarette against his watch, lit it, took a long drag. Shaking his head, he blew out the smoke. "I wanted to marry you. I wanted us to be a family, but that's not what you want. You left because you wonder if he'll ever be right."

She recoiled. "No. I left because *I'm* not."

"I need you to leave."

"Okay. I'll go home." A busy street wasn't the right place to have this out anyway. "We can talk after you get off."

"You don't understand. I need you to *leave*."

She breathed in his statement. She must've heard wrong. "Leave the duplex?"

He nodded. Wouldn't meet her gaze.

I won't cry. I won't *cry.* "No, Hal. You don't mean that. We can work this out. I'm sorry."

"Sorry?" He looked up, eyes blazing. "Sorry is for serving dinner late. Sorry is for spending too much on groceries. Sorry isn't what you say after vanishing without a single word." He tossed the cigarette on the ground and stamped it out. "The thing is, darlin' . . ." He paused. When he spoke again, his voice was soft. "It was kind of peaceful while you were gone."

Mariah gasped. "What?"

"Hear me out. I was mad the first day. Then I came home that night. The apartment was quiet and clean. The baby was happy. And the girl serving me dinner didn't have red-rimmed eyes."

Ida Mae just happened to be there, had she? That galled Mariah. Had the other woman planned this? Set a trap for Mariah to step into?

As suddenly as it had flared, her fury drained away. If this had been a trap, Mariah had jumped in willingly.

He shook his head sadly. "Why, darlin'?"

"I don't know. I haven't been the same since . . ."

"The baby was born."

"No, since . . . before that." Since their trip to Dealey Plaza. "You've been different too. We never talk about it."

"I never want to. I can't."

Yeah, she got that. The nightmare that never ended.

"I don't think we'll ever get past it, darlin'."

"Get past what?"

"What happened that day." He blinked rapidly. "Every time I look at you, it all comes back. Them waving. The pops. The . . ."

He stopped before he said more, but she saw it on his face. *The red mist.* Everything had changed in that moment. The end of innocence.

"We've been ruined, Mariah. You and me. *We* will never be right." He swiped at his mouth. "Kenny's happy without you."

She shook her head rapidly. No, her son loved her. *Needed* her. "That's not true."

"Ida's taking good care of him, and he don't cry for her."

Mariah didn't believe it for a second, but Hal seemed to. "You might not see him cry around her, but he does. He's a baby. That's how he talks."

Hal's expression hardened. "Go on and clear out your things."

Was he serious? He couldn't be. "No. Kenny is my son. I'm not leaving him."

"You already did."

"It was a *mistake*, Hal. I'll make it up to you. Both of you. I'll fix it."

"Some things are too broken to fix."

Oh God. This isn't happening.

She wouldn't give up. Hal was upset, and he had a right to be. Someone had gotten to him in the past three days, chipping away at his confidence. It would take time to build him back up, but she was a patient girl. She would come up with a plan. As soon as her mind cleared.

"Where am I supposed to go?"

He shrugged.

"Hal. Really. I have nowhere to go. No money. No job. Your family hates me. My only friend is Paul, and he can't take me in. What am I supposed to do?"

"Where did you stay in Galveston?"

"The Baptist Mission."

"I bet they have one of them in Dallas."

Her lungs heaved with panic. She had to slow down her breathing. Think clear thoughts. "Okay, I'll, um, . . ." She would figure this out. Wait for things to cool down. Everything would be fine. "I'll find somewhere and let you know."

His face crumpled. He looked up at the sky, breathing through his mouth, then slung an arm around her shoulder and pulled her against his chest.

That embrace was more devastating than any words he could've said. It felt like a goodbye. She buried her face in his shirt. Sobbed in the familiar smell of oil and grime and him.

A car slowed on the street, bumped into the gas station, the ding-ding alerting the staff of its presence.

His voice shook. "I'll get Reggie to take you wherever you want."

She didn't want to go. "Please, Hal. I love you and Kenny. So much."

"It's not enough."

"But it's true." She looked up into his sad blue eyes and tried to smile. She would *not* believe this was hopeless.

His lips pressed to her forehead. Then her mouth. "I love you too."

CHAPTER 25

Reggie's jaw was clenched as he gunned it out of the station. "Where to?"

"The duplex." Mariah would pack a few things, but not all, because she would be back soon.

They'd driven a couple of blocks before he spoke. "What's wrong with you, Mariah? Why did you do this to Hal and the baby?"

"I had no way home, Reggie. I tried." As sick as she was of the story, she gave him a summary of the past three days.

At its end, he let out a long stream of smoke. Stubbed out his cigarette in the overflowing ashtray. "You left messages with Ida Mae and my pa, and neither passed them on?"

"Yes."

"I don't have any trouble believing a word of that. They didn't tell me either, 'cause I woulda come to get you straightaway." He slammed a fist against the dashboard. "Did you tell Hal?"

"Yeah. He said it didn't matter. Said it was peaceful while I was gone."

Reggie ground his teeth. "They worked him over good."

"He told me to leave."

"He loves you, Mariah. You'll be back."

"I'm not so sure." She wasn't, but she wouldn't let doubts creep in now. "I gotta find somewhere to stay tonight." She'd have to get a copy of the yellow pages and look for possibilities. But first, she had to see her son. "Can you take me out to your folks' house next? I want to hold Kenny."

"'Course."

As they turned onto the block of the duplex, Reggie bellowed a curse. There was a familiar car in the driveway. They were silent as he parked at the curb.

"Why is Ida Mae here, Reggie?"

"I don't know. I thought Ma had the baby."

Mariah was so upset, her teeth chattered. "Come in with me. Please."

"No. I can't be around her." He squeezed her hand. "Don't let 'em win. Hal is wild about you. You can stay with me till this all blows over."

"Thank you." She wouldn't turn down the offer. He lived close. She could come over each day and take care of her son.

She hurried to the front door. Inside, it was like walking into an episode of *The Donna Reed Show*. The duplex smelled of lemon Pledge, roasting chicken, and apple pie. Ida Mae stood in the center of the spotless living room, in a dress and apron, tall and proud, cuddling Mariah's son.

She gaped in outrage. "What are you doing?"

"Somebody had to watch the baby while you were gone."

"I would've been home hours after I left if you'd told Hal I was stuck in Galveston."

"You got yourself down there. I figured you could get yourself back."

"Well, it's over now. We don't need you here anymore." She started across the room toward her son.

"Hal asked you to leave."

Mariah stopped, shocked by the woman's audacity. "What happened between Hal and me is none of your business."

"Oh, I think it is." Ida's lip curled. "You have everything a woman could want. The best man either of us will ever meet. A beautiful baby. All you had to do was take care of them and this place, but that wasn't good enough for you."

"What are you talking about?"

"Even though Hal has proposed to you a thousand times, you've been dangling him on a hook like some kind of flopping fish that's unable to break free. Hal deserves someone who wants to be his wife. The baby deserves someone who wants to be his mother."

"You don't know anything about me."

"I know you don't love Hal enough to marry him. I also know you've been standing there and the baby hasn't reached for you once."

That last statement shuddered through her. It was true. Kenny watched her with detachment, perfectly content with where he was. Was Ida right? Mariah came closer and held out her hands. "Kenny, Mommy's here."

He lifted his head. Wobbled. Raised his fist, banged it awkwardly against his mouth, and started sucking.

"Come to Mommy, sweetie." She stood there, frozen in place, silently begging her son to reach for her.

He flopped his head back on Ida Mae's shoulder.

It was a knockout blow, and Mariah was reeling.

"There you go, hon. You're not wanted here."

Mariah had to escape the triumph flashing in the other woman's eyes. She stumbled to the bedroom, desolation stealing through her limbs, and looked around at the room where she'd lived and loved for the past year. It had been tidied up too. Another woman had touched her things. It made her ill.

She dragged her duffel bag from the closet. Yanked two pairs of underwear and a bra from the dresser drawers. Crammed in two changes of clothes. Added her camera and sneakers. From an old pair of hose beneath her period underwear, she drew out the wad of cash from Stephen, peeled off five tens for herself, and put the rest in Hal's Sunday shoes.

She took one final look around the room she'd shared with Hal, blinking as if in a dream. For the second time in four months, she'd awakened to a different world.

Hoisting the bag, she walked out to the living room, crossed to her son, and kissed his soft cheek. "Mommy loves you." He didn't respond. Just blinked.

She spun on her heel and opened the front door.

"You're doing the right thing, Mariah. You know Kenny's better off with me."

No, that wasn't true. It would never be true. She would fix this.

Some things are too broken to fix.

She shut the door and ran to the truck. Reggie tossed the bag in the back. "Ready to go to my place?"

She nodded, trying not to cry, trying not to think about what lay ahead.

Mariah propped herself up in a corner of Reggie's living room for the rest of the day, eyes trained on the door, waiting for Hal to walk in. Or call. He did neither.

When Reggie got home, he came over and knelt beside her. "He isn't coming."

"What about tomorrow?"

"I don't know." He patted her hand awkwardly. "Want me to get you something to eat?"

"No, I'm not hungry."

"Okay. Let me know if you change your mind."

She wouldn't.

After Reggie left for the gas station early Saturday morning, Mariah rolled off the couch, too listless to bathe, and stumbled to the kitchen. After pouring herself a cup of coffee from the dregs of the pot, she ate the leftover crusts from Reggie's toast and started out of the house for the half-hour walk to the duplex.

It was locked up tight. No one there. And her keys had been stolen.

She stopped at each window, but none would open. As a last resort, she jimmied the sliding glass door off its rails, went inside, and ran to the bedroom. Her things had been heaped in a corner.

She was puzzled about what to do. And where was her son? Had they taken him away so she couldn't find him?

Calm down. Wherever Kenny was, he was safe. Hal wouldn't let anything bad happen to their son.

She scooped her belongings into two paper bags and walked back to Reggie's. But when she got to his house, his truck was at the curb. Home on a Saturday morning? She went through the front door and found him waiting in the middle of the living room.

"Reggie, what's going on? Where's Kenny?"

"With Ma." His gaze swept over her uncombed hair. The coffee stains on the ugly outfit she'd been given at the mission. He shook his head, his expression haggard. "This is worse than I knew, Mariah."

His voice gave her a chill. "What do you mean?"

"Pa told Hal that you're crazy and he's afraid you'll hurt the baby."

"He did what?" She started to shake. "How does he think he knows? He never sees me."

"You must've said something to Hal about being crazy yesterday. He doesn't know what to think. So I came to check on you, but you need to be careful. No one's letting you near Kenny until we're sure he's safe with you."

She gasped. "He *is*."

"I hope you're right." He headed for the door. "I'll be back later."

She couldn't understand what was happening. How could people be saying such things about her? How could Hal believe them?

She wandered the room restlessly for hours, her thoughts going round and round, until she dropped to the floor, exhausted. But as she stared up at the ceiling, she wondered if there was anything to their worries. She'd felt *off* since November. The crying spells. Her seesaw moods. The days when she couldn't make herself think or care. It was like there was a sickness in her head that was robbing her of herself.

Were they right?

She'd heard whispers about what they did to women who admitted there was something wrong in their minds.

No. Stop. Whatever was wrong, she would never harm her son. That would be . . . crazy.

◆　◆　◆

On Palm Sunday, Reggie got up early, dressed in his Sunday best, and tiptoed out the door without speaking to her. Without offering to take her to Mass. He wasn't the churchgoing type, but maybe his folks had insisted.

She used the bathroom. Brushed her teeth with her finger. Then walked to the living room and lay on the carpet. It smelled like cigarettes and felt sticky to the touch. Gross, but her limbs were too heavy to move. So she stared at the flickering sunlight on the ceiling and cried, the tears trickling over her cheeks, pooling in her ears.

What could she do now? She'd lost Hal. She'd never had help from Fred and Vera. She despised Ida Mae. And she wouldn't force Reggie to choose sides. He'd pick family if she did.

But she still had Kenny. And he loved her. On Friday, he'd simply been slow to recognize her. That was all. She'd given in too soon.

Fresh tears welled up, but tears of anger this time. She was his mother, dammit. She should march over to the duplex and take him. Who could stop her? Then she'd just . . .

She closed her eyes. What would she *just* do? She had no job and no way to get one with a baby to care for. Nobody would rent to an unwed mother. The Highcamps might pitch in to help Hal, but they wouldn't move a muscle for her.

She missed her son. Needed him.

Had Hal taken Kenny to church? No, not likely. They might be home, and with the other Highcamps at worship services, she could have her guys to herself, hold Kenny, and reason with Hal. It was a fine plan.

Her new goal gave her a burst of energy. She scrambled to her knees and crawled to her duffel bag, then fumbled around inside until she found her nicest outfit. The hose were in shreds, so she tossed them in the trash. The dress was horribly wrinkled, but she didn't care.

She walked the two miles to the duplex. When she arrived, though, there were lots of cars. Dread coiled in her gut. She wanted Kenny and Hal to herself. She stood indecisively in the street. Go in? Go back to Reggie's?

What was she thinking? The duplex was hers. She marched up to the door and went inside.

It was too quiet for guests. It was also spotless, except the kitchen, which showed signs of a feast. Bowls, pots, and pans were stacked by the sink. The floor could use a mopping. Where were they? Not far, because the cars were here.

She followed the sound of laughter through the backyard, across the next street, and into the park. A group of ten was under the picnic shelter, their voices stopping abruptly at her approach. A living sculpture, staring at her. Mariah headed for the strange woman cradling a sleeping Kenny in her arms.

"Thank you for holding him," Mariah said with a smile as she scooped him up and cuddled him against her chest. She walked out of the shelter and into the sunshine. The voices buzzed again, the laughter absent.

Footsteps drew closer, snapping twigs. She was surrounded by the scent of Aqua Velva and Marlboro smoke.

"What are you doing here?" Hal bit out.

She turned to him. "What do you mean? I'm his mother."

"You gave up that right when you—"

"No," she shouted. The baby startled, squirmed, then stilled as he looked up at her. When he smiled, her heart melted. He did remember. "I gave up nothing," she said, kissing Kenny's nose.

Uncle Fred yelled, "Ya want us to call the cops, Hal?"

She stiffened. Call the cops on Kenny's *mother*? She didn't want the cops. They hadn't been nice to her in Galveston. Would Dallas cops be as bad?

Hal yelled back, "Don't butt in, Uncle Fred." He dropped his cigarette and stamped it out. "Mariah. You're a mess."

"Kenny doesn't mind."

"Darlin' . . ."

She breathed in the endearment. He loved her. She was still his darling.

"There's something bad wrong with you. We all see it."

Bad mother. "What are you saying?"

"It's no good, Mariah." He took Kenny from her and held him against his neck. "You have to go."

"No, Hal." She would *not* cry. "Don't say that. Please."

"Kenny'll be fine, okay? He's got plenty of people taking care of him. You have to fix yourself, darlin', and I can't help you."

There was defeat in his eyes. It poured over her and whittled away her hope.

"I'm his mother."

"Don't you want what's best for him?"

"Of course I do. I *am* what's best."

"Are you?" He lowered his voice, even though there was no one near. "You said yourself something crazy's got hold of you. What if you really hurt him?"

She wouldn't. It wasn't possible. Yet . . . a week ago, she would've sworn that nothing could drag her away from her family.

She was so confused, and Hal was staring at her with . . . fear? Did he really fear what she might do?

She looked back at the group. They watched her, standing here with her guys. Uncle Fred and Ida Mae smirked. Vera smiled sadly. Reggie saw the reproach in her gaze and frowned at his feet. She didn't know the others. Never would.

"Mariah, please. Fix yourself and come back when you're better."

Fix herself? How did he expect her to do that? "Where should I go?"

"I don't know."

Do what's best for Kenny.

"Okay." She tried to smile at Hal, but her mouth wouldn't cooperate. "Okay." She cupped his cheek with her hand, pressed her lips to his, and turned to her son. She kissed his sweaty brow, her heart breaking, and whispered, "Mommy loves you, Kenny. Always."

She walked away, not looking back, afraid her courage would fail her if she did. Just kept putting one foot in front of the other. A cool breeze whipped at her hair, blowing it across her face. She was too numb to feel a chill.

Outside the park on the main road, a truck pulled up beside her. "Mariah, hop in," Reggie called. "I'll drive you home."

"I'd rather walk."

He waited a beat. "You sure?"

"Yes."

"Okay, Mariah, except . . ." He looked embarrassed. "You have to find somewhere else to stay."

She stared at him, hollow-eyed. He'd been the only person left she could count on. But not anymore. The future terrified her. She was utterly alone.

Inside his apartment, she packed her duffel bag. Then picked up a pen and a piece of paper, sat on the floor, and wondered what to do. Where to go.

She was sad and sick and scared. She needed her mother.

Left for the bus station. I'm going home.

CHAPTER 26

Mariah rested her head against the bus window, looking forward, not out. If she weren't longing fiercely for her son and Hal, she would be numb.

She felt so odd, as if she were no longer in control of her mind or body. It reminded her of once when she'd been little, walking in the ocean, trying to reach the shore. The sand had sucked at her feet, dragging her backward with each step. The water had pulled at her hair, towing her under. When fighting it got to be too much, she'd simply let go, and everything had become so peaceful. Then Ma had screamed and come running and pulled her to safety.

That's where Mariah was headed now. To the safety of home.

She was sick, and she needed her ma.

◆　◆　◆

"Miss." A hand shook her shoulder. "Miss, wake up. We're here."

Her eyes fluttered open. Through the cracked window came the hum of another bus and a whiff of fumes.

"Miss?"

She turned toward the kind voice.

The bus driver smiled. "We're in Raleigh. You have to get off."

"Okay," she said, forcing the word through a throat that was scratchy and dry. She pushed up from her seat and trudged along the aisle of the empty bus. Down the stairs. Into a blast of bright sunlight, noisy motors, and more fumes. Her duffel bag lay on the curb. Alone. Forlorn. She picked it up and wandered into the station. She had two hours until the bus to Wilmington. So she used the bathroom, washed her face, and found a seat in the waiting room.

She would see Ma soon. Five hours? Six?

What would her welcome be? The twins were twelve now. Still at the Catholic school. Loving baseball and fishing, no doubt. Not noticing girls yet.

Mitchell would be long gone, she hoped.

And Pa? She felt a whimper of fear. There would be no welcome from him. How could she have forgotten about Pa? What would he do?

It was only fair to warn Ma so they could decide what to do. Jumping up, she crossed to the pay phone, dug out a dime, and dropped it in the slot. "I'd like to place a collect call . . ."

Ma picked up, gravely accepted the charges, then whispered, "What are you doing, Mariah, calling here?"

"I'm sick, Ma. I'm coming home."

There was a stunned pause. Then . . . "No. You can't."

"But, Ma, I have nowhere else to go."

In the background, Pa shouted, "Who's on the phone?"

"Wrong number," Ma yelled back, then whispered again, "I'm sorry. You can't come home." There was a sob, and she hung up.

Mariah gently replaced the receiver. Looked around the lobby, staving off panic.

Another big mistake. She hadn't been impulsive this time. She'd made a plan to go home and ask for help. Her mother loved her and would think of something.

Mariah had known she couldn't stay at the house, but there were other possibilities. Maybe her mother could ask a friend or the nuns at Saint Adalbert's or make a pallet in the barn.

But it hadn't occurred to her that there would be an immediate hang-up.

It had been a foolish oversight. Maybe because she'd never imagined Ma would turn her away so completely.

She'd made no second plan if the first didn't work. When she'd needed help, she'd wanted her mother. So she'd headed home, only to discover she had no home.

Mariah tossed her ticket to Wilmington in a wastebasket and walked out of the bus station. She couldn't go back to Texas until her affliction had healed, and she couldn't go home. The remaining option was to wander around in the sunshine of a place she didn't know.

She came to a large square in the heart of Raleigh with a wide lawn and trees and a huge domed building. The State Capitol. She sat in its shadow on the grass, a spectator of the bustle of the city. She watched the birds, the squirrels, and the people. All moving and making noise. Around her were big white granite buildings. The halls of justice.

The sun crept past overhead, then over to the west. A clock tolled the hour. She'd been sitting here for hours. Snapping open her purse, she dug around for cash. Twenty-six dollars and thirty-seven cents. That wouldn't last long.

Where would she sleep tonight? She'd passed several churches. Might one of them have a mission where they would lend a cot? She stood and ambled down a wide street, studying the hodgepodge of architecture.

A sign caught her attention. Looking unashamedly out of place, a county library had been fitted into an old department store, mere yards from the stolid majesty of the Capitol.

Inside, the place was hushed and smelled of old paper and Pine-Sol. There were rows and rows of stocked shelves, a semicircle of chairs around a low table dotted invitingly with magazines. As far as she could tell, she was the only one in the library besides the eagerly approaching woman.

"May I help you?"

"Oh, I'm just . . ." Mariah hesitated, searching for what to say. Visiting? Stalling? What was the right word?

The fog in her brain wavered. Why not sit in the library and think until she had a better idea? Or until closing. "I'm new to Raleigh."

"Welcome. Would you like a library card?"

She blinked at the word. She was *welcome* here. "Oh. Um." She tightened her grip on the bag. Maybe Raleigh could be a place where she stayed until she wasn't so empty anymore. Until she'd fixed the broken parts well enough to return to her son.

"I've just arrived," she told the librarian. "I don't have a job or anywhere to stay."

The woman smiled. "Well, you've come to the right place. The Salvation Army might take you in for a night or two. And if you'd like to consider something more permanent, we could look at the Sunday paper. Even better, the bulletin board. People advertise all sorts of things there. Let me show you."

They studied the want ads and notices of rooms for rent.

"Have you ever worked as a waitress?"

"Yes."

"Plenty of those jobs available. How much can you pay for rent?"

Mariah winced. Nothing yet.

The librarian smiled in understanding. "Don't worry. I know a place. A boardinghouse for young women. The landlady will be patient for a week or two. Let me get you Mrs. Bridges's address."

By nightfall, Mariah had a job waitressing and a tiny cell of a room.

Who would've known that hard work could rest an overwhelmed body? It seemed to be true for Mariah. She awakened each morning at five, put on her uniform, and hurried through dark streets to reach the diner near the State Capitol for her six o'clock shift. She returned home midafternoon, her pockets full of coins. Politicians tipped well.

She didn't bother to make friends. Why should she? She didn't expect to remain in Raleigh. As much as she hated the thought of living in Texas again, her son was there.

Her life took on a routine. Nine hours at the diner, six days per week. Sunday mornings at the cathedral, sitting in the back, saying prayers, lighting candles—but not confessing or receiving Communion. Sunday afternoons found her at the library. Reading magazines. Chatting with Alice, the kind librarian. Or, sometimes, simply sitting quietly.

She wrote letters at least monthly to Stephen, although she didn't really expect replies. He would answer if he could.

To Hal and Kenny, she wrote as often as she had sufficient cash to fill the envelopes. She mailed theirs to Reggie's address since she didn't trust sending it to Hal's. It took six weeks before she received his first response, a short note thanking her for the money and a Polaroid of Kenny. The note went in a hatbox she stored under her bed. The Polaroid stayed in her purse.

Throughout the summer, she and Hal exchanged more letters and pictures. And she made a new goal. Save enough money to buy another bus ticket. She'd even picked the date. If she was better, she'd go back for Kenny's first birthday.

Mariah stopped attending Mass after the priest pressured her to come to confession. She wasn't ready, and when she was, she wouldn't like confessing to Father Ambrose. He was old and pinched, not at all like Father Tim.

So she replaced attendance at church with studying the stars. Each night, she went to the front porch of the boardinghouse, rocked in a rocker, prayed her prayers, looked up at the night sky, and wrestled with her guilt.

Her landlady joined her a few nights later. They rocked together, each lost in her own thoughts. And so they continued, night after night. Eventually, Mrs. Bridges talked about her life, her voice cracking with pain. During World War II, she'd been a widowed mother in England who fell for an American soldier. Her new husband had brought his bride and stepson home to North Carolina, only to die a few years later in a work accident. Her son lost his life in Korea. Now she rented rooms in her beautiful old house, not because she needed the money, but because she enjoyed the company.

Mariah listened and sympathized but continued to hide her own painful secrets behind a wall of silence.

Months passed in quiet monotony. She was eating better at Mrs. Bridges's table, and she didn't fear sleep as much. However, the odd fuzziness in her head had proved tenacious, detaching her from the world, keeping her separate.

She wrote to Hal that she was *less sick*. His *keep trying* response hadn't reassured her.

It was in September that things started to go wrong, all through letters. Three, in rapid succession. Each dealt a blow.

The first was from Hal. She read eagerly until the third paragraph.

The doctor says Kenny has problems . . .

Hal described what the doctor had told them (who was "them"?), but it sounded jumbled. Bewildering. Though he ended the paragraph with something perfectly clear.

More money would help. Please send what you can.

More? How? She gave him every penny she could spare. Should she work more hours? She rocked on the porch and stared dully at the sky, unable to corral her thoughts.

Stephen wrote her next.

Dear Rye,

I know you'll worry, but don't. I'm heading to Vietnam soon. Twelve months. Or maybe eighteen. The army needs a photographer over there, and I'm one of the best. But I'll be safe. They'll have me hanging around generals, and those guys don't go anywhere dangerous.

I've enclosed some money. I'm hoping you'll use it to go to college, but I suspect you'll give it to my nephew. That's fine too.

Love,

Stephen

She would worry. She'd worry every single day until he returned home safely, but she was grateful for the cash. She withdrew enough to buy a bus ticket to Dallas, then sent the rest to Hal.

The third letter came from Reggie. It contained a Polaroid of Hal in his Sunday best, standing on a downtown sidewalk, gazing solemnly at the camera. A smiling Ida Mae stood beside him in an ivory suit, a jaunty feathered hat on her head. She grasped a bouquet of daisies in one hand and Hal's arm in the other.

Dear Mariah,

Hal married Ida last week . . .

CHAPTER 27

The television station staff received an email in their inboxes midafternoon, with the subject **Open positions**. Jessica skimmed it until she found the details she sought near the bottom. Applications would be accepted today through next Friday. Eight workdays. The announcement should've given her a thrill. A huge step closer to a goal. And all she could think was . . . *How will I fit everything in?*

And her newest priority? She had an uncle, whom she would meet this weekend. The thought filled her with a kind of tremulous joy.

"Jessica?"

She looked up. RJ was leaning against her desk. "Are you okay? I've been trying to get your attention."

"Sorry. I'm just—"

"Dazed? Yeah, Charlie's announcement is a stunner. But we need to put that on hold. There's breaking news. Warehouse fire near the airport. Arson, likely."

"Right. On it." *Wow.* There had been a school shooting in a nearby county they'd first reported during the noon news, and now an arson fire. Bad news Wednesday. But it was also a relief to have something so absorbing command her thoughts.

She didn't leave the station until after eight, exhausted and energized. Tonight's show reminded her of how critically important her job was. Two heartbreaking stories. Loss of life in both. And they'd told them with humanity. News production was where she was meant to be.

It was only after she'd gotten in her car that she checked her phone. A text from her husband.

We made the playoffs

Congratulations. Do you know when you'll play?

Saturday afternoon in Greensboro

He was typing more. It took a minute before the message came through.

Can you make it?

There was too much pulling at her. Her mind was buzzing with the promotion. She had to stay visible at the station. She had to meet her uncle this weekend *and* attend Luke's game. She wanted it all. She just had to do a better job of defining what "all" meant.

I can

Driving home, she called her sister. "Hey. About this weekend?"

"Luke's team won." Raine sounded glum.

"Yes, they did. I have to go to the game Saturday."

"Yeah, I know. I called Alder Creek today. They said Kenny has a routine that he doesn't like to change. The best time to see him is between one and five in the afternoons."

"I can't get there until Sunday."

"And you think we should go together, right? So Sunday afternoon?" Raine's frustration was barely contained. She was ready to go.

Jessica ached at her sister's concession. Raine was champing at the bit to meet their uncle. The only thing delaying her was Jessica's impossible schedule, yet her sister wasn't complaining. Raine was willing to swallow her disappointment and wait. No, that wasn't okay with Jessica. "Go sooner. You'd prefer to meet him one-on-one anyway."

Slow exhale. "It would be my preference. Are you sure?"

"Yes. Go. I'll get there Sunday."

"Okay." A long, relieved sigh. "Jessica? Thanks."

At home, she was scrounging in the refrigerator for something to eat when footsteps came bounding down the stairs. She pulled out a platter with hummus and raw vegetables. That would be enough. She wasn't very hungry.

Luke oozed pride. "The team played great. You should've seen them."

They both froze. She'd had the whole season, and she'd missed every game.

"Will you really be able to come Saturday? You're not on call or anything?"

"I'll be there." One of three number-one priorities she had.

"Okay." His smile was only half-believing. "Hey, why don't you sit? I'll take care of your meal."

"Thanks." She drooped onto a barstool, propped her chin in her hands, and watched him through half-closed eyes. After being on high alert for the past few hours, fatigue was finally hitting her.

He filled a plate for her and slid it over. "You had a tough day," he said soberly.

She nodded.

"Are you okay?"

"I'm fine." She picked up a carrot and munched.

"Anything new about your uncle?"

"Not really. Raine's meeting him tomorrow. She'll let me know whatever she learns."

"What about the promotion?"

"I have until next Friday to apply. The morning senior producer position is available." She looked up from twirling a carrot in hummus. Her husband was lounging against the counter, his expression watchful. "What do you think?"

"I think I'll support whatever you decide."

She would love to take his response at face value, but there were things he wasn't saying, and she had to hear them. "You have to be part of this decision. The promotion affects both of us."

He straightened. "I don't know what else you expect me to say. I believe you'll make the right choice. I can't say I'm delighted you'll be in bed early on weeknights. But if the trade-off is having you home in the afternoons, that'll be great, especially after we have kids. And it *will* delight me to see you loving your job. As far as I see it, my primary role in this decision is to support my wife."

Kids? That was another discussion she longed to raise, but there were other more urgent topics to cover. Yet her husband had mentioned it so matter-of-factly, as if it was a given with details they would get to. That was so very good.

He kissed her. "See you upstairs." And he was gone. The floor creaked overhead as he walked to the spare bedroom.

She pushed away the plate, walked out to the porch, and flopped in the glider. The coming week would be difficult. Not enough hours in the day to do everything well. So where would she screw up?

No, she wouldn't screw up. It all had to be perfect.

CHAPTER 28

Raine would be visiting Alder Creek this afternoon to meet her uncle. It might be hard to concentrate on work this morning, but she would try.

Fortunately, a distraction popped up in her email. The second opinion contract from Patrick. She DocuSign-ed it, then took her first peek at the case and felt her interest engage. She loved the kind of projects he provided. It was time to find out why Patrick always asked about her certification. She texted him.

Can we talk?

Sure. When?

Now?

Her phone rang with a video call. "Hi, Patrick. Thanks for responding so promptly."

"No problem." He smiled. "What do you need?"

"Do you always ask me about certification because you might offer me a job when I have mine?"

"Yes."

Good start. Interest on both sides. Now if she could only get through the next part without messing up her chances. "I don't like testifying."

He laughed. "I don't know many who do."

She doubted he'd ever met anyone who hated it as much as she did, but okay. "How often would I have to?"

"It's hard to say. Just depends on the cases you have." His smile faded. "Look, you have an incredible talent in forensic accounting, but you have to be willing to show up in court. Have you ever testified?"

"Once." And it had been a miserable experience. It still bothered her, and the opposing attorney hadn't even been that good.

"Testifying as an expert witness is a learned skill. You'll get there." He looked away suddenly, then back. "I have to go soon. Why don't I let you know when one of our accountants heads to court? You could show up and listen."

Yeah, that might help. "Sure."

"Any idea when you'll take the exam?"

She grinned. He never missed a chance. "August."

"Good. Stay in touch about the second opinion."

Raine waited until after lunch to drive to Alder Creek. Alone, which was probably for the best. Their uncle might find going from zero to two nieces overwhelming.

After plugging the address into her GPS and putting her music therapy playlist on low, she drove southwest from the city. Traffic was light and easy. After leaving the state highway, she passed through a charming town, then spent the final ten miles on a quiet two-lane road cutting through small farms and dense woods.

At a discreet sign, she pulled through an open gate in a brick wall and drove up the long driveway as it snaked through a tunnel of old oaks, their branches creating a green canopy. She looked around, feeling an odd sense of déjà vu.

She emerged in a burst of sunlight and slowed in awe. The building had the look of a sprawling one-story farmhouse. It was painted white with dark-green shutters. Two people rocked in a wooden swing on the front porch. The place looked comfortable. Homey. She'd heard about residential facilities, and not all were good. She'd worried what she might find, but she shouldn't have. Papa would've wanted the best for his stepson.

She parked in a small gravel lot, turned off the engine, and walked toward the building, passing a small fountain and an arbor of roses. The fountain looked familiar too, like an out-of-focus but happy memory crystallizing. Even as she grabbed at it, it slipped away.

Jessica thought they'd been here before. Maybe she was right.

Raine entered a small lobby decorated in cool greens and blues. A reception counter waited to one side with an open door behind it. A staff member came out with a friendly smile. "May I help you?"

"I'm here to see Kenny Highcamp."

"Ms. Elliott?"

"Yes."

The receptionist inclined her head as she picked up the phone. "Ms. Bright, Kenny's niece is here." She listened, gave a nod, and hung up. "The administrator will be right out. Would you care to wait?"

"Sure."

Alone again, Raine looked around, absorbing the peace of this place. The lobby was sparsely furnished. A padded bench, a side table, and a silk fig tree. Three hallways branched out from the lobby, two in opposite directions, the middle hallway straight back. It was as pleasant on the inside as the website suggested.

The office door opened, and out came a woman. Tall, thin, with a prematurely silver cap of hair, dressed in stylish business casual. "Ms. Elliott? I'm Norah Bright, Alder Creek's administrator. Thank you for coming. I'll take you to your uncle, but if you'd like to speak with me, drop by before you leave."

Raine followed the administrator down the glassed-in middle hall, excitement blooming inside her. She was about to meet her uncle, who'd lived nearby her entire life. She calmed her breathing. She would get through this.

Ms. Bright opened a double door at the end, and they stepped into a recreation room. A half dozen residents were present. Two were playing Parcheesi. Three were gathered around a TV, watching an Avengers movie. The two people in navy-blue scrubs were observing.

On the far side, a middle-aged man sat alone on a couch, bent over a coffee table, staring intently at a jigsaw puzzle.

"Let's check with one of the caregivers," Ms. Bright said, then called out, "Ian?"

The caregiver standing nearest the man with the puzzle looked up, his gaze going from the administrator to Raine. He approached. "Yes, Ms. Bright?"

"Ian, this is Raine Elliott. Please take her to Kenny, and let his reaction guide what happens next."

"Sure." Ian gave her a brief nod and crossed to the couch. "Kenny, Raine's here."

"One second," the man said.

She halted, throat aching with words she couldn't speak, overcome by the moment. They were using her name as if she were a routine part of his life. Until two days ago, she'd never had the slightest inkling her uncle existed.

He fitted another piece into the puzzle and looked up. "There you are."

"Hi, Uncle Kenny."

"Hi, Raine." He patted the cushion beside him. "Sit here."

She perched on the edge of the couch. He had Mariah's black-brown hair and his father's blue eyes. He was staring at the puzzle with brow scrunched and lips pursed.

Seconds ticked past, then a minute. Being here beside her uncle was awesome. Why had they been kept away?

She leaned forward to check out his puzzle. An aquarium of tropical fish. "Can I help?"

"No."

She suppressed a smile. Okay, then. She was good with honesty.

"Want something to drink, Kenny?" the caregiver asked.

"Yes."

The guy looked at her. "How about you?"

"No, I'm fine."

With the caregiver gone, she attempted to talk with her uncle, but he answered in monosyllables or not at all. Something else she liked. Small talk was overrated. So she took an interest in the puzzle, intrigued by the way he was solving it. Steadily, confidently, top down.

When Ian returned, he set a can of Coke on the table and went over to offer drinks to the three people by the TV. Kenny ignored his drink as he continued to work, not speaking but aware of her, twisting his head toward her occasionally, as if reassuring himself she hadn't left.

An hour passed before Kenny rose awkwardly. "It's almost time for dinner."

The caregiver appeared at his side. "Thirty minutes."

"I have to wash my hands."

"Sure thing." Ian cupped Kenny's elbow, helped him navigate around the table, and handed him a cane.

"Will my puzzle be all right?"

"I won't let anyone touch it." The guy smiled. "They'll be leaving for dinner soon too."

Kenny gestured at Raine. "Let's go."

Their progress was slow, but that was okay. She enjoyed listening to whatever he had to say, whatever was important to him. It was cool to take these first steps together, to catch up on what she'd missed. Kenny commented on the state of the vegetable garden, visible through the windows of the hallway. The residents were responsible for the garden, and he'd weeded his section that morning.

When they reached the main lobby, he turned into the left hallway and pushed open the first door. The room was small, with furniture creating two spaces. The living area held a brown couch and a wall-mounted TV. Dividing the room was a low bookcase holding DVDs, books, and baseball memorabilia.

"Follow me, Raine."

Kenny shuffled past the bookcase into the sleeping side of the room. Sunlight poured through the window onto a twin-size bed draped with a bright-green quilt. The walls were bare, except the wall across from the bed. It was covered with black-and-white photographs in matching black frames. She gasped as she identified the subjects of the photos.

Her uncle awakened each morning to a wall of Jessica and Raine.

All the information and emotion flying at her were making her breathless. She stood beside her uncle, her shoulders stiff under the weight of betrayal, and clamped her trembling lips together. *Do* not *lose it.*

They'd been part of his life, and he hadn't been part of theirs. A tragedy none of them deserved. Maybe one day she'd be able to get past the grief and forgive whoever had kept them apart. But that was hard to imagine in this moment.

"Do you like my Nieces Wall?"

"I do." Her voice sounded husky and thick. "Mariah took a lot of them."

"She gave them to me," he said matter-of-factly. "And I put them up."

Raine shuddered with relief. Here was evidence her grandmother had been part of his life. That was . . . good, but it just made it harder to understand why Mariah had kept their uncle from them and why Papa had gone along with it.

Kenny frowned. "Are you mad at me?"

"No. I'm happy to be here." And she really was, so she gave him a reassuring smile. "Do you have a favorite picture?"

He pointed. "That one."

It was one of Raine's favorites too, taken at her grandparents' beach house by Mariah. Raine was with Jessica at the water's edge, their backs to the ocean. The day had been overcast and the beach empty. The best time to be there. They'd both acted so typically. Jessica smiled fully at the camera, an arm wrapped protectively around her younger sister. Raine stood in profile, staring into the distance, not interested in the now.

"Will you come back this time?" Kenny asked.

This time? That was confirmation of her previous visit to Alder Creek, those memories of the lane and fountain shimmering in her mind like pixelated images. What a waste. She tamped down the wisp of anger. "Yes."

He sighed. "Gregor is gone."

"He . . . is." Her grief had added a new dimension, disillusionment at how her grandfather had plotted her path to this story.

"I have to set the tables in the dining room. You can go now."

"Okay."

He waved as he entered the bathroom.

She stopped in the lobby at the reception counter. "Is Ms. Bright available?"

"Follow me." The woman led her through to a tiny office.

Ms. Bright indicated a chair opposite the desk. "Do you have any questions?"

"What are the arrangements for Kenny?"

"Mr. Azarian had everything handled. Kenny can live at Alder Creek for the rest of his life . . ."

Raine listened as she explained the details. But the bottom line? The family would never have financial worries about his care. "Can you tell me . . . ?" She paused, not sure the best way to ask. "Why is he here?"

"He had jaundice as a newborn. Because it's so common, medical staff usually watch for it and treat it before there are complications. But it's my understanding that the hospital staff were distracted, and by the time they noticed how severe his was, he had brain damage."

Oh wow. Mariah had only been nineteen. She'd witnessed a terrifying event, delivered her baby the same day, and the people responsible for caring for them had made a horrible mistake. More information to fit into a story that seemed to get murkier the more she learned.

"Did my grandmother . . . ?" She could hardly form the words, too afraid she would regret the answer.

"I've never met Mrs. Azarian, but I've only been here for two years."

Mariah had lived in the memory-care unit for longer than that. Raine wanted to believe that was the reason. "What about my mother?"

"I've met Ms. Elliott."

So her mother had come, but Ms. Bright's wording was muted. An indication of frequency? Raine filed that away without assigning any emotion to it yet. She'd dealt with enough for now. Rising, she said, "Thank you."

"Return anytime. No need to make an appointment. It's just best if you come in the afternoons between meals."

On the way to her car, she made a detour to the arbor, its red roses so heavy the branches bobbed in the breeze. She sat on a bench, hugged her knees to her chest, and willed her mind to calm. She would stay a few minutes, delaying the need to act.

She watched as the sun disappeared behind a line of storm clouds. The breeze began to strengthen. Still she sat, her energy sapped by all the feelings she'd experienced this afternoon. She could deal with them later, when she was home and balanced.

Would it have been better not to know?

On the lane, several cars drove past. A short pause. Then a minivan raced by. They bypassed the visitor spots and parked at the back.

Papa, why did you give us your final wish now?

Why didn't we know the secret years ago?

The four most important adults in her life had known and formed a pact to hide it. What had bound them together?

She was too close to this. It skewed her objectivity.

Tires crunched on gravel and sped from the facility. It must be shift change. She'd been at Alder Creek over three hours, more than one of those hours in this spot. She rose and went to her SUV, dreading the drive back to Raleigh, alone with her thoughts. She hadn't been to Larkmoor since Monday, too upset to face Mariah so soon after discovering the news about Kenny. Raine was still grieving Papa, and now she had to grieve the person she'd believed her grandmother to be.

How did she get past her disillusionment with Mariah? There was no talking. No arguing. No granting forgiveness. She had to debate both sides of the problem within her own mind, without understanding the other person's reasons.

Raine drove back through the small town, two blocks of brick buildings with business names in curly script on matching gray awnings. One of the businesses had **ROONIE'S DINER** painted in dark green. It was past seven. She should eat. After parking nose-in to the curb, she went inside.

The owners had been aiming for a stereotype. Striped curtains. Vinyl-covered booths. Sassy waitstaff in tight black miniskirts, white shirts, aprons, and big hair with pencils tucked behind their ears. The only thing saving the place from being a total cliché was the color scheme. Tangerine and lemon.

She slid into the only empty booth and checked the menu. Within seconds, a waitress materialized beside her before she'd assessed the options.

"You vegetarian? Any allergies?"

"No and no."

The woman leaned a hip against the table. "I recommend the burger and fries, then."

"That works." Raine closed the menu and set it back in the rack holding the salt and pepper shakers. "Medium well."

"Iced tea? With chocolate cream pie for dessert?"

"Yes." The waitress probably said the same thing to every new customer.

She'd finished the burger and was about to start on her pie when a man in navy scrubs entered the packed restaurant and scanned in vain for an empty table. It was Ian, Kenny's caregiver. His gaze slid past hers. Slid back.

She would be gone soon, and the guy wasn't a complete stranger. She gestured at the empty seat across from her.

She cataloged his appearance as he approached. Brown hair, brown eyes, clean-shaven. Average height and better-than-average build. He looked pretty good in scrubs, which, in her opinion, was quite an achievement.

When he hesitated beside her table, she said, "You can have my booth. I'm leaving after I finish the pie."

He dropped onto the bench opposite her and flashed a grin. "Thanks." He placed his order by nodding at the waitress, accepted a glass of tea, and looked back at Raine. "I'm Ian Romero."

"Raine Elliott." She'd be done in five minutes, which wasn't really enough time for a conversation, but they probably shouldn't sit here in silence either. "Have you worked at Alder Creek long?"

"Three years."

"Do you like it?"

"Yeah. For a nursing assistant, it's awesome. Great pay and benefits. They treat us well. Positions are competitive." He inclined his head. "But I won't be there much longer, actually. I'm leaving at the end of next week."

"Why?"

"I'm going to be a nurse. I've just finished my ADN." He must've seen the question on her face because he explained. "My associate's degree in nursing. I'm taking time to focus on studying for my board exams."

"Yeah, I get that. I'm studying for my certification exam."

"For something in accounting?"

Papa must have talked about her. It gave her a warm feeling of pleasure, but it was frustrating too. They could've shared the relationship with Kenny and Papa. She couldn't wait until she knew all. "So you've known my uncle . . . ?"

"Three years."

"Will you tell me what he's like?" She took a bite of the silky, smooth pie.

Ian's smile widened. "Kenny? He's great. Happy, mostly. Sometimes lazy. He can have a bad temper, but his anger fizzles fast. Did you see his bookcase?"

She nodded.

"All his favorite things are there. Baseball, anime, cars. He has lots of friends, although he liked your grandfather best." Ian's smile faded. "Mr. Azarian's death bothered him, but he's doing better. Mr. Azarian had prepared him. He said he was eighty-nine, that he felt good, but tomorrow was never promised."

Wow. Not pursuing that thread. Papa had seemed ageless to her. She hadn't been prepared at all.

After the waitress slid a plate in front of Ian, he sat back and ate a bite of his burger.

Raine dipped her fork in the whipped cream of her pie, then licked it off. "What was my grandfather like around Kenny?"

"Fun. They'd watch TV. Tell bad puns. Play cards."

"Cards? Really?"

His eyebrow arched in question.

"My grandfather wasn't very good at card games."

"No, he really wasn't." Ian laughed as he added a spiral of ketchup to his fries. "I've never met your grandmother."

Raine wasn't usually so forthcoming with people she'd just met. Or even after she knew them, for that matter. But this guy had insider knowledge of her uncle, and he seemed open. "Mariah has dementia and has lived in a memory-care unit for years. She doesn't go to see anybody."

"That explains it. Kenny says she's too sick to come. He does talk about her, though." He looked out the window. "I've seen your mother around a couple of times."

A couple of times in three years? She hoped he'd seen Mom so infrequently because he wasn't there every day. There weren't any excuses that could make right what the three of them had done to Kenny and his nieces, but at least they should've been coming to see him themselves. It made her head ache. She couldn't wait until Jessica met him, so they could figure this out. "My sister and I only learned we had an uncle on Tuesday."

Ian's gaze slid back to hers. "He has a photograph with you when you were kids."

"Jessica and I only have vague memories of ever visiting Alder Creek." How often had they visited? Another thing to check. "Does he ever question our absence?"

"Not around me. He's not shy, so he must have known why and was okay with it." He frowned at his empty plate. "Look, I'll be honest with you. Our residents don't get many visitors. If you asked their families, some would say Alder Creek is too far. Others might claim the resident isn't interested, which, for some, is totally true. They can be strained by disruptions to their routines pretty quickly, but it was different with Mr. Azarian. His visits were regular."

When the waitress showed up with Raine's check, she gave a slight start. Her five minutes had turned into thirty, and she had the drive to Raleigh ahead. She picked up the bill and slid from the booth. "Enjoy your meal," she said, feeling awkward. "Maybe I'll see you next time."

He nodded. "Thanks for the booth."

She headed out to her car, so glad she'd made it to Alder Creek today. Meeting their uncle had been surreal and amazing. The facility was nice, and the Nieces Wall? Both beautiful and sad. She'd had a helpful conversation with Ian that would add new data to the shareable folder. New questions too. How involved had Mariah been with her son? Why had she moved to Raleigh? And why hadn't she told Papa from the beginning?

CHAPTER 29

November 1964

Hal's next letter was agonizing to read. His *wife* had quit her pediatric nursing job to take care of Kenny. Ida had skills that would help him grow stronger. There were special shoes—expensive shoes—they were considering. Special toys. Kenny relaxed around classical piano music, so they were buying albums. Could Mariah please send more money?

Mariah wasn't sure how she'd do it, but she would try.

She couldn't wait to see her son on his first birthday. The thought of being with him made her smile, and she didn't do that often, not genuine smiles. But otherwise, November made her uneasy. It included the first anniversary of Dealey Plaza, and the newspapers and TV were flooded with stories about President Kennedy and . . . that day. Over the past months, she'd had some success at burying the memories. The nightmares had become less frequent. But now she felt herself being tugged back toward the darkness. She'd nearly poured coffee into the lap of a diner customer today, anything to get him to shut up about the Warren Commission and its findings about JFK's . . . death.

She'd made it through the shift, walked home, skipped dinner, and gone to bed. But a nightmare jolted her from sleep. She'd stared into the dark, heart pounding, lungs heaving, hands burning. In three weeks, she'd get on a bus to Dallas. Where *it* had happened, on its anniversary. And she was afraid of how that would feel.

Fred and Vera were hosting the birthday party. Had that been a deliberate choice? She would also have to face Reggie, who'd let her down. Ida Mae, who'd envied her life and managed to get it. Hal, who'd said he loved her, then rejected her twice, first by shoving her away when she'd been at her lowest and then by marrying her nemesis.

But, despite her fears, Kenny was there, so she would go. Hal said their son still reacted badly to strangers, but she had to see it for herself. She was his mother, and he would *know* her. If she could just hold him, see him smile, hear him laugh, it would be worth it.

The next night, Mariah finally poured out her sorrows to her landlady, from her childhood to fleeing to Texas to the reasons she'd moved to Raleigh. When she was done, she waited, hardly daring to breathe, to see if her secrets would cost her a friend.

But Mrs. Bridges simply said, "So that's what the rocking's all about. A way to endure the guilt and grief."

Mariah had never thought about it quite that way. "Yes, ma'am."

"Call me Elsie." She reached over and patted Mariah's hand. "Oh, pet. My first reaction is that . . . I don't understand how a mother can choose to live so far from her baby." At her gasp, Elsie said, "No, wait. I'm not done. This tale isn't about just any mother. It's about *you*. When you got here, you were a terrified little thing, jumpy, beaten down, on constant guard for more hurting. The change has come slowly, and I'm seeing tiny glimpses of the lovely woman you will be. But every time you receive a letter from Texas, I hold my breath and worry about which Mariah we'll have after you've read it. Your son's father . . ."

"Hal."

". . . treats you more like a bank than a person."

Mariah closed her eyes, holding back a sudden rush of tears. That same thought had occurred to her, before she'd dismissed it as unworthy. Whatever she did for Kenny was a pleasure.

"You're healing—but not healed. What ails you won't be cured with a pill. Only you can know when you're well, so I'm not judging the choices you've made."

"Others will."

The rocker stopped. "Yes, pet, they will. There's nothing more irresistible to some people than to judge another woman's mothering. But unless they've lived your life, they have no right. Don't let them stop you from doing what you know is best for Kenny. Now," Elsie said, rubbing her hands together, "if you wish to earn more money for your son, waitressing won't get you there. What else can you do?"

Mariah felt hope stir. She hadn't lost her friend. "Office work. Cleaning. Sewing."

"How good are you with sewing?"

"Very." No need for false modesty. "But I don't have a sewing machine."

"I do. Give sewing a try." The landlady tapped her fingers on the rocker arm. "I'll barter a week's rent for a good cleaning of the kitchen, dining room, and upstairs bathroom."

"That's a deal."

Mariah began the housework the next day. She told the other boarders about her sewing skills and took in all their repairs. Word spread, and soon she was tailoring all the clothes she could manage. The envelopes to Texas would bulge.

Three days before she was due to leave for Dallas, the phone in the boardinghouse rang during dinner. Elsie answered, then looked toward the dining room table where five pairs of eyes waited. "Mariah," Elsie said quietly and held up the handset.

She hurried over, pulse racing. "Hello?"

"Mariah." It was Hal. In the background, Kenny was wailing. "This'll be quick."

Not wanting the other girls to hear, she turned her back on the table and lowered her voice. "What is it?"

"We moved to a bigger place, and Kenny's been screaming ever since. It's really bad." Hal sighed. "We've called off the party. It's better if you don't come."

She started to shake. "Hal. Please."

"Can't you hear him? It's terrible. He won't even go near Vera. You could get here and not be able to touch him. I'm sorry, darlin' . . ." He stopped. Swallowed hard. "I'm sorry, Mariah. Don't come." He hung up.

She replaced the handset and stayed where she was, one hand pressed to the wall to keep her from falling.

"Bad news?" one of the other boarders asked.

Nodding slowly, she met Elsie's gaze over her shoulder. "A family member is . . . unwell. I'll have to postpone seeing him." She walked out of the kitchen and up the stairs to her room. It would be a long night.

The next day, after her shift at the diner, she went to the bus station and got a refund for her ticket, then to the post office and mailed a package to Texas with two handmade gifts—a stuffed turtle and a blanket—and a card with enough money to buy a pair of special shoes.

Then she wandered aimlessly around the streets of downtown Raleigh with no destination in mind, so numb with grief that the gray clouds and cold wind whipping at the edges of her coat didn't register. But the sudden downpour did. Pedestrians ran for cover. She looked around, and seeing the library across the street, headed for its warmth and shelter.

There were more people inside on a weekday afternoon than she was accustomed to. And the librarian wasn't her favorite, Alice. Newspapers lay about, JFK's anniversary featuring prominently in the headlines. When she averted her face, her gaze landed on the bulletin board, with its multitude of cards and scraps of paper.

Should she add her seamstress services? She asked at the desk for an index card and pencil, wrote out an announcement, and returned to the bulletin board to thumbtack her card.

Above it, a want ad caught her eye.

> Secretary needed for a construction company
>
> Experience required
>
> 30 hours per week at $1.50 per hour
>
> Apply in person to Mr. G. Azarian on 23 November between 8 and 9

Office work. Part-time. Nearly double what she earned per hour at the diner.

She'd never gone to secretarial school, but she had been a receptionist in Dallas. Really, she'd been more. She could become what this company needed too. At a dollar fifty per hour, she could work half the hours and still bring home almost the same money. And she'd get off in the early afternoon, freeing up time to take in more sewing projects and earn more money to send Hal.

She reread the ad. The handwriting of Mr. G. Azarian was efficient. Bold. She would like working for someone with his kind of confidence. He'd listed no phone number, but the downtown address would be an easy walk to her lodging. This could be the perfect job for her.

After her breakfast shift Monday morning, she left early and rushed home to the boardinghouse. She bathed, shaved her legs, and put on her best dress, hose, and shoes. Against the chill of the day, she slipped into her green tweed Goodwill coat and took off for a two-mile walk.

She reached the address on the flyer, then faltered to a stop. The storefront was narrow and gloomy. It was well past noon—late for the interview period—but she hadn't expected the office to be empty. Peering between the blinds, she could make out an ugly wooden desk sandwiched between a gray metal filing cabinet and two mismatched chairs. The lobby was dirty and unappealing, not at all what they should present to potential customers.

Her mind sparked with ideas. She could already imagine what it might look like with a mopped floor covered by a cute rug. Framed photographs of their completed houses on the walls. A pretty pillow or two to enliven the chairs. And potted violets on that atrocious desk.

At the end of a dim corridor, light spilled from beneath a closed door. She might be late, but she was pinning her hopes on that light. She plopped onto the curb, elbows on knees, chin on fists.

The squawk of a door yanked her from a drowse. Scrambling to her feet, she watched a young, tall Black man cross the sidewalk to a beat-up red truck and put an armload of rolled papers onto the passenger seat.

"Hello?" she called.

He turned.

She waited for him to speak, but when he said nothing, she smiled nervously. "I'm here to interview for the job."

"Interviews were this morning." He slammed the truck door and headed around to the driver's side.

"Is the position filled?"

"Don't know."

"Will Mr. Azarian be back today?"

"No." The man climbed into the cab and cranked the engine.

She wouldn't give up. Not yet. She wanted this job, and not only for the extra income she could earn for Kenny. This company could use her ideas, and it would be nice to feel useful again. Hurrying to the passenger side, she spoke through the open window. "Do you know where he is?"

The man's smile flashed. "At a construction site." As he yanked the gear into drive, he added, "Two blocks from the big church on Oberlin." The truck pulled away.

She wasn't sure where Oberlin was, and the man hadn't told her. But if this was a test, she would pass. She went to the post office and studied a city map. Two hours and three buses later, she got off at the big church on Oberlin. She followed the sound of hammers through the neighborhood until she saw the red truck parked at the curb before a house under construction. Three workers stood in the carport listening to a fourth. The guy who'd given her the hint tracked her progress up the driveway.

"Gregor, you have a visitor."

The man at their center turned, stared at her, then stepped into the sunshine. He wore the same uniform as the others—dungarees, denim shirt, boots—on his tall, muscular body. Laugh lines bracketed his mouth. While she wouldn't call him classically handsome, most women would consider him attractive.

His gaze swept her head to toe, then he smiled. "May I help you?"

She stared at that lovely smile and basked in its kindness. "Mr. Azarian?"

"Yes."

"I've come to interview for the secretarial job."

His eyebrows rose. "How did you find me?"

She exchanged a conspiratorial glance with the red-truck guy and smiled. "Luck, I guess."

"Indeed?" He shot a glance over his shoulder. "Phil?" The man grinned unrepentantly before heading around the side of the house. Mr. Azarian looked back at her. "I'm afraid the interviews were conducted this morning."

"I was busy then."

"I'm sorry, but it's too late." The words were dismissive, but his expression was not.

Was he waiting to see what she'd do? His gaze dared her not to give up. She felt a tug to meet that dare. "You could interview me now."

Crossing his arms, he repeated his study of her, this time more slowly. "Why should I do that?"

"Because I'm here," she said, as if that clinched the argument.

"Wouldn't that be unfair to the applicants who arrived at the correct time, in the correct place?"

"It was unfair to me for you to schedule interviews in the morning only, during my shift."

His lips twisted, as if he struggled to suppress a smile. "Perhaps you have a point. Very well, then. I am Gregor Azarian."

"Mariah Byrne."

"Shall we?" He gestured for her to precede him into the house.

They walked through a mudroom and into a kitchen. She stopped in the doorway to take in the room. The cabinets and sink were already installed. A large window bathed the breakfast area in sunlight. At its center, an unpainted door lay on two sawhorses, paper and pencils littering its top. The makeshift desk took up most of the space.

He dug a sheet of paper from his pocket and frowned as he read. "Did you bring a résumé?"

"No."

He met her gaze. "Can you take shorthand?"

"No, but I can type."

"What speed?"

Her two index fingers could fly across the keys. But, *what speed?* "Fast."

"Have you ever been a secretary?"

She might not have attended secretarial school, but she knew she could do this job well. "Not exactly."

"I see." He folded the paper and pushed it back into his pocket. "Miss Byrne—"

"This is a nice kitchen," she interrupted him, delaying his imminent dismissal. She walked to the sink, rose on tiptoe, and looked at the backyard. "Although . . ."

"Although what?"

She would be honest. How could it hurt? "A woman my size would enjoy the view better if the window was about three inches lower."

"Are you trying to distract me from your lack of qualifications?"

She spun to face him. "Is it working?"

He grinned slowly. "You're still here, yes?"

She had his attention, and she was feeling inexplicably bold. "May I see the rest of the house?"

"To what purpose?"

"If I'm going to be your secretary, I ought to know about your business."

A laugh burst from his lips, full and rich and infectious. "Very well, Miss Byrne. Follow me."

He gave her a tour through the three-bedroom one-bath house, his voice ringing with pride as he described its "special touches." Floor-to-ceiling windows in the living room. Built-in bookshelves in the main bedroom. Black-and-white tile floor in the bathroom. Louvered doors on the closets. She asked a lot of questions, and he patiently answered them all.

The tour ended where it had started.

"What do you think, Miss Byrne?"

"There's a lot to like." She poked her head into the pantry and pictured how she would organize groceries on its shelves. A bit larger would be better, but it wasn't bad now. She backed out and saw him watching her intently. His interest in her opinion pleased her. "Will the secretary have any input into how the houses are built?"

A long pause. "That isn't something I've considered."

The truth might sound rude, and she didn't consider herself a rude person. But everything about this interview had been unconventional. The wrong time. The uninvited visit. The request to tour the house, as if *she* were the one who had to be impressed. But why not? She should be impressed, shouldn't she? To be a good secretary, she ought to be interested in the business, and she actually was. She'd lived in enough dreary places to know what a home should *not* be. Her opinions might help them build houses where families could thrive. "Mr. Azarian, are you married?"

His eyes narrowed. "No."

"Is your architect?"

"I haven't asked."

"If he is, he didn't seek his wife's advice about the kitchen. Small changes would make big improvements."

"Oh?" He shifted back a step, scowling at her like she was an unknown creature to be cautious of. "Like what?"

"The pantry could be closer to the stove. An automatic dishwasher would be cool, and the window over the sink could be lower. For women my size."

He snorted softly, his lips curling into a half smile. "It is an intriguing tactic in an interview, Miss Byrne, to insult your prospective employer."

"I'm insulting your architect, not you."

He threw back his head and laughed. A moment later, the door to the carport creaked open. Phil, the driver of the red truck, appeared. Smiled. Retreated.

As his laughter faded, Mr. Azarian glanced at his wristwatch. "All right. Do you have any work experience that applies?"

"I've been a receptionist at a photography studio."

"Were you? What types of duties?"

"Answering the phone. Managing clients and schedules. Tracking supplies and equipment. Light bookkeeping." And soaking up everything she could about photography. She'd cared about that business too.

"For how long?"

"Six months."

"Would they give you a reference?"

"I'm sure they would. A very good one." And she *was* sure. She'd loved that job, and they'd loved her.

"How old are you, Miss Byrne?"

"Twenty."

"Are *you* married?"

"No." Her smile vanished. *Almost* didn't count. It certainly hadn't counted with Hal.

"How soon could you be available?"

"Tomorrow, but only afternoons this week." Mariah wouldn't desert the diner at Thanksgiving. "I could do whatever schedule you like after that."

He gestured toward the door. She preceded him outside and hesitated in the carport, not ready to say goodbye, worried she'd ruined everything with her critique of the house.

When he started down the driveway, she hurried to catch up. "Mr. Azarian?"

He inclined his head. "Yes?"

Was there anything she could say to repair the interview? To let him know how much she wanted this job? No, probably not. It would be hard for her to compete with other applicants who had actual experience or education as secretaries. "Thank you for hearing me out."

"Of course." He stopped on the street, his smile polite. "Do you need a ride somewhere?"

"No, I'll be fine." She turned to go.

"Will you give me your phone number? And the name and number of your reference?" He held out a scrap of paper and a stub of a pencil.

"Sure." *Please let this be a good sign.* She jotted down the requested information and handed the paper back.

"Thank you." He tucked it into his shirt pocket. "It's been a pleasure, Miss Byrne. Truly."

◆ ◆ ◆

When she reached the boardinghouse, she went straight to her room and flopped on the bed, staring at the wall. What had gotten into her? Mr. Azarian's kindness had drawn something out of her, a glimmer of the hopeful Mariah from long ago. But now she was worn out. Scared she wouldn't get the job. And scared she would.

She skipped dinner that night, preferring to stay in bed and watch the moon rise through the window. Around eight, another boarder banged on her bedroom door. "Mariah? Phone."

Was it the call she was expecting? She rolled off the bed, dodged a towel-clad girl leaving the bathroom, and skipped down the stairs. In the kitchen, the handset dangled by its curly cord.

"Hello?"

"Miss Byrne." It was Gregor Azarian.

Please. "Yes?"

"I would like to offer you the position of secretary for my construction company. If you're willing."

The news fanned a forgotten ember of joy. She took a deep breath to compose herself. "I am willing."

"Good. Come to the office tomorrow at one."

"Okay." After their goodbyes, she hung up and leaned against the wall in the drafty kitchen, disoriented by the news, as if waking from a nap after a long sleep. Maybe this was the change she'd needed, a job that would be about more than earning money. Maybe this would be the place to make a difference.

CHAPTER 30

February 1965

It took ingenuity, elbow grease, and multiple raids of the petty cash drawer, but by mid-January, Mariah had brought the Azarian Construction office into the modern age.

One of her first acts as secretary had been to purchase a new IBM Selectric typewriter, speeding up her typing, allowing her to wrench the paperwork into order by Christmas. After returning from the break, she'd used pockets of free time to update the lobby into an appealing place to greet potential customers. Geometric-print pillows turned mismatched chairs from ugly to fab. Framed photos of their best houses formed an enticing gallery on the wall. The cracked linoleum sported a fuzzy new rug.

She'd set her sights next on the break room. Why shouldn't the crew be taken care of too? She kept a fresh pot of coffee brewing all day, homemade cookies in a tin, and fresh fruit in a basket. Once word got out, the men came by for more than their paychecks. It was lovely seeing them more often, accepting their appreciation, being treated like a member of the team.

But her favorite part of the job was the business lessons Mr. Azarian gave her. Each Friday afternoon, he'd come in to teach her something new. The terminology of residential construction. The subtleties of their bookkeeping. How to deal with the local government. The lessons often ended with praise for the changes she'd made or a request for her opinion on an idea he was considering. His approval boosted her confidence.

Hal's letters continued to arrive regularly, with photos and pleas to *send money*. Each time she wrote back, she asked to visit Kenny. Hal always had the same excuse to put her off. Kenny was terrified of strangers, which was all Mariah was to him. If she could just be patient, they would work something out. Although he never mentioned his wife, Mariah wondered if Ida Mae was a factor too.

Then Hal surprised her. He'd gone to his aunt Rosalie's funeral in Virginia and brought Ida Mae and Kenny with him. They stopped in Raleigh on the way back.

In a matter of minutes, she'd gone from hemming a dress to holding her sleeping son in the formal living room. It was like being in a dream. Hardly daring to breathe, she was caught between wanting to savor each second and wishing the audience watching her like two hawks would go away.

"He's so handsome," she said, memorizing every inch of him. "He's getting so big." She loved the solid weight of him in her arms.

"Shh," Hal said softly. "You do *not* want to wake him."

But it was too late. Kenny startled, his eyes popping open. When he focused on her face, he screamed, arching his back, desperate to get away.

"Let me have him, Mariah." Hal lifted their son into his arms and backed up a few steps. As Kenny's howls died, he sucked his thumb.

She waited in stunned silence on the couch, hiding her shaking hands in the folds of her skirt.

When Ida stood, Hal shook his head at her and gestured toward the door. She left with a humph. Mariah watched her go with relief. It would've been unbearable to see her touch Kenny.

She looked back at Hal. Felt her face flush with anger. How could he spring this on her? "Why didn't you warn me?"

"Whoa, darlin'," he said, his eyebrows rising as he shifted a squirming Kenny in his arms. "I didn't plan this. I'm sorry I couldn't let you know, but we came. Okay?"

Nodding, she controlled her temper. It had been an unexpected joy. "Thank you."

"We got a long drive ahead. I gotta go."

She followed him outside but remained on the steps. After they drove away, she retreated to her room and lay down on the cot, curled on her side, and relived the delight of cradling her son. The heartbreak of hearing his screams. The flood of grief now that they'd left. And the fear that their visit might reawaken the stupor she'd fought so hard to banish.

Once night fell, she went down to the porch and dropped onto a rocker.

It wasn't long before Elsie joined her. "You saw your son. I had my doubts about what that young man's been saying to you about Kenny. But it seems to be true."

It certainly was. Mariah hoped it didn't set her back.

"You haven't asked for my advice, but I'll give it anyway." Elsie cleared her throat. "Long ago, your mother was faced with a choice about her baby. She made what she thought was a good decision, only she ended up living in pure misery, and so did her kids. I don't fault her for wanting to keep her son. But good decisions don't always bring good results.

"You made a decision for your baby. He needed you to be well, so you found somewhere to heal. And you *are* healing. But you're a stranger to him, for now."

Mariah didn't bother to brush away her tears.

"I'm sorry, pet, but it's true. Kenny will need you again one day. I know that everything inside you is yearning to be near your son, but you have to be patient. What your child needs matters more than what you want.

"Coming out here each night, stewing in your guilt and grief and regrets? That's a natural reaction, but it doesn't help anyone, least of all Kenny. Channel some of those feelings into getting better. *Being* better." She reached for Mariah's hand. Held on a brief moment before releasing her. "Become the mom your son deserves when he's ready."

Long after the screen door thwacked behind Elsie, Mariah gazed at the stars and wondered if her friend's words would ever take root.

◆ ◆ ◆

Kenny's rejection had created cracks in Mariah's recovery. Although that dreaded sense of numbness hadn't succeeded in taking control, it was relentless in its efforts to try. She had to marshal all her energy to hold her anxiety at bay.

Her work suffered. Elsie was helping as a backup seamstress, but there was nowhere to hide at the office. She completed the minimal amount of paperwork. Handed out paychecks. But after that, she had nothing left.

The crew noticed and reacted with kind words and gestures. They made coffee and brought sweets. Scraped their muddy boots without reminders. Left bouquets of spring flowers on her desk. Told her corny jokes.

One morning in early March, Mr. Azarian drew a chair up to her desk. "Miss Byrne," he said solemnly. "Are you all right?"

She nodded, gaze lowered.

"It seems to me that you've experienced a recent sadness."

More like a deep anguish. "Yes."

"Is there anything we can do?"

"No." She looked up, touched by the compassion from him and the crew. "But thank you."

A phone call from a local magazine triggered the first small change. Mariah had pitched an article to *Raleigh Now*, hoping to get a bit of free advertising. Gregor Azarian, an American-born son of immigrants and a veteran of the Korean War, now built sturdy homes for first-time buyers. A man who'd lived the American Dream was helping others to live it too.

The offer from *Raleigh Now*'s editor was simple. *Write the article, take photos, and we'll talk.* She dropped the handset onto the telephone, folded her hands in her lap, and stared at the clean desktop in disbelief. Had she really been asked to submit an article? Not only would this be great advertising, but it might be, after many years, a place for her "hobby" and her job to intersect. It wasn't precisely the hard-news journalism she'd considered as a teen. But if she did this well, her words, her photos, and her byline would be published in a magazine.

She flipped through a mental inventory of the houses in progress, with their different stages of completion and the lots they were on. Not much color yet, but there were some with forsythia in bloom.

A burst of energy launched her from her desk. She slipped on a jacket, placed the CLOSED sign in the window, grabbed the office camera, locked up, and took a bus to the site Mr. Azarian was supervising this afternoon. As she hurried down the residential street, she could see him standing with Phil as they considered the chimney, their conversation lively.

She composed a picture. The men had their faces lifted heavenward. Phil pointed while Mr. Azarian listened with his muscular arms crossed, the sleeves rolled up his forearms on the mild March day. Sunlight made a dappled pattern on the ground around him. She took two shots. If they turned out, they would be stunning.

"What are you doing, Miss Byrne?" he asked.

"Taking pictures of you."

A grinning Phil entered the house through the open front door.

Her boss approached her. "What possessed you to do that?"

"I'm writing an article for *Raleigh Now*."

"Why?"

"It'll be good advertisement for the business."

"And what will this article entail?"

"An interview with you about your past and present. Pictures of your houses. If we feature the Oakwood house, it might make the cover. You'll be impressive."

"Will I?" He grinned.

She gave a decisive nod. "Trust me."

He stood so close that she could feel the warmth of his body, smell his spicy aftershave and the Juicy Fruit on his breath. "I do trust you. If you believe this is wise, I believe you."

He trusted her judgment as wise. What a lovely thing to say and a lovely thing to be. When she raised her gaze to his, she nodded. "I do think it would be wise."

He edged back a step. "Would today be too soon for the interview? Perhaps I could drive you back to the office and stop on the way for lunch."

The speed of his capitulation surprised her, but the sooner the interview was over, the sooner she could write the article. "That would be nice."

She suggested the diner where she used to work, and he readily agreed. She chose a booth near the cash register, placed their orders, and prompted him to talk. He was such a fabulous storyteller that she rarely had to ask questions. He spoke first of his Armenian grandparents. The grandfathers who had both been murdered. The grandmothers who had separately immigrated to the States, settling in Virginia. He reminisced over his childhood. His postwar college education. Mariah gave up all pretense of being in control of an interview that held her enthralled. She didn't take notes, but no matter. She wouldn't forget.

"I came to Raleigh after getting my degree," he said, pushing away his plate. "I miss my family and friends in Richmond, yet I don't regret moving here and finding my own way. Now, Miss Byrne, I have a favor to ask of you."

She blinked, as if from a daze, reluctant to leave behind the magic of his story, wary about the favor. "What?"

The waitress startled them by slapping a ticket on the tabletop and striding away. Mr. Azarian reached for it, considered it for a long moment, then looked up. "Are we ready to go?"

"Sure." She slid from the booth and stepped outside while he paid the bill. But as they reached his truck, she looked up at him. "What was the favor?"

"It was nothing." He opened the door for her. "Another time."

It had been rewarding to write the article, and once it was published, the calls poured in. They had all homes in progress sold by the end of May and deep interest in whatever came next.

Mr. Azarian was beside himself with glee and invited her out for lunch to celebrate. "Your advertising idea has been a great boon for the company."

His praise warmed her. Eased a tightness in her chest. She smiled across the table at him, enjoying their moment of shared triumph. It felt good to be viewed as more than just a secretary filing paperwork and answering phones. She liked being part of his success. "Thank you. It was a pleasure to help."

"Miss Byrne?" He licked his lips nervously. "The chamber of commerce has invited me to a cocktail party on Friday, and I may bring a guest. Will you join me?"

She fought to keep her smile from fading as she considered his question. Was he asking her on a date? She'd never thought of him as anything more than her boss. Was this a professional request? She liked her job and wouldn't want anything to happen that might be . . . uncomfortable. "Why?"

His smile was polite. "The article piqued their interest, and they want to learn more. Although it's a social event, business is conducted. It would only be natural to bring the writer of the article."

"Oh." She relaxed. It *was* professional, and he would be publicly acknowledging how important she was to his company. She might find this type of event interesting, but they had to be clear about their roles. "How would you introduce me? As your date or as your friend?"

"That is your choice."

His response reassured her. It might be instructive to go together, mingle with other local business owners, and spread the word about Azarian homes.

Really, the invitation made perfect sense. It could be yet another way for her to be useful. "Yes, I'll go with you. As friends."

Mariah enjoyed her evenings out with Mr. Azarian—*Gregor* when they were socializing. As soon as they left the office, they dropped their roles as boss and secretary and simply became friends.

Mariah had been overwhelmed by that first cocktail party. So many people talking, drinking, smoking. She'd watched from a quiet corner as Gregor charmed the crowd with his wit and infectious laugh. Another reason to admire him.

They were invited to more events with other groups. She soon relaxed enough to brag about the beautiful, affordable homes Azarian Construction was building. She would glance up at Gregor and find him smiling down at her with approval—as if her participation was making a difference.

When it was just the two of them, they never ran out of things to talk about. Their preferences in books, plays, and movies. Places they'd visited or would like to visit. Politics. He talked a lot about his family. She barely mentioned hers. If he noticed, he didn't press.

Mariah had never experienced a friendship like this before with a man. It was lovely.

The change came before she expected.

After an evening out in July, he walked her to the front porch of the boardinghouse, and as she looked up at him, he asked gravely, "Mariah, may I kiss you good night?"

In the months they'd been attending events together, there had been no indication he wanted anything other than friendship. His behavior had been courtly and charming. But a kiss would elevate what they had to more.

She wasn't sure how to respond. Her time in Texas had scarred her, and she suffered still. But there was something good and kind about this man. Her friend. When she was around him, she felt hopeful.

She would let the kiss decide. "You may."

He rested his hands on her shoulders, his brow creasing in concentration. He leaned forward in a rush. The kiss was tentative, his lips closed, their noses bumping. Straightening, he stared at her, eyes wide and anxious. Waiting. Was he seeking permission for another?

She tilted her chin up in invitation. The second kiss was much like the first. Endearingly inept. He didn't know what he was doing. His lack of experience, his sweetness roused longings she'd denied too long. "Ask me to dinner."

"As a date or a friend?"

She'd locked down her heart because she believed she didn't deserve more. Shame had prevented her from fully embracing her life. Maybe it was time to let someone—no, *this* man—in. She smiled. "Your choice."

Those summer days brought another change. The *Raleigh Now* magazine had been so taken with her photography they asked her to freelance on other articles. Flush with Gregor's encouragement, she'd said yes and had already completed another assignment. The pay had been modest, but it allowed her to send more for Kenny.

She was working three jobs now: secretary, seamstress, photographer. But she reserved every moment she could spare for Gregor.

Sometimes dates would be just the two of them. Sometimes with other couples. She'd even attended his friend's wedding in Richmond, met his mother and brother, and had been warmly welcomed by the congregation at his Armenian Apostolic church.

On an unusually mild evening in September, Gregor told her he'd planned a particularly special date. As he often did, he surprised her by picking the most unique spot possible. The state fairgrounds.

"What are we doing here?" she asked as he helped her from the car.

"This is the place."

"What place?"

"You'll see." His grin was nervous.

After he tucked her hand into the crook of his arm, they headed up the wide concrete apron toward Dorton Arena. The odd structure rose like a mammoth, an inverted saddle made of steel and glass. With few other vehicles around, there couldn't be an event tonight.

He gazed up, his face glowing with wonder. "It is magnificent, is it not?"

She hid her smile. He would be lecturing her soon on its architecture and history. "It is."

He held the door for her and ushered her in. Their footsteps echoed eerily as they crossed the concourse and into the arena. At its center, a picnic basket waited beside a small table set with a linen cloth, crystal and china, and a vase with a single rose—its white petals tipped with crimson. Above them, the building soared in a strangely compelling mishmash of cables, beams, and windows streaming light. The arena could hold thousands, but today, despite its size, it felt intimate. "Are we dining here tonight?"

He gave a jerky nod. From his pocket, he pulled out a flat, square box and lifted the lid. Inside lay the loveliest brooch she'd ever seen. It was circular, made of rose-gold swirls with a small diamond at its heart.

"How beautiful!"

"It is an Arevakhach. For Armenians, a wheel of eternity." He held the box out to her. "For you, if you will accept it."

She cradled it in her palm. A wheel of eternity. Words of promise. Her heart beat faster. "Why, Gregor?"

"I wrote your brother."

Never in her wildest imagination would she have expected him to say that. "Stephen?" Of course Stephen. He was her only family member she'd truly discussed with Gregor.

"I have asked him for your hand."

"In marriage?"

"Yes." The single word came out gruff. "Mariah, will you do me the honor of being my wife?"

She'd known they might be headed toward marriage, but she hadn't expected the question so soon. Gregor had crept softly and steadily into her heart. Like with her brother, when she was with Gregor, the impossible felt possible again. "Why?"

"Because we are right for each other."

She looked around at the empty stands in this large, echoing arena. Stephen was in Vietnam, and mail there was so unreliable. If Gregor had been able to write her brother and receive a response, he'd been planning this for weeks. This wonderful man had recognized how important her brother's blessing would be. Another gift to treasure.

She'd met his family. He would never meet hers, if it was up to her. Except Stephen. Of course the two men she loved most must someday meet.

Gregor cleared his throat, his brightness snuffed out. He'd anticipated the answer quickly. Happily. And she hadn't given it, because this man didn't know her secrets.

How could she tell him about Kenny? She loved her son enough to wait until he wouldn't scream or shrink from her. Until he was old enough to want her back. Because she couldn't bear to watch him turn away from her again.

Family was so important to Gregor. He wouldn't understand how she could patiently bide her time to reclaim her place in Kenny's life. *Their* place in his life.

Gregor couldn't comprehend the choice she'd made, and she didn't know how to explain. Were there even words to capture what she'd experienced? The eternal horror of Dealey Plaza? The terrifying months of worrying whether she'd lost her mind? The grief of surviving what was best for her son and the relentless guilt of wondering if it was the right decision?

When she shared her secrets, she had to tell them perfectly, and he had to be ready to hear them. When would that be?

Gregor loved her. He hadn't spoken the word, but she knew he did. Not the sweet young love Hal had offered. Gregor's feelings were big and bold and complete and wise. She yearned for his kind of love. Unconditional. Filling the cracks of her life. She would promise to love him as well as she was able, but her heart wasn't whole or healed. Would that be enough?

"Mariah, I'm sorry. I thought—"

"Yes, I will marry you."

He blinked down at her, his grin slowly widening, then threw back his head, laughing with pure joy. Swooping forward, he yanked her high into his arms and kissed her with enthusiasm.

His lips slid to her cheek, to her temple. He groaned. "Why did you make me wait? It was agony."

"I was conferring with my heart."

"Its answer delights me." He lowered her to the ground. "We shall be happy."

Ducking her head, she was hit by the urgent desire to wear her brooch. After fumbling with the clasp, she pinned it on, the perfect engagement gift, representing his heritage and eternity and love.

We shall be happy.

There was one secret she would tell him now, and she hoped it wouldn't change his mind. In that moment, she knew marrying him was the right decision, because not marrying him had become unthinkable. "Gregor, you are not my first love."

He smiled tenderly. "Perhaps not, but I will be your best."

CHAPTER 31

The smile Luke shot Jessica when he spotted her in the bleachers made her efforts to get to the baseball game worth it. She cheered, groaned, and screamed herself hoarse at their win.

Although he'd taken the team bus to Greensboro, he rode home with her. Luke was so buzzed about the team moving on to the next round in the playoffs that she was content to listen to him relive the best moments.

But once they closed in on Raleigh, it was time to fill him in. "Can I give you an update about the promotion?"

"Sure. What have you decided?"

"I'm applying for the senior position of the morning show."

"Great. What's the process?"

His smile was easy. Genuine. Such a relief. "There's a web form I fill out."

"No résumé?"

"I can submit one, but it's optional."

He was shaking his head. "No, it's not. Take it from a business communication teacher."

"Oh?" She eyed him curiously. "Why? They've watched me for three years. They know what I'm capable of."

"They know what's important to them. They don't necessarily know what's important to you." He smoothly passed another vehicle before adding, "You can state your career objective at the top, then have the rest of your résumé demonstrate your commitment to your goals. Emphasize what you're most proud of."

She thought that over. Using a résumé to give insights into what she loved most about news production sounded smart. "If I write it, will you edit?"

"I will, but don't expect me to cut you any slack because of our relationship." He laughed. "So, when do you plan to visit your uncle?"

"It has to be tomorrow. I'm on call next weekend."

"Do you want me to come with you?"

Jessica glanced at Luke. With his sunglasses on, she wasn't able to gauge his reaction. "No, I thought I'd ask Raine."

He nodded, a faint smile curving his lips. "I approve."

After Sunday brunch, Luke went out to do yard work, and Jessica texted her sister.

I'm meeting Uncle Kenny this afternoon. Want to come?

Are you sure you don't want to meet him alone?

That's your preference. Not mine. We can talk on the way

Sure. What time?

Leave at noon

Okay

I'm going by Larkmoor first

Pick me up after. I'm not ready to see Mariah yet

Okay. See you at noon

Jessica let Luke know her plans, then left for Larkmoor. When she reached her grandmother's suite, Mariah was sitting beside the parlor window, staring into the courtyard.

Jessica dragged a chair closer. Here they were, granddaughter with her grandmother. Something that had happened so many times throughout her life. But this time . . . Jessica saw Mariah from a new perspective. She was someone who had left her son behind. Someone who had been Jessica's idol and had deceived her. It hurt to be here.

And right now, Mariah didn't even know who Jessica was. Didn't know that she'd caused Jessica's pain.

"Good morning, Mariah. Are you ready for a visit?"

"I can be." Her grandmother clutched a small bouquet of flowers, petals falling like confetti on her lap and around her feet. "What day is it?"

"Sunday."

Mariah lifted the bouquet to her nose and breathed in. Roses, daisies, and a single gardenia. The scent was as wonderful as the sight.

Jessica had come here hoping to get answers, and now she didn't know how to begin. "Your flowers are beautiful. Where did you get them?"

"From Gregor."

Her heart stuttered at the response. "Gregor died. He couldn't have sent them."

Mariah snorted, then gestured vaguely at a side table. "I can read, young lady."

Jessica picked up the card and read with surprise. Papa had written the note.

You have been my heart for 58 years. I only wish I met you sooner so I could have loved you longer.

Gregor

Papa must have set the delivery up in advance. Would there be other bouquets? Would they all come with handwritten cards?

Had he known he wouldn't be there to deliver them himself?

Papa, did you know you were sick? Did you keep that from us too?

Her grandmother asked imperiously, "Have you come to take me home?"

"No, Mariah."

"I'm tired of this place. I'd like to leave now." She shifted in her chair until they faced each other. Her lips were obscured by a clown-like layer of red lipstick. She wore no jewelry, and her shirt wasn't buttoned correctly. Obviously, she'd dressed herself. It was the sloppiest Jessica had ever seen her. Another source of pain.

Pity crowded out anger. What was the point of arguing with someone who couldn't defend herself? "You smudged your lipstick. May I repair it?"

Her grandmother dropped her head wearily against her chair. "Would you?"

"Certainly." She pulled a makeup wipe from her purse and gently dabbed the skin around Mariah's mouth. She lay limply in her chair, eyes closed, breathing evenly. Had she fallen asleep? Jessica tossed the wipe into a trash can and debated leaving.

Her grandmother's eyes popped open. "Thank you. That was nice." She held up a hand and wiggled her fingers with their unpolished nails.

Jessica swallowed past a lump in her throat. Why was her grandmother picking today to be playful? "Would you like me to paint your nails?"

"Please."

"Any particular color?"

"Pink, I think." Her smile was sly.

Jessica blinked against the sting of tears. Mariah had used a code phrase from Jessica's childhood. A clue that meant she would be getting her Mima's complete attention. *Let's retire for girl talk and nails. Pink, I think.* It had been a silly thing to say since neither of them liked pink particularly. A week ago, Jessica would've been overjoyed to hear those words. Now, it made her sad.

She hunted through her grandmother's dresser and found a bottle of Plum Delicious polish, then returned to the sitting room. Mima was waiting patiently, fingers splayed on a lap tray.

Jessica finished a thumbnail before asking, "Ready for some girl talk?"

"Sure." The word was hesitant. "Shall I start?"

"Please."

Her grandmother averted her head. Gazed out the window. "I have grandchildren."

"Yes, you do," she said as evenly as possible. "How many?"

"Why don't you guess?"

She sucked in a breath. Mariah didn't remember. "You have two granddaughters."

"Correct."

The joy of *Pink, I think* faded. Had Mariah been slipping even more since Papa's death? "Okay, I have a question. How many children do you have?"

Mariah pursed her lips. "Two."

A punch to the gut. She'd admitted the truth. Jessica felt light-headed. *Please acknowledge him.* "Do you know their names?"

"Stop that. It's my turn. How old are you, young lady?"

Opportunity missed. She felt let down. "Thirty-one." She patted her grandmother's left hand, then reached for the right.

"How old am I?"

"Seventy-eight."

"That's nice." Mariah grew quiet, her gaze making a slow circuit of the gardens beyond the window. "Okay, your turn."

Jessica couldn't afford to waste a second try. Her grandmother's attention could be gone any moment, and they'd already touched on the subject. "Would you like to talk about Kenny?"

"No." Mariah drew the word out mournfully.

Jessica wasn't giving in yet. "Do you remember him?"

"A sweet boy."

"How often do you see him?"

"When I'm allowed."

That made her breath catch. What did *allowed* mean? Maybe she understood that it wasn't easy to transport her from Larkmoor to his home. It was something Jessica would have to check into. "Do you know where Kenny lives?"

"My husband knows." Her grandmother started humming "What a Wonderful World." A lone tear trickled down her cheek.

"Mariah?" Jessica waited. Hoped. Her grandmother had known she had two children. Called Kenny "a sweet boy." She might not visit him now, but how often had she gone in the past?

Could Jessica trust what Mariah said?

The humming grew louder. Girl talk was over.

After leaving Mima, Jessica plugged Alder Creek into the GPS before making a quick detour to her sister's condo.

Once they were on the highway, Raine initiated voluntary sharing. "I'm working on getting another certification. I need it to progress in forensic accounting."

"Why?"

"It's time. It'll let me be taken seriously as an expert witness."

"Is that something you want to be?"

"No, but it comes with the job. You're not as valuable if they can't drag you into court occasionally." She played with her headphones. "Which is why I have a podcast to finish. Thirty minutes left. Now or on the way back?"

"Now." Jessica smiled. "On the way back, we'll want to talk."

Her sister slipped on her headphones and closed her eyes. She didn't stir again until they were pulling through the gate to Alder Creek.

At the end of the narrow driveway, the main building sat in the middle of a small lawn. It resembled an old farmhouse with a wing tacked on here and another there, gleaming with white paint in the afternoon sun. If Jessica had ever seen the building before, she didn't remember. But her memory of the gazebo returned clearly. A table decorated in red, white, and blue. Cupcakes with white frosting, sprinkles, and tiny toothpick flags instead of candles. Her sister beside her, focused with absorption on the treats. Adults standing on the periphery, singing.

After parking, she turned to her sister. "Ready?"

"Yep." Rained placed her headphones on the back seat and slid out.

They entered the coolness of the lobby and crossed to the receptionist. "We're Kenny's nieces."

"He knows you're coming." The man smiled. "He's in the garden. I'll take you."

They followed him down a middle hallway—really more of a glassed-in portico—and through a large rec room buzzing with activity to an inconspicuous door in the back corner. They emerged into a yard, an acre or more, dominated by a garden of vegetables, herbs, and flowers.

A man was kneeling in front of squash plants, busily weeding. A woman, wearing long-sleeved navy scrubs and a lovely silver headscarf, stood nearby with a rake.

"There they are," the guy said. "Kenny and Amina are working in the garden today."

"Thanks," Jessica said, then looked at her sister, her stomach twisted with nerves.

"Yeah, I know. It's overwhelming."

She continued toward her uncle, glad she'd worn sandals instead of heels over this spongy ground. When they were a few feet away, the woman looked up, her hand shielding her eyes from the glare.

"Hi," she said with a smile. "Kenny, you have visitors."

He turned. "Hi, Raine. Hi, Jessica."

"Hi, Uncle Kenny," Jessica said. She would *not* cry. He was speaking to her like it had been a week, instead of more than twenty years.

As he labored to his feet, she took in his appearance. Taller than average. Medium build. Clean-shaven. Dark hair pulled back into a nub of a ponytail. Bright-blue eyes.

He looked uncertainly at Amina. "Is it okay to stop?"

"Sure. Should we offer your nieces something to drink?"

"Good thinking." He slipped off his gardening gloves and laid them on Amina's outstretched hand. "We can sit under the dome, but I have to wash my hands first."

Amina smiled at the sisters. "If you want to sit in the shade, Kenny and I will be right back. Would you like tea, water, or lemonade?"

"Lemonade," Jessica said.

"Me too." Her sister waited until the other two were out of earshot before turning to her. "You okay?"

Jessica nodded, not yet trusting herself to speak. He seemed comfortable with them. She wanted to be comfortable with him too. To find a way to catch up quickly. She had so many things she wanted to say to her parents right now. She and Raine deserved answers, explanations, and apologies.

Jessica followed her sister over to the pavilion. The structure had a stained concrete floor under a wooden roof. It was furnished with wrought-iron chairs made comfortable by cushions in floral fabric. She chose a chair facing the garden. Raine stood to the side, both distant and near, and leaned against the wooden railing.

Kenny returned with Amina, who carried a tray with three plastic tumblers of lemonade. After setting the tray on a table, she disappeared inside the facility.

Kenny sat across from Jessica. "You work on TV."

"On the news."

He nodded. "Sometimes Gregor and I watched your show together. But not much. He usually left before dinner."

"I hope you liked it."

"We did."

She bit her lip and looked out. A white wooden fence separated them from a pine forest and a glint of water beyond. But she hardly registered it, too weighed down by the sense of loss. He'd been here their whole lives. They'd missed so much.

Kenny had drained his glass. "Raine's already seen my room. Do you want to?"

She smiled. "That'd be great."

"After you finish your lemonade."

They carried their empty glasses inside, then Kenny gave them the grand tour, which Raine hadn't received. He pointed out the two residential wings, the rec room, the dining room, and kitchen. Other residents and staff called out or waved as they passed.

When they finally made it to his room, he introduced Jessica to his bookcase and, therefore, his interests. Their last stop was the wall opposite his bed.

It was as her sister had described. Black-and-white photos, double matted in gray. In the center were several shots of the sisters, all taken by their grandmother. On his dresser was a smaller version of the same collection of three brides that Jessica had hanging over her mantel, each wearing the same gorgeous lace gown Mariah had made herself.

Her presence was everywhere. The realization eased a knot of fear. "Uncle Kenny, these are great pictures."

"Yeah. They're from Mariah." He pursed his lips. "When I was little, Dad said she had to be my secret mom."

"Why was she a secret?" Jessica asked. Beside her, Raine seemed to hold her breath.

"My other mom, Ida Mae, didn't want Mariah to be part of my life."

CHAPTER 32

November 22, 1967

Mariah had been pressuring Hal for months to schedule a visit for their families. She hated keeping the secret from Gregor, and Kenny was nearly four. Surely his anxious stage with strangers had calmed?

Hal remained reluctant. Yes, he wanted Kenny to know her family. No, the time wasn't right.

Mariah believed Ida Mae was the problem, not Kenny. If Hal wasn't willing to beg his wife, Mariah was. So when Gregor had proposed traveling to New York City for Thanksgiving, Mariah agreed. He could travel by himself in advance and visit alone with his family for a day. She and Stephanie would fly in later.

Then Mariah asked Ida for a meeting on Kenny's fourth birthday. It had surprised her how easily Ida had acquiesced. Was that a promising sign?

Gregor left early on Tuesday in their Lincoln, his kisses and gratitude profuse. Once he was safely on the road, Mariah packed a suitcase, dressed Stephanie, and took a taxi to the airport. They were flying to Dallas.

It was the flight from hell. Stephanie didn't like air travel. Cookies and juice did little to compensate. But eventually she napped, and the passengers and stewardesses sighed with relief.

Mariah and a cranky Stephanie got off the plane and were mercifully whisked to a hotel. Her daughter fell asleep quickly, but not Mariah. She lay in bed far into the night, staring through the open curtains, too agitated to sleep.

She'd hated deceiving Gregor about this trip. When she finally did reveal the news about Kenny, Gregor would be furious with her. He'd also be impatient to meet his stepson, to bring him into the heart of their family. But Gregor didn't understand the rules that would govern their interactions with the Highcamps. She'd experienced how they could be when they didn't want someone around, and it had nearly destroyed her. Without Ida's full cooperation, the blending of families would be unpleasant, if not impossible. Mariah would wait to tell Gregor until she had Ida on board.

Mariah had been preparing—for years, really—what to say to Ida and how to say it. Mariah had brainstormed various options for visits that could be fun and enjoyable for them all.

What she hadn't prepared for was how it would feel to be back in Dallas—on the fourth anniversary of JFK's death, no less. Nightmares were rare now. She no longer thought of Dealey Plaza every day. But as she and Stephanie had flown in, the spectacular lights of the city spread before them, a familiar sense of detachment threatened.

Mariah got her daughter up early the next day—Kenny's fourth birthday—though the visit wasn't until ten. She'd sewn special holiday dresses for the two of them for Thanksgiving, and Stephanie looked adorable. They had breakfast, took another quick nap, and hailed a taxi. But as they rode through the streets, Mariah felt her tension rising. And her hope. She was about to see her son.

Once the taxi dropped them off at the park, Mariah held the suitcase with one hand and balanced her daughter on a hip with the other as they made their way to the meeting place. Even at ten in the morning, the park was busy. Stephanie was mesmerized by the shrieking children running around in the mild weather.

Ida Mae waited at a picnic table. The years had taken a toll on her. Under the open coat, the hourglass curves had widened to a solid block. The bottle-blonde hair had gone a dull brown streaked with gray.

At her feet sat Kenny, dressed in his Sunday best topped with a pullover sweater and beret, playing with pine cones. Mariah stopped, savoring the sight of her son. She had recent pictures of Kenny, but they hadn't prepared her for seeing him. To know she could touch him and hold him close.

"Hello." Ida's expression was sullen.

"Hello." Mariah set her daughter on her feet. Stephanie steadied herself, then toddled over to her brother and plopped onto the ground beside him. She grabbed a pine cone, dropped it immediately, and looked up, her mouth in a stunned *O*.

Kenny calmly added the cone to his pile. He pointed at his new playmate. "Who?"

"Stephanie," Ida Mae said.

"Your sister," Mariah said, riveted by her son. He was eyeing her suspiciously. But there were no screams. No shrinking from her presence. She would call that a victory.

He pointed at her next. "Who?"

Ida Mae was already answering. "Mariah."

He went back to his play.

She turned to Ida Mae, who flinched. Mariah didn't react. She'd promised herself to be calm. She had a sensible plan for bringing the families together. Stephanie was walking, soon to be talking and ready to know her brother. Azarian Construction was booming, so well that they'd been able to hire an office manager. Whatever schedule Ida proposed, Mariah would accommodate.

"Why are you here?" Ida asked.

"To reach an agreement about having my family visit Kenny." Mariah had stayed as involved as possible from a distance since the Highcamps' drop-by visit in Raleigh. Cards and letters and photographs. Ida knew little of that.

"What would the agreement entail?"

"Vacations in the summer. A week or two. We could come here. Go to the zoo or Six Flags or the lake."

"Is that all?"

"I'd like to come over the holidays too. Thanksgiving or Christmas." She would prefer Thanksgiving and Kenny's birthday, but they could do whatever the Highcamps thought best. She would save her final idea—to have Kenny visit them in North Carolina—until he was older.

"I thought you might want to bring your family around." Ida wearily tucked a stray lock of hair behind her ear. "And here you are with your daughter."

"His sister."

"He doesn't know or care about that." She gestured at him, playing with pine cones. "Has he shown you any interest? No. You're a stranger to him."

"We won't be strangers to him if we visit."

"No."

No, what? Was Ida refusing outright? Mariah must have misunderstood. She'd have to be more persuasive. "No?"

"This won't work. A week or two in the summer? Do you think that's enough? He'll forget you in between."

"At first, maybe. But he'll be old enough to remember soon."

Ida shook her head. "He isn't ready, and neither are we. Why this sudden interest?"

"Sudden?" She took a breath. Calm. "I've been asking for years."

"You're asking for the fun without taking any responsibility. Sure, you send the occasional envelope with your puny contributions. But that doesn't say much for a woman who can afford to dress herself and her daughter in designer clothes and buy an airline ticket for one day."

Mariah felt her cheeks heat. Her contributions hadn't been puny. She'd given Stephen's life insurance money to Hal. Twice what Hal earned in a year. He'd put it into the bank, saving it for his dream of starting a business for him and Kenny to renovate old cars. But Hal hadn't told Ida.

She would pester him to buy a bigger house. The dream business would get them there—just later. Mariah would not betray his confidence, but that left her with no defense. "A week in the summer, Ida. Please."

"Strangers traipsing in for a few days? Having fun, then disappearing?" Ida scoffed. "That's not what he needs."

Anger flashed. Mariah was tired of being polite. Now she would demand. "Ida—"

"No, Mariah. You need me on your side, and I'm not." She said it calmly, but it felt like a threat.

Was this the source of Hal's reluctance? Ida was alone with Kenny all day. Surely she wouldn't try to sabotage his future relationship with Mariah's family? "Then what can we do?"

"Nothing, for now." Ida's smile was strained. "We have a wall of pictures at our house. And your family is there in a pretty frame. Hal points it out to Kenny at night. *Our friends.* That's why he's ignoring you right now instead of clinging to me. He recognizes your face."

"That's something, isn't it? We could—"

"No!"

Kenny pushed to his feet and lurched across the ground to Ida, wrapping his arms around her leg. Like any child who wanted his mom to be okay. Would he ever look at Mariah that way?

"Hi, buddy," Ida said, her voice changing to warmth as her fingers combed his hair. His lips widened into a smile, drool bubbling at the corner. She looked up, firmly shaking her head. "If you love Kenny like you claim, this has to be about him."

What your child needs matters more than what you want.

Would those words have to keep her sane a little longer?

Mariah would be going home without the agreement she'd hoped for. Without the opportunity to introduce Gregor to Kenny. What would she do now?

"Your husband doesn't know, does he?" Ida smirked.

Mariah didn't respond, but the answer must have been written across her face.

Ida smiled, not so much in triumph as in resignation. "When Kenny's ready to handle his other family, we'll let you know. But not before." She opened a picnic basket, pulled out vanilla wafers, and handed two to Kenny. While Kenny munched, Stephanie wobbled to her feet and joined them, laughing, her grimy hands eager.

Mariah watched her son and daughter eat their snack. They looked so sweet together. Good for them. Unbearable for her.

Stephanie pivoted, then toddled over to Mariah, her hands smeared with wet cookie.

"Is that good, sweetie?" she asked her daughter, smoothing her hair.

Kenny came over but stopped at a wary distance. She smiled at him tentatively. Held her breath.

He scooted closer and offered up the mushy remains of his cookie. Was this a snack for her? When she held out her hand, he mashed the sticky crumbs on her palm.

She smiled wider, struggling not to weep happy tears at the contact. "Thank you, Kenny."

He grunted and stumbled back to his pine cones, with Stephanie close behind.

Oh, how she ached to tell her husband, to end the lie. It had gone on too long. And learning the truth would hurt him so badly. If only he could meet Kenny. It wouldn't prevent the wound, but it might help to heal it.

Should she tell Gregor anyway? *You have a stepson, and sorry, you can't meet him.*

The betrayal he'd feel would be unspeakable. How would he react?

Storm down to Texas? That could have disastrous consequences for everyone.

Storm out and take Stephanie with him? That possibility would be unbearable. She couldn't lose them too.

No, she wouldn't take the risk. She would wait a little longer. Surely Kenny would be ready soon.

CHAPTER 33

Raine studied her uncle. There were so many lies in this story, it was hard to keep them straight. "Mariah was your secret mom?"

"She was, but I don't keep her a secret anymore."

"Does she come to see you?" Jessica asked.

His face fell. "Not in a long time." There was no anger or censure in Kenny's tone.

How long was long for him? For the past few years, their grandmother hadn't left Larkmoor often. If they took her out, she'd become too agitated and beg to go home to the old house. Was that when she stopped visiting him?

Raine shifted into his line of vision. "So she came to see you before."

"Yeah. Before she got sick." He nodded. "Ask Reggie. He knows."

"Do you talk often with your cousin Reggie?"

"Whenever Ian or Amina calls him for me on FaceTime. Reggie and I are baseball fans. He likes the Texas Rangers. I don't, but I don't let on." He shuffled over to his sitting area, dropped onto the recliner, and picked up the TV remote, holding it against his thigh.

The sisters exchanged glances and smiled. Clearly, it was time for them to go.

After saying their goodbyes, they headed out of the building. Raine preceded her sister down the veranda steps, blinking at the brightness of the day. As they walked toward the parking lot, she ran through the last part of their conversation with Kenny. On the drive to Raleigh, her sister would want to talk about it, and in this case, Raine agreed. "We learned new data."

"Yeah, but I'd like more clarity," Jessica said, circling around her car to the driver's side. "He spent time with Mima. But how much?"

"Ida Mae died in 1972. If Kenny had to keep Mariah a secret from his stepmom, then Mariah was already playing some type of role in his life before he was nine." Raine shook her head, astonished by the web of lies. "I don't know how they got away with it."

"I guess it's easier to lie successfully when the people around you trust you not to."

The car locks clicked. As she was reaching for the door, someone called out, "Raine."

She and her sister turned. Ian was jogging down the veranda steps.

"Just a sec." She strode back to him, meeting him halfway. "Yes?"

"Hi." He smiled. Crossed his arms. Fidgeted. "You and your sister visited Kenny?"

She nodded. "Jessica hadn't met him yet."

"Good." Ian looked down at his shoes. Then up again. "Okay. So. I'm just going to say it. Would you like to go out with me?"

Raine tried not to gape. She hadn't been expecting that question at all. *Wow.* Her initial feeling was pleasure, until her wariness muscled in. She was curious about Ian, although she didn't get why he might be interested in her.

She hadn't been on an actual date in five years. Could she trust her curiosity?

Okay, she needed to be logical about this. Ian had been at Alder Creek for three years, where jobs were highly competitive. She doubted he would've been allowed anywhere near Kenny if Papa hadn't approved.

There was a measure of confidence in knowing that.

Raine's gut reaction was to . . . accept. Not just because he was attractive—which, yes, he was—but also because he'd been comfortable to talk to. He'd been honest with her, even with things that weren't easy to say. He seemed to treat everyone well, from residents to waiters to other staff, which implied how he would treat her. All positives.

There had to be negatives. If she tried, she'd come up with some.

Ian's smile faded. "Did I misread this?"

"Not exactly. I'm thinking through all the angles." Like . . . probably he lived near here, an hour from her, inconvenient if they made it past the first date. And there was an obvious age difference. "How old are you?"

"Twenty-five."

"I'm four years older."

Her comment must have reassured him, because his smile returned. "Is that a polite way of saying I'm too immature for you?"

She laughed. "No."

"Then I'll ask again. Will you go out with me?"

Her heart was pounding. Was she about to do something stupid? "Yes."

His smile was beautiful. "Are you free Saturday night?"

Friday was his final day at Alder Creek. Would he be celebrating the transition with her? Did she want the pressure?

She ought to chill. It would be fine. "Will you come to Raleigh?"

"I will." He handed her his phone. "Around seven?"

Nodding, she texted herself, then handed his phone back. "See you then."

She had barely gotten inside her sister's car when Jessica asked, "What was that all about?"

Blushing, Raine took her time with buckling her seat belt. "He asked me out."

"Really? And you said yes."

She nodded.

"If he works there, he's met Papa's standards."

"I've already thought about that."

"Does that comfort you?" There was a smile in her sister's voice.

"It does, actually," she said, glad her sister had picked up on that. Raine slipped on her sunglasses and gripped the armrest as Jessica reversed from her parking space and drove a bit too fast down the lane.

"Okay. Back to Kenny. What questions remain?" Raine opened the notes app on her phone and created a file for items to research. "We need to uncover the reasons for the conspiracy of silence."

"What really happened in Texas? Why did Mima leave? How much did she and Kenny interact over time?"

"Why didn't she return?" Raine added the questions to her notes and looked up. "Who would know the answers?"

"Mom."

Raine sighed. "If she'll tell us."

"I have a plan for that. I'm sure I can make her spill more." Jessica accelerated, passed a tractor, then made a swift right onto the highway's on-ramp.

"Be my guest." Raine looked out the side window. Anything to avoid seeing the speedometer. Her sister liked fast everything.

"Mariah."

"If she remembers." Raine hadn't seen her grandmother in nearly a week, too upset to be in the same room with her, but it was time to let that go too. "It's hard to stay mad at someone who doesn't understand why."

"I get that. We have to talk to Dad."

Raine had already confronted him. And in the days since, she'd let her disappointment go. He'd been hurt too. "I wrote up notes from talking with him."

"I wasn't satisfied with his answers."

Too bad. Raine wasn't asking him again. "Reggie Highcamp."

Jessica nodded slowly. "He's the only eyewitness still living. Besides Mima."

Reggie had been a part of the story, almost from the beginning. "He might know more than she does. He was there after she left. He watched Kenny grow up. If he was in Hal's confidence, he could tell us what roles they played in what happened."

"Yeah, we definitely need to talk with him. The caregivers have his contact information. I wonder if they'd give it to us."

"I'll ask Ian."

"Ian." Jessica's voice had that *aww* sound. "That's sweet."

It helped knowing that Jessica didn't think it was weird to be going out with him. So when the anxiety twitched, Raine pushed it away.

"Do you want me and Luke to come by? Check him out?"

"No, thanks," Raine said, keeping her tone even. Her sister was probably teasing, but Raine was capable of handling one date. She bent over her notes. "Papa's wish was for us to claim the story. It feels like we have all the major pieces. We just need the motivations that connect them." She looked out the windshield at the highway stretching ahead. "When Papa said to do the right thing, he must've meant forming a relationship with Kenny."

"True, and we're doing that. But the story still has gaps. There might be multiple right things to do."

"Like what?"

"Forgive Mariah. Mom." Jessica paused. "Dad."

Raine swallowed a retort. She wasn't arguing with her sister about Dad. *Nope.*

"And Papa."

Raine nodded. She and Jessica would have to find a way to forgive the conspirators, including the man who'd sent them on this journey, who'd learned seven years into his marriage of his wife's deception and still managed to forgive her.

CHAPTER 34

September 1972

Mariah had been dragged into politics by her camera strap.

The connection had been made through Stephanie's kindergarten class. Mariah had been their de facto photographer, showing up at every event, snapping photos of every child, sending the extras home. Last spring, she'd been approached by another parent. Would she be willing to help him photograph public school buildings?

"Why?" she'd asked.

"Some members of the Raleigh business community are working with local leaders to merge the city schools with the county system. We'd like to improve our schools without the courts getting involved." He went on to explain how groups in Raleigh and Wake County were collaborating to find the right path toward integration.

She was curious to learn more about what they had in mind. "How can I help?"

"Take pictures of schools across the whole county, so we can compare the county facilities to those in the city."

She'd agreed, spending months snapping hundreds of photos, stunned by the differences in the quality of the facilities. She'd been drawn into the fight.

But afternoon meetings had to end by two. Stephanie was in first grade now, and one of her parents picked her up every day.

Today was Mariah's turn.

"Mama, see what I painted," Stephanie shouted as she hopped onto the front seat.

It was a respectable house beside an oversize rabbit on blue construction paper. "Beautiful."

She listened to her daughter chatter the whole way home. When she pulled into the driveway of their home, she was surprised to see Gregor's Cadillac parked at the curb. Unless it was his day to pick up Stephanie, he rarely got home until dinner.

"Daddy," Stephanie screamed, racing down the hall to his study.

Mariah could hear the rumble of his voice. Even without hearing the words, she could feel the pulse of underlying tension.

She entered his study, then hesitated at the cold fury in his eyes when his gaze landed on her. "What—?"

"Stephanie," he said, his tone gentle, "go to your room, please, and start your homework." He looked down again at a letter on his desk.

She stepped farther into the room. "What's wrong, Gregor?"

He folded the letter with precise movements, stuffed it into a grubby hand-addressed envelope, then set it into a drawer. "I have an unexpected meeting tomorrow. It will take all day. You'll be here for Stephanie?"

"Yes, of course." She wanted to yank open the drawer, fetch the letter, and see what it had done to her husband. But she wouldn't. That wasn't the kind of relationship they had. "Where's the meeting?"

"It remains to be seen." He stared at her, jaw tight. "If you'll excuse me, I have work to finish."

"Okay." He'd never looked at her that way before. She racked her brain but couldn't think of what she might have done. "I'll have dinner ready at five."

He gave a curt nod.

She shut the door behind her and went down the stairs. Pausing outside Stephanie's room, she listened to the happy sound of her daughter reading to herself. Mariah continued into her bedroom, removed her makeup, changed, then went back upstairs to prepare their meal.

Gregor joined them promptly at five, spoke only when spoken to, and disappeared back into his study when he was through.

She waited for him in bed, but he never came. She lay awake until late into the night, her sense of foreboding increasing with each hour. She could think of only one reason that explained his behavior. Had he found out her secret?

◆　◆　◆

Gregor was gone the next morning before she awakened. He'd left a note on the breakfast table.

I have gone out of town. Not sure when I'll be back.

A sudden trip out of town?

Fear pooled in her belly. Was his trip to Dallas? It must be. She sagged onto a chair and gazed out the picture window. The sky was laden with thick gray clouds, as bleak as she felt. He *knew*.

After years of negotiations, she and Hal had planned the long-overdue family reunion for this summer. Kenny was finally ready to meet his sister and stepfather. Before Mariah could break the news to Gregor, Hal had called to cancel. Ida was ill. Could they push out the reunion to Christmas?

Mariah had lived in terror of discovery for too long, but she'd agreed. If the fury in Gregor's eyes was an indication of how their next conversation would go, she'd been right to be afraid.

She took Stephanie to school, stopped by the Azarian Construction office to answer messages, then cleared the rest of her day. From the top shelf of the linen closet, she retrieved a hatbox and drew out her most recent letter from Kenny. He loved mail, so once he'd learned to write, they'd become pen pals. It was such a joy to exchange letters with him. She sat in her rocker, smoothed the sheet of notebook paper, and smiled as she read. Then she slipped it into her pocket and rocked while she shuddered at what might happen in the hours ahead.

Stephanie must have sensed her tension because she was unusually subdued that evening. No whining about a second night of macaroni and cheese, although there were complaints that her daddy wasn't there.

Dinner came and went. No word from Gregor.

Homework, bath, and bed for Stephanie. Still no sign of him.

It was past nine before Gregor's car pulled up the driveway and stopped halfway. He got out and closed the door with a heavy thunk. She rose and walked to the parlor entrance.

He'd been furious the night before. And now this. Alarm squeezed her chest. His behavior was out of character, unseen in the seven years they'd been married. The fear of his reaction to her secrets had long kept her silent. She'd been hoping that the joy of meeting Kenny would take away part of the sting.

Had Gregor found out?

No, it couldn't be that. Hal would *never* tell.

But something dreadful *had* happened.

The front door closed with a soft click. He stood in the foyer, staring at her with an implacable anger.

Dear God, who sent that letter?

Mariah clasped her hands against her waist to stop their shaking. "How was your trip?"

His eyes were hard. Slipping a hand into his pocket, he drew out an envelope. With exquisite care, he extracted a Polaroid, nostrils flaring, then held it out.

She reached for it, then recoiled. It was a photo of Hal and Kenny. A *current* photo. For so long, she'd lived with guilt and remorse. She'd tried to atone. She'd deceived her husband to avoid *this* moment. This awful moment. "How did you find out?"

"I received a letter."

No, Hal. You promised. "I can't believe he contacted you."

"He did not. The letter came from his wife."

Rage sizzled in her veins, but she suppressed it ruthlessly. Ida Mae had known better too.

"I flew to Dallas this morning to meet Hal and Kenny."

The names shuddered through her. Hal had grown from a beautiful boy into a far better man than their hometown would've ever believed. He was her hero. And her sweet son? She was as much a part of his life as she could be. Had Hal explained that?

The way Gregor was looking at her chilled her. "How are they?"

"They're fine. Do you care?"

Was there a response Gregor would believe? Probably not. One of the reasons she'd hidden it from him. She'd lived in anguish since she'd left all those years ago. How one stupid mistake and a malaise she didn't understand had led to a broken mess, and the girl she'd been before hadn't had the ability to make repairs. "I care."

Gregor strode toward her. She backed up until the wall stopped her, surprised but not scared. Her husband would never hurt her. Not physically.

"Here is what I heard in Dallas. You ran away from North Carolina with Hal. Had his baby. Then left one night without warning. You returned a few days later for long enough to pack your things and leave again, this time for good." Tilting his head, he gave her a nasty smile. "Does that sound about right?"

The version he recounted was factual, but it missed crucial information. How hard she'd tried to stay in touch, provide what she could, make amends. But Ida Mae had left those details out, because she didn't know all of them. "That's Ida's version of the story. But it's not complete. She doesn't know the whole truth."

Gregor's hands splayed, then clenched. "Did you abandon your disabled son?"

"*No.*" She shrank from the word, shocked that he could even think it. "I did *not* abandon Kenny."

"Then how would you describe it?"

Her husband's fury at her was justified, but he'd already convicted her of the charges before he knew all the crimes that had been committed. And by whom. If he would only listen . . .

No, she'd had seven years to make him listen. Seven years to present her side of the story. She was to blame for what he believed. "I'm in contact with Hal. I send money. Letters. Pictures. I get letters back from him and Kenny."

There was a flicker of surprise in her husband's eyes. "How often?"

"Monthly or more."

His expression remained grim, but he was listening. "Neither one of them said this."

"Ida Mae thinks I've been cut off from most direct contact with my son. Hal hasn't told her any differently." What had possessed the woman to write Gregor? Ida Mae knew where they lived. If there was something the Highcamps needed, she could've addressed the letter to Mariah.

"Hal didn't tell me either." Gregor bowed his head, as if it was too heavy to hold up any longer.

"Were you ever alone with him?"

"No." He looked up again. "The timing of the letter isn't incidental. She has grown too sick to care for the boy. Her liver is failing, Mariah."

She'd known Ida had been ill this summer, but she hadn't known how serious. Mariah's outrage drained away. How terrible for them all.

"Why didn't you tell me?" Betrayal colored Gregor's voice.

"Because I was scared of how you'd react, of how you would look at me once you knew."

"You were right to be scared." Accusation blazed in his eyes. "I wouldn't have married you if I had known."

She gasped, pressed against the wall for support. That was the anger speaking, surely. His mind had filled in the gaps of what he didn't understand. "No, Gregor. You don't mean that. You love me."

"I loved the woman I thought you were. Now, I can't stand the sight of you."

The statement hit like a blow. "No." She touched his arm, but he spun out of reach and returned to the front door, his hand grasping the knob.

"Where are you going?"

"A hotel tonight. I'll find somewhere to live tomorrow."

"Gregor, please." So many blows had struck she almost couldn't feel them anymore. "Don't leave us."

He looked over his shoulder. "I'm not leaving Stephanie. I'm leaving *you.*"

"Please, don't. She needs you." *I need you.*

"She's the center of my world. That won't change." He went out to the porch.

Mariah ran after him, desperate to head off this decision. The life she'd created with him, with Stephanie, was wonderful. And she'd thought that they were close to bringing both sides of the family together. She'd been foolish to think redemption might be in sight. "What do I tell our daughter?"

He pressed his fists to either side of his head, as if in unbearable pain, and moaned. "Ah, Mariah. You've had years to come up with a plan. You'll find a way." He rushed down the steps and slammed into his car. The taillights flashed as he raced down the lane.

Mariah collapsed onto the steps and stayed there, long after Gregor's car had vanished from view. She'd known for years that pure joy could never be hers. Regret and lies stood in its way.

She'd made an awful mistake, from which she'd never completely recovered. No amount of wishing could fix it.

CHAPTER 35

The ringing of Jessica's phone broke the silence. When the car's console displayed *Luke*, Jessica ignored the call, unwilling to interrupt their discussion. "I'll call him back."

Immediately, her sister's phone rang. "It's Luke."

Something must be up.

"Yes." Raine listened, then tapped a button on her phone. "You're on speaker now. Go ahead."

"Stephanie called," he said, his voice strained. "She tried you both first, but you didn't pick up." There was traffic noise in the background. "Your grandmother fell and likely has a hip fracture."

Jessica's hands gripped the wheel as Luke continued. He relayed what he knew, using phrases like *stable condition, surgery possible, rehab required.*

"Where are you now?" Raine asked.

"Driving to the hospital. Stephanie rode in the ambulance."

Jessica breathed in her husband's calm. Let it center her. "Which hospital?"

"WakeMed Raleigh."

"We'll be there in thirty minutes." The call ended.

Raine's head bowed over her phone, fingers flying. "I'm searching on hip fractures in the elderly."

"Good idea."

Over the next half hour, Raine shared carefully curated information from the internet about their grandmother's possible treatments and prognosis. By the time they were hurrying through the hospital's lobby, Jessica felt well informed. And frightened.

"The statistics are grim," Raine said.

"Got it." Sometimes, her implacable honesty bordered on the irritating.

"But Mariah isn't a statistic."

They stepped on the elevator. Jessica pressed the button for the surgical floor. "Let's talk about Mom."

"Like . . . how upset we are with her?"

"Yes, but now isn't the time to tackle her about Kenny." Jessica drank in a steadying breath. "She needs our support."

"Of course." Raine met her gaze. "Mariah has to be our focus."

When the sisters entered the surgical waiting room, they found their mother sitting in a corner alone, eyes closed.

Jessica approached quietly, trailed by her sister. "Mom?"

Her eyes opened, fear reflected in their depths. "Hi. I'm glad you're both here." She looked down at her hands clenched in her lap.

"Where's Luke?" Jessica asked.

"He went to get me something to drink."

"What are the doctors saying?"

Mom inhaled. Exhaled. "It's definitely a hip fracture," she said, her voice faint. "Once they're sure she's medically stable, she'll have surgery. The orthopedist on call is coming in."

"How long before we know more?" Raine asked.

"Not too long."

Jessica glanced at her sister and saw the same awareness in her face of how strange the next few hours would be. The meeting with their uncle was still fresh, yet they would have to put any confrontation on hold until they were past this crisis. Their grandmother had to be their concern, and Mom needed their support.

Luke came in, carrying a Coke Zero and a small cardboard tray with an array of snacks. "Here, Stephanie," he said and handed her the drink.

She accepted it absently and twisted off the cap.

He gave Raine a hug before sliding an arm around Jessica's waist. "Any updates?"

"Not since you left," Mom said.

They remained in the waiting room throughout the afternoon and into the evening. The surgeon had estimated a couple of hours. It had been longer than that.

Jessica reclined against her husband, watching her family in a daze. Raine was in a chair across the room, curled in on herself. Mom drooped on a couch, arms crossed, foot wiggling.

What could Jessica do to help them? She strained closer to Luke's ear and whispered, "Raine and I didn't get a chance to eat lunch. Why don't you tell her you're picking up a snack for me in the cafeteria and ask her to go along?"

He gave her hand a squeeze. "Good idea. Know what you want?"

"I'll text you."

"Okay." He crossed the waiting room to Raine. They spoke briefly, then she nodded, stood, and followed him out the door.

Jessica joined her mother on the couch. "Need anything?"

Mom gestured toward the door Luke and Raine had just exited. "Are they going to get food?"

"Yeah."

"A Coke Zero."

After texting Luke an order, Jessica looked up. "What else?"

Mom shook her head.

Another hour passed—sufficient time for Jessica to finish a rather tasteless protein bar—when a tall man in scrubs strode through the doorway. "I'm looking for the Azarian family."

Her mother was already halfway across the room, with her sister a step behind. Jessica rose more slowly and joined them as the surgeon was saying, "Wednesday, perhaps."

"That soon?" Raine asked.

"If all goes well." He glanced at his wristwatch. "Someone will come and get you when you're allowed to go back." He spun on his heel and walked out.

Mom stared at the now-empty doorway. "She can have PT at Larkmoor. They're good, and the surroundings are familiar."

Jessica didn't want to get into the details now. Of course the sisters would want to help out with Mima's care, but it would make more sense to wait until she was discharged and they understood the magnitude of what they were facing. "We can work that out later."

While they were waiting for Mima to come out of recovery, Raine and Luke went out again, for dinner takeout this time. Jessica sat on an uncomfortable faux-leather love seat by her mother, who was texting rapidly. She listened to the intermittent tapping for ten minutes or longer before asking curiously, "Letting your friends know?"

"Yes. And your father."

There were a couple of interesting tidbits of information in her response. First, Dad was excluded from the wide, loosely defined pool of people she referred to as friends. Not unexpected. But Mom texting her ex at all? Yeah, that was a surprise. "You and Dad stay in contact?"

Mom flushed. Looked up. "More since Daddy's death. Donovan understands how hard it's hit me."

Jessica was glad for even this small sign of civility. She made a mental note to pass that along to Raine.

They'd all eaten before a nurse came to fetch Mom. After she left, Jessica leaned wearily against her husband. Raine paced the room, scowling. After three laps, she stopped before them.

"Should we visit Mariah every day?"

"Yes, we should. It'll take pressure off Mom." Now for the tricky question. Knowing what they did about their uncle, having met him, he was part of the family. They wouldn't deny him. "What should we say to Mom about Kenny?"

"I'm saying nothing. If she notices me acting tense, she'll just think I'm withdrawing again." Raine shrugged. "You can't get away with that."

"True, but I can't avoid her. Should I hold off until we get Mima home? Even past that?"

"It would be the kindest reaction, but it might also be hard for you to maintain." Raine pursed her lips and stared at the overhead lights, thinking hard. "I'd say . . . we don't lie to her about Kenny. That's what they did to us, and we're not reflecting it back. So maybe we say nothing until Mariah settles down or the right opportunity pops up."

"Okay." Avoidance sounded good for now. It would give Jessica more time to craft the message. "What about Kenny? Should we let him know?"

Raine blushed. "I texted Ian. He's handling it."

"Oh?" She turned to her husband. He was trying not to grin, so obviously her sister had told him about the date.

"No big deal." Raine spun around and left the waiting room.

"Yes, it is," Luke said.

Jessica nodded. *Agreed.*

◆ ◆ ◆

By Wednesday, Mariah was doing well enough that the hospital discharged her. As expected, she was reluctant to do physical therapy.

Jessica coordinated a schedule of visits with their mother. For the first week postsurgery, each sister would visit once per day. They would reevaluate after that.

Luke had already returned her résumé with comments. She accepted the changes she liked, brought up the web form, typed in the appropriate fields, uploaded the résumé, then called him to their home office.

He walked in, freshly showered, ready for bed. "Yes?" He looked over her shoulder. "Ah. About to apply."

She nodded. Breathless. Scared. Excited. She clicked the submit button and waited for the confirmation page. "Okay, it's done."

"Congratulations, Jess. You'll get it."

She shivered, hoping he was right. "Have you submitted your grad school application?"

"Nah. Still trying to make up my mind about the program. I have four weeks until the deadline." He kissed her, then straightened. "See you soon."

After he left, she decided to check the programs he was considering. The Global Literacies program sounded amazing. International themes, engagement with global communities and educational systems, heavy on the technology. She switched to the leadership program—and again, it sounded great. Luke was exactly the kind of leader North Carolina ought to nurture and promote up the ranks.

The delivery method caught her eye. On campus. When were classes held? Nights? Weekends? Both?

She flipped back to the global program. Completely online.

Her husband was faced with a similar choice to hers. Busy either way—but one would be better for family balance. She'd included him in her decision. Would he include her in his?

◆ ◆ ◆

Jessica was planning to stop by Larkmoor Thursday on her way home from the TV station. Gathering her purse and iPad from her desk, she made her way through the building.

As she was passing Charlie's office, he gestured her over. When she walked in, she was surprised to see the news director sitting in the visitor's chair.

She had a sick feeling in the pit of her stomach. She'd submitted her application last night. Were they already letting her know it wasn't happening? Had "lie goals" been too big? Had the time she'd spent with her family been too much?

"Have a seat," Charlie said.

They both smiled, so probably nothing terrible. She smoothed her expression into a polite mask and perched on the edge of a credenza. "Yes?"

The news director hitched forward in her chair. "We got your application for the morning show, but we have two senior positions open."

"Two?" She'd only seen the one.

"Morning and evening."

Wait. "Evening? What about RJ?"

"He's accepted a new job in Charlotte," Charlie said. "He'll be leaving in two weeks. We'd like you to throw your hat in the ring for evening."

She looked at the two of them, trying to take in what they'd said. Senior producer for the evening news? "Really?"

"Yes." The news director smiled back at her.

"I . . . Wow . . ." Her heart was brimming with joy. "Are you sure?"

"Yes. Let us know by Tuesday," Charlie said.

She left their office and hurried out to her car in a fog of excitement. She loved working the evening news. She was sure she'd like morning news too, but the atmosphere wouldn't be the same. And senior producer in the evening was more prestigious. Her career plan hadn't accounted for such luck.

This was amazing. She couldn't wait to tell Luke.

Luke.

Oh no. He wouldn't view this as great news. He'd said he would support her, whatever decision she made, but he'd only known about the morning option. While a promotion to senior for the evening brought prestige, it also brought higher stress. Much higher. She'd have a similar schedule to what she had now but with many more hours. Was this what she wanted for herself? For her marriage? For their family?

She and Luke both had choices to make about their careers. Before raising the topic with him, she would have to formulate her thoughts about her decision—and his.

CHAPTER 36

Raine had been restless all day. Tonight, she'd go on her first date in five years. She'd exchanged texts with Ian a couple of days ago to ask for Reggie Highcamp's contact information. Ian had reminded her he'd be at the condo by seven on Saturday. As if she could forget.

And here she was, pretending to study litigation support, waiting for the clock to tick down. By five o'clock, her nerves were on fire. She jumped into the shower, trying to relax, then stayed so long she was in danger of shriveling. Fortunately, the hot water showed no signs of running out. So she remained, eyes closed, water sluicing down her body, thoughts churning.

What had she been thinking to accept a date? With a guy she'd met only a week ago?

Ian seemed like a nice guy, but her ex had seemed nice too. He hadn't been. *Nice* was not a word anyone would use to describe Coulter. *Enthralling, forceful,* or *relentless,* maybe. But not *nice*—as he'd proven so clearly.

What would he think if he knew how long it'd been since she'd gone on a date? Probably he'd be proud of his lasting effect on her. She could almost hear him taunting her. Of course a loner, a loser, a *freak* would drop off the relationship radar after one little misstep.

She still couldn't understand why she'd put up with the crap Coulter had dished out. Or why she hadn't listened to her grad school friends' warnings sooner. She was much happier single.

She should cancel.

Raine got out of the shower, dried off, and dragged on shorts and a shirt. Taking her phone with her out to the balcony, she sat on the love seat and brought up Ian's number. It would be best to call him and apologize. Tonight wasn't going to work.

But wouldn't it be good to finally move past whatever was blocking her?

Nope. Not fair to him. She should call.

But she didn't want to be reluctant forever, and he'd seemed like a good guy.

She glanced at the clock. It was later than she thought. He would be on his way. Decision made.

When the doorbell chimed, she was jittery. She opened the door. Ian was facing away, but he turned with a smile, radiating happiness. He wore Levi's and a green polo. He was freshly shaven, and his hair had been trimmed. He looked . . . really good.

As she stepped aside to let him in, her gaze locked on the huge magnolia bloom he was holding out to her. "Thank you. That's nice." Her heart clutched. *Nice* was too tame a word. The flower was amazing.

"My pleasure."

She sniffed at the bloom, breathed in the scent. Sweet and distinctive. No one had ever given flowers to her, not even herself.

It should go in water, right? Did she have a vase? If she did, it would be in the kitchen. She bolted there, away from Ian, face averted so he couldn't see how his gift had affected her.

One after the other, she banged open the cabinet doors. No vase. Of course not. She'd never needed one before. What could she use instead? She looked in more cabinets, frantically seeking a substitute. What kind of *freak* didn't even have a damn vase?

"Hey," Ian said. "What's wrong?"

Ignoring the question, she opened the pantry and frowned at the top shelf, the place where she stored useless things. It held a cut-glass pitcher. Another impractical Christmas gift from her mother. Ornate and completely un-Raine-like.

She shifted to the side, head bowed. "Can you get the vase?"

He lifted it down, crossed to the sink, added water. But when he reached for the magnolia, she shook her head, plopped the stem into the vase, and carried it to the table. For a long moment, she silently admired this alien bit of frivolity in her home.

"Raine?"

She wasn't ready to look at him. What would she see when she did? She was acting strange, and she couldn't help it. Would he be put off? A first date was too early for *strange*. Swallowing hard, she steeled herself. Glanced his way.

"Have I upset you?" he asked, his expression mild.

"No, I'm not used to . . ." She looked at the magnolia. Felt her face burn with embarrassment.

"Raine. Everything's okay. It's just you and me here."

She met his gaze. Breathed in what he'd said. Let it fill her. Just the two of them. The simple words reassured her. She could do this. She'd delivered enough *strange* for one date. "Okay." She tried to smile.

"Kenny approves of the idea of bringing you a flower."

That made her smile genuine. "Will you report back?"

"Next time I see him." Ian stuffed his hands in his pockets. "We're having an old-fashioned date. Kenny saw one on a *This Is Us* rerun and insisted."

"My uncle watches *This Is Us*?"

"He does, and he loves Beth best."

"Good to know." Her date showed no signs of wanting to leave. Of being spooked. She relaxed a bit more. "What will an old-fashioned date entail?"

"Manners, of course. They are key."

"Naturally."

"Plus dinner."

"Did he plan that too?"

"No, he left those details to me." Ian shoved his fists in his pockets. "There's no rain in the forecast, so I thought we could walk. It looks like there are plenty of places to eat nearby."

"Sounds good."

Ten minutes later, they were on the street, strolling toward a retail district with a variety of restaurant choices. The conversation started out light. Their summer plans. His studying for his nursing boards. Her progress toward her CFF exam.

They ended up at a pub but could only get a high-top table near the bar. They didn't speak until the server brought their drinks and took their order.

He sipped from his beer. "I passed along the message you sent about your grandmother. How is she?"

"Really confused. We're hoping that clears up." Mariah was back in her suite, unhappy and complaining. Raine had gone to visit earlier today, and it hurt to see how miserable and confused her grandmother was.

"A fractured hip at her age is serious."

"I know. I've researched, and that's how it sounded."

"The anesthesia can have an effect too. Her dementia might appear to worsen."

She hadn't heard that, but she would pay attention. "Thanks for telling me."

He watched her quietly for a moment, then asked, "Want to tell me what happened earlier?"

Honest and open. She approved, but she also wasn't ready. "Not yet, but thank you. Your response helped." She held his gaze. "Is it okay if we talk about something else?"

"Sure." He segued into sports, which lasted until their food arrived. Then he switched to a getting-to-know-you topic. "So tell me about forensic accounting. How did you get into it?"

Had he searched on First Date 101 like she had? Because asking the other person about their jobs or hobbies was at the top of the list. "I was at a public accounting firm, mostly doing forensic type work.

Valuations. Asset tracing. Then the pandemic hit, and the firm folded. I picked up some freelance projects in the interim and really liked the freedom of choosing my projects and clients. I have a home office. Three years later, I'm still at it." She grimaced. Here came the hard part. "Papa thought I should upgrade."

"To what?"

"Something that's not freelance."

"Is that a bad idea?"

"No."

"So what's the holdup?"

"Papa asked the same thing the last time I saw him. Basically, I had to let him know that fear was holding me back."

"Fear of what?"

Okay, wow. They were talking about feelings. Yet, surprisingly, she wanted Ian to understand. "Testifying in court. Being grilled in front of a live audience. Seeing the people whose lives I might be ruining with the conclusions I've made."

"It's okay to not be ready." Ian set down his beer and leaned forward. "I get that. It's something I'll worry about as a nurse. I could be the only person available to help a patient. What if I freeze up and do the wrong thing? But when I start wondering if I'll be good enough, I turn it around. What if I'm the person who saves them?"

Raine straightened, struck by what he'd said. Her thoughts had tiptoed around that same contrast before, but never in such a stark way. What if, instead of financial ruin, she was the person who restored a lifestyle?

"Thank you. That . . . makes me think." She'd told Ian about her job fears, which she never did. Not even to her family, unless they dragged it from her. But with Ian, it had just come out. He'd empathized. Not ridiculed. Not judged.

She was moving from curious to interested, and it scared her. Maybe her relationship fears would be too much for a first date, but if he wasn't interested back, she'd rather shut things down now than invest in a relationship and lose him a few dates later. She'd had all the personal loss she could handle for a while. "I haven't dated anyone in five years."

"Well, then, thank you for taking a chance on me," he said, apparently not put off by the topic. "Can I ask why?"

"The last one was a total jerk." She frowned at her beer.

"I've had bad relationships. I get that."

"He fooled me."

"He *hurt* you, and that's on him."

She looked up. Ian was right. She shouldn't blame herself for the way Coulter had treated her. She hadn't invited it. She'd just . . . taken too long to wake up. "Okay, I didn't want to be hurt again, so it's been easier not to date."

He smiled slowly. "Are we dating?"

Did she have a deer-in-the-headlights look on her face? Because it sure felt like that. What was she doing? Should she put on the brakes? "I think dating requires three dates."

"Let's call the meal at Roonie's our first date, which makes this the second." He grinned. "Our next date will make it official."

She smiled, not agreeing exactly, but it gave her more to think about.

After dinner, they walked back to her condo, a slight distance between them as they listened to the laughter from neighborhood bars and whoops from students at the nearby university. When she stumbled on a piece of uneven sidewalk, Ian gripped her arm firmly. She gently disengaged but sent him a smile of thanks.

When they reached her building, he stopped on the sidewalk and faced her, his stance that of someone about to say good night. Outside. No uncomfortable moment at her door. Ian was just about perfect.

"Thank you," she said. "Tonight was great."

"For me too." He smiled uncertainly. "Can I kiss you?"

She didn't know whether he was a naturally tuned-in guy or if he was reading her extraordinarily well, but she was choosing *yes*. Resting her hands on his shoulders, she leaned closer, felt his hands at her waist. Their lips clung for hardly longer than a breath. One brief, sweet, awesome kiss.

Their evening together had been simple and fun and the best date of her life. Ian had called it their second date. It wasn't, really, but it must mean he was in it for actual dating. Was she? It was a big step for her. Big, scary, and . . . *good*. Before she lost the courage, she asked, "Will you go out with me?"

He clenched his fist in victory. "*Yes.*"

Oh wow. He was so excited. She laughed. So happy. "How about Thursday?"

"Thursday works." He grinned. "You ask, you plan."

"Of course." She was already thinking through the possibilities. "I'll text you the details."

"Or call."

"That too." She wanted to kiss him again, but Thursday would be soon enough. Anticipation would make the heart grow fonder. "I'll definitely call."

CHAPTER 37

Jessica had signed up for the Saturday evening shift with Mima. When she arrived in her suite, Mom was dropping keys and a paperback into her purse.

She looked up and smiled faintly. "Hi, sweetie."

"How is she?" Jessica asked.

"Asleep." Mom stood and stretched. "She's probably out for the night."

They crossed to the bedroom. Mima lay in bed, breathing evenly, bed rails pulled up protectively around her. The room was dim, lit only by a night-light on the opposite wall.

"They have a bed alarm on if she attempts to get out," Mom said quietly. "You don't have to stay."

Jessica wouldn't mind reclaiming an evening at home. "Are you sure?"

"Yes. Go home to Luke."

She looked at her grandmother, resting so peacefully. "What do they say about her recovery?"

Mom leaned her head wearily against the doorframe. "Physically, okay. She's not happy about the PT, but she is doing some and they say her progress is fine. But mentally?" She shook her head. "She's barely speaking and seems to be even more confused."

"What does that mean?"

"They're hoping that it's temporary. It'll take a few days to know more." Mom pushed from the wall and turned. "I'm leaving. I could use a good night's rest."

"I'll walk out with you."

They went to the parking lot together in silence. Jessica's stress heightened with each step. Should she say something about meeting her uncle? Or was it too soon? Mom was already struggling with Mima's health concerns.

"Luke said you and Raine were out together, doing a sister-bonding thing Sunday." Their mother smiled as she stopped beside her car. "I'm glad to hear that."

Mom had made an opening, and Jessica would take it. She hoped she wouldn't regret this. "We were at Alder Creek, visiting Kenny."

"*No.*" Mom stared at her in wide-eyed horror. "No, no, no."

"We have to talk about it."

"No, Jessica. *No.*" She blinked back tears. "Why couldn't you leave this alone?"

"We told you we wouldn't give up."

"I can't bear this. It's too much." Mom wrenched the car door open, slid onto the seat, and rested her forehead against the steering wheel. "My mother is lying in that room," she said on a sob, "recovering from surgery. Hip fractures are hard on the elderly. Do you get that?"

"Yes—"

"Stop. I won't talk about this." The car door slammed. Mom reversed and pulled away.

Jessica got in her car and sent an update to Raine.

I tried to talk with Mom about Kenny tonight. You were right.
She refused

Sorry. That'll slow us down. Not stop us

Before she could text Luke, her phone rang. The station.

"Jessica, we need help, and you're up."

"Okay. I'll be there in fifteen minutes." After she ended the call, she shook her head. It was the first time she'd been called in since a snowstorm in December. She sent a message to her husband.

On my way to the station. I've been called in

Okay. Keep me posted

I will

◆ ◆ ◆

Jessica spent a lot of hours at the TV station Memorial Day weekend. A state senator had drowned at the beach Saturday. The holiday weekend traffic had netted a higher-than-usual number of accidents and traffic pileups. When she returned to the town house on Monday night, she was almost numb from exhaustion. She was on the screened-in porch, sipping a glass of wine, when Luke came out.

"Hey," he said. "Want company?"

She shifted over on the glider so he could sit beside her.

"Tough weekend?"

She nodded.

He grinned. "If you're too tired to talk, we can just sit here."

"No, I'll catch you up." She filled him in on Mariah's health. The tension with her mother. And the newest update on the family secret. "I've talked with Reggie Highcamp."

"How'd that go?"

"Not as well as I'd hoped. He seemed off. I'm not sure if it was the natural aversion of an eighty-three-year-old to a Zoom meeting, or if he was hedging his answers because he was uncomfortable with the truth. I think he knows more."

"So you'll try again?"

"Yes. Raine thinks we should consider doing an in-person inter-view. It might help him relax to talk with people in his own home."

"Raine suggested that? As in flying to Dallas?" At Jessica's nod, he laughed. "Do you know how much she hates flying?"

Jessica hadn't known. Well, if her sister was serious, Jessica would be hearing from her soon. "We'll see. I'm definitely curious about what he's holding back." She was weary, and the wine was loosening her tongue. Since she'd been worrying about Luke's grad program for days, she ought to get it out there. "Over Guard weekend, you said our rela-tionship needed an overhaul."

He turned to her, tensing. "Yes, I'd like us to spend more time together."

Why had she started this? She was worn out and vulnerable. But it was on now. She had to see it through. "I don't have enough time for you during the week. And you don't have enough for me on the weekend."

"One weekend per month." There was an irritated edge to his voice.

"Sometimes two," she added. Might as well put it all out there. "Charlie called me into his office again."

"A decision already?"

She shook her head. "To let me know a second senior position has come available. For the evening news."

Luke coughed. Stood. Stalked over to the opposite side of the porch. "Same schedule you have now, except longer hours."

"Yes." She rose too, but remained on her side of the porch. Lights spilling from the house made it easy to see. "I have until tomorrow to let him know if I'm interested."

Luke crossed his arms. "Are you asking my opinion?"

"I'm confident you don't like the idea." She raised her chin. It was time to let him know what was really bothering her. "I looked up the two programs you're interested in for grad school. The delivery methods are significant."

"One's on campus. The other's online." He paused. Thought. Shook his head. "Okay, I get what you're driving at."

She waited for more, but when he remained silent, she asked, "Are you still leaning toward the leadership degree?"

"It'll open more opportunities."

"And take time away from us." For so long, she'd felt guilty about how much she worked, but no more. They shared the blame. "I sometimes feel as if you think my job is the problem. That if I would just choose to come home sooner, I could."

He narrowed his eyes at her. "What's this all about?"

"The overhaul isn't one sided."

"I never said it was." His face slipped into a blank mask. "I'll give what you've said some thought," he said quietly, then went inside.

She quashed the urge to follow him. *Don't push.*

For her, the morning show option would be a good decision for her career and her marriage. The evening position would be fabulous for her career and wrong for her marriage. When she thought of it that way, the choice was clear. She would choose the morning option for *them.* If only she could be sure that Luke would choose them too.

CHAPTER 38

Jessica had told her sister that if she was serious about the in-person interview with Reggie, it would have to wait until the May ratings period was done. So it shouldn't have surprised her when she received a text from Raine a few days later.

Reggie suggested a week from Saturday. Ok?

It was Luke's drill weekend, which was perfect.

Yes, if we can do same-day travel

On it

Raine made all the arrangements and forwarded the details an hour later.

The following Saturday, they arrived in Dallas on an early-morning flight, rode the light-rail into the heart of the city, got off near Dealey Plaza, and emerged from a wind tunnel of tall buildings into one of the most infamous corners on earth. Elm at Houston.

Standing there, Jessica felt an incredible sense of loss on behalf of their country. But knowing Mariah had witnessed that horrible moment in history—and the domino effect it had on their family—made the loss more personal.

Her sister nodded toward the Sixth Floor Museum. "Our tour starts at ten. Let's take a look from the grassy knoll before we go in."

Jessica dutifully followed her sister up the hill. The area was crawling with tourists, all murmuring in respectful tones. Gesturing, staring, shuddering. It was still holy ground.

They took in the white *X*s painted on Elm Street, the traffic as cars gained speed before disappearing from view under the bridge. Jessica didn't look at the plaza across from her. Wasn't ready to pinpoint the exact location where her grandmother's life had taken its dramatic turn.

The sisters spent an hour going through the museum, immersing themselves in the Kennedy era. Jessica's emotional response became so intense she looked away from the exhibits, observing instead people from all cultures, locked in this same experience.

Afterward, she and Raine took the elevator down and exited into the hot, bright city. Her sister led them to Dealey Plaza, searching for the spot where Mariah had stood so long ago. It was on the slope, with a clear line of sight.

"Wow," Raine said.

Jessica nodded, her throat too tight to speak. Their grandmother had been a pregnant, unwed teen in 1963, expecting a joyful event. But she'd witnessed horror instead. If the assassination had happened in the twenty-first century, Mariah could've sought therapy. Allowed others to help her heal. But that kind of mental health care wouldn't have been available to her in the sixties. Jessica ached for the girl her grandmother had been.

"All right, I've taken in as much as I can," Raine said. "Lunch, then Reggie's."

◆　◆　◆

Reggie's home was in an upper-middle-class neighborhood of newish houses with manicured yards. He awaited them on a covered stoop, a tall man with thinning hair, the Highcamp blue eyes, and deeply tanned skin. He was in his eighties but looked younger by a decade.

"Hello, Mr. Highcamp," she said. "We're Jessica and Raine Elliott."

"Reggie. Nice to meet ya." He ushered them through the house to a family room with tiled floors, photos crowding the mantel, and sliding glass doors overlooking a small garden.

"Tea?" He indicated a pitcher beside a plate of brownies.

Jessica accepted a glass, more from politeness than desire, surprised by how nervous she was. "Thank you for letting us come."

"Glad to help." He sprawled in an overstuffed chair, relaxed. A good sign.

"Reggie, are you okay if I record our conversation?"

"Go ahead." As Jessica set up her phone, he asked, "How's Kenny?"

"He's great."

"Yeah. He always was." Reggie looked them over, nodding as if he'd found the answer to a mystery. "So you're Mariah and Gregor's granddaughters?"

"We are. You knew our grandfather?"

"Well enough. They came here often after Hal's wife died." He pronounced *wife* with a caustic edge. "I woulda been happy to take Kenny in if anything happened to Hal. But Mariah and Gregor wanted him. Kenny was a little nervy about leaving Texas, but in the end, he wanted to live near them."

"What about before Ida Mae died?" Raine asked.

"That was trickier. Mariah visited sometimes, but that mostly stayed a secret. Ida Mae would've blown a gasket."

Jessica wanted to know more about the shadowy Ida Mae Highcamp. "What was Ida Mae like?"

"She was a piece of work." His gaze fixed on something in the yard. "But she loved Kenny. I had my problems with Ida, but I have to admit she was devoted to him. She and Hal were proud of him, and they shoulda been. Kenny's a great guy. Full of personality. And great with cars. When Hal got his auto restoration business going, Kenny was his main detailer."

Jessica was poised to ask questions if needed, but Reggie was doing well on his own.

"Back then, the schools didn't have much patience with kids like Kenny. But President Kennedy had seen to making changes. Kenny went to special classes. He could read and write and do some math. Ida and Hal worked with him until he graduated."

Jessica waited a moment before holding out a black-and-white photo of the two couples.

He took it. Smoothed a finger across his lips. "Mariah was an angel, but she was so young. Naïve. Her parents had her too damn sheltered. She didn't know anything about anything, and she and Hal were dirt poor. Once they knew the baby was on the way, it got even harder.

"My parents never gave her a chance, 'specially my father. He was furious that Hal brought a girl with him. It didn't help she weren't a Christian. Their attitude burned my butt."

"Not a Christian?" The phrase burst from Jessica before she could stop it. Her grandmother had converted to the Armenian Apostolic Church at marriage, but she'd been raised in the Roman Catholic Church. "My grandmother was Catholic."

"That didn't count back then. Not unless you were born again." He gave a soft snort. "Mariah was gorgeous. Sweet. Bubbling over with joy. All the guys wanted her. Hal wasn't even jealous. She adored him. He adored her back. Which made it so awful—" Reggie picked up his glass of tea and stared into its depths. His hand trembled.

Raine threw Jessica a glance. Took over. "The president's assassination changed everything."

"Yeah. They'd gone downtown to get married."

The sisters stiffened in shock.

"November twenty-second should've been her wedding day?" Raine asked.

He nodded. "She wanted the baby raised Catholic. She held out until Hal finally gave in and set the date for the very next Friday. They stopped at Dealey Plaza on the way to the courthouse. I'm sure Mariah was beside herself with excitement. Then they got there . . ." His face creased into grim lines. "When Hal heard the gunshots, he did what any man would do for his woman. He threw her to the ground. Covered her body with his. Kenny shoulda been a Christmas baby, but he came a few hours later. A month early. Hal blamed himself." Reggie cleared his throat. Stared at a spot on the carpet.

Jessica waited, giving him time to compose himself. When the silence stretched, she asked, "What kind of relationship did our grandmother have with Hal afterward?"

He inhaled a whistling breath. "It was sad. You could see them cracking. They couldn't shake it."

"About what happened to the baby?"

"They didn't really believe what the doctors said about Kenny. Nah, it was the assassination they couldn't shake. What they saw that day broke their relationship. Nearly broke each of them. They both refused to talk about what happened at Dealey. We'd call it PTSD now." Reggie scratched his jaw and sank into his memories. "After she went to North Carolina, Hal wouldn't let people say bad things about her. He wasn't bitter. Just . . . sad."

"How often did he hear from Mariah?"

"Regular like. Pretty near every month, she sent letters and money. Mostly to my address, so she could be confident Hal'd get them. She couldn't be sure that Ida Mae would pass 'em along."

Jessica wanted to drill into that relationship. He'd alluded to it twice now. Maybe he was ready to go deeper. "Tell us about Hal and Ida Mae."

Reggie shook his head. "They just up and got married at the court-house one day." He rubbed his chin, as if it pained him. "Ida wasn't the only one keeping secrets. Hal didn't tell her about Kenny's disabilities. Babies had jaundice all the time, and the doctors couldn't know how it would turn out for Kenny. Mariah left before anyone could see how it affected him. Hal loved Kenny just the way he was, and so did Ida. I'll give her that." He looked out the window. Bounced to his feet. "My wife has some prized rosebushes. Want to see?"

When Jessica stood, Raine did too. The man had made it through an emotional explanation. He needed a break. "Yes, sir."

They followed him outside, listening politely as he described the types of roses. Then they moved on to his tiny patch of a vegetable garden, seemingly unaware of the hot Texas sun beating down on them. When his phone buzzed, he said, "'Scuse me a minute," and started back toward the house.

"How do you think it's going?" Jessica asked.

"Good," Raine said. "We're getting new information, although he hasn't volunteered anything about why Mariah and Hal split. I'll ask."

When they reentered the house, Reggie had poured more tea and added grapes to the brownie tray. "That was my wife. She'll be home in fifteen minutes." He picked up his glass.

"Reggie," Raine started, "can you tell us why Mariah left?"

"It wasn't like their split was planned. It just . . . happened." Reggie drained half of his tea. Inhaled a big breath, preparing himself. "Mariah had a terrible time after Kenny was born. Bills and chores and a baby who needed a lot of holding. She had the worst case of baby blues I ever seen. They might call it postpartum depression now, but back then, we didn't know what the problem was." He shook his head sadly. "So there was Mariah, desperately needing help, and no one would give her any. Hal wasn't okay either, but he went to work each day. Hard, physical work. Got stuff out of his system. Mariah spent all her time in that tiny duplex taking care of the baby. She was wasting away, sad, lonely, and sick. It was pitiful. Then her brother came for a couple of days, and she perked up. Afterward, though, it made her worse. She'd been so happy while he was there, then right back to sad, lonely, and sick.

"Anyways, one day she decided she wanted to see the beach. Didn't warn anyone. She just went." He shook his head again. "To Galveston."

Jessica reached for her sister's wrist, accepting the lead. "What happened?"

Reggie rubbed his face with both hands. "Mariah got stuck there. Her purse was stolen, and she didn't have the money to get back. Hal didn't know where she was, so he didn't know to go get her."

"She didn't call?"

"Oh, she did, but Hal never received the messages. She got home a couple of days later and showed up at the station. They talked. Not angry. Just . . . sad. Then they kissed, and he asked her to move out." Reggie's eyes grew soft. Distant.

"What did she do next?"

"She stayed with me for a while. When I drove her to their apartment to pick up a change of clothes, I stayed in the truck while she went inside. Ida was in there with the baby. Mariah came back out again all upset." He stopped. "Then there was Palm Sunday . . ."

His face reddened. "My parents were having a picnic. Invited family and friends. But not her. I was so ashamed. Couldn't even face her. Well, she came anyway. She looked . . . terrible. Wrinkled dress. No stockings. No makeup. Hair all wild. The whispers started. That she was plumb crazy. She walked off with Kenny, and Hal followed. He convinced her that she was a danger to Kenny. Hal wasn't letting her near their son again till she got herself together. And she had to leave my place, 'cause my girlfriend didn't like her staying there. Mariah looked back at us, and you could tell from her face that she'd lost all hope.

"And that was it. When I got back to my apartment, she'd left a note saying she'd gone home."

Raine frowned. "She left without a fight?"

He shot her a disapproving glare. "Young lady, you don't know what it was like back then. Pa threatened to call the cops on her. If they'd come, they coulda locked her up and thrown away the key. That might've been what broke her. She had nothing left to fight with." He shrugged. "Hal changed his mind 'bout a week after Mariah left. He came over kinda frantic and begged me to tell him where she was, but I didn't know. It was another week before the first letter showed up. After that, they rolled in steadily, and I handed 'em over."

So much had gone wrong, piling on relentlessly. Jessica said, "Ida Mae sent a letter to my grandfather when Kenny was eight."

"Yeah. Ironic, that." A faint smile curled his lip. "Ida created her own downfall. They had a good life before she sent that letter, but I guess she couldn't resist.

"Hal was at work the day Gregor showed up. I answered the phone when Ida called to say they had a visitor.

"Hal had been worried about her. Her liver was failing, and Kenny was getting to be too much. Ma had been going over there to pitch in. But no, that wasn't good enough for Ida. She thought Mariah shoulda been paying more. What Ida didn't know was that Mariah gave her brother's life insurance money to Hal, and he'd saved it.

"But the joke was on Ida. When Hal told Gregor about his dream to own a business restoring old cars, Gregor made an investment. Between that and the money from Mariah, Hal got his wish. Did real good at it." Reggie smiled. "Gregor was a fine man. Kenny took to him too.

"After Gregor left that day, Hal confessed to Ida that he and Mariah were planning to bring the families together at Christmas. That they'd been in regular contact. All those years, she'd sent money, and they'd exchanged pictures and letters.

"Ida Mae died a few weeks later. Finding out how much Mariah had remained in the picture? It took some of the joy from Ida Mae's final days. For that, I'm sorry."

CHAPTER 39

January 1973

Four months had passed since Gregor had learned about Kenny and moved out. He still wasn't speaking to her, other than the minimum required to arrange Stephanie's schedule.

Mariah and her daughter were sitting on the front steps of the house, bundled in a blanket, waiting for Gregor to pick Stephanie up for the evening. She'd insisted on being outside fifteen minutes early. She didn't want to miss a second with her father.

"Mama," Stephanie said, patting her arm, "when will Daddy move into our house again?"

"I don't know. I hope soon."

"Me too. He's sad. Like you."

Tears stung Mariah's eyes, and she blinked them away. "I miss him. Very much."

Stephanie leaned into her side and whispered, "Sometimes, daddies never come back."

She wanted to reassure her daughter that he'd be back, but she didn't know. He wouldn't talk to her. Wouldn't listen to her explanation. And she was guilty. In hindsight, the reasons seemed feeble. She could've told him so many times about those hard first months of

Kenny's life, why she'd left, and why she'd chosen to remain silent. She hadn't trusted Gregor to do the right thing.

The Cadillac pulled into the driveway and idled. Gregor stepped out and met his daughter halfway, swinging her high in the air. "How are you, pumpkin?"

"Good. What are we doing tonight?"

Mariah didn't catch what he said as he buckled their daughter into a seat, then straightened and shut the door. "We'll be back by seven thirty."

"Okay." She smiled, loving the sight of him. "Have a good time." She went inside and into her parlor, dropped into her rocker, and stared out the bay window at the gathering dusk.

Ida Mae had passed away in November. Gregor had attended the funeral alone.

Mariah had flown to Dallas at Christmas, but without her daughter or husband. It had been good to openly visit her son, even though he'd been sad and quiet. She still hoped for a reunion for them all.

If only Gregor would come home.

When the mantel clock tolled half past seven, the front door banged open, and Stephanie's excited voice rang through the foyer. "Daddy. Will you come tomorrow?"

He glanced into the parlor and met Mariah's gaze. "Of course, as I promised."

Feet thumped down the stairs to the lower level. "Daddy, will you tuck me in bed?"

"Yes, pumpkin."

"I don't have to take a bath 'cause I already had one . . ."

Their voices faded.

Mariah rocked, incapable of concentrating with her husband so near. It had been this way for the four months of their separation. He was the model father, picking Stephanie up often from school, spending time with her at the library or park. Sometimes preparing her a meal in his apartment and helping her with her homework. But he always brought her back to the house so she could sleep in her own bed. He never stayed to say anything to Mariah other than ensuring they had what they needed. Polite and impersonal. It hurt to have her husband treat her as if she were nothing more than an acquaintance.

Socializing had become awkward. Friends stopped inviting her after a while, which was really for the best. She hadn't heard he was dating again, but stumbling across him with another woman would be intolerable.

She'd had the good luck to fall for two wonderful men. She'd lost them both through her own efforts. With Hal, her mistakes had been the result of pain in her body and mind, of being unable to think straight. In attempting to make herself feel better, she'd made everything worse.

But she didn't have that excuse with Gregor. She'd chosen her mistakes. She'd been clearheaded about deceiving him—because she feared.

Gregor's tread thudded with measured force up the stairs. She looked into the foyer, waiting for him to pass, holding her breath. A floorboard creaked. A light flickered, its glow faint in the hall. Gregor had gone to his study.

He hadn't left immediately. Why? It was unusual, but she wasn't ready to hope. She walked into the foyer. Glass clinked. His old leather chair squeaked. She went to the study door, hands clasped to her waist. He sat in a wingback chair, swirling whiskey in a tumbler, watching the doorway as if he'd been expecting her. The silence was broken only by the ticking of a clock. If anything was said, it would have to come from her.

For the first time in months, he'd remained in her presence. She had to make him listen. They'd had a beautiful family and a beautiful marriage before she'd broken it. She'd do whatever it took to make things right. "I'm sorry I deceived you."

He sipped from his glass, waiting for more.

"I could never think of how to tell you."

"You're an articulate woman. It would seem that sometime in the seven years of our marriage, you could've found the right words."

"The truth is bigger than me. Bigger than Kenny."

"What is the truth?"

"I doubt I know everything." She only knew her side. But not Hal's or Ida Mae's or the other Highcamps'.

"I doubt you do too."

How much did he know of their stories? Would he tell them to her? She wanted to understand. "My story is long and twisted. If you'll hear it, I'll tell you." She had so many regrets. But as difficult as it would be to remember, she couldn't wait to share it with him.

He poured more whiskey in his glass and set the decanter down. His gaze never left hers. "I flew to Dallas last week."

That shocked her. "Why?"

"From your perspective, the outcome was good. I've had many long conversations with Hal. It would seem everyone has secrets." Gregor tossed back the rest of his whiskey, set it with precision on a leather coaster, and rose. "Anything else before I go?"

Her heart fluttered with fear. He might reject her, but she had to try. "Please move home."

His eyebrows rose. "Why?"

"I miss you." *I love you.*

"That's not reason enough."

Hal had said something similar right before she left Texas. She'd fought too feebly. She wouldn't repeat the mistake of not trying hard enough. Of giving in too soon. "Stephanie misses you. She needs you in her life every morning and every evening. She's innocent in this."

"I miss her as well. Our visits only make me wish for more." He rubbed his face, his sigh heavy in the silence. "We can't go back to the way we were, Mariah."

"I know." Was he considering it? She was afraid to hope.

"I'll give it thought." He walked across the study and past her with deliberation. The front door clicked shut seconds later.

Her shaky legs buckled, and she fell into a chair, a fist pressed to her mouth to hold back a sob. His absence had been an endless nightmare. The days had been busy. There was much to do with her role with the school merger. With Stephanie. But the nights? They'd been sad. Longing for her husband. Her best friend. She'd missed his wisdom, laughter, and love. If only he would come back, she would do whatever he asked.

◆　◆　◆

It had been a week since Mariah had asked Gregor to move home. He had Stephanie tonight. She'd spent most of the evening at a meeting downtown about the school system merger, not wanting to be in an empty house.

When she returned, they were already there. He'd pulled his car into his half of the garage. After turning off her car, she sat motionless, listening to the engine tick as it cooled, not daring to believe. Had he come home?

Please.

As she went down the stairs, she heard Stephanie shouting from her bedroom. "Daddy, when will you read with me?"

"Soon," he answered from their bedroom.

What was he doing in there? Mariah gripped the banister, hardly able to breathe. Hope had been a fickle friend. She needed proof before she could give in.

Stopping in the doorway, she watched Gregor remove T-shirts from a suitcase and place them in a drawer. Her chest heaved with the effort to take in a breath. Was he back? Oh please, let him be back.

When he turned and saw her, he paused. "I'm home," he said quietly.

She choked on a sob. "For Stephanie's sake?"

"And ours."

A wave of relief and joy surged through her. She clutched the door-frame for support and fought to get through the next moments with her dignity intact. "I love you."

He moved to her, caught her against him, and covered her mouth with his, the taste of his favorite whiskey mixing with the salt of her tears.

They broke apart, breathing hard.

"I have missed you," she said. "My best love."

He kissed her again.

"Daddy!"

He drew away. "I must tend to Stephanie."

"Don't take long."

"I won't." He stepped back. "I'll return in ten minutes."

"To talk?"

"We'll talk tomorrow, and you'll tell me everything, Mariah. What you did. How you felt. What you regret and why. I want to know it all."

"Gladly." Speaking of her time in Texas would be hard. Honesty wouldn't come easily. "Will we start the conversation tonight?"

"No." He smiled, his gaze heating. "Tonight is for touch. Words can wait."

Mariah awakened to a lingering kiss. She was almost afraid to open her eyes and have the magic return to her former reality, but the second kiss reassured her.

"Good morning, my heart. My wife."

She smiled and stretched and looked into her husband's beloved face. "Morning."

"Stay. I'll get Stephanie to school." He brushed a finger against her lips. "We'll talk when I return. I will hear the truth."

"I agree." And she did. She would be relieved when they were on the other side of this discussion. But having it? The telling would be torture.

He straightened, already dressed in slacks and a button-down shirt. Not work clothes. Once he'd disappeared into the hallway, he called out, "Let's go, pumpkin."

She rolled to her side. Gregor was everything to her. Joy and sorrow. Pride and pain. Now he would be alongside her as she came to peace with the past.

The garage door whined up and then down. She slipped from bed, put on a robe, and went upstairs to the kitchen. The coffee machine held a full pot. In the sink sat a single bowl with the chocolatey-milk remains of Coco Pops. So Gregor had indulged their daughter, but he hadn't eaten. She scrounged in the refrigerator for omelet fixings and had them ready when he returned.

He came into the kitchen and straight to her, then kissed her brow. "Thank you."

She nodded, not trusting herself to speak.

"Shall we eat in the sunroom?"

She nodded again.

"Then we talk."

They carried plates and coffee out. He ate while she picked at her eggs. When he finally set down his fork, she set down hers. He stood, offered his hand, and led her to the sunroom's glider. They sat side by side, facing the backyard.

She didn't want to do this, but she'd promised. "When I look back, it's as if the memories are dim and out of focus. As if I'm a spectator rather than a participant. From the moment we took Kenny home from the hospital, I was locked in fear. Afraid of everything. Eating. Sleeping. Driving. Waking him up. Dropping him."

Gregor gave a grunt of surprise.

"Yes, it was strange. My arms would grow weary, and I'd imagine dropping him. So I paced by the couch." She laid her head against his shoulder. "Then Stephen came, and it was wonderful. After he left, it got even worse. Hal babysat one night, to give me an evening off. I got on a bus and didn't get off until I reached the beach."

"Galveston."

She nodded. "I don't remember making the decision, as if something else controlled my brain. Once I returned to Dallas, they'd all decided I was crazy. They convinced me that I was a danger to Kenny."

"Ah, Mariah, you would never harm him."

"I agree, but I couldn't take the risk." She told Gregor briefly of taking a bus to North Carolina, seeking help from her mother and being rejected. How fate stepped in. "So I stayed in Raleigh, and Elsie Bridges took me in." If Mariah closed her eyes, she could still see the two of them, rocking on the porch, talking her way to healing.

"Why didn't you go back?"

"It took me a long time to get well. My body felt better before my mind. Hal and I would mail back and forth. Then he got married." That had set her back so much. "I would ask to see Kenny. Hal would say *not yet.*"

"Why?" Gregor took her hand.

"Kenny was afraid of strangers. It hurt so much to hear my child scream when I came near, a stranger to my own son." She looked up at her husband. "Then I met you, and you were so kind. You treated me like I mattered. I needed that." Her eyes stung, and she looked away. She couldn't watch him when she made her next admission. "I made a mistake by not telling you the truth before we married."

"Indeed."

"I'm sorry. I will always be sorry." She licked her lips. Another admission. "I've been to visit Kenny several times over the years." His eyebrow rose, but he didn't speak. "We're pen pals."

"So I've heard." Gregor wrapped an arm around her and pulled her close. "Hal has given me details you don't know. He has many regrets. About who he listened to. What he said. How he reacted. He assures me that you've stayed in touch. Hal claims you sent your inheritance from Stephen."

She nodded.

"His wife didn't know that." He smiled lightly. "Hal bears you no ill will. He regards you fondly."

He should. They hadn't destroyed their relationship. It had been ground down by other forces, too weak to survive. They were at peace with each other, and she could prove it. She stood. "I'll be right back."

She went into the parlor. From the bottom drawer of her desk, she lifted out a hatbox, carried it out to the sunroom, and handed it to her husband.

"What's this?" He opened it.

She didn't answer. He would learn soon enough.

He thumbed through folded letters. Drew out a stack of photographs of Kenny. Gregor flipped over the top snapshot.

November 22, 1972

"His ninth birthday?"

"Yes. I get several photos a year, but always a birthday shot."

Photo by photo, he looked, one from each of Kenny's birthdays. When Gregor reached 1967, he stopped, gasped, and rubbed his face, the photo slipping from his hand.

The picture from Kenny's fourth birthday was her favorite. Her treasure. After all, she'd taken it.

"You went with Stephanie."

"Yes."

He flipped through the rest, then set them neatly in the hatbox and restored the lid. "How can you bear being apart from him?"

"How does any unwed mother bear knowing someone else is taking care of her child? You must convince yourself that what you're doing is best for *him*."

His eyes were incredulous. "Do you believe that's true?"

"Yes."

He cleared his throat. Took a breath. "Did you leave him because he was disabled?"

"When I left, he was a baby, and I was nineteen. The doctors had warned us of what *might* happen, but I hadn't seen any signs yet. I didn't believe . . ." She stared at her clenched hands. If she looked at Gregor, she couldn't make it through this next part. "There were so many reasons to leave. None of them were enough by themselves. But piled on together, they were more than the girl I was could fight."

"Your son was born on the day President Kennedy was assassinated."

"We were there."

He gasped. "Who was where?"

The words ached in her throat. She'd never spoken them before. "Hal and I. We were there at Dealey Plaza. We saw everything."

"Oh, my love." He drew her onto his lap, cradled her in his arms. "Do not hide your secrets anymore. Tell me all."

She'd never told anyone the whole story before, but with Gregor, it poured out. Raw and horrifying. But she managed to falter through it until the very end. "I was smiling at Mrs. Kennedy, and she was waving at me. Then—" The words choked her.

He hugged her tighter. "The memories are burned into your soul, and not only the sights. You cannot forget the sounds. The smells. The feel."

She nodded, tears squeezing past her defenses. "I couldn't stop thinking about it. Every time I closed my eyes, I relived those minutes. Hal and I . . . just couldn't escape its grip. He said it ruined us."

"I understand."

She looked up into his eyes and recognized the sheen of remembered horror. "How?"

"I have fought in a war, my love. I lost many friends. I saw them . . . go."

Korea. Of course. He would understand. She rested her cheek against his chest. "We are forever changed."

"Indeed," he said. "But we don't have to yield."

CHAPTER 40

Raine could see how much the interview was costing Reggie. He'd already shared much they hadn't known, and he'd been honest, even about his own culpability. It was time to go.

She exchanged a glance with her sister and nodded in unspoken agreement. While Jessica did the kind of small talk to politely wrap things up, Raine called for a Lyft. A car was five minutes out.

An hour later, she and her sister were sitting in an airport bar, each nursing a glass of wine.

"We learned a lot." Jessica toyed with her glass.

"Especially about Mariah's mental health issues," Raine said. "I've done some searching on the internet. Mental health care back then, especially for women, sounds pretty horrible. And Mariah was a poor teen mother all alone with her baby. She almost certainly had PTSD from witnessing the assassination and possibly postpartum depression. If Hal's family had turned her in, she could've been committed to a mental hospital or given electric shock treatments. Mariah might have been fleeing the possibility of that."

"But I still wonder if she gave up too easily."

Raine tensed. She didn't want to talk about this, but she had to, or Jessica wouldn't get it. "Have you ever been depressed?"

Her sister shook her head.

"Then you can't understand." How could she explain this to someone who'd never experienced it? "Depression is a beast. It makes you believe things that aren't true. It robs you of your will. Your hope. Depression is hard enough to defeat *with* help. I can't imagine fighting it on my own."

She felt a hand on her arm. An offer of comfort? She closed her eyes and nodded.

"Okay," Jessica said. "Maybe Mariah realized she needed help, so she went home to get it."

"But either she didn't stay in Scottsburg or never got there." Their grandmother had been nineteen, depressed, and scared. She hadn't known what was happening with her mental health and had nowhere to go. How must that have felt? "Her father would've refused her."

"Maybe," Jessica said slowly, "it was her mother. That would explain why they were never really close again. When Mariah needed her mother most, Lorraine rejected her."

A plausible and sad possibility. "But Mariah would've recovered eventually. Why didn't she return to Texas?"

"Reggie said there were secret visits."

"Yeah, and he also said that Hal and Mariah were planning some kind of reunion for Christmas 1972. But I don't get why they waited until Kenny was nine to create a more open relationship between his families." Raine frowned into space, trying to organize the new information into a logical explanation, but the facts stubbornly refused to align. "Why didn't Mariah insist on telling her son-in-law sooner? And why did she never tell us?"

They both took a sip of their wine.

When had Mariah told Mom? They had to ask and make Mom answer. "When we first talked about this, you said there might not be good reasons, but there could be varying degrees of bad. So what are the degrees of bad?"

"The worst, she didn't want to be the mother of a disabled child."

Raine shuddered. "I don't want that to be true."

Jessica was shaking her head. "I don't think it is. She threw her life into supporting special education."

"Atonement?"

"Sure, but it has to be more than that. She stayed in politics for twenty-five years."

Raine groaned. "I'm ready to move on to a less-bad reason. Postpartum depression can last up to a year. And untreated PTSD can last a lifetime."

"Maybe by the time she knew she was well, she decided it was too late to be part of his life."

"Or the Highcamps wouldn't let her come near him."

"Hal did, though, in secret."

Raine considered that. "Let's consider the best case—that she genuinely thought she was doing the right thing for Kenny. I might not agree, but I also can't fathom the stress she was under."

"The best case?" Jessica nodded. "Maybe so. The end results support that, although it took a long time."

"But she did get there," Raine reminded her sister.

"True. But I still don't see why she didn't go back to Texas."

"I'd say that's more evidence for PTSD. After I dumped Coulter, I stopped going where we'd gone together. I refused a job offer because he was at that firm. I didn't date for five years because I wasn't willing to risk making another mistake. Avoidance can be an effective coping strategy until you get better. Stronger."

Jessica nodded slowly, thinking that through.

When their flight was called, they picked up their carry-ons. Raine followed her sister to their gate. But once they were in line, she said, "Maybe we'll never know."

"We have to confront Mom."

"I agree."

Jessica blinked in surprise. "Really?"

"Yes, even though she's refused so many times. We have more information now. Possibly some she doesn't."

"Mariah's surgery changed her. She's worried, and this lie hangs between us."

On board, Raine leaned closer. "You're welcome to confront Mom alone."

"You can't go through life avoiding confrontations."

She tried not to smile. "I can try."

Jessica snort-laughed. "We're a team. We have to do it together."

"Agreed." Raine faced forward. She dreaded that conversation, but she got why it was necessary. Reggie had filled them in on what life had been like for Mariah and her involvement with Kenny until he'd left Texas. Their mother would have to give the eyewitness account of what had happened once their whole family got involved.

The plane lurched and rolled back from the gate. "I don't like flying," she said.

Jessica laughed. "You might have mentioned that a half dozen times on the flight over."

"I'll do the same on the flight back." Raine closed her eyes. "We're about to take off. I'll be ready to talk again once we reach thirty thousand feet."

Now sit back, relax, and enjoy the flight. She shook her head. Not a chance.

CHAPTER 41

Jessica had expected more pushback from her sister over scheduling the conversation with their mother, but it was Raine who'd insisted until Mom agreed.

So the three of them were meeting on a stormy Saturday afternoon. Jessica was waiting in her car as she watched the gates to their mother's neighborhood. It wasn't like her sister to be . . . punctual. Raine was usually fifteen minutes early, impatient to begin. Was she caught in traffic?

Raine's SUV rolled through the gates and over a speed bump, then turned into the parking lot. She braked and cut the engine on the stroke of five o'clock. Sliding from the vehicle, she walked over.

"I'd like to lead off," Raine said without greeting. "I'll explain some of what we've learned, then let you run the questions."

"Okay. When you have anything to add, jump in."

Raine looked at her feet. "Watch for my reactions, because it'll be hard to maintain calm."

"I understand." Jessica pulled her sister into a hug. "Okay, let's do this."

Her sister led the way to their mother's door, tapped the code on the keypad, and stepped inside. They entered a darkened living room, drapes closed tightly.

Mom sat in her favorite chair, her back to the window. "I don't want to do this."

"We know," Raine said, flicking on a table lamp, sinking beside Jessica on the love seat. "But it's time."

Mom reached for a brandy snifter of red wine and drank deeply. "Go ahead."

"Papa gave us a letter," Raine said. "It was his final wish for his grand girls to discover the truth of our family's story. He left us photographs, home movies, and old documents. We've interviewed Uncle Duane, Reggie Highcamp, Kenny, and even Mariah."

"Not your father?"

"I talked with him," Raine said. "He doesn't know much."

Mom shrugged.

"Jessica and I have most of the story now, but we have a few questions, and we need you to answer them."

"Like what?"

Raine released a shuddery breath. "Who made the decision to keep Kenny a secret from us?"

Mom closed her eyes. A long moment passed. When they opened again, her eyes were wet. "I did."

Raine's body visibly quaked. Jessica wrapped her fingers firmly around her sister's wrist as they both tried to absorb their mother's betrayal. They'd known it might have been her, but to hear it confirmed was stunning.

Jessica paused to catch her breath. "That's horrible."

"Why?" Raine asked plaintively.

Mom swirled her glass. "Daddy left Mama when he found out. I was six. Do you know how frightening that is for a first grader?"

"Almost," Raine said. "I was thirteen when my father left."

Mom's hand jerked, splashing a drop of wine. When she spoke, her voice was faint. "I was traumatized. Then I met a brother I'd never known about. He had special needs, and they became totally focused on helping him." She bowed her head, her hair sliding forward around her face. "Ken didn't like to travel, so we spent our vacations and holidays with him. Mama ended up devoting her life to improving special education here. I got . . ." Her voice trailed off.

"Less time?" Jessica suggested. Her sister stirred. Quieted.

"Yes." Mom took a sip. "Then Hal died, and Ken wanted to move here. My parents offered to have him move in with us or to Alder Creek. He visited both and chose Alder Creek." She looked up, met their gazes. "You've both been there."

They nodded.

"It's a great place. He loves living there."

"So why did you hide him?" Raine asked.

"He's not hidden." Mom frowned at her younger daughter. "The staff know who his family is. They knew Mama was in the general assembly. When he moved here, Mama wanted to make this big splash, and I convinced her not to. Politicians' kids should be protected from the public. And if it had gotten out about Ken, the scandal might've made a difference in Mama's election. Or the media might've shown up at Alder Creek and harassed him."

"Seems low risk," Jessica said.

"You're right," Mom said defensively. "But it didn't make sense to take even a low risk for something she didn't need to do. She never had to deny him."

"Except for us." Raine was shaking her head. "If his nieces didn't know about him, there was denying."

Mom sniffed.

Jessica nudged her sister. Her turn to ask questions. "Do you ever visit Kenny?"

"Of course. I go around his birthday every year and redecorate his room. I visit other times too, but mostly I write him. He likes mail."

"What about Papa and Mima?"

"Daddy went often. He and Ken had a lot in common. Checkers, puzzles, old TV shows, baseball. Mama would go with them to ball games. They had picnics. But she also visited separately. She and Ken liked to shop together." Their mother looked down at her glass. Swirled it. "It's been a while for Mama. Once long car rides started agitating her, Daddy didn't take her anymore. Too disturbing for everyone."

Raine asked, "Did she talk about him openly?"

"She did around me and Daddy, of course. I don't know about all of her friends, but definitely Mrs. Bridges knew."

"Yet you managed to hide Kenny from Dad," Jessica said.

Mom nodded.

"Why?"

She dropped her head into her hands. "Because I was scared."

CHAPTER 42

September 1986

Stephanie's Beetle sputtered to silence in the driveway. She'd come home for the weekend to celebrate her twentieth birthday. Then it would be back to Chapel Hill on Sunday and a return to the more typical contact when she ran out of money or had too much laundry.

Minutes later, the front door opened. "Mama, Daddy, I'm home."

Mariah and Gregor were side by side on the love seat in his study. She squeezed his hand. He nodded. They were ready for this discussion.

"We're in here, pumpkin."

Sandaled feet slapped down the hall. Stephanie came in. "Hi." She hitched her backpack more securely on her shoulder. "What's up?"

"We have news." Gregor gestured at an empty chair and waited until she sat. "Hal has cancer. He's dying."

"Oh, man. I'm really sorry to hear that." Stephanie hugged her knees to her chest and squirmed for comfort. "How long does he have?"

"Weeks."

"That's sad." She bit her lip. "What'll happen to Ken?"

Mariah exchanged a glance with her husband. She wanted her daughter to be all right with their plan. It would take their whole family to make it work. "He's moving here."

"What?" Frowning, Stephanie released her knees and shifted to the edge of the chair. "*Here* here? Like in the house?"

"We gave him the choice," Gregor said. "Here or a group home we've found nearby. He's chosen the group home."

She relaxed. Thought that over. Wrinkled her nose. "Those places aren't . . . nice."

"This one is. Very nice. It's small and rural, on a pretty piece of land in Lee County."

Stephanie reclined in the chair again. "Are you helping them, Daddy?"

"Yes. Azarian Construction is working out a deal to double its capacity." He smiled proudly at his wife. "Your mother has contacts. She'll check into grants and cut through the red tape."

Mariah listened to them talk, faint with relief. Her daughter seemed to be okay with the idea. Although she hadn't spent a lot of time around her half brother, she was taking this in stride.

Stephanie leaned over the arm of the chair, fumbled in her backpack, and pulled out a pen and notebook. "Does he want to keep working?"

"I'm already talking with an auto repair shop in a nearby town," Gregor said.

"What about decorating his room? I can help."

"They're careful about that," Mariah said. "Not all residents can afford to decorate."

"No problem." Her daughter jotted down some notes. "One of my classes this semester is about decorating on a budget. If the group home has some storage space available, I could stock it with home decor, like lamps and pictures and pillows. We could scrounge stuff from thrift stores or take donations. Then any resident who wants to fix up their room could."

Gregor gave Mariah's hand another squeeze. His smile seemed to say this was going well. She turned back and watched her daughter make more notes. They were about to get to the hard part. "We want to include him in the family."

"What?" Her daughter looked up. "Like . . . tell everyone who he is?" She shook her head rapidly. "No. Uh-uh."

"Stephanie—?" Her father started.

"You can have a relationship with him there." She frowned at her mother. "You're running for the general assembly, Mama, and it's going to be close. Your whole candidacy is about disability education. You can't let them find out that you abandoned your disabled son."

"I didn't *abandon* him." Mariah breathed in as the remorse that was never far away flooded her.

Stephanie's lips pinched. "Well, that's how they'll see it. Once it's out there, it'll hang over your head for the rest of your life."

Gregor made a dismissive sound. "She's the better candidate."

"She's running against an incumbent, and she's a woman. Throw in a scandal, and she's done."

Stephanie had been serving as an unofficial campaign manager, brainstorming slogans, printing flyers, going door to door, showing a surprising amount of political savvy. But Mariah thought she was wrong about this. "He's my son, Stephanie. I'm not hiding him."

"Okay, fine. Make a splash. It'll destroy everything you've worked for. The story becomes Ken. You'll be a hypocrite, and your career will end."

"So be it."

"No, Mama. Not *so be it*. The instant the wrong people find out about Ken, everything you've achieved will be viewed with contempt. You—and anything you've touched—will become a joke. *The woman who doesn't live near her disabled son wants to help you take care of yours.*"

Mariah gripped her husband's hand tightly. For strength. She hadn't imagined it would get this hard. "The truth is more complicated than that."

"You won't get the chance to explain. If the truth doesn't fit in a headline, you're screwed."

"Stephanie," Gregor said in warning.

Mariah tried for calm. "Why are you being like this? We can make this work."

"Why am *I* being like this?" Stephanie rose, stormed to the bookshelves, and braced herself against them. Made a muffled scream. "Do you know what it's been like for me?" She whipped around, face reddened, tears flowing. "When I was six—six!—my dad moved out. It was horrible. I wanted my parents to be together, and they weren't. I had nightmares. Would I wake up in the morning and find out Daddy was gone for good? If he was, would he love me anymore? Then suddenly, he moved back in and I had a brother. In Texas. My parents almost divorced over Ken."

Gregor shook his head. "It wasn't about Kenny."

"Try explaining that to a six-year-old," Stephanie said bitterly. "Then everything became about Ken. What he wanted. What he needed. While my friends spent their vacations at the beach or in Orlando or the Caribbean, I got to go to Texas. Because my brother didn't like to travel, and we always went to him."

Mariah looked at her husband and saw the same shock in his expression.

"And don't forget the holidays," their daughter added. "Do you know how scary it is for a little kid to wonder if Santa can find her—not at home, but in a motel room in Dallas?"

"We didn't know you felt that way," Mariah said softly.

"Because you never asked. And if I'd told you, I don't think it would've made a difference." Stephanie flounced back to her chair and sprawled. "And you know what? I love my brother. When it's just the two of us, we have a good time. Board games are our thing. And he likes to talk about cars. I don't, but I don't mind listening." She straightened, lips trembling. "But let one of you two walk into the room, or a letter show up, or the phone ring, and I disappear." She dropped her head forward, sucking in loud breaths. "Please, Mama. Give it a year. Get through the election. Find out how well Ken likes the place."

Mariah stared at the top of her daughter's head. How had she not noticed this? Had she really neglected her daughter? Made her feel somehow less important?

Gregor said, his voice shaky, "You're the center of our world."

"No, not even half." Stephanie seemed to deflate. "Please wait and see. You don't want reporters hunting for a sensational story where Ken lives. Please."

"I'm running for a state House seat from Wake County," Mariah said. "It's not important enough for reporters to show up."

"You can't count on that, and you aren't the only one who stands to lose. The scandal could set back special ed in our state. Even if you got elected, you wouldn't be able to accomplish anything. No matter how good a bill is, it'll be tainted because of your support. And Ken won't care. He just won't. You know what'll make him happy? Working on cars. A fun place to live. Daddy taking him to ball games or you making his favorite kind of cupcake. You can give him all those things without sacrificing your career."

Mariah shook her head. "We won't stop seeing him. We'll spend as much time with him as he wants. Someone will figure it out. Wouldn't it be better to admit it?"

"He has a different last name than us. No one will know." She shot them pleading glances. "Most politicians keep their children out of the limelight. They get to choose what's best for their family. We ought to be able to choose what's right for us."

Of all the reasons Stephanie had listed, Mariah worried most about hurting the people she'd hoped to help. She looked at Gregor.

He sighed. "It's worth considering how this could impact the people you seek to serve."

He was right. She turned back to her daughter. "What does Donovan think?"

Stephanie flushed with uncertainty. They'd been dating for a year, with an engagement on the horizon. "I haven't told him."

Mariah gasped. "Why not?"

"I can't have him . . . disapprove of my parents. I'll tell him someday. But not yet."

"This is wrong, Stephanie," Gregor said quietly. "He deserves to be told. If you wait too long, it will crush him."

"You should know, Daddy."

Her response jolted through them. Gregor looked at his wife, his words echoing across the years.

I wouldn't have married you if I had known.

They'd gotten past it, but only after he'd listened to her, to Hal, to Kenny. Once he understood all the complexities, he'd forgiven. But neither of them had forgotten those terrible months of separation.

If Mariah could go back in time, she would tell Gregor. Believe that his love was strong enough to accept her mistakes and fears. If only Stephanie would learn from the past. That the guilt of secrets was too painful a burden to bear. Marriage required trust. When Donovan found out—and he would—his sense of betrayal would be total. He was a remarkably idealistic young man. Life and the law would file his idealism down, but discovering that Stephanie hadn't trusted him with the knowledge of her brother? Mariah didn't think he would get past that. "You have to tell Donovan."

"It's my decision."

"We're not hiding our son," Mariah said. "My friends know. The staff at Alder Creek will know."

"Then I won't bring my . . . family around."

The statement shocked Mariah into silence.

Gregor's hand held hers in a punishing grip. "You would cut us off?" he asked gruffly.

Stephanie's chin jutted forward. "Not if you let me decide what to tell Donovan and when."

Mariah glanced at her husband. His face reflected the same strain and disbelief that claimed her. Would Stephanie really keep them from her future husband? Their grandchildren? Did she not understand that she was taking the same terrible risk Mariah had? Why would Stephanie repeat her mother's mistake?

"Will you promise to let me handle Donovan?" she asked implacably.

They leaned into each other, like they would have to in the coming days. "Yes."

◆ ◆ ◆

October 1986

The phone rang, too shrill to ignore, dragging them both from sleep. Mariah peered at the alarm clock beside the bed. It was 5:20 a.m.

There could only be one reason why.

Gregor groaned and rolled over. The handset rattled in its cradle.

"Hello?" he grumbled. His body went on instant alert. "Yes, Reggie. What?" A long, sorrowful sigh. *Just a moment,* Gregor mouthed at her as he stood, lifted the phone base with his free hand, and crossed to the walk-in closet, the phone cord unspooling behind him. He glanced back at her before closing the door.

Hal had died.

She sat up on the edge of the bed and breathed in. Her first love. The person who'd held her after witnessing a horrific event from which neither of them ever fully recovered. Her son's father. Now her husband's friend. Hal had only been forty-two.

She slipped on a silk robe, tightened it about her waist, and went to the sliding doors that led to their private patio. Their backyard was beautiful in October. It wouldn't be sunrise for another hour, but her mind filled in the glorious display of colors. She pressed her hands to the cold glass and waited.

The rumbling of Gregor's voice stopped. The closet door opened. The phone tinked as it was returned to the nightstand.

"Mariah." Her husband's warmth surrounded her as he rested his hands on her waist and drew her back against him.

She laid her hands over his.

"The funeral is Wednesday. A simple graveside service. Will you go with me?"

"No," she whispered. Uncle Fred and Aunt Vera would resent her presence. They ought to be able to mourn without her as a distraction.

"I'll fly to Dallas tomorrow. Meet with Reggie and Kenny and the lawyer. All is in place." Gregor rubbed his unshaven cheek against hers. "Hal has deeded me his car, a Chevy Impala they restored quite beautifully. Kenny and I will return with it this weekend."

She smiled. She knew the car well. "Natural air-conditioning?"

"It will be comfortable enough for October. I understand Kenny has a portable tape player." He chuckled. "Do you worry about the news getting out?"

She turned in his arms. The battle for a seat in the general assembly had grown even more brutal in the closing days of the election. Her opponent was trying to fuel hostility over her early interest in desegregation and her current focus on special-needs education. "It's unlikely. But if I'm ever asked, I won't deny him." She added fiercely, "It will be so good to have him here."

"Yes, it will." He kissed her temple. "*Very* good. How often will we see him?"

She'd been thinking of that question often. Wondering what Kenny would want. How soon he would find a comfortable routine that they could fit into. "I think Kenny will have opinions."

"Yes, he certainly will. For us to see him together and separately."

Mariah pressed against her husband, feeling as if she was drowning in a vortex of emotion. Grief for Hal. Regret over her choices and their consequences. Relief that after twenty-two years of living apart, her son would be near her again.

CHAPTER 43

Raine felt pity stir at the anguish in her mother's voice. "Scared of what?"

Mom pressed a fist to her lips. "I was so afraid of what Donovan would do. We'd just become engaged. I was worried about how he'd react if he found out Mama had abandoned her disabled child in Texas."

Raine glanced at her sister and nodded. It was time to tell their mother the truth. To claim their story. "*Abandon* is the wrong word," she said.

Their mother looked up. "What?"

Raine couldn't be the one to share what they'd learned. She shifted on the love seat, knowing that her sister would understand.

"Reggie told us what really happened," Jessica said. "Mariah had serious mental health issues. PTSD. Possibly postpartum depression."

"Why PTSD?"

"She witnessed JFK's assassination."

Mom's mouth dropped open in shock. "What?"

The sisters watched her steadily as she struggled to absorb the news.

"Why did she never tell me?"

"It was too traumatic for her," Jessica said. "Reggie told us that she'd been acting mentally unstable, and no one knew what to do about it. Hal convinced her it would be safest for Kenny if she left and didn't return until she was better. For reasons we don't know, she came home to North Carolina to recover, but she never lost contact with them. She sent child support, communicated often with Hal and Kenny, and visited. Reggie said everyone knew Kenny would go with Mima and Papa if something happened to Hal."

Tears dampened Mom's cheeks. She shook her head, over and over. Raine studied her mother's face and saw something unexpected. Relief?

Jessica noticed too. "Wait. Did you ever ask Mariah the reason she left Kenny in Texas?"

"No." Her mother mopped her cheeks with her sleeve.

"Why not?" Raine asked, shocked. It seemed like such an obvious question.

"I was afraid of the answer." Mom drained her wine glass and set it unsteadily on a coaster. "My mother is an amazing woman. An angel. I wouldn't let myself believe she could've done something so terrible."

"Why would you think that? The moment she could, Mariah moved him here."

Mom's hands trembled. She clasped them together and dropped them in her lap. "I was twenty. I wasn't thinking clearly."

"Mom," Jessica said, her voice edged with reproach. "You've had years to think clearly, both for Dad and us."

Their mother simply shook her head.

Raine exchanged a glance with her sister. They waited for an explanation, but apparently none was coming. She prompted, "We visited him once when we were kids."

"Yeah, the Fourth of July. America's birthday party." Mom gulped in a sobbing breath. "It didn't go well. You two were crabby. It was hot and humid. Ken hadn't been around children often, and you were getting on his nerves. So he went inside for the air-conditioning, and we left." She brushed her hand against her cheek, smearing a thin trickle of mascara.

She tried, it went badly, and that was enough? "So you only tried once to let us know?"

"Not exactly. I tried again in 2007, starting with your dad, and that went horribly. I planned another attempt after Raine graduated from high school. Then Mama was diagnosed, and that was it. I could *not* run the risk of losing you when we needed you most."

Raine groaned in frustration. Losing them? Why would she think that? Did Mom believe her daughters were incapable of listening? Of understanding? Of forgiveness?

"Why did Papa and Mima keep it from us?" Jessica asked.

Their mother closed her eyes. Paled. "I extracted a promise."

"What kind of promise?" Jessica narrowed her eyes, then widened them again in horror. "Oh my God. Did you threaten to keep us away?"

Mom nodded.

Raine welcomed the firm pressure of her sister's hand on her arm. If she'd ever actually considered all the possibilities, she might have arrived at this explanation, but she was glad she hadn't. It was better to have heard the awful truth from their mother than to have believed it possible of her before. "Mom," she asked wearily, "why was it so important to you that we not know?"

"It was a big lie, and the longer it went on, the harder it got to tell the truth. Until it felt too big to admit."

If Mom had only faced her fears and told the truth years ago, so much pain could've been avoided. Such a waste.

The grandfather clock in the foyer went through its complete song, then tolled the hour. Six o'clock. They had answers. Raine was saturated with loss and grief. She had to leave. To return to the haven of her home and recover. When she stood, her sister did too.

"What did you think would happen once we knew?" Raine asked.

Mom looked up at them. "My father left my mother when he found out. My husband left me when he did. I couldn't have my girls leave me too."

They were silent as her statement sank in. Their mother had made the wrong decisions because she was scared of losing her loved ones—and those decisions had actually pushed them further away. But she was their mother. They would find a way to forgive.

"We won't leave you." Raine slid the strap of her purse over her shoulder. "But we've lost decades with Kenny. It's too late to talk with our grandparents about what they went through. We love you, Mom, which won't end because you made a really bad choice. But we're not going to say it's okay either."

"We love you, and we're still a family," Jessica said. "You haven't lost us, and someday we'll get over this. But you hurt us, Mom. Give us time."

CHAPTER 44

As Jessica left the townhome, she had to breathe consciously. In and out. Willing her heartbeat to slow. That had been one of the hardest conversations of her life.

Raine went straight to her SUV, its lights flashing as she reached for the door.

"Wait," Jessica said. "We have to talk."

"We can do that later." Her sister got into the car.

"When?"

Raine leaned forward until her head bumped against the steering wheel. "I barely survived the past hour. Now isn't the time for a rehash."

"I want an explanation from Dad."

"He's already explained it to me." Raine shook her head. "You weren't around much during the divorce, Jessica. They lied to Dad too. He's suffered just like we have."

"What do you mean I wasn't around? I was here for two years after their separation."

"Physically, yeah. But you had detached. You didn't *see*."

She couldn't argue the truth of that. She had plunged herself into school, friends, finding the right college—anything that got her away from home. Being busy had been a relief. "I still have questions."

"Then talk to him if that's what you want, but leave me out." Raine powered on the engine. "And watch his expressions carefully. You'll see." Raine pulled the door shut.

Jessica watched as her sister drove away. "Okay, I will."

◆ ◆ ◆

Luke found her on the living room couch, lights off, listening to the storm through the open porch door.

"Hey," he said, sitting beside her. "How'd it go at Stephanie's?"

"Tough."

"Want to tell me about it?"

She leaned against him, liking the weight of his arm pulling her closer. Yielding to the comfort he was offering, she relayed their mother's version of the story. He listened without comment. When she was done and silent again, he kissed her brow and brushed his thumb over the bare skin of her thigh.

"What are you thinking?" she asked.

"That you and Raine were brave to confront Stephanie, especially knowing how hard her side of the story might be to hear."

"But?"

"No buts. I don't condone what they did to you or Raine or Kenny." He linked their hands together. "Just remember that I teach at a magnet high school. I come across all kinds of parents. I witness the good, the bad, and the heartbreakingly ugly. It's hard to surprise me anymore."

The heartbreakingly ugly? She could only imagine the things he'd seen. Dropping her head to his shoulder, she said, "Once we were done, I asked Raine if she wanted to discuss what we'd heard."

Her husband snorted softly. Fought off a smile. "And she did not."

"No, she didn't. I'd like to talk to Dad. She's not interested."

"What would you ask Donovan?"

"Why didn't he tell us when he found out?" Beside her, Luke stiffened. She angled to see his face. "What?"

"Raine couldn't have taken it back then." He shook his head slowly. "The divorce hit her hard, maybe more than you know. Your dad took her from therapist to therapist until she finally got the help she needed. There's a bond of shared pain between them that she won't want to revisit."

"The divorce hurt me too."

"I know, but you coped in a different way."

Was that what her sister had meant about not seeing? "I still want answers."

"Then get what you need. You don't have to include Raine."

"Okay. I'll call him tonight."

After they returned from eating out, Luke went upstairs while Jessica crossed to the couch. She flicked on a lamp and placed a video call to her father. "Hi, Dad. Got a moment?"

"Yes." He propped his phone in a stand and leaned back. He was in the study of his home. Only one lamp was on, casting the bookcase behind him in shadows.

"Raine and I talked to Mom this afternoon."

"Yes, I know," he said. "She called me. Raine has too."

Jessica could understand the contact from her sister. She'd want to warn him. But their mother? Jessica would hold that thought for later. "Did Raine tell you what we've discovered?"

"Yes."

Jessica was studying his reactions intently, as her sister had suggested. So far, he was hard to read. "How much did you already know?"

"I knew most of what's happened in the past thirty years. Before that, only a little." He had his lawyer face on. Curious yet guarded.

"We were lied to, and you went along with it for years. Why?"

"I thought it was important for your mother to be the one to tell you."

"But she didn't tell us."

His mouth twisted, as if controlling a strong wave of emotion. "I handle a lot of divorce and custody cases in my practice. I see ex-partners tearing each other apart every day—and their children in the process. I couldn't be that dad."

Even if *not* knowing hurt the children anyway? "It was a bad decision."

"I agree. It *was* a bad decision, and I'm sorry it hurt you and Raine and Kenny. But all my choices sucked." He leaned closer to the camera. "Raine struggled to get over the divorce for a long time, even after you left for college. She needed all four of the adults who loved her to get her through it."

Both Luke and Dad had mentioned Raine's difficulties. Why hadn't anyone said anything before? Had Jessica been so caught up in her own despair that she failed to notice her sister's? "There've been other opportunities since."

"There have, but I couldn't be the one to break the silence." Something flickered in his eyes, a sorrow so profound he had to look away. "Gregor started to tell you several times, but something always came up to make him reconsider. The divorce. Mariah's diagnosis. Then his."

"His?" That was news.

"He was diagnosed with heart disease not long after Mariah moved into memory care. He wasn't sure he could tolerate the fallout of your learning the secret."

Oh wow. The fallout? Had Papa really worried about their reaction? And why hadn't he told them about his heart? She and her sister had been adults long enough to be trusted with the truth. It hurt that they hadn't been. "Did anyone consider Kenny?"

"He's their son. Of course they considered him. We all did."

"And how was this good for him?"

"Your grandparents didn't like any of the options they had. But Kenny having his nieces at war with their parents or grandparents didn't promise a good outcome either."

"That wouldn't have happened."

"We didn't have a crystal ball, Jessica." He sighed. "We did what we thought, at the time, was the best of the options, and we failed. I'm sorry."

They stared at each other for a long moment. He'd said he was sorry twice, and he'd sounded genuine, weary. Raine was right. The tale had haunted him too. "You talked to Mom tonight?"

"She gave me a heads-up." He cleared his throat. "We're civil when it concerns our girls."

The echoes of his past were reflected on his face. There was much that Jessica hadn't seen. A kind of sad heaviness settled over her. "Thank you, Dad," she said, her gratitude sincere.

"I love you, Jessica. Be safe." He ended the call.

She set her phone on the side table, flicked off the lamp, and closed her eyes. It was her hope that all apologies had been said and forgiveness granted.

On Monday, for the second time in the past three weeks, Jessica was called into Charlie's office after work. The executive producer for the morning show was there, along with the news director. This time, she had only the faintest fluttering of nerves.

The EP smiled. "Congratulations. You're my new senior producer."

Jessica briefly considered an undignified squeal but channeled her delight into a wide smile. "Thank you. This is an honor."

"Your skills have always impressed us," Charlie said, beaming.

The news director added, "The ability to own up for the 'lie goals'—without pushing the blame on anyone else—helped. Not that we want you to make another mistake like that."

They all laughed. Then it grew quiet. The others were staring expectantly at Jessica, waiting for her to say more, when all she wanted to do was leave and tell Luke. "This is amazing news. When do I start?"

"The first Monday in July. The third," the EP said. "It's a holiday weekend, which can be loads of fun." She rolled her eyes.

It was also Mima's birthday and only two weeks away. Management wasn't wasting time. She smiled, wishing she could think of something to say.

Charlie chuckled. "A speechless Jessica Elliott."

She bobbed her head.

He gestured toward the door. "Okay, get out of here."

She texted Luke as she hurried to the parking lot.

Any plans for supper?

Leftovers. Why?

Meet me at Village Grill?

Sounds good. On the way

She arrived ahead of him and had two beers waiting when he joined her.

"What's going on?" he asked, his smile puzzled.

"I'm the new senior producer for the morning news."

"Whoa. Congratulations." He kissed her and reached for her hand. "I'm not surprised."

"Thanks. I start July third."

They clinked bottles and sipped.

"So . . . we have something else to celebrate." His expression turned serious. "I submitted my application package today—for Global Literacies. I chose it over the other program mostly because it was right for us. But then, a strange thing happened. I started thinking hard about what I'll learn, and I'm really excited. The leadership program is about ambition. The global program is better aligned with what I love about teaching."

"That might be true for me too. Or partially true. I enjoyed six o'clock as a news producer. But would I enjoy it as much as a senior? I'm not so sure. I'm confident I'll love the morning show."

"Except the wakeup hour."

"Indeed." She picked up her menu. "Okay, let's order—and then we'll talk about how the whole go-to-bed-by-eight thing will work."

CHAPTER 45

In the two weeks since the showdown with Mom, Raine had only seen her at Larkmoor. That wasn't conscious avoidance on Raine's part. It was just how her schedule had worked out.

There was a stiffness, a formality to their interactions. She supposed that was natural. But if it continued much longer, maybe they'd have to address it directly. And *not* think of it as a confrontation next time.

She'd visited her uncle twice. They were making their way through an anime about baseball. *Big Windup!* It was pretty good, and she wasn't really into anime. She'd also discovered the criticality of learning his TV schedule so she knew what afternoons to avoid. Fortunately, Ian's experience with Kenny's preferences was only a text away.

Ian wasn't coming over tonight, wanting to invest the two-hour commute in studying. That was fine. She'd been studying too. She would take her exam next month. As long as she passed, the only thing left to do for certification was to apply.

When her phone beeped, she frowned. It was after ten o'clock. A group text to Stephanie, Jessica, and Raine. From Andres, the night charge nurse at Larkmoor. *Oh no.*

As soon as you can, please come

It must not be a medical emergency or he would've sent them to a hospital. If he was calling in the family, this was something else, something Raine didn't want to face. She threw her phone into her purse, slipped her feet in sandals, and was out the door. Once in her car, she responded.

On the way

When she reached Larkmoor, the lighting revealed a mostly empty visitor lot. She didn't see her sister's or her mother's car, but that didn't mean they hadn't arrived yet. Checking her phone, she found two messages.

From Jessica. **Nearly there**

From Mom. **Caught in traffic**

Raine texted Ian as she raced inside and down the corridor. Quiet voices spilled from the open door to her grandmother's suite. Andres and a nursing aide turned as she walked in.

He gestured her closer, sympathy on his face.

"She's dying," she whispered.

"Yes."

"How long?"

"It's hard to say." He pulled her into a hug. "Talk to her. She'll hear."

Raine hugged back briefly and then stepped into the bedroom, her complete focus on her grandmother. Mariah was reclined on the hospital bed, its head raised. She wore a mauve nightgown with a scarf at her throat, pinned with the engagement brooch. Someone had brushed her hair. Her breathing was uneven. Her left hand plucked restlessly at the bedspread. Yet she seemed . . . beatific. Raine had researched the signs and knew what they meant, but she wasn't ready to say goodbye. Sliding onto a chair, she sucked in a shaky breath.

"I'm here, Mariah. It's Raine."

Her grandmother made a choking sound. A gasp. Then relaxed.

Raine placed her grandmother's cold hand between both of hers, warming it.

"Dear," Mariah mumbled.

Raine stiffened. Was her grandmother trying to say *dear one*? Had Mariah recognized her? No, she'd probably imagined it because she wanted it to be true.

Footsteps came running into the room. Jessica appeared on the opposite side of the bed, eyes reddened.

"Is Luke away this weekend?" Raine asked.

"He was." Jessica sank onto the other chair. "Premobilization training. He was supposed to stay for night operations, but he's on his way home now."

"Did you speak with Andres?"

Jessica nodded. Coughed. "How has she been?"

"Mostly like this. Ragged breathing. Eyes closed. I've heard her mumble, but it wasn't clear." Those gasping breaths would replay in Raine's dreams forever. It hurt to listen.

"She looks angelic." Jessica reached for Mariah's other hand.

Mariah made odd, buzzy sounds with her lips, then clearly, "I love them."

What? Raine met her sister's gaze and saw the same shock. "Did she say *I love them*?"

"That's what I heard too."

They both exchanged tremulous smiles.

Raine was so happy to have heard those words. She laid her head on the bed and pressed it to her grandmother's side. This was going to be a long, hard night.

A half hour passed before Mom strode in. "Girls," she said quietly. She angled her head toward the parlor. They looked at each other across the bed, rose, and followed her.

"I've talked with Andres." She drank in a closed-mouthed breath, eyes shiny with tears. "They don't know how long. But soon. A few hours. When she shows signs of discomfort, he'll manage that." She swallowed. "We can talk or sing. Whatever we want. But she probably won't respond."

"Okay," Jessica said. "How do we do this?"

"I'll be in there unless I need a break. You two can decide what you'd prefer."

"Mom," Raine said and put an arm around her. Jessica joined from the other side, and the three Elliott women held each other and cried.

"Okay," Mom said and hiccuped. She dropped her arms, dashed at her cheeks, and walked into the bedroom. "Hi, Mama," she said brightly. "It's Stephanie." A chair screeched.

Jessica blew out a noisy breath. "So . . ."

"Go on in," Raine said. "I'll take a turn later."

Even though the staff didn't expect Mariah to regain consciousness, Mom and Jessica held her hands and spoke to her softly, sharing old family stories. Raine stood at the foot of the bed, listening. Retreating to the parlor if the story choked her up, which happened a lot.

Luke arrived around midnight. Raine went into the bedroom so her sister could greet him. Seconds later, she heard Jessica's muffled sobs. How lucky she was to have her husband here.

The hours ticked past. Raine relieved Mom. Then Jessica. None of them were out of Mariah's suite for long, just a bathroom break or to stretch their legs. Luke kept them supplied with coffee.

At five, Raine took another shift at Mariah's side, and when Mom returned, Raine paused briefly at the entrance to the room. Her grandmother looked beautiful in the faint light of a lamp.

Jessica came into the parlor a few minutes later, wrapped her arms around Luke's neck, and whispered in his ear. He nodded, stepped back, and went into Mariah's bedroom.

"I'm afraid I'll fall asleep and miss . . ." Jessica hung her head.

"Come out and watch the sunrise with me. We'll only be seconds away," Raine said.

They walked silently down the corridor and out the door to the enclosed courtyard. In the gazebo, they sat side by side, watching the fountain and the faint lightening of the sky.

"She loved this place," Jessica said.

"Well, this courtyard. She didn't love Larkmoor."

"Take me home," they said in unison, then smiled.

"She'll be seventy-nine tomorrow," Raine said. "I planned to bake cupcakes. With sprinkles and tiny flags."

"Tomorrow is my first day as senior producer for the morning show."

"Oh wow, that's right." She glanced at her watch. "I have an alarm set."

"You do?" Jessica turned to her with a pleased smile. "Thanks."

"I have job news too. Sort of. My favorite client made me an offer."

"Did you accept?"

"Not yet, but yeah, I probably will." Raine focused on the stand of pines beyond the courtyard, a dark silhouette against the softening blue of the sky. "He'd like me to start August first."

"But you won't have taken the exam yet."

"He's sure I'll pass." A mere formality, he'd said. Which was nice to hear. It gave her confidence a boost.

"Have you talked with Ian?"

"We've texted. He's passed along the message to Alder Creek." Her life had changed so much since Papa's death. Two months ago, she'd been in ignorance of key elements of her family's history. Now she knew her uncle. She'd had to forgive her parents, although the forgetting part wasn't quite there yet. She would have someone to lean on this time. Really, two someones, because she wouldn't have asked her sister for help before.

"So much is different since Papa died," Jessica said, as if reading Raine's thoughts.

The sun chose that moment to pop out, sending ribbons of yellow and pink and purple along the horizon. Time to face the day. She stood, slid her fists into her jeans pockets, and nodded toward the door. "Let's go back in."

Mariah's breathing had grown more labored while they were outside. A quick look at Andres's face let Raine know it wouldn't be much longer. So they sang Mariah an early happy birthday. Whispered a prayer. Said *I love you.*

And when her breaths ceased, they all looked to Andres, who nodded in sympathy.

Mom wailed and laid her head against Mima's chest.

Jessica fell into Luke's arms.

And Raine watched from the foot of the bed.

We'll miss you, Mima.

Rest in peace.

She'd heard that phrase spoken so many times, but today she actually understood why the words brought comfort.

As Mariah had requested long ago, the funeral was elegantly simple and private, with only a small group of family and close friends at the cemetery. In the front row, Mom stood on the end. Then Luke and Jessica, Dad, Raine, and Ian. Without the ritual of the military service, they wouldn't be here long.

The priest conferred quietly with the funeral director as the other mourners slowly made their way to the graveside. Uncle Duane had come with his wife and sons. So had Phil Jones and his grandson Damian. Mariah's first friend in Raleigh, Alice, a retired librarian. Papa's brother from Richmond.

Raine watched the main gate for one more vehicle, then breathed a sigh of relief as a silver minivan pulled in and parked. Kenny got out of the passenger side, looking handsome and eager in his baggy khakis and blue shirt. He clutched a handful of roses from the garden at Alder Creek.

Amina walked beside him until they reached the family. "We got a late start," she whispered.

"That's fine," Raine whispered back. "Thank you for bringing him."

The priest had just crossed to stand before those gathered, holding up his hands for silence, when Mom turned her head and spotted the new arrivals.

"Ken." She held out her hand. "Want to stand with me?"

"Okay, Steph." He started toward her, roses in one hand, cane in the other.

When he reached his sister's side, she looped her arm through his, then nodded at the priest. "We're all here now."

EPILOGUE

Three months later

Raine and Ian worked all morning raking leaves and mulching beds at Papa's house. At noon, she called a break, and they went inside, cleaned up, and took sandwiches out to the sunroom. She smiled with pride at all they'd accomplished. "Papa's backyard looks good."

Ian laughed. "Your backyard," he corrected for the hundredth time this month.

"Yeah, it is." She'd hated the idea of selling Papa's house. So she'd worked out the finances with her sister and now owned it.

The past three months had been busy.

Ian had passed his nursing boards and started a new job at an urgent care in Lee County. He still lived near Alder Creek. When she drove to Ian's for a date, it often included a visit with her uncle.

Raine had been working at Patrick's firm since August and received notification of her certification not long afterward. She was remote three days per week. She didn't get to pick her projects, but Patrick had, so far, assigned the types of cases she liked best. Cheating spouses hiding assets. Cheating companies underpaying employees. She hadn't been there long enough to testify yet, but it was coming. Patrick and the other accountants had promised to coach her. Raine believed Papa would've agreed she'd found the right job for her.

"Ready to get back to work?" Ian asked.

Before she could answer, her phone buzzed with a text from her sister.

We're cooking out tonight. You and Ian should come

She glanced at Ian. "Jessica's invited us to dinner."

"I'm on board."

Raine texted back.

Sure. What should we bring?

Vegetables to grill

No request for dessert? She would bring one anyway. "My sister likes the way you grill vegetables."

"Onions, mushrooms, peppers, asparagus?" His forehead creased as he made a mental checklist. "How about a pumpkin?"

He and Luke both loved her pumpkin cheesecake. Dessert solved. "Can we head over to the farmers' market?"

He stood and gestured for her to precede him into the house. "Let's go."

Raine gripped the dessert container like it contained precious gems. Ian shifted the tray of raw vegetables to one hand and reached past her to ring the doorbell.

Luke answered. "Glad you could come," he said and led the way to the kitchen.

Jessica was arranging steaks and chicken breasts on a large platter. "Hi," she said. "Welcome."

Raine passed her sister to get to the refrigerator. "I brought cheesecake."

"Grill's ready," Luke said, picking up the platter of meat. "Heading outside."

Ian followed him with the tray of vegetables. He paused at the door and looked around not-so-surreptitiously.

"Beer's in a cooler on the deck," Jessica said.

Ian flashed her a grin and caught up with Luke. The door closed.

Raine looked back at her sister, who was preparing salad dressing from scratch. "What can I do?"

"Set the table." Jessica pointed to a stack of four complete place settings and napkins on the bar. "He's good for you."

"Agreed." Raine carried the dishes to the table and got to work.

"Have you watched the morning news recently?"

"Yes. It's pretty good." She folded napkins and carefully laid one at each plate. "Do you like being a senior producer?"

"I love the work. Getting up at two a.m.? I don't love that. But it's best for the family plan. I have afternoons free to spend with my . . . family."

"Has the family plan kicked in?" Maybe that was bold, but her sister had introduced the subject.

"Oh yes."

Raine looked over her shoulder. Her sister's smile was wide and happy. "Are you pregnant?"

Jessica nodded. "Due in May."

"During ratings month."

She laughed. "Yeah, well, we'll make it work."

Raine put the last fork in place and turned to face her sister. "How does Luke feel?"

"Over the moon. Already picking names." Her sister lifted a hand to her abdomen. "He's taking a leave of absence next fall for grad school. He'll have more time to stay at home with the baby, and I'll have afternoons free." She gave a swift shake of her head. "We're not telling anyone else yet, but we knew you would keep the secret."

"That I can do. Does Mom know?"

"We'll tell her when she gets back from the cruise."

"And Dad?"

"We'll wait to tell him the same day."

The sisters exchanged understanding smiles. Their parents' relationship had eased somewhat, but there were limits to how good it would ever get.

Raine looked out the window. The guys were talking, drinking beer, pretending to watch the food grill. Good. They would be busy for a while, and the sisters had an issue they'd never completely resolved.

She crossed to the bar and leaned on her forearms. "Can we talk about Mariah's film?"

"Sure." Jessica washed her hands at the sink, dried them on a towel, and carried the salad bowl to the table. "Do you want something to drink?"

"Yeah." Raine went to the refrigerator for a bottle of hard cider. Carrying it back to the bar, she climbed onto a barstool. "Go ahead. I know you have ideas."

"I have a friend of a friend who has a contact at the Smithsonian. They have a process for acquiring donations of artifacts. It's rare that they accept items, but ours might be of interest."

Raine grinned. "I think it might."

"I've asked if the donors can stay anonymous. So those details need to be clarified, but it's a conversation we can have."

"Why not the Sixth Floor Museum? Or the JFK Library?"

"I like that the Smithsonian is national. They'll do the right thing about where it should really be."

Another way to *do the right thing*. "It's a good solution."

Jessica's eyes widened. "That's it? No argument?"

"None."

Her smile was relieved. "Who do we tell?"

"Mom should know, and we should tell her before everything's settled, but we'll make it clear that it's our decision. Papa gave the film to us."

"Agreed. Luke already knows everything. Whatever you decide about Ian is fine with me."

"I trust him, and I'm done with secrets." Raine pointed at Jessica's abdomen. "Although I can wait on the baby secret."

"You can tell him. It'll be obvious soon enough."

Male voices drew closer to the door. It rattled and squeaked. Time was running out on their conversation, which was fine. The decisions were made. All that remained was implementing the details.

"Do we know the whole story?" Jessica asked.

"We know what's important."

The guys were inside now, laughing, bringing with them the scent of grilled food.

"So it's over," Raine said. Both the decisions and the turmoil of the past five months. "The end of secrets."

ACKNOWLEDGMENTS

I'd like to thank the many people who contributed to bringing this book to life. Mike Cochran for his insights as a journalist in Dallas-Fort Worth on the day President Kennedy died. My parents, Teresa Coleman, Larry Langston, and Tom Brodie for describing what life was like in the sixties and during the Vietnam era. Jessica Patrick, Lori Grant, Stella Shelton, and Randy Merritt for the ins and outs of television news production. Thomas Buckhoff, PhD and Sheila Hensley for explaining forensic accounting. Kathryn Bradsher, Mike Mazzella, and Mary C. for their patience with my health-care questions. The North Carolina Armenians and Tina for sharing their culture and faith. Nancy and Dennis on their Roman Catholic faith. Jaime for his wisdom about the National Guard. Marcia Abercrombie for her family's experiences with disabilities.

My deep gratitude goes to those on my publishing team. Melissa Valentine and the wonderful editorial and production staff from Lake Union. My retreat friends and beta readers—Angie, Marcia, Merle, and Rebecca. Laura Ownbey, my remarkable developmental editor. Kevan Lyon, my amazing agent. Amy Langston for being my copyeditor, sounding board, and resource on all things neurodiversity and faith traditions.

Finally, I couldn't be an author without the support and encouragement of my family. I'm forever in your debt.

THE MEASURE OF SILENCE

Book Club Discussion Questions

1. At the end of the first chapter, Mariah reflects on how quickly the world "split into *before* and *after*." Have there been pivotal events that served as defining moments in your life? How did they affect you?

2. Throughout the book, there are multiple instances where characters make choices that have unexpected consequences. "Good" decisions go wrong. "Bad" decisions turn out all right. What makes a decision good or bad, right or wrong? When judging a decision, should you consider good intentions? Should you weigh positive outcomes?

3. Mariah experienced PTSD and depression during a time when mental health care was notoriously poor. After Hal's family threatens her with police intervention—and possible institutionalization—Mariah is frightened enough to flee to somewhere she feels safe. What do you think of the support she found within the community she built? With the improvements in our current mental health care system, why might people still be reluctant to seek therapy?

4. Although Mariah betrays her husband's trust, Gregor comes to forgive her and works toward reconciliation. After Stephanie betrays her husband's trust, Donovan forgives her but still

pursues divorce. Why do you think Donovan responded differently? When you forgive others, where is the line between betrayals you can reconcile and those you cannot?

5. Gregor and Donovan were complicit in not sharing family secrets with Raine and Jessica. Why do you think they remained steadfast with that choice—despite years of opportunities to change their minds? Was Donovan right to insist that it was "their story to tell"? Have you had to keep family secrets despite disagreeing with the silence?

6. In the final confrontation with Raine and Jessica, Stephanie tells them she hid the truth for so long because the act of lying "felt too big to admit." Can you relate to her choice? Has anyone ever hidden secrets from you because they were too ashamed to confess to lying?

7. Raine has a unique way of thinking. Family and friends may wonder if she's neurodivergent, yet Raine doesn't have a diagnosis. Are you familiar with neurodiversity? If a person suspects they're neurodivergent, what factors might they consider when deciding whether to be diagnosed?

8. Jessica struggles throughout the story to resolve how she should balance her career, her marriage, and, someday, children. She "wanted it all" but "had to do a better job of defining what 'all' meant" for her. What does *all* mean for you? How has *all* been redefined from the baby boomer generation to now?

ABOUT THE AUTHOR

Photo © 2016 Wesley Smith

Elizabeth Langston is an award-winning author who spent a career as a software engineer before discovering she loved writing stories more. When she's not researching her next book, she enjoys traveling the world with her family, binge-watching mystery shows, or curling up in her North Carolina home with a cup of coffee and a good book. For more information visit www.elizabethlangston.net.